MW00941151

SOUTH OF THE CITY

A NOVEL

W.H. HERMAN

This is a work of fiction. All of the names, characters, organizations, places and events portrayed in this novel are either products of the author's imagination or used fictitiously. Any resemblance to real or actual events, locales, or persons, living or dead, is entirely coincidental.

Text copyright © 2017 by W.H.Herman

ISBN-13: 978-1545040478
ISBN-10: 1545040478

Cover design and interior formatting by Damonza
Cover image by W.H.Herman

Dedicated to Sally - my wife, best friend, and support system.

CHAPTER 1

Carthage, Iowa
August 1990

"COME ON, STITCH, be on time for once in your damned life."

Standing at the crumbled shoulder of Route 79, Jim Wright took a final searing drag of his unfiltered Lucky Strike, inhaling until the tobacco embers burned the yellow callouses on his thumb and forefinger. He held the smoke captive in his lungs for a moment, as if it would somehow calm his nerves, before reluctantly flicking the butt out onto the pavement.

The roadside meeting with Mitch Goren had been scheduled as a final review of their plans for that night, but now Jim was having second thoughts, and those misgivings made it urgent that he speak to his partner before Mitch took action on his own. His initial concern was giving way to an uncomfortable feeling of panic as Wright realized that his accomplice might already be out getting drunk somewhere, having decided that a dose of liquid courage took precedence over another run-through.

"Where the hell is that boy?" He continued speaking aloud, to no one.

The mid-day cloud cover had been ushered away by a breeze that could barely be felt at ground level, allowing the direct sunlight to scorch everything within its reach. Heat radiated from the cracked asphalt as he lowered his Ray-Bans and squinted to his right, towards the western horizon where the ribbon of road disappeared in a shimmering haze. A short distance to the east a pair of crows picked at a road kill, their blue-black feathers iridescent in the brilliance of the day, departing noisily as a vehicle approached. Its appearance was preceded by the sound of a diesel engine laboring under a heavy load, disappointingly different from the one that Wright was listening for.

The large squat truck came into view, slowly overcoming the slight incline in low gear. Jim recognized it as a tanker from the local septic service and although he didn't recognize the honey dipper at the wheel, they traded friendly waves as the hulking metal dinosaur rumbled past. He retreated a couple of steps from the roadside, holding his breath until the stench of its wake had washed past him. The crows called to each other as they returned to their grisly meal and once again there was stillness, interrupted only occasionally by the shrill chirping of a cicada, adding its solo performance to the background chorus of crickets as they reveled in the sweltering day.

Jim felt drops of sweat gathering at the nape of his neck, trickling down the hollow of his spine and creating a dark streak on the back of his faded grey Iowa Hawkeyes tee shirt. He grimaced and glanced down at his watch yet again, a habit that had more to do with a comforting memory than with the passing of minutes. It was a quality timepiece, a twenty-year old gold-plated Hamilton that had been his father's prized possession. For an instant Jim once again savored a flashback of the day he came into possession of the watch, how good it felt to remove it from his daddy's wrist and to be finally free of his drunken tyranny.

"Sonofabitch." he muttered, somehow directing the curse at both of the men who now occupied his thoughts. He slicked back his thick black hair with both hands, wiping them off on the thighs of his jeans, considering the possibility that he may just have to track Mitch down if he wanted to speak to him before leaving town.

At that moment, the growing roar of an almost unmuffled engine reverberated from the distance to his right, accompanied by an occasional loud pop from one of its six poorly timed cylinders. Somehow recognizing the discordant racket, Wright took an expectant step forward and craned his neck as Mitch Goren's ancient Ford pickup appeared, trailed by a plume of oily blue smoke.

The wreck crossed lanes and lurched to a stop on Wright's side of the road, uncomfortably close, as its driver threw the column shift into neutral and turned the engine off before settling back into the seat. Casually draining the last of a can of Bud, Mitch Goren tossed the empty onto the floor of the passenger side where it clanged against several others.

Wright placed his palms on the roof of the cab and was sure he could smell weed as he leaned in close, frowning to convey his displeasure at having been kept waiting in the broiling sun. He was an imposing figure, well over six feet tall and brawny, but despite his comparatively small stature Goren was not one to be intimidated. Their history together dated back to junior high, where they had enjoyed a well-earned reputation as a feared bullying tandem. Since then their secret crimes had steadily increased in brutality if not frequency, committed not for monetary gain but simply to blow off steam, satisfying shared compulsions that they recognized but rarely spoke of.

"'bout time you showed up. Are you lit?"

"Nah, I ain't had more than a six-pack the whole day, and I can't be more than a few minutes late anyway. What, are you afraid she'll see us talking, Jimbo?" He kept his mirrored aviators in place, knowing that his red eyes would betray the lie.

Wright glanced back towards the house, which was obscured by an overgrown hedgerow that fronted the property.

"I'm supposed to be out for a walk while she makes dinner, but she'll be careful not to come out and catch me smoking." He flashed a smile of superiority. "She knows full well I didn't quit, but she's too damned timid to call me on it."

Goren's knowing grin creased the ragged scar that ran from his left eyebrow down to his jaw. It served as a constant reminder of the fierce bar fight five years earlier that had started when he taunted a biker who was twice his size, and ended with a broken longneck being dragged across Mitch's face. In time, he came to regard the disfigurement as a badge of honor, identifying him as some sort of street warrior, but only his closest friends could use the nickname without fear of a perceived slight. Jim Wright was one of those chosen few.

Wright looked around somewhat nervously before leaning even closer, lowering his voice to a more conspiratorial tone.

"Stitch, I'm calling it off. Just forget I ever mentioned it."

Goren stared straight ahead through the cracked windshield, working his jaw as he struggled to control himself, then violently pounded his palms against the steering wheel as the battle for self-control was lost.

"No! Why? Goddammit Jimbo, you know how much I been countin' on that money! I was about to ask you for a little down payment right now so I could look for a new truck. This thing is fallin' apart, even the goddam frame is rusted through!"

He pointed a finger at Wright in a gesture that was clearly meant as a threat.

"Don't you *dare* go soft on me now, you know this has got to be done."

Wright put both hands up in stop-sign fashion, breaking eye contact and cocking his head to one side in a seemingly submissive gesture. He knew how volatile Goren could be.

"Calm down, we'll figure something out. I'm just thinking that maybe I jumped the gun here, she doesn't know as much as I thought she did."

Goren snatched the last can of Bud from the back seat and pulled the tab, ignoring the eruption of white foam that dripped onto his already filthy denim shirt. He shook his head side to side as he took a long swig.

"You can't call this thing off, Jimbo. You know it 'n I know it. I need that cash, and she knows too much. Your smokin' habit ain't the only thing that girl has figured out. She's just keeping things to herself for now, waiting until the next time you screw up. You got to nip this thing in the bud!"

Wright's patience was already worn thin. "Listen, I don't have time to argue with you Mitch, just stay cool for now and I'll be in touch. Maybe we'll take another road trip, have some fun."

Goren poured the remaining contents of the can down his throat and tossed the empty onto the pile, leaning over and spitting through the opposite window. He jabbed his finger towards Wright's face, adding emphasis to his next words. "You're a fool, Jimbo. You said yourself she's been snoopin' around, how long you think it'll be before she finds out where we go on those road trips? And you said you got all drunk and told her about your daddy, do you think Little Miss Kim will keep quiet about that? When she starts thinkin' on what happened to her mom and puts two and two together?"

The wine stain birthmark on Wright's forehead turned a shade darker, a sign that his own penchant for sudden fury was nearing the surface. He grabbed Goren's sinewy shoulder and squeezed hard, angered by his partner's resistance but more irritated with himself for having put them in this situation.

"Shut up about that! She will never tell anyone about my father, and you're the only other person that knows. As far as Melanie, she fell off a ladder and tumbled down the stairs. It was an accident, just like the sheriff said." He grabbed Goren's wrist, turning the hand upward and holding it there as he pulled a crumpled twenty from his pocket and slapped it into his palm. "Now you go get drunk and have a good time, I gotta get back."

Goren disgustedly shoved the bill into his shirt pocket and cranked the engine over, reviving the noise and vibration. A cloud of bluish gray smoke seemed to emanate not from the end of the tailpipe but from somewhere under the passenger compartment. He raised his voice to be heard.

"You give me a call when you come to your senses, Jimbo. That woman can put you in a bind, and you need a way out."

Having regained control of his emotions, Wright took a step back from the fumes. "She won't do that, Stitch, that girl loves me. I just need to give it some time."

Goren didn't hear the last part. He let the clutch out, mashed the accelerator and attempted a defiant burnout, but the dilapidated Ford couldn't deliver anything more than the ping of pre-ignition. Wright watched him pull slowly away, smoke trailing behind the old pickup as it dog-walked down the road and out of sight. He headed back to the rear of the house, trying to convince himself that he had done the right thing.

*

When her husband suddenly declared that he was going out for "some fresh air before dinner", Kim Wright naturally assumed that he was giving in to his not-so-secret smoking habit. Jim proudly claimed to have given up cigarettes months ago, and although the evidence to the contrary was obvious, Kim chose to ignore it in order to avoid the inevitable confrontation and indignant denials that would surely follow. Jim's past behavior had always made it clear that their relationship would run smoothly only as long as certain subjects remained outside the boundaries of open discussion. She would gladly put up with the faint odor of tobacco on his clothing if it meant keeping the peace between them.

He had been gone much longer than usual and dinner was nearly ready, so Kim left the kitchen and wandered out front to look for him, eventually hearing voices from beyond the thickly overgrown hedgerow. Stepping cautiously into the barrier of tangled vines and dogwood to part the branches, she managed to catch sight of her husband as he stood at the road about fifty yards away. He seemed to be engaged in an animated conversation with the occupant of an old blue pickup truck, and although she couldn't see the driver she knew that the battered vehicle belonged to Mitch Goren.

The two men were close friends, a fact that distressed Kim greatly. She didn't like Mitch, and couldn't understand what bond her husband could possibly have with such a crude, ignorant hayseed. They were hunting and fishing buddies and drinking partners, and sometimes spent weekends together pursuing those interests far from home. They seldom spoke of the details of these ventures in her presence, and when they did she was excluded from their drunken whispering, high-fiving and inside jokes, behavior that seemed more suited to memories of a bachelor party than a trout stream. Kim wanted badly to trust her husband and was determined to give him the benefit of the doubt, but his wing man received no such consideration.

The voices were louder now, to a shouting level, and although Kim couldn't make out their words she could see fingers being pointed in anger. Jimmy took a quick step back from the cab of the pickup and shrugged his shoulders, palms up as if he refused to argue any further. Intrigued but fearing discovery, Kim took this as her cue to turn and hurry back to the house, and as she did so the roar of an engine signaled Mitch Goren's departure.

CHAPTER 2

January, 2016
Grove Park, NY

JACK FERRIS DROVE slowly into the village of Grove Park, taking pleasure in the natural beauty of a January snowfall. The virtually weightless flakes floated slowly downward, swirling in the occasional breeze, blanketing the frozen ground and coating every branch and twig with a layer of white. Intuition honed by a lifetime in upstate New York told Jack that a lake-effect storm could be brewing, about to dump a foot or two of snow overnight, but he wasn't going to worry about that possibility. He was headed to Woody's bar for a beer, or ten. It had been a long workday, nine hours without a break, but he had managed to finish the job by Friday afternoon as promised. He had been painting three rooms in one of the mansions of the nouveau riche in Heron Ridge Estates, and the lady of the house insisted that it must be done in time for her daughter's sweet sixteen party. Normally Jack was his own harshest critic but he had to admit, the faux pattern he had applied in the dining room looked fantastic, better than any wallpaper, and he knew that he could expect several referrals once the neighborhood ladies had an opportunity to admire it.

Rather than take the time to stop at home to shower and change, he had quickly washed up before leaving the job site and grabbed a clean tee shirt from the duffle bag that he kept in the van. Hopefully, he would get to Woody's in time to get a seat at the bar, but right now he was enjoying the ride, listening to The Boss sing about something going on at "the edge of town." He mused that you just didn't hear that phrase anymore, unless there was an old western on late-night cable. That's where Jack was coming from, the edge of town, and into the heart of the village.

Pressing the source button, he switched over to AM radio just in time to catch the weather forecast.

" — will bring a projected snowfall of four to six inches in the Buffalo metro area, at least a foot south of the city, and possibly two feet in the ski areas further south. Temperatures will — " His suspicions confirmed, Jack turned the sound system off so he could better enjoy the peaceful scenery for the remainder of his ride.

As he approached the "four corners", Grove Park's equivalent of downtown, Jack thought about how much had changed here in the last ten years. Main Street was wider now, and lined with decorative street lamps from which baskets of poinsettias and politically correct holiday banners still hung. These would soon be replaced with something appropriate for spring, in keeping with the town council's concerted effort to promote and maintain Grove Park's picture-postcard appearance. There were cobblestone crosswalks at each intersection, and sculptures contributed by local artists accented the six-block stretch where restaurants and shops were located.

Most of the buildings had been renovated, and yet the village retained its quaint, intimate small-town feel. Jack had long expected an influx of fast-food joints and franchise retailers, but that fear, shared with many of the town's citizens, had not been realized. There had been plenty of housing development and commercial building in the last decade, including a 40-store shopping mall nearby, but since the town of Grove Park actually covered 38 square miles, the village and its four corners district was unaffected.

The town population was growing and the signs of affluence were obvious. New home construction was booming, and in developments like Heron Ridge and Heritage Heights the horseshoe driveways were filled with luxury cars and the largest SUV's available. Still, the wealthy businessmen and professionals who lived there managed to coexist comfortably with Grove Park's less notable citizens, the working class that Jack was proud to be a part of. He loved the upstate area, winters and all, and Grove Park seemed to him to be the ideal place to live.

CHAPTER 3

August 1990

HAVING RETURNED TO the safety of her kitchen, Kim tried to relax and catch her breath, expecting Jim to return at any moment. Using a cloth napkin to dab perspiration from her face and neck, she set the usual two places for dinner with practiced precision, scanning the table one last time to make sure that nothing had been overlooked. Getting up during the meal to retrieve the salt shaker, or any other forgotten item, would be an imposition that would aggravate him into a mood of passive aggression that made light dinner conversation impossible.

Stepping into the bathroom to quickly check her appearance in the large oval mirror, Kim studied her reflection for a moment. She had been blessed with natural good looks, her tanned face featuring deep blue eyes framed by light brown hair that was now bleached almost blonde by the summer sun. Satisfied that she looked presentable, she smoothed the skirt of her white linen sundress and returned to the kitchen. As she removed the main course from the oven Kim heard the door open behind her as Jim entered and, without a word, headed straight for the bathroom to wash up.

She had made a favorite meal of his, roasted chicken, and took comfort in the knowledge that, for at least this one meal, Jim's frequent criticism of her cooking might be avoided. She tried to put aside the disconcerting roadside scene that she had witnessed, and certainly had no intention of mentioning it.

A light mood was especially important today, since Jimmy was to depart right after dinner for a two or three-day business trip to meet with clients and scout for potential property listings. Kim hoped that this meal would be an opportunity to finally speak to him about some of the things that had been on her mind in recent weeks. She wanted to discuss their future, and the possibility of starting a family.

Once they were both seated and facing each other, Kim watched as Jim's eyes quickly surveyed the space between them. He looked up and gave her a wry smile that seemed to convey congratulations on a job well done — or was it disappointing to him that he couldn't dramatically rise from his chair with an exasperated sigh and point out an oversight?

"Picked a pretty hot day to roast a chicken" was his only comment, spoken without a trace of levity.

After about five minutes of alternately eating and engaging in halting conversation about the weather, it seemed like an opportune time to put her recent concerns into words. She had been looking forward to this moment for days with great anticipation and no small amount of dread, and her heart was pounding as she took the plunge.

"Jimmy, are all these out of town trips really necessary? I mean, you must know how much I hate being alone here at night. Maybe you could do more over the phone, even set up an office here at home. That way you could take care of a lot of details without leaving the house at all. Wouldn't that be more convenient for you?"

Jim stopped eating and looked up at her, the increasing redness in his cheeks reflecting his resentment of Kim's advice. His facial expression alarmed her, and her stomach tightened as she realized that her carefully planned wording may not have been tactful enough. She desperately wanted to finish her thought, to express her feelings for her husband and raise the notion of starting their own family, but now she was afraid to continue.

"What the hell are you talking about, Kim?" He spoke in a mocking whine as he repeated Kim's words. "'*Are these trips necessary?*' Of course they're necessary! I have to speak to my clients face to face! Do you know what it's like to try to convince a fifth-generation farmer that selling his property is the right thing to do, because he's in debt up to his ass? Or to get a buyer from the city to part with hundreds of thousands of dollars to

buy it and turn it into a country estate? I have to develop a rapport, a relationship, with them. You can't do that over the goddamned phone!"

Kim's first instinct, the one her husband expected, was to be apologetic in order to quell Jim's building rage, to explain that she wasn't trying to tell him how to conduct his business, she simply wanted him to
travel a little less. Somehow she managed to suppress that reaction and
decided that this time she would hold her ground and not allow herself to
be steamrolled.

"Well, take this trip, for instance — I understand the purpose of it,
but what will you be doing for three whole days? Maybe if you shared
more with me I'd understand."

To Kim's surprise, he seemed unable to provide an immediate reply to
what should have been an easy question. She was merely trying to restore
their dialogue to a civil tone, but now Jim seemed flustered by his wife's
unexpected temerity.

"Well," he stammered, "I don't have a firm schedule. I just intend to
meet with these people and try to sell them a property."

Suddenly gaining an uncharacteristic boldness, Kim pressed on. "But
why three days? I'm sure your pitch won't take that long, what else will
you be doing? Are you meeting Mitch to do some fishing or something?"

Jim's demeanor had changed completely. Kim's bold questioning had
put him on the defensive, a situation that was totally unheard of in their
relationship. His cheeks were flushed by a sudden rush of blood, and
the oddly shaped birthmark on his right brow had become an ominous
red flag.

"Jesus Christ, Kim" he blurted, "What do you think I'm gonna do
there? Are you saying you don't trust me? You think I'm cheating on you
or something?"

Now it was Kim's turn to be speechless. The conversation had taken a
totally unforeseen turn, and seemed to be careening out of control.

"Of course I trust you!" was Kim's attempt to restore order. Then,
unable to resist voicing her true thoughts, she added "Is there some reason
I shouldn't? Are you meeting someone there?" Now her tone was soft and
tentative, as if she was afraid to hear the answer to a question she might
regret asking.

Several heartbeats of silence followed, and Jim looked down at his plate as he deflected the question with a sarcastic "Yeah, right Kim, I'm meeting someone there, right!" He tried to sound confident and dismissive, making light of such a ridiculous idea, but he wasn't able to carry it off. As Kim stared at him Jim went silent and continued pushing food around his plate, unable to make eye contact. The only sound in the room was that of Kim's chair sliding back across the hardwood floor as she slowly stood, horrified by a sudden realization. Her words came out slowly, barely audible, as she gave voice to her biggest fear.

"Oh my god, you are — you're cheating on me, aren't you?"

Her eyes filled with tears, and Kim didn't hear her husband's words as he struggled to attempt a denial. She saw the lapse of confidence in the eyes that still couldn't look at her, and interrupted his reply with a derisive, mirthless laugh. "Jesus, I'm such a fool! My mother was right about you!"

That remark triggered Jim's full rage, a fearsome event that she had experienced only a few times in their relationship. Before Kim could move, his chair was flying back against the wall with a crash as he sprang up to confront her. He moved closer, his face now inches from hers, and appeared to be enjoying her fright.

"What does that mean? She was right about what? That old bitch, you're just like her!" He shouted the words like a madman, and Kim could feel his spittle on her face.

Frightened now, Kim backed away a step, just as Jim unleashed a vicious backhand that struck the right side of her face with a blinding flash. She staggered backwards and found herself with her back against the wall, and for a few seconds her legs felt so weak she thought she might collapse to the floor. Just then some form of self-preservation took hold, and she found the strength to push past him toward the staircase.

He took a step forward to follow up but, in a rare display of self-control, decided against it. Chest heaving, adrenaline still pumping, Jim watched her retreat, stunned by the sudden events that had just taken place. He sat down heavily in the chair his wife had just vacated and felt the sting on the back of his right hand, a reminder of what he had just done. Predictably, his immediate reaction was not one of remorse, but a familiar feeling of satisfaction.

*

Rushing up the stairs towards the sanctuary of her bedroom, Kim sobbed uncontrollably, fearful that her husband might be in close pursuit. She had climbed these thirteen steps a thousand times before, and her feet pounded furiously on the risers without a stumble despite the flood of tears that blurred her vision.

Throwing herself onto the bed with a groan of agony, Kim buried her face in the pillows and succumbed to the convulsive sobs that shook her body. She felt wounded to her very soul, as primal emotion asserted itself over any form of reasoning. Her tortured sobs gradually dissolved into a quiet, steady stream of tears. The pulsing throb under her right eye was fading into numbness as the swelling grew.

Eyes closed, the argument replayed in her mind in brief, increasingly dreamlike flashes, and she was only vaguely aware of the distant sounds of Jim's departure drifting up to the second floor.

Mercifully, Kim's brain recognized her need for relief from the pain and exhaustion she felt, and provided the anesthetic she required — she fell into a deep sleep.

CHAPTER 4

January 2016

WOODY'S PUB WAS located on the main drag, but Jack anticipated the lack of street parking that would be available out in front. He turned down a side street and drove toward the back entrance, pulling into the parking lot that Woody's shared with the adjacent Grove Park Lanes. Approaching the door, Jack spotted a huddled group of five patrons who had braved the snow and cold to come outside for a smoke. He interpreted the size of the shivering group as an indication that the bar must be unusually crowded for this early hour.

Walking through the lobby of the Lanes, Jack heard the familiar explosions of hardwood pins being struck by 16-pound urethane missiles, and reminded himself to check the standings of his Wednesday night league on his way out.

He passed by the shoe rental counter and entered Woody's through a portal that connected the Lanes to the pub, a heavily traveled route on league nights as the bowlers took turns buying rounds between frames.

Entering Woody's, Jack had an immediate sense that he was a late arrival to a great party. "Piano Man" was playing loudly, accompanied by a group of patrons who were attempting to sing along without full memory of the lyrics. Raucous laughter and the clinking of glasses punctuated their version, and Billy Joel was allowed to fill in the words they had forgotten. Jack walked carefully past the pool table and dart board, both occupied even at this early hour, and approached the large three-sided bar.

He was surprised at the sight of what appeared to be a standing-room only crowd. This had always been a working man's bar, but it seemed that quite a few office types had blown off work this Friday afternoon to enjoy the atmosphere that Friday night brought to Woody's.

"Jackieee!" came a shout from the opposite side of the bar, in a volume that was somewhat louder than necessary. He looked through the crowd and saw the familiar face of Pete Webster, a Grove Park detective and one of Jack's closest friends. Jack was glad to see Pete, even if he was a little inebriated, and was even more pleased at the sight of the vacant bar stool next to him.

"Come on, man, I saved a seat for ya!"

The two had been buddies since high school, and hung out together as often as Pete's schedule allowed. Their friendship was based on common interests such as sports and beer, and the two had a long history as teammates on various bowling, softball and hockey teams, although in recent years it seemed that the beer drinking had become more important than the sporting challenges.

Pete's life had been forever changed a few years before by the death of his wife, Mary, and he was still trying to recover. He had lost some weight in the process and seemed to have aged more than the three years that had passed. Still, he was one of those rare nice guys, a good-looking guy who was attractive to women but didn't seem aware of it, as if it wasn't important to him.

"Tough day at work, Jackie?" Pete laughed, looking at Jack's paint-splotched jeans.

"Yeah, thanks for noticing, asshole. I wasn't feeling self-conscious enough." Despite the joking, Jack was confident in his appearance and didn't have any regrets about his chosen vocation. Approaching forty, he maintained an athletic build and exuded a humble sort of self-assurance. Along with a full head of chestnut hair and a light manly stubble, his chiseled features completed the all-American look that the ladies seemed drawn to.

Jeff "Woody" Woodward, the proprietor, was one of two bartenders working feverishly to keep up with the demands of this seemingly parched early crowd, but Pete was oblivious to their plight as he issued a loud command. "Woody, a bottle of Blue for my man Jack, and back me up too!"

Embarrassed, Jack added, "When you get a chance, Woody."

"Sure thing," the barman replied good naturedly, and a minute later Jack was sipping from a cold bottle of Labatt Blue.

"Be right back, man, I gotta whizz," Pete volunteered as he shoved himself off of his barstool. Jack noticed the slur in his friend's words, and was surprised to see how unsteady Pete was as he walked towards the men's room. Noting the number of empty shot glasses on the bar, Jack made a mental note to make sure Pete didn't drive himself home.

Scanning the room, his attention was drawn to a boisterous group at the opposite corner of the bar. They appeared to be sharing a terrifically funny joke, and in the center of the group Jack recognized the storyteller as James Wainwright, the Town Supervisor. At his side was his knockout wife Nicki, and as Jack's idle gaze wandered to her, he was surprised to find her looking directly back at him. The eye contact seemed unexpected for both parties, and each quickly looked elsewhere.

Jack remembered the same thing happening once before at the local fitness center, as if he and Mrs. Wainwright had been interested in getting a good look at each other but were embarrassed to admit it. Maybe next time he'd strike up a conversation, rather than continue to act like some socially inept lurker.

Jack had seen a couple of the guys before, they were assistants to Jim Wainwright and at present seemed to be charged mainly with laughing at his jokes. One was Joey Garrity, a sort of personal aide to the Supervisor and manager of the Wainwrights' real estate agency. The elder gentleman was Al Kaplan, a former Town Attorney who, in addition to his law practice, also served as an advisor to Wainwright and was a respected town councilman. The only other female in the group was Jill Sherman, a recent client of Jack's. He had done some painting and stenciled borders in her kitchen a few months earlier, and she had seemed happy with the results. Jill was a striking redhead who apparently was a close friend of Nicki's, and Jack had noticed that they usually worked out together. Continuing his visual tour of the bar area, Jack was once again struck by the diversity of the Woody's crowd. The regulars were well represented as always, middle-aged blue-collar types, factory workers, local tradesmen like himself, town employees, and the unemployed. They sat around the bar in their favorite places and traded opinions on sports, current events, politics, and whatever else might appear on the big-screen television above the bar.

Sitting at tables next to the bar, and further back near the pool table and electronic dartboard, were groups of younger patrons. Judging by their apparel, Jack would guess that some were college students and others were local working kids. They preferred to sit with their peers, avoiding the conversation at the bar. The presidential primaries were underway, and vocal Trump and Clinton supporters had engaged in too many heated arguments of late. Thankfully, at the present time the two factions enjoyed their chosen beverages in peaceful coexistence.

Sprinkled throughout the place were a number of local businessmen, professionals, and the usual ski buffs who stopped in for a beer and a bite to eat before heading home. On summer nights, the ski crowd would be replaced by the local bikers. Those were mostly weekend riders, baby boomers who had reached a point in their lives where they could afford that Harley Davidson and reclaim a portion of their lost youth.

They all were seemingly drawn to the unpretentious ambience of the place, and Woody's had enjoyed a revival along with the rest of Grove Park. On this day, even the upper crust of Grove Park society was represented, in the persons of the Wainwright party. These were not the old-money descendants of the town founders, but rather the local political and business circles' most recognizable faces, the Town Supervisor and his posse.

Jack was watching Woody work, hoping to get his attention to request another round, when he heard the click of spike heels approaching. Turning to his left in order to check out the legs above those heels, he was surprised to see the face of Nicki Wainwright, flashing her perfect smile from less than two feet away.

Sensing that he was lost for words — maybe she was accustomed to having that effect on men — Nicki rescued him by extending a hand.

"Jack, right? I'm Nicki Wainwright, glad to meet you."

"Hello Ms. Wainwright, nice to meet you, too."

Ms. Wainwright? What the hell was he thinking, not calling her Nicki? After all, she wasn't his former high school English teacher. Jack considered himself to be pretty good with the ladies, but this one seemed to fluster him. Maybe it was because she actually *wa*s a lady, he wasn't sure. She was definitely an attention-getter, the heels making her stand taller than her natural 5"6", stylishly sculpted pixie hairstyle highlighted to almost blond, and an oval face that featured greenish eyes and that devastating smile.

He attempted a recovery with "I've seen you at Strong's gym, right?"

"Yes, you may have. My friend Jill Sherman pointed you out for me and said you were the best *faux* painter in town. I've seen some of your work since then, she was right."

At that moment, Pete wandered back and stood behind Nicki, awkwardly waiting to reclaim his place at the bar but unable to get around her. Nicki finally sensed his presence, and stepped aside.

"Look, I don't want to intrude, I just was wondering how booked you are. I have a few rooms that need freshening, and I was hoping you could come over sometime and give me some ideas, and maybe an estimate."

"Well, sure, yeah, I could do that. I'm actually kind of caught up right now."

Nicki was obviously pleased to hear the answer that she knew was coming all along. "Great! Here's my card, call my cell anytime and we'll set up a date, okay?"

"Sounds good, thanks, Ms. Wainwright." Jack took the card, trying to hide the undeniable excitement he was feeling at the prospect of meeting with this woman.

"Call me Nicki, please!" she laughed. " Don't forget me, now."

"No, I won't." *Not a chance in the world I'd forget you*, said Jack's inner voice.

Just then they were interrupted by the arrival of Mr. Wainwright, who strode to his wife's side and took her arm. He completely ignored Jack and Pete — well, for that matter, she had ignored Pete, too — and seemed a bit aggravated as he blurted, "C'mon hon, you ready to go? I'm starving. We're going across the street."

Jack thought that the Supervisor may be telling the truth about being hungry, he looked like a man who didn't miss many meals, but the real motive for his visit was borne of jealousy. Nicki looked to be around the same age as Jack, but this guy had to be at least ten years older. He had undoubtedly come over as a reminder that this was *his* woman they were talking to, hitting on, lusting after, or whatever the hell they were doing. Of course, he couldn't blame them, she really was fine, but he had seen enough.

"Yes, I'm ready." Nicki answered, still focused on Jack. Then, favoring the handsome painter with one last smile, just to tweak Big Jim a little more, "Goodbye Jack, talk to you soon." Grove Park's power couple made their way to the front entrance, headed across Main Street to Barton House.

"Yeah, right, get your ass across the street where you belong," Pete mumbled.

Jack watched them go, and couldn't deny that a part of him wished that they had stayed. He would have preferred that Nicki Wainwright return to her group of friends before her boorish husband had felt it necessary to intervene. At least that way Jack could have stolen a few more glances at this captivating woman, who seemed to know that she had his full attention.

CHAPTER 5

August 1990

STARTLED INTO SUDDEN consciousness by a sound from downstairs, Kim lay perfectly still, staring into the darkness. The origin of the noise was unknown, but it had been loud enough to cause her to flinch, and she thought there had been an accompanying vibration. Had something struck the house? Had a door been slammed closed by a breeze or, even worse, been forced open? Maybe it had been a car door closing. She didn't know, and that frightened her.

The world had continued to turn as Kim slept, bringing the inevitable sundown and shadows, and she felt disoriented. It had been full daylight when she fell asleep, and now the house was cloaked in total darkness. Raising her head from the pillow, Kim winced as she felt the pain from under her right eye, and the ugliness of that day's events came flooding back to her. It hadn't been a nightmare, the argument with Jim had actually happened. Sleep had provided a temporary escape, but there were harsh realities that must be faced.

Now that the façade had been ripped away, uncovering the truths that she had conditioned herself to ignore, it was time for Kim Wright to take control of her own life for the first time in years. She would have to begin by investigating this disturbing noise.

She had always hated being alone in the house at night. When it came time for bed she would nervously, reluctantly, turn off the last of the downstairs lights and hurry up the stairs to her bedroom. Once there she would usually toss and turn restlessly, sometimes for hours, listening to the creaking and snapping sounds emanating from the wood framing of the hundred-year-old farmhouse that she had grown up in and inherited from her parents. Somehow those sounds went unnoticed when Jim was home, although she was sure they must be just as loud.

Kim listened intently, trying to hear any further sound from downstairs. The symphony of a Midwestern summer drifted in through the open window — the steady chirping of an army of crickets, accompanied by the rhythmic bass of tree frogs and the occasional gust of wind ruffling cottonwood leaves softly in the background. She realized that *the sound* had so alarmed her that her only movement since hearing it had been to open her eyes and slightly raise her head so her ear was above the pillow. She heard the dull internal roar of blood pushing through her arteries, its flow increased by a rapid heartbeat. Remaining on her left side in a near-fetal posture, eyes locked on the shadows of the hallway outside her bedroom, Kim tried to calm herself. She wanted to move her limbs, to at least relax them, but the rigor of her fear would not yet allow it.

It was so dark. When Jim left there were no lights on inside the house, and Kim pictured the doors and windows left open, at the very least unlocked, as he stormed out of the house. Could he be coming back to apologize, to make amends? She hoped so, but in her heart Kim did not believe that contrition was a part of her husband's character.

Kim was reminded of her childhood fear of the dark, when she refused to go to bed without the comforting glow of a nightlight, or her bedroom door left ajar to provide a sliver of light. Since her marriage to Jim she had adapted to his preferred sleeping environment, which meant total darkness. There were no streetlamps near their house, and the waning crescent moon struggled to send its dim light into their bedroom window. The only discernible shapes were cast in the faint glow of the digital display of the clock-radio on the nightstand. It read 10:45, and Kim estimated that she had been asleep at least five hours.

Silently berating herself for over-reacting to what was probably nothing more threatening than a wind-blown door, Kim resolved to overcome her fear as any sensible adult would do. She would force herself to get up, go downstairs, and prove to herself that no psychotic killers lurked in her kitchen. The alternative was to lie in bed motionless, a quaking bundle of nerves, afraid and unable to face her life. After all, she reasoned, why would anyone break into their home? There were no outward signs of affluence to attract a thief, and violent crime was nearly unheard of in this rural community. The only instances she could recall were far from being random acts. The victim usually had had some personal history in common with the perpetrator, and more often than not the two were blood relatives.

Listen to yourself, she thought — when had the word *perpetrator* become a part of her vocabulary?

After a full five minutes — it seemed like thirty-five — of lying still, listening, and rationalizing, she summoned the will to move her body into an upright sitting position. Kim moved gingerly, slowly, as if she were sitting in a minefield, in spite of the knowledge that, from downstairs, the sound of her movements couldn't possibly be heard.

Heart pounding despite her attempts to be calm, Kim swung her legs — rather, she slid them, ever so carefully — over the bedside. Once again all movement was halted as she listened for any new unexplained noises, and her eyes peered through the doorway of the bedroom, seeing only the darkened hallway. Her feet were suspended above the floor, not yet able to reach it, and she steeled herself for the push that would remove her from the safety of her bed. She was vaguely aware of the gathering beads of moisture on the back of her neck, on her forehead and her upper lip.

Somehow, this fear was taking on a life of its own, possessing Kim's mind and interfering with her attempts to control physical movement. Still, she clung to her underlying sanity, the belief that she was being silly, there was nothing to fear at all. She was determined to fight and win this internal battle, and her fingers dug into the edge of the mattress as she pushed forward, until her toes rested on cool hardwood. She exhaled.

Rising to her full 5'3" height on legs that felt surprisingly weak, Kim was aware of the soft creaking sounds created by the mattress and box spring returning to normal thickness after being compressed by her weight. Had there been another sound from downstairs? It seemed like a bump, or a thud — the phrase "bump in the night" flashed by, immediately lost among her racing thoughts — but the sheer pressure of blood being pumped by her thumping heart was so loud in her ears, she couldn't be sure what she had heard, if anything. There was no turning back now, she told herself.

Summoning every bit of courage in her possession, Kim moved closer to the doorway, developing a technique of stealth as she moved. She would slide a foot slowly forward, never quite losing contact with the floor, gently transfer her weight to it, then pause to listen before moving the other foot forward. Feeling through the darkness to locate the dresser on her left, she kept her hand there to provide balance as she crept around it into the doorway. Directly across the narrow hall was the bedroom that had been Kim's for most of her life.

For an instant her mind flashed back three years, to the night she decided to leave her childhood home to move in with Jim. Standing in that doorway her widowed mother first attempted to calmly reason with Kim, and when that didn't work she tearfully begged her to reconsider, all the while knowing that the battle was already lost. Any weight her words may have carried had been washed away in the wake of Jim's Svengali-like influence on Kim.

A year later her mom was gone, taken by a tragic accident. She had somehow fallen down the staircase and succumbed to her injuries, laying there for two days before a visiting friend discovered her body.

After that, it had been just Kim and Jimmy. Now she was alone.

CHAPTER 6

January 2016

BARTON HOUSE WAS a Grove Park institution, having been owned and operated for more than five decades by one of the village's founding families. The gourmet food was highly rated and more highly priced, and the intimate bar room had long served as a gathering place for the town's prominent political and business figures.

Seated at his favorite table, Jim Wainwright sipped his Grand Marnier aperitif and tried to appear interested in the after-dinner conversation, although it bored him tremendously. Joey Garrity and Al Kaplan were arguing about politics, specifically about Donald Trump's viability as a presidential candidate.

Who gives a damn? thought Wainwright, glancing towards the restroom alcove every few seconds to see if Nicki and Jill were planning on returning to the table. It had been fifteen minutes since they had excused themselves, supposedly to visit the ladies room, and Wainwright suspected that they had decided to forego the inevitable talk of politics for a fresh drink at the bar.

Just as he was considering tracking them down Wainwright felt the beckoning vibration of his phone, and automatically plucked it from his breast pocket as he nodded in apparent agreement with one of Joey's increasingly passionate statements. Wainwright shrugged as if the call was an unwelcome interruption, but in truth he had stopped listening to Joey a while ago and the phone call was a welcome distraction.

"Yeah, Wainwright -" was his terse greeting, an indication that he fully expected the call to be of a business nature rather than personal. He rose from his chair and walked toward the restrooms, appearing to retreat from the noise of the dining room as he took the call. In fact, he was more interested in finding out where his wife had gone.

"Hello Jimbo."

Wainwright paused momentarily as his mind flipped into free browse mode, trying to identify the familiar voice. Before he could respond, the caller continued.

"This *is* Jim Wright, ain't it?"

Wainwright stopped in his tracks, feeling his stomach tighten in an involuntary response to the question. "Who is this?" he demanded, tugging at his tie as he felt himself break into a sweat. The room temperature seemed to have risen to 90 degrees, and he felt a bit outside of himself.

"Well, I'm not surprised you don't remember me Jimbo — but I've never forgotten you. It's your ol' buddy Mitch."

Wainwright had pegged the voice just as the caller identified himself. Mitch Goren was a former schoolmate and friend – not to mention partner in crime — from his early days in Iowa. Wainwright had been known as Jim Wright then, but changed to the longer surname shortly after leaving the heartland behind to head east. He hadn't been addressed as 'Jim Wright' by anyone in over two decades. His first instinct was to buy time by feigning ignorance as if he didn't remember the name, and with someone other than Mitch he might have, but somehow that didn't seem like the right play.

"Mitch Goren?" he asked, sounding more surprised than pleased to hear from his old friend. "How the hell are you, man?" The question was insincere, but it was all Wainwright could think of. He told himself to remain cool, in spite of the growing dread he was feeling.

"Not bad, Jimbo, not bad, doin' better all the time. Nice of you to ask. I know *you're* doin' okay."

Wainwright couldn't bear the small talk any longer. "Mitch, what's — how did you get this number?" He felt a knot in his stomach, and felt the need to sit down. He hadn't thought about the Mitch Goren period of his life for many years, and didn't wish to revisit it.

Goren chuckled at the other end, sensing the bewilderment in

Wainwright's tone. "Just lucky Jimmy, just lucky. I'll explain it to you in person, how would that be? We have a lot to catch up on, huh?"

The wheels of Wainwright's thought process were still turning, but found little traction. He looked across the darkened dining room to make sure no one was listening to his end of the conversation, and saw his dinner companions carrying on without him, illuminated by the decorative twinkle lights overhead. No one was paying any attention to him, and he relaxed a bit, finally able to respond.

"Sure Mitch," he agreed, not wishing to upset Goren by putting him off. Now that contact had been initiated, Wainwright had to find out what Goren's agenda was. They shared a lot of history, things that only the two of them knew about, and he had to keep it that way. "Do you plan on being in town soon?" He had the feeling that Goren was already in Grove Park, and was attempting to illicit a confirmation.

Goren stifled a laugh, an audible snort escaping into the phone. "I'll call you soon Jimmy, and we'll set it up. I know you're real busy, bein' the Town Bigwig and all."

Wainwright was at a disadvantage, wondering how much Goren knew about him. He had absolutely no knowledge of Goren's current situation, or for that matter his last twenty-five years.

"Fine, Mitch. You call me and we'll meet somewhere, catch up on things." Wainwright was trying to sound at ease, and failing miserably. He wanted the call to end. He could picture Goren's smug grin, those crooked teeth, the scar.

"Right, Jimmy. Now you get back to your dinner group, especially those two luscious ladies! I'll be in touch." Goren disconnected, leaving a stunned Wainwright scanning the restaurant, open-mouthed, still holding the phone to his ear.

CHAPTER 7

August 1990

HAVING FINALLY REACHED the doorway of her bedroom, Kim leaned forward until she could see the stairwell to her right, without exposing herself to the view of anyone who might be downstairs. Her vision was now fully adjusted to the darkness that seemed to have dissolved just enough to allow a murky view of the steps and landing. To someone descending the stairs, the living room came into view over a railing on the left, but a solid wall separated the stairs from the kitchen on the right. Kim would not be able to look into the kitchen area until she had crept down to the end of that wall, and poked her head around the doorframe. Earlier, she had been convinced that the unnerving noises had come from there, but she was beginning to feel foolish for being so alarmed.

She was gaining confidence now, breathing more easily and, most important, quietly as she moved toward the first of thirteen steps, six feet away. She passed the bathroom on her right, and was momentarily startled to see movement in there. She gasped and flinched at the sight, and then realized that the figure was her own reflection in the mirrored shower doors. She paused, hand on her chest, relieved to have survived the instant of terror. Her heart pounded with renewed frenzy as she paused for a minute to collect herself, and then cautiously resumed her journey until she arrived at the first step.

Kim stood frozen at the edge of the stairway. It loomed in front of her like a bridge that linked her safe upper region to the uncertainty, and possible danger, that might lie below. She allowed a few silent minutes to pass, bolstering her belief that she was truly alone in the house, and then was able to move forward.

Taking a deep breath, she began her descent, hugging the wall and placing her feet only on the extreme right side of the steps. Kim had been up and down these treads countless times, and knew how to avoid the areas that would give in to her weight and then spring back with a loud creaking sound when the pressure was removed. Pleased with her silent progress and growing determination, she soon found herself perched on the next-to-last step, and now she had only to peek around the opening to her right to finally glimpse the kitchen area. Summoning all the nerve she possessed, Kim was about to move forward when she heard something. Her brain identified the sound immediately, processing the meaning of it within a split second. It was the screen door slapping closed, softly but still audible, an indication that the solid inside door was not closed and locked as Kim had hoped. The outer door was wood framed, made by her father many years ago, and it was held in closed position by a spring rather than a more contemporary pneumatic cylinder. It would sometimes clatter open and shut if the wind gusts were strong enough, but on this night, that was not the case. Someone had just entered, or exited.

There were no follow up sounds — no footsteps or voices, nothing. Kim was so unnerved that tears welled up in her eyes and she pressed her back to the wall. Once again, a flood of thoughts came to her in an instant.

Oh my God, there is someone here!!

Jim, please come home right now!

Wait, it must be Jim, what intruder would make such a careless racket?

Once again she listened, but heard only the sounds of nature coming from the open window above her new stainless steel double sink. It was somehow comforting, a familiar non-threatening background noise. Somehow her instincts told her that the door had closed upon someone's exit, and that someone had to be Jim, probably gone back out to the car to retrieve his bags. She wanted so desperately to end this darkness. She had to switch on a light, even though the sudden brightness may temporarily impair her vision and leave her exposed.

Turning toward the wall and placing one foot to the floor, Kim reached a hand around the blind corner, groping for the light switch on the kitchen side. Just as her fingers felt the switch plate, the wall seemed to explode as something was crashed into it, sending plaster and lath flying and nearly breaking through to her side. Something heavy, swung with a vengeance, had come within inches of crushing her hand.

Kim was unaware of the volume and pitch of her first scream, as her attacker reveled in the abject fear that it reflected. She turned to run up the stairs, but sheer panic further blinded her and she stumbled.

Helpless, she turned to face her assailant. There was a whistling sound as something moved through the air towards her at a high velocity, and for Kim the darkness became complete. There was no further sound as she lay at the foot of the stairs, virtually the same spot where her mother had drawn her last breath two years earlier.

CHAPTER 8

January 2016

AFTER TWO HOURS at Woody's, Jack Ferris finally convinced himself that it was time to make a move for the exit while he was still somewhat sober. His frequent glimpses of the outdoors as patrons entered or exited had made it clear that the intensity of the snowfall had increased, and visibility was trending in the opposite direction. The large white flakes he had seen earlier were now smaller, multiplied in volume and driven by a gusting wind.

It was one of those occasions when atmospheric conditions had made the call easy for meteorologists, and their predictions of a heavy snowfall had been on the money. The concentrated squalls had continued non-stop while Jack had been inside as arctic air was blown across unfrozen Lake Erie, picking up the required moisture to create a magnificent snow-making machine. The white fluff had piled up to a depth of least eight inches already, deep enough to fall into Jack's unlaced workboots as he trudged to his van. Once there, he stopped for a moment just to watch it fall, enjoying the landscape of pure white. He was awed by the tranquility a blanket of snow could bring, muffling even the sound of nearby traffic.

He would have to be careful on the drive out of town, and was relieved that Pete had called his usual "taxi service" to take him home so that Jack wouldn't have to drive him. Pete assured his friend that the Grove Park patrol car had been right in the area anyway, and the officer owed him one. It turned out to be Marti Lucas, the only female patrol officer on the force. Jack knew her through Pete, and they had sometimes chatted at the gym. Her sexual preference was a subject of conjecture among her fellow officers, but Jack had never understood why. Marti was very fit and could bench nearly as much as Jack could, but wasn't butch at all. He had once seen her at a fundraiser dressed in a short skirt and heels, and had found it difficult to keep himself from staring at her. She was quiet and rather serious, and probably just hadn't yet found the right guy. Hopefully, Pete wasn't so drunk that he would raise the subject during the ride home.

After pushing the wet snow from the Chevy's windshield and clearing space for the wipers with his bare hands — *would he ever be prepared for a heavy snowfall with gloves and a decent car brush?* — Jack got in and fired up the engine, steeling himself for the ride ahead. He jacked up the defroster to it's highest setting, turned the CD volume high enough to drown out the noisy heater fan, and pulled out of the lot to head toward Main Street. Heartbreak Hill awaited, and he hoped he could keep the rear-wheel drive Cargo van from sliding off the road as he climbed it.

Reaching the corner, Jack looked left just in time to see blinding headlights approaching, and waited as the vehicle passed by in front of him, cutting through the unplowed snow like a tank. It was a bright yellow Hummer H2, and Jack didn't need to see the BIGJIM1 vanity plates to know that it was driven by Jim Wainwright. He grunted to himself, struck by the coincidence that their paths had crossed twice in one evening. Suddenly exhausted and eager to get home, Jack made his right turn and began the journey.

*

"I love this freaking truck— goes through all this snow as if it wasn't even there!" exclaimed Jim Wainwright, once again convincing himself that his Hummer was a necessity for suburban survival rather than an ostentatious status symbol.

His wife made no response, preferring to stare out her side window and enjoy the warm buzz that three martinis provided. Nicki had been enjoying their evening out, and wondered aloud why Jim had insisted on leaving.

"You know I have an early meeting tomorrow, try to think of someone besides yourself for a change! Christ, I've been up since five! I think you're just pissed because I broke up that little private party you and Jill had going at the bar. Who were those other people anyway?"

Nicki glared at him. "Those 'other people' were prospective clients. They're both attorneys, and they both have wives who are pushing for that first big house, the one that screams 'success' to all their friends."

"Yeah," Jim sneered, "and what else are they in the market for? I didn't see any wives at the bar. It looked like you and your buddy Jill were really trying to close the deal."

"Hey, don't be so insulting, Jim! What is it about Jill that upsets you so much? She's always nice to you, and you're always so condescending, as if you're better than her. Tim's out of town, couldn't you make her feel like she was welcome to join us?"

Now her husband hesitated, reluctant to bare his true feelings, but he couldn't let the moment pass once again.

"You two are like two horny teenagers lately. Always confiding in each other, whispering, giggling, enjoying your private jokes —" Even as he spoke, Jim hated the way that sounded, so whiny and petty.

"Don't be so paranoid Jim, we're friends! Can't you be glad that I have a close friend, someone to confide in?" Her tone was conciliatory, hoping to reason with him.

"What the hell am I? You can't confide in me?"

Nicki exhaled an exasperated sigh. "It's different, you know that. A female friend is different. There are things that you just can't discuss with a man, not even your husband. That doesn't mean it's something sinister."

"Uh huh. Well, don't think I'm not aware of your little secrets. Like tonight, when you both went off to 'powder your noses.' You think I didn't get that little inside joke? You were gone fifteen minutes, and came back all giddy and bright-eyed. Do you think my friends and I are stupid?"

"Not all of them", she shot back, "Joey asked if we had a bump for him." Nicki immediately regretted her careless remark. Joey was a good guy, why had she dragged him into their argument? She knew that Jim's silence was a sign that he was already planning to confront his trusted aide with this new bit of information, and interrogate him about his drug use. He'd look at Joey differently from now on.

Nicki wanted to change the subject, and she thought of just the thing to put Jim on the defensive.

"I know you have secrets too, Jim, things that you don't share with me. Did you think I didn't notice those visitors you had at the house last week, that unexpected company? The ones you called 'business associates'. They looked like they just walked out of Bada Bing! But I didn't pry, did I?"

Jim was obviously uncomfortable at the mention of that meeting. He had hustled the two goons into the den, and until now had been relieved that Nicki let it pass without comment.

"Nicki, that really *doesn't* concern you, and it's not the same thing! I'm not hiding things from you, and I don't do drugs, or — " Jim stopped there, possibly because he was groping for words, but more probably because he was about to deeply offend his wife.

"Or what, Jim? What were you going to say? 'I don't flirt? I don't cheat?' What are you accusing me of, exactly?"

Her husband didn't respond, pretending to be preoccupied as he carefully made the slippery turn into the driveway. He was suddenly eager to exit the vehicle, and put an end to this conversation.

Nicki was unruffled, inwardly celebrating the way she had shut him up. She decided to press a bit more before letting him off the hook.

"Why do you have a meeting on a Saturday morning, anyway?"

"The Council is meeting with the Planning Board tomorrow. We need to go over a proposal for a new housing development, a big one. These board members have real jobs, and it's tough to get them all together on a weeknight. So, I arranged a Saturday meeting. If I left it up to them, they'd schedule it for a month from now."

As Nicki opened her door and turned to leave the car, Jim held her arm to stop her. He looked into her eyes for a long moment, wanting to open up to the woman he loved, but he couldn't bring himself to involve her in his recent shady dealings.

"Nicki, I don't want to fight, I want us to be happy. Let me take care of some things I have going on, and when the time is right I'll explain everything. Just not now."

Nicki Wainwright gave her husband a quizzical look, wondering how well she really knew him. It seemed that he had been harboring some dark secret for weeks, and she had assumed his motives for doing so involved an affair. Now she was unsure, and it felt as if he was protecting her from something. In any case, Nicki was weary of the entire subject.

"Okay, Jim. When you're ready to share your life with me, let me know. But don't wait too long."

As Jim tried to interpret what seemed to be an ultimatum, Nicki Wainwright pulled her arm away and left him sitting in the car, disgustedly shaking his head, as she slammed the passenger door and stalked into the house.

CHAPTER 9

I T HAD BEEN difficult to refuse the handsome young lawyer's repeated offer of one last drink, but Jill Sherman knew it was time to leave Barton House. She had given in once already, and this time managed to politely but firmly decline. It was the right decision, given her elevated blood-alcohol content and the eager barrister's increasing aggressiveness.

Jill was uncomfortable at being left on her own in that situation, without Nicki nearby to lend support. An hour earlier, Big Jim had rudely interrupted their conversation to inform Nicki that they were leaving. Jill was so stunned by the sudden end to their fun, it never occurred to her to ask for a lift home, as she had planned. She thought Nicki would offer to bring her back the next day to retrieve her car, and of course Jill would accept.

Unfortunately, the Wainwrights' abrupt departure had not allowed time for Nicki to raise the subject, or perhaps Jim's demeanor kept her from asking. In any case, she now found herself driving her husband's classic 1975 Jaguar through the snowy, rutted streets of Grove Park.

The Jag was a beauty, white with plush red leather seating, but Jill knew it had been a foolish decision to risk driving it in January. In these conditions its rear-wheel drive transformed even gradual acceleration into a thrill ride, featuring spinning tires and the occasional sideways slide. Normally she would be behind the wheel of her beautiful 2013 all-wheel-drive Range Rover Sport, but the dealership was still trying to determine what had recently been triggering its maddening "check engine" warning light. Jill would have given anything to be driving that car just then.

*

Jill and Tim Sherman had moved to Grove Park three years earlier, when Tim had been transferred to the northeast division of Graham Aerospace. Tim was a brilliant engineer, and seized this opportunity to attain the management position he coveted. Within two years he had been named Vice President in charge of Northeast Operations and was pulling down 250K annually, plus stock options. On the downside, there were 60-hour work weeks and frequent trips out of town to put out fires and placate Graham's demanding customers.

Tim and Jill had become distant in more than geographic terms, and though they rarely argued it had become clear that she had no intention of playing the role of the lonely housewife. With no children to occupy her time, Jill indulged herself in shopping, decorating, and travel, usually accompanied by her closest friend, Nicki Wainwright.

The two women turned heads wherever they went, and admitted only to each other that they loved the attention. Like Nicki, Jill was somewhat younger than her husband — 37 to his 46 — and possessed a classically beautiful face adorned by long auburn hair. She wasn't the type of woman who wished to cheat on her husband, and had never given much thought to leaving him. She did have needs, however, and one of those was the need for the attention she received when she was with Nicki. Jill felt an inner satisfaction in the knowledge that she was still attractive and desirable, and it was Nicki who affirmed that for her.

*

Following the path formed by the tires of preceding vehicles — none of which were in sight — Jill made a slow, deliberate turn onto Route 19 and headed toward the Heron Ridge development. The five miles remaining to be traveled would seem like an eternity, and Jill was thankful that she had refused that last cosmopolitan at Barton House. Without taking her eyes off road, she felt for the controls of the compact disc player, and soon the soothing sounds of Bonnie Raitt filled the car's plush interior.

As she passed the intersection of Bowman Road, less than two miles from home, headlights appeared in the rear-view mirror. Jill was somehow comforted knowing that she wasn't alone on the road, but the other car closed quickly and now the headlights reflected in the rear and side view mirrors were blinding her.

"Hey buddy, I'm glad to see you but get off my ass!" She spoke out loud, a symptom of her sudden feeling of vulnerability.

She was hoping the guy would pass her, and slowed down to give him every chance to do so safely. Instead, the anonymous driver turned his bright lamps on, filling the Jag's interior with blinding halogen light. Jill momentarily lost sight of the road, and her first reflex was to tap the brake pedal. As she did so, there was a sudden surge of momentum as the mystery vehicle made contact with the Jag's rear bumper.

Jill was panicked, and sped up to distance herself from this crazy person behind her. Was this a pursuer, or someone else who wasn't used to driving in these conditions? The Jag gained speed, and the intensity of the follower's headlights decreased as Jill pulled further ahead.

Scanning the roadside for a glimpse of the stone pillars that marked the entrance of Heron Ridge, she spotted them too late. Jill was afraid to suddenly brake into a turn for fear of sliding sideways into the pillars, and made a split-second decision to continue past the entrance. Now a feeling of dread overtook her as she realized there would be no convenient place to turn around for a few miles, as the grade increased and Route 19 snaked on into a sparsely populated wooded area.

Within minutes, Jill's worst fears were realized as the unfriendly headlights again drew closer, and once again her tormentor kept coming, sometimes crossing into the opposite lane as if attempting to pass the Jaguar but always dropping back. She still was unsure if she was the victim of harassment or randomly unfortunate to be on the road with an obnoxious, possibly drunk, driver.

There was a yellow sign up ahead, illuminated by the Jag's headlights. The thick snowfall made it difficult for Jill to read, but she recognized the symbol for an upcoming cross road. She wasn't familiar with this area, but it was a welcome opportunity to turn off of 19 and allow the other vehicle to pass by, freeing her to turn back towards home.

Jill exhaled in relief as she flicked the turn signal on and made a slow, deliberate turn onto what she thought would be Powers Road, only to find circumstances that made the Jag even more difficult to control. The snow appeared to be over a foot deep, and hers was the first car to plow through it. And now, adding to her fear, the headlights of the *Other Car* appeared again in the rearview mirrors. She still had company.

It took Jill's full attention to follow this road's unfamiliar twisted path, and although she didn't dare take a glance at the mirrors, peripheral vision confirmed that the headlights were once again getting very close. As the road straightened out a bit in front of her, lights behind her suddenly increased in intensity and then shifted, as her anonymous enemy began to parallel the Jaguar.

Jill wanted to know who was driving this vehicle from hell, and as it pulled alongside her vision was distracted from the road ahead for a second too long. She recognized too late that she had to bear left, but was being forced straight ahead by the position of the *Other Car*. The Jag's undercarriage made grinding contact with a sloping guard rail, and from outside the car Jill's scream was unheard as the classic coupe became airborne, destined for a tragic end to its pampered life.

CHAPTER 10

AT SEVEN O'CLOCK Saturday morning Powers Road remained treacherously unplowed. The county employees who would normally have been manning the trucks with their huge winged blades stayed home that day. Their union was currently embroiled in a bitter dispute with County Executive Joseph Spano over what Spano considered excessive overtime hours. Ultimately it was his use of the term "padding" during an interview for the local television news outlet that had enraged the rank and file, and their stewards had decided to teach Spano a lesson. In a satisfying act of malicious obedience, the drivers were not authorized to work any overtime hours that weekend, in spite of the early storm warnings that had been issued.

As Ed Flanders slogged his way through the snow along Powers, adhering to his rigid dog-walking schedule, he was unaware of the political bickering. He wondered where the county trucks could be, and was wary of having one of them come up behind him, burying him and his pet under an avalanche of white. Normally, the shoulder would be cleared by now and the walk would be easy, but today it was proving to be more than he could handle. This exercise was supposed to be a benefit to both man and beast, but even the yellow Lab didn't seem willing to continue the struggle against chest-deep snow.

"Milo, we're both getting too old for this shit", Ed muttered as he pulled up to catch his breath, well short of their two-mile goal. Approaching the small bridge that crossed Silver Creek, common sense told him that it was time to turn around and head back, and live to walk another

day. Just as he was about to do so, Ed's attention was drawn to a distur-
bance in the blanket of white in front of him, something that seemed out
of place. Although partially filled by snowfall, a set of tire tracks could still
be seen, making it clear that a vehicle had left the road and hit the leading edge of the steel guard rails that led to the bridge. Ed could picture
only one result; a car vaulting into space before plunging down the ravine
towards the creek bed that lay twenty feet below.

Coaxing Milo to follow him into a three-foot drift, Ed moved closer
to get a look into the ravine. Cautiously high stepping towards the drop-
off, he squinted downwards. The morning sun reflecting on newly fallen
snow was blinding, and he placed a gloved hand above his eyes to better
enable him to see the place where this vehicle had come to rest. A chill
ran up his spine as Ed spotted a white car near the edge of the shallow
creek. It was lodged against the immovable trunk of a huge willow tree, its
crushed front end boding ominously for the unknown driver. He couldn't
be sure, but Ed thought he had seen that car before.

For the first time, Ed Flanders wished he hadn't refused his daughter's
offer to buy him a cell phone for emergency use. At the time his vanity
hadn't allowed him to accept, and therefore admit that he had reached the
age of "I've fallen and I can't get up". Now it would be half an hour, mini-
mum, before he reached home and was able to call for help. Hopefully, a
car would come by and provide assistance, but with these road conditions
he wasn't counting on it.

Ed's first instinct was to attempt to reach the car and help the victim in some way, but at his age the steep decline made that impossible.
Shouting for Milo to follow, he reluctantly turned away from the scene
and began the trek homeward to call for help. He hoped it wouldn't arrive
too late.

CHAPTER 11

NICKI WAINWRIGHT PULLED the lat bar downward, keeping her back straight to concentrate the tension in her shoulders and upper back. She counted off fifteen reps and paused to rest between sets, dabbing sweat from her forehead with a small green towel that matched her outfit perfectly. Nicki's workouts were strenuous, but she welcomed the exertion and the feeling of self-esteem that it brought. As long as she was capable of completing her circuit of the Nautilus machines, Nicki felt that she was successfully fending off the ravages of time.

She actually enjoyed working up a sweat — within reason, of course. Looking trim and toned in her yoga pants and snug Spandex tank top, Nicki remained perfectly groomed as ever. Outside of the gym she routinely wore designer clothes and expensive jewelry, but Nicki felt most attractive at the gym, after a workout had increased her heart rate and left her glowing with perspiration, flushing her cheeks to a healthy pink.

She thought that Jill would be at the gym today as usual, but so far there was no sign of her. Nicki's search for a true soul mate had led her to Jill, but she didn't want to appear too needy and upset the chemistry of a valued sisterhood. Nicki had made that mistake once before, and didn't wish to repeat it. Still, she wished Jill would show up so they could chat and work out together.

Rising from the bench after a third set of pull downs, she noticed a familiar figure disappearing into the adjoining weight room. It was Jack Ferris, the painting contractor whom Nicki found so intriguing. She didn't know what it was about him that piqued her curiosity, but Nicki definitely wanted to get to know this guy, to see what he was like. These were thoughts she hadn't even shared with Jill, but they were persistent, and now the opportunity for a conversation had presented itself. Nicki didn't normally venture into the weightlifting room with its regular crowd of grunting muscle heads, but today she would make an exception.

*

Jack Ferris had arrived later than usual for his Saturday workout, having chosen to sleep in that day. He thought the previous night's snowfall would discourage most of the early morning crowd, but to his dismay he found the Nautilus room fully occupied, with some people standing around and waiting for a machine to be freed up. Jack headed for the dead weights, where he found an empty bench and began a series of warm-up bench presses.

When his trembling arms had completed their last possible extension against the hundred pounds of resistance, Jack returned the bar to its rest and sat up to catch his breath. As he did so he found himself looking into the captivating eyes of Nicki Wainwright.

"Well hello again — really, we have to stop meeting like this!" she laughed. "Working off the hangover?"

Jack broke into a sheepish grin, much to Nicki's delight.

"Yeah, I guess I did need to sleep in a little bit today. I'm usually out of here by now."

Suddenly feeling flirtatious, Nicki answered with "Well, how lucky for me."

Sensing that Jack wasn't sure how to respond, she added, " Now I can pressure you to stop over and take a look at the space I'm redecorating."

It wasn't pressure that Jack felt, in fact he was eager for the chance to get to know this woman a little better. She was married — to the Town Supervisor, no less — and he knew plenty of single women, but at the moment they didn't interest him nearly as much as Nicki Wainwright did. Jack had to find out if she wanted him for anything more than his home improvement skills.

"Oh, I think I could spare some time from my busy schedule" he replied, pronouncing the word as "shedjule" for some reason unknown even to him. Nicki didn't react to the attempt at cute humor, but mercifully she acted as if she hadn't noticed.

"How about stopping by right after this?" she pressed on, inwardly admonishing herself for sounding so desperate. "Do you know where it is?"

"Amelia Drive, right? It's hard to miss that bright yellow Hummer in the driveway."

"Oh, that's Jim's toy", she said with a dismissive wave of her hand, "it won't be there, he's working this weekend. It's number 29, look for my red Volvo."

"Got it", Jack confirmed, and got up from the bench, sensing that the chat was ending. Nicki hadn't moved, though, and now he was unintentionally close to her, and wondering if he should back off a bit. He could smell her perfume, or maybe it was scented shampoo or body wash, who knew? Whatever it was, he was compelled to stand his ground and enjoy the experience.

"So, this is how you stay in shape. What else do you do to pass the winter months? Let me guess, you're a skier, right, Jack?" Then, accompanied by that devastating smile, "I'm sorry, may I call you Jack?"

"Certainly — Nicki."

She nodded her approval. "Thank you!"

"No, I haven't put on skis for years. My only winter sport, if you can even call it that, is bowling. And that's more of a boy's night out than a sport. I'm waiting for spring so I can get the golf clubs out."

Now Nicki displayed a renewed interest. "Oh, you play? I love golf! I've been playing since middle school, my grandfather got me hooked on it. You should be my guest at the Club sometime, I'm always looking for a playing partner. Jim doesn't play much, and the ladies just aren't very serious about it. I prefer to golf with men, when I get the chance."

From there, the conversation moved to handicaps and golf anecdotes, and before either one realized it, twenty more minutes had passed. Sensing that Jack was about to excuse himself and return to his workout routine, Nicki decided on a pre-emptive move to make things easier for him.

"Jack, I'm going to let you get back to your workout. See you later, then?"

"Uh, sure, when I'm finished here, I could do that. What time would be good for you?"

"Why don't I meet you out front, we can go right from here. Don't rush, though, I don't mind waiting for you. I'm just glad we ran into each other!"

"Okay, see you later." They exchanged grins as Jack returned to his exercise routine, fighting off the urge to do a celebratory fist pump at his good fortune.

*

Nicki Wainwright and Jack Ferris had been so involved in getting to know each other, they were totally unaware that someone had been watching them.

Marti Lucas had been standing in front of the mirrored wall at the back of the weight room, critiquing her muscle definition as she caught her breath between sets. She was identifying the areas of her arms and shoulders that needed work, and those that had been developed to her satisfaction. It may have seemed like pure vanity to an outsider, and in truth there was an element of that, but it was enjoyable to see the results of her hard work. Marti loved the way her arms and shoulders looked during a workout, especially after three sets of curls. The possession of physical strength was satisfying, and came in handy on the job, but soon she would have to back off on the weight to avoid the look of masculinity. Marti was just about to turn away from the mirror when she noticed familiar faces reflected in the glass, over her left shoulder. She stopped flexing and looked on with interest at Nicki Wainwright and Jack Ferris, wondering what their connection could be. Marti immediately suspected romance, and just as quickly dismissed that possibility. Still, she felt an unmistakable pang of jealousy, even resentment, that she wasn't one half of that couple in the mirror.

Forcing herself to look away before one of them noticed her staring, Marti reclined onto the bench and focused her attention on the weight she was about to lift, calming herself. She lifted the bar from its cradle and began her set of skull crushers. Pushing the bar above her chest until her arms were fully extended, she took a quick breath and then lowered it to within an inch of her forehead, hinging at the elbow in perfect form. She exhaled and pushed the weight back up, feeling her triceps pushing against the resistance. Twenty reps later Marti sat up, breathing heavily, and couldn't resist stealing a direct glance at the unlikely couple. To her surprise, they were gone. Had the conversation ended, or did they move it elsewhere? Marti was left to wonder as she finished her routine.

CHAPTER 12

A BREATHLESS VICTOR HARMON strode into the Town Supervisor's office and tossed his overcoat onto the rack, pausing briefly to straighten his tie. He had dashed up the stairs two at a time to get there, but made no apology to the group for his late arrival. Looking down with dismay at his soggy Italian loafers, he realized that they would never be quite the same after their trip through the slushy Grove Park sidewalks.

"God, I hate friggin' winter."

Jim Wainwright, Al Kaplan, and Joey Garrity had been waiting impatiently for Harmon to appear so they could discuss what might take place at the Town Council meeting that morning. Members of the town Planning Board would be there for a scheduled discussion of the proposed Cedar Ridge development project, and this four-member secret alliance hoped they could influence the Board's recommendation. They all had a personal interest in the project's approval, Wainwright and Harmon most of all.

Jim Wainwright was beginning to wish that he had never met this man, in spite of the rewards it had brought. As he waited for the latecomer to seat himself, Wainwright's mind flashed back to an earlier meeting with Harmon, right in this same office.

Shortly after his election to the office of Grove Park Town Supervisor, Wainwright had been approached by Harmon, who introduced himself as a representative of Kevin Cochran, a local developer who had contributed to Wainwright's campaign fund. As president of New Century

Corporation, Cochran had built a reputation as a successful and innovative developer who had made a fortune by building strip malls and office buildings in suburban communities. Although they had never met, Wainwright was flattered that someone of Cochran's status would become one of his backers.

Of course, Wainwright should have guessed that it was not his political philosophy that inspired Cochran to support him. New Century was interested in building a gated community of no less than eighty upscale homes near the village of Grove Park. A tract of land had been purchased a few years earlier, but there were political hurdles to be cleared before the plan could be implemented.

The property acquired by New Century was zoned agricultural, meaning the Town Planning Board would have to approve a rezoning application before any request for development could even be considered. That would be the easy part, as New Century's legal staff had been through that process many times before in other locations and was nearly always successful.

Once the scope of the project was submitted to the town, there would be mandatory traffic and environmental impact studies, and the local and state governments would be asked to help fund the necessary improvements to infrastructure. A three-mile stretch of Powers Road would have to be widened and repaved to handle the increased traffic. This included the redesign and total rebuilding of a bridge over Silver Creek that had been built in 1952. The existing structure's width was considered inadequate by present standards and the curving approaches were unsafe, especially to drivers who were unfamiliar with the area. Conservative estimates placed the cost of these improvements at about four million dollars.

The support of the Town Supervisor was considered critical at the inception of the project. He had influence over members of the town council and its' various committees, some of which had been formed with the specific intent of slowing, even discouraging, any further commercial development in Grove Park. In fact, tighter control of growth and development had been a plank in Jim Wainwright's election platform. He had promised to say "no" those who lobbied on behalf of national restaurant chains and the dreaded superstores that would hurt small business owners, thereby preserving the small-town aura that the Grove Park voters cherished.

That being the case, what would provide sufficient motivation for the Town Supervisor to become the leading proponent of a development plan in the face of voter dissent? That was the question that Kevin Cochran had asked himself, and the answer seemed obvious. He would offer His Honor a pile of cash.

Cochran dispatched Victor Harmon to meet with the Supervisor on the premise of simply breaking the ice, explaining the details of the proposed community so Wainwright could visualize it and appreciate the benefits Grove Park would realize. After just thirty minutes, Harmon's instincts told him that Wainwright was approachable, and he raised the possibility of other, more personal, benefits that could be realized. He suggested a discreet payment of fifty thousand dollars in cash to show New Century Corporation's appreciation of Wainwright's anticipated support. When the plan was formally approved by the town council, there would be a second payment of fifty thousand, and still another when Cedar Ridge became a reality, on the day of the official groundbreaking.

The Supervisor postured indecision for a short time, but he had realized immediately that this was a no-brainer. He was confident that it could be accomplished without too much political damage, and Harmon's obviously practiced style in closing the deal convinced Wainwright that no one would discover the illegal payment. In his usual self-important manner, the Supervisor agreed to "provide assistance in bringing the plan to fruition", and the next evening he received a visit from the "goons" that Nicki had seen. The two men were middle-aged, well dressed but somehow rough around the edges, with what Nicki thought were New York or New Jersey accents. They mentioned Harmon's name but not their own and asked to speak in private, and Wainwright had hustled them into his home office. Behind closed doors, with only the briefest exchange of words, Harmon's associates opened a briefcase and counted out the promised down payment, piling packets of cash on top of the polished walnut desk.

Long after they had left, Wainwright sat in his office behind locked doors, counting the bills repeatedly and celebrating his good fortune with a bottle of Jack Daniels that he kept in his desk. He thought about how he could best use his influence to win approval of the New Century plan, and eventually locked the money in the wall safe, one to which only he had the combination.

One thing Jim Wainwright didn't need to consider was what to do with the money. His wife loved to spend, he loved gambling, and this windfall would give him a comfortable cushion which could help to support their lifestyle. As it turned out, some portion of it might now have to be used to solve a more pressing problem in the person of Mitch Goren.

*

Finally seating himself in the remaining chair, Harmon addressed the group with interest. "Well, gentlemen, fill me in. Where are we on this?"

Harmon wasn't a bit surprised when the three amigos exchanged blank looks as if no one knew where to begin. He had long ago lost confidence in them, but it was his job to prod them through the approval process.

It was Al Kaplan who was finally able to voice a lucid thought in response. "Okay, why don't we begin with a review of the situation, so we're all on the same page?" This would be solely for Harmon's benefit, since they rarely met with him in person.

"An hour from now, the Town Council will meet with the town's Planning Board to discuss the Cedar Ridge proposal. The petitioner, New Century Corporation, will be represented by Mr. Harmon, who will present a brief overview of the project. We hope to gain the Council's approval today, but if not we'll move on to plan B. We would schedule another review, possibly a public hearing, in thirty days or so. That would give us time to regroup and sway public opinion, but we hope to avoid such a delay."

Harmon grimaced at the latter part of Kaplan's assessment, and began writing notes as the explanation continued.

"There are six Town Council members, two of which are in this room. I'm confident that at least two others, Brady and Fronczak, will vote in favor of the project. The other two, Fremont and McGregor, may put up token resistance just to please their constituents, but as far as I can tell they have no real personal commitment either way."

It was a fairly positive description of the project's chances for approval, and Harmon felt a renewed confidence. Then Jim Wainwright spoke.

"Our problem here is the Planning Board. They can only recommend of course, the council will make the final decision, but we must tread carefully. If the planners put up strong resistance and we approve Cedar Ridge anyway, how will that look? Our reputations are at stake here, not to mention the possible investigation that could follow."

Harmon wanted to hear more from Kaplan, who seemed to have the best feel for the players involved. "Al, what's your take on the Planning Board members? How are they leaning?"

Kaplan referred to his own notes. "Well, that body has eight members. Four of them haven't taken a clear position up to now. Three members seem solidly in favor of the proposal."

Wainwright interrupted "That would be Fisher, Brennan, and Volek?"

"Right."

Harmon's pen hovered over his notebook as he looked at Kaplan and asked "and the eighth member?"

Now Joey Garrity chimed in, feeling that it was his turn to contribute. Wainwright had assigned the task of getting a read on the remaining Planning Board member to him.

"Brenda Jackson. She's the Planning Coordinator, meaning she works with the town's engineering department on these proposal reviews. She makes sure all the required documents are submitted and in order, determines the adequacy of the Draft Environmental Impact Study, that sort of thing."

Joey was speaking directly to Harmon now.

"Brenda's an attorney, extremely intelligent and well spoken. She's very well connected to the Independent party."

Having done a little homework of his own, Harmon recognized the name. "Black lady, good-looking, around forty?"

"That's her. Her husband is a lawyer too, they have three kids. They aren't natives of the area, moved here from Pittsburgh, but they've become a very prominent family in Grove Park."

Garrity avoided making eye contact with his boss as he voiced his next thought. "A lot of people think she'll be taking a run at Town Supervisor next time around."

Wainwright snorted. "We'll see. For now, just tell us her position on Cedar Ridge."

Garrity locked eyes with Harmon as if to emphasize the point. "She strongly opposes the project. Not only this one, she's against any further development at this time. Brenda is by far the most vocal and influential planning board member, and to be honest we're just not sure how many other members are with her on this. Today's meeting will give us a better read on that."

Harmon appreciated Garrity's candor, but wanted more information. "So, you believe that she's against our proposal based on that general 'no more building' principle, nothing more specific?"

Garrity had to admit that he wasn't sure of the answer. "As far as I know, nothing specific. We'll know in a little while."

Harmon was irritated at Joey's response, and Joey found his steely gaze to be unnerving.

"I don't like surprises, Joe."

"I know that, but I can only ask so many questions without seeming like a spy."

Harmon's glare softened a bit. He quickly checked his watch and stood up, making it clear that, at least for him, the meeting was over.

"Okay. I have a few calls to make. I'll see you at the meeting."

CHAPTER 13

DRIVING SLOWLY TOWARDS her home, Nicki checked the rear-view mirrors frequently to make sure Jack was still following. It wasn't really necessary, since she had given him the address and he could easily find it without her help, but Nicki felt strangely excited at the prospect of being alone with this man. She felt as though she was about to open the door to something that could be wonderful, but also quite dangerous, and irrevocable. There was something special about Jack Ferris, and Nicki felt that he was interested in her in spite of her marital status. If she was totally misreading the situation and no sparks flew between them, the worst-case scenario would be a chance to discuss her decorating ideas with an attractive, highly regarded professional.

When they reached the Wainwright house, an impressive Victorian in one of Grove Park's old-money neighborhoods, she unlocked the double entrance doors and waited for Jack. He followed her in, carrying a large book that contained wall covering samples as well as a portfolio of patterns he had created for previous clients.

"Why don't you have a seat in the dining room Jack, I'll be right with you." She left the room, the scent of her perfume lingering behind, and Jack could hear her checking the message machine. She returned with a perplexed look on her face, posing a question aloud but seemingly to herself.

"Where could she be?"

Jack looked at her quizzically, and Nicki seemed to dismiss the worry with a wave of her hand.

"Oh, sorry, it's probably nothing." Once again she flashed her engaging smile, and then bounced into the adjacent kitchen. "What can I get you? Coffee, water, a beer?"

"Water would be fine, thanks."

She returned with two chilled bottles of water and cut glass tumblers, and took a seat across from him.

"So, which rooms are we going to talk about?" he asked, having noticed that the dining room seemed to have been recently updated.

"Well, I want to change the look of the entry foyer and the living room, you've seen those. And there's a large guest bedroom upstairs that's been ignored for years. Come on, I'll show you."

Nicki gave Jack a quick tour of the house, including her comments on almost every room. She spent a few minutes showing him the bedroom that she was planning to update and then they returned to the parlor. As Nicki tried to put her vision into words, her guest took in his surroundings. Jack's line of work took him into countless homes, and he had learned that their interior was often a reflection of the occupants' lives. This room was tastefully decorated, filled with quality furnishings that exhibited little or no sign of wear. There were no antiques or heirloom pieces to lend a sense of history, and none of the usual picture frames filled with family photos or favorite vacation snapshots. There was one large portrait of the Wainwrights, posing somewhat stiffly in formal attire, which was hung above the mantel of the stone fireplace. It appeared to be hand painted, and judging by their clothes and Nicki's hairstyle, it must have been a few years old. There was no sign of the birthmark on Jim Wainwright's forehead, a testament to the skill of the artist or perhaps a request by the subject.

Studying the room, Jack was reminded of the model homes that local builders set up, accented by attractive furnishings but absent of any trace of actual habitation. It was pleasant to the eye and yet somehow seemed rather empty, and he wondered if it was an accurate reflection of Nicki Wainwright.

A baby grand piano sat in a corner of the room, with sheet music neatly displayed above the keyboard. It seemed out of place to Jack, taking up space that this room couldn't afford to give up.

"Do you play?" he asked.

"A little, but not very often lately. I took lessons as a kid, and always wanted to pick up on it again, but" — her voice trailed off as if she felt embarrassed. "I mentioned the lessons to Jim once, and he surprised me with this on my next birthday. It was nice of him, but my skills really don't deserve such an extravagant piano." She chuckled, and added "I think he was kind of angry when he actually heard me try to play it. I never said I was good! Adds something to the room though, don't you think?"

"Yes, it's a nice touch" he said, unable to give a more positive endorsement. In truth, the idle piano struck him as an enormous waste of space, and money.

Nicki took his arm as one would do with a close friend, and led him back to the dining room. Having heard her rather vague conceptual explanation, Jack was still unsure what to suggest.

"Tell you what. Why don't you have a look at my book, and see if there's anything close to what you're looking for."

They returned to the table, where Nicki sat next to him as he leafed through the pages. She moved her chair close to his, pretending to be very involved in studying the patterns as Jack turned the pages. She noticed the woodsy smell of his cologne, and her eyes refused to stay focused on the pages as she frequently looked at his face while he explained the techniques he might use in the bedroom. She had wondered about those, but her private musings had not included paint.

Jack was having trouble finding something appropriate for the application, and Nicki was so near he was having difficulty concentrating. It was becoming obvious that the decorating was an excuse for them to become better acquainted, and he was in favor of that, but wasn't sure what Nicki wanted, or when.

He turned one of the few remaining pages in the book, and revealed a page covered in a washed pattern of blue and white, a muted effect reminiscent of a cloudy mist against a blue sky. He realized that Nicki might have seen it before, since he had used it in the Sherman home. He turned his head to say as much and was stopped speechless as he found himself looking into Nicki's green eyes, mere inches from his.

They slowly leaned forward in unison, as if their close proximity caused some magnetic pull that brought them together, and their lips touched and moved softly against each other. They parted for a moment, and then wordlessly renewed the kiss in earnest, with a hunger that had been building for more than just these last few hours.

It was Nicki who spoke first.

"Jack, what are we getting into here?"

"I'm not sure, but I can't help myself." He kissed her again, unable to resist, and bared his soul a bit. "There's something about you Nicki, I can't stop thinking about you."

She smiled and nodded, confirming that she had the same type of feeling about him. "I have to be careful, Jack. I want to get to know you better, but — you understand my situation, don't you?"

Jack didn't get a chance to respond, as their tender moment was interrupted by a ringing telephone nearby. Nicki seemed startled, then recovered and rose to answer it.

Jack stood, considering whether he should make his exit and allow Nicki to return to her real life. The Wainwright home felt like the wrong setting for the beginning of an affair anyway, and he hoped to make plans to meet elsewhere.

"Hello? Hello? Jim?"

"Is anyone there?" She listened for a few more seconds, and then returned the phone to its cradle.

She turned to Jack again. "Wrong number I guess. Lousy timing, too."

"Yeah. I should probably get going, don't you think? I'll leave the book with you, look through it and see if anything catches your eye."

"Oh, sure, I will. But I think I know what interests me." She took his arm and leaned into him as they walked toward the door.

"I'll be in touch, Mr. Ferris." She smiled and they kissed one more time, and then stood apart discreetly as he opened the door to leave.

Jack walked to his van as she watched from the window, and both were left to consider the thrilling possibilities that lay ahead.

CHAPTER 14

PETE WEBSTER HAD been on his way to headquarters that morning when his scanner crackled to life with the first reports of a single-vehicle accident on Powers Road. Since he was not officially on duty and had been on his way in only to catch up on some of the dreaded paperwork that he had been ignoring far too long, Pete took the next turn east.

As he made a left turn onto Powers, heading towards the village, Pete heard transmissions from the first responders. From the description of their location, Pete knew that they would be in sight soon, and within a minute the first flashing lights came into view. They would need officers to direct traffic here, as the site was adjacent to a narrow bridge and the presence of the rescue vehicles completely obstructed one lane.

Pete pulled onto the shoulder closest to the accident site, a few car lengths away from the emergency response vehicles sent by the local volunteer fire company, and left his car to survey the scene. A car had gone off the road as it reached the bridge, landing on a steep embankment and continuing downward towards the stream that ran below. From his vantage point, Pete was unable to see exactly where the vehicle, and its unfortunate occupant, had come to rest. He pushed forward through the snow to get a better look just as the Grove Park accident investigation officers arrived.

"Hey Max, Eric — mind if I go down there with you? Heard the report on my scanner and decided to have a look."

Max Jennings grinned at him, sensing an opportunity to needle a senior officer. "Sure Pete, no problem. Looks like it'll be a bitch getting down to it, though. You sure you're up to it?" Max and his partner, Eric Bronski, were both considerably younger than Pete, and had known him for some five years. As rookies, they had frequently sought his opinion on how to best conduct investigations, and the trio had hoisted more than a few beers together after hours.

"I'll do my best to keep up, smartass." Pete replied, suddenly realizing just how steep the slope would be as he began sidestepping downward, trailing one hand on the wet snow to keep his balance. They could see the wreckage now, about fifty yards ahead, resting against the massive base of an old willow. The rumpled hood had been thrown back over the windshield by the impact, and it occurred to Pete that the driver's injuries would likely be severe. Two paramedics were already at the car, struggling to open the driver's side door.

Stumbling the last few feet to the bottom of the hill, and hoping the younger guys hadn't noticed how clumsily he had accomplished his descent, Pete stopped to catch his breath and took another look at the car. Before he could say anything, Bronski identified it for him.

"Hey, I know that car. Classic Jag, I've seen it around town. That good-looking redhead drives it. Jesus, I hope she isn't in there."

Bronski realized that sounded inappropriate, as if he would trade someone else's life for that of any attractive female, and he quickly added "I mean, I hope whoever's in there is still alive."

"No airbags in it, that's for sure" his partner offered, reinforcing Pete's fears for the driver.

As they approached the scene, one of the paramedics left the car and walked towards them, shaking his head as if to indicate bad news.

"Driver's a female, probably in her thirties, severe head and chest trauma. Died on impact, I'd say — looks like she's been here all night. You guys do your thing, I'm gonna make a call and see if County wants us to stick around to transport the body."

Pete hung back a few feet, allowing the investigators to begin their process by taking digital photos of the scene. As they moved in he stayed close behind, until he could see the body of Jill Sherman. The paramedics had leaned her back into the seat to check for signs of life, and now Pete could see why it had been so obvious that there would be none. She was barely recognizable, and the white silk blouse that Pete had seen her wearing the night before was now covered with her frozen blood.

Max was at the passenger side, collecting items from the floor of the car. They were the scattered contents of a handbag, and he was about to open a red leather wallet.

"Maxie, I know who this girl is — Mrs. Jill Sherman, lives in Heron Ridge. I think her husband's name is Tim. I actually saw her in Woody's last night, with a group of friends. Man, what a friggin' shame."

Max pulled a driver's license from the wallet, studied it for a moment, and nodded in agreement. "Jill Sherman, 14 Oriole Road. Yep, that's in Heron Ridge."

"There's something else here that's interesting." He reached down and picked up what looked like a brass or gold tube, and unscrewed the top. "White powder in here, looks like coke. I'll bag it for testing."

Pete had seen enough, and the freezing temperature was getting to him. He had snow inside his boots and up his pant legs, and dreaded the climb back up to his car. "What a depressing start to a weekend" he remarked, turning away from the scene. "Catch you guys later. I'll get someone to send coffee down."

His cohorts grunted their replies and continued their work, carefully recording the details of the scene so that they could later piece together the chain of events as accurately as possible.

Having finally completed the climb back to his truck, Pete started the engine and sat inside, waiting for the heated seat to thaw him out a bit. If he had been on duty Pete would have left the engine running and returned to warmth, but this was his personal vehicle and gasoline was just too expensive to waste when it was on his nickel. He was about to grab the shift lever when his cell phone rang.

"Webster." He barked his usual greeting, and heard the caller reply "Hey, how *you* doon?"

Pete recognized the voice of Jack Ferris, doing his terrible Joey Tribbiani impression.

"Hey, Jack. I'm at an accident scene, just about to leave. What're you up to?"

"I was gonna grab breakfast in town, you interested?" Jack sounded so exuberant, Pete hated to bring him down with what he was about to say.

"Ah, sorry Jack, maybe later, if you can wait. I think I should stop in at the station for a bit."

"I'm pretty hungry, Petey. Make it quick and give me a call, okay?"

"Yeah, I will — listen, Jack, about this accident — there was a fatality."

"Oh, jeez — " Jack offered, becoming aware that he was interrupting serious business. Something in Pete's voice told Jack that the deceased might be someone he knew. "Who was it, Pete?"

"You know that lady who hangs around with Nicki Wainwright, the one she was with at Woody's last night? Jill Sherman."

"Oh my God, Pete, what happened?"

"She missed a curve on Powers Road right near the Silver Creek Bridge, went down the embankment and hit a tree head-on. A real mess."

"You're kidding" was all Jack could say. He knew the ladies had been drinking, and would have assumed that someone in the group would see them home safely. "She might've been driving too fast, with the snow and all."

Pete hesitated, not wanting to reveal more than he should, but found himself confiding to his buddy. "Maybe living too fast, Jackie. Looked like there was a vial of coke in the car."

Jack wasn't sure how to respond to that, his mind was already distracted with thoughts of Nicki, and how the news of her friend's death would affect her. "Pete, it's weird but I ran into Nicki Wainwright again this morning, at Strong's. She mentioned that she usually worked out with a friend on Saturday mornings, and she wondered why this friend hadn't shown up today. I'll bet she was talking about Jill Sherman."

"I'll have someone interview her, let her know what happened and get some information about when she last saw the victim" Pete offered, firmly entrenched in cop mode.

Jack reluctantly offered, "After the gym, I stopped at Nicki — Mrs. Wainwright's house to take a look at a room she wants painted, and while I was there she checked her messages and mentioned it again."

Listening to the tone of Jack's voice, Pete was struck by the level of concern his friend felt for this new acquaintance. It was obvious that Nicki Wainwright had made quite an impression on Jack.

"Thanks for letting me know, Jack, we'll take care of it. But first we have to find the husband and notify him."

"But you're sure it was Jill Sherman, Pete? No chance it's a mistake?"

"No, it's a positive I.D. I saw her myself, Jack, and it was the same woman we saw last night. Listen, I gotta run. Catch you later, okay?"

"Yeah, later. Give me a call when things calm down." Jack replied, and ended the call. He decided to skip the breakfast in town and head straight home.

CHAPTER 15

WHEN ALL PARTIES were in place, Grove Park Town Supervisor James Wainwright called the meeting to order and read aloud the petition of New Century Corporation, outlining the scope of the proposed development to be called Cedar Ridge.

He introduced Victor Harmon, who guided the attendees through a PowerPoint presentation that provided some of the same information, with the addition of artistic renderings of the concept homes.

The planning board members occasionally interrupted Harmon with questions, mostly soft tosses that he handled easily. They were the usual concerns over increased traffic, possible detours during construction, additional load to the school system, all the queries a developer should anticipate and be prepared for. As far as Harmon could tell, there was no real opposition to the proposal. At that point, Brenda Jackson addressed the meeting for the first time.

"Gentlemen, I have a few questions."

"Certainly Mrs. Jackson, you have the floor." Wainwright loved any opportunity to act as if he were in control of the proceedings.

The planning board coordinator picked up a sheaf of papers, and held them at shoulder height for all to see.

"Mr. Harmon, are you familiar with the Environmental Impact Study submitted by New Century?"

"Well yes, I'm not an engineer but I reviewed it, of course."

"So, you're aware of the problems with the site regarding approximately five acres of wetlands that would be affected."

"I know that our engineers have been communicating with the proper local, state and federal agencies to meet all their requirements. It's my understanding that any loss of wetlands will be mitigated by the creation of new wetland areas near the building site. We're very sensitive to environmental concerns, as we've demonstrated in the past on other similar projects."

Harmon was smooth and confident, but seemed a bit too condescending to this new interviewer.

"Mr. Harmon, shouldn't mitigation and replacement be a last resort? Has there been a genuine effort to rearrange the layout of this development, so that the existing wetlands might remain natural and undisturbed?"

"I assure you, our site development staff worked long and hard to come up with the most environmentally-friendly plan possible."

"Sir, what about the residential lots that will be located on the former wetlands? There is no county-approved soil sample survey included in the DEIS. How can we be sure that the homes built on former wetlands will remain structurally sound, and not subject to foundation problems due to settling of the underlying soil? This has been a huge problem in your existing Windsong development in Harrison, New York, hasn't it?"

Harmon was beginning to feel ambushed, as his adversary appeared to be better prepared than he.

"The Windsong problems are still being investigated, there hasn't been a final determination as to the source of the problems there. We think the subcontractor's concrete mix may have been flawed. That, combined with pouring foundations in unusually cold temperatures, may have resulted in some unsound foundations."

Jackson was fully prepared for rebuttal. "The lawsuit that has been brought against New Century by 27 homeowners alleges that there was no testing of the soil layer after the wetlands had been cleared. They have brought no action against any subcontractors."

"Mrs. Jackson, I assure you and all the members of the board that these tests are being conducted at the Cedar Ridge site, and additional core samples will be taken if and when any lots are readied for the construction phase. The problems in Harrison were an anomaly that we could not have foreseen, and we are working with those homeowners to provide a solution."

Jackson pressed on. "But sir, at the end of the day it's the homeowner who must bear the burden of those very costly 'solutions', isn't that true?"

"As I said, we're working with them. I can't comment further, except to say that we now take additional steps in the testing process, even testing beyond the new state requirements to avoid any foundation problems down the road. These problems are not typical of New Century's developments, and will not occur at Cedar Ridge."

"Alright Mr. Harmon, but this board will need a much more detailed explanation of the testing procedure, whenever that is completed. As you know, there are always consequences to the draining and regrading of a wetland area. Aside from the loss of an ecologically balanced area, as small and inconsequential as it may seem to a developer, there are drainage and runoff patterns that will be affected. The flow of local streams may be dramatically increased during even the most typical rainfall. Where are the studies and projections that deal with that? I don't see them in the DEIS."

Harmon could see that he needed to wrap things up. "I will certainly take your concerns back to our engineering staff, and all of these concerns will be addressed to your satisfaction. We will provide all the details you need to feel comfortable with our proposal."

"That would be a welcome change. These documents," again she was waving the DEIS in the air, "seem to have been hastily prepared, as if approval has been taken for granted. For example, the aerial photos of the site are confusing to the viewer. There are no compass arrows for directional orientation, no gridlines, no scale of measurement, no names of roads or streams. We need more than a vague concept, this should be very specific information that the board can use to form a recommendation."

Now Harmon's discomfort was becoming visible, although he continued to force a smile. He knew that it was time to get off the ropes and limit the damage, then return to the fight another day.

"I apologize for any perceived slight to the board. That was certainly not our intention. We may have allowed time constraints to affect the integrity of the printed materials that were submitted, and that's something we can correct. The information you require is available and will be provided to your satisfaction. After all, it's the goal of New Century to be a partner with the community, not an adversary."

Jackson was inwardly pleased with Harmon's submission, but her quiver contained one last arrow.

"One more question, and then I'll yield. I noticed in your presentation that 82 residences would be built, ranging in estimated sales price from five hundred thousand to one-point-five million dollars. However, the plans you provided show only 80 lots. Our drawing shows no revision letter, is it current?"

Harmon had not expected anyone to pick up on the last-minute change in his presentation. He had decided to add two lots to the total, to be used in place of cash if it became necessary to buy additional support for the project. Now he would have to find a way to avoid a direct answer.

"That may be a typo, I'll check into it." Harmon knew he was dismissing the subject too easily, but it was the best he could do. This lady was a combination of pit bull and Sierra Club member, and he had had enough.

"Thank you, sir. We look forward to your response, hopefully within an acceptable time frame."

Finally, the Supervisor intervened. "Are there any other questions for Mr. Harmon?"

The second of silence that followed was all Wainwright needed. He smacked his gavel to end the questioning.

"I move to schedule another meeting, date to be determined, at which time we will hear the board's final recommendation, followed by the council's vote. That meeting will be open to the public. All in favor?"

The board members murmured assent, and once again the gavel struck its base.

"My thanks to all for attending."

Wainwright rose and turned to head for his office, avoiding eye contact with Victor Harmon. He knew Harmon would be eager to have a few words with him before they left the building, and he wasn't in the mood.

CHAPTER 16

NICKI WAINWRIGHT LEANED closer to the mirror, trying to study her reflection as a detached observer, an objective appraiser who had no personal bias or self interest. In recent years this had become an almost daily ritual for her, following her morning shower. Nicki would begin by carefully wiping the fog of condensation from the glass, voluntarily giving up the advantage of its soft-focus effect. Then she would examine her face, searching for the first signs of any new line, crease, or blemish.

Satisfied that no epidermal crisis loomed on the horizon, she moved on to her hair, all the while preoccupied with thoughts of this new love interest, Jack Ferris. Something about this guy was enthralling, and he didn't seem to be put off by her rather aggressive pursuit.

Nicki's introspection was interrupted by a noise that managed to get her attention despite the roar of her blow dryer. She turned it off to listen and was met by the sound of the door chime. Tightening her silk robe about her waist, she walked towards the front door, half expecting to open it and find that Jack Ferris had returned to take her in his arms once again. She was surprised to discover that the visitor was not Jack, but a tall, stern-faced man who looked vaguely familiar to her. He wore a brown leather jacket, with an open collared shirt and loosened tie. It was still early in the day, but he looked weary.

"Mrs. Wainwright, sorry to disturb you" he started, after a quick glance at the robe. "I'm Detective Webster, Grove Park P.D., may I speak to you?" As he spoke he flipped open an I.D. wallet, and Nicki saw a badge and a card identifying this man as Detective Peter Webster, with a photo that confirmed that fact. Satisfied that he was indeed a detective, Nicki pushed the storm door aside and allowed him to enter. She felt that a change of clothes would be appropriate, but was too curious to take the time to accomplish it.

"What's this about, Detective?"

Pete Webster, on the other hand, was in no hurry to break the dreadful news of her friend's death to this unsuspecting woman. Beside that, she was wearing a very short, thin robe and her killer legs would be a complete distraction.

"Mrs. Wainwright, this may take some time, would you like a few minutes to change before we begin?"

Feeling embarrassed that she had not excused herself to do so on her own, Nicki could only manage to say, "be right back" as she turned to momentarily retreat to her bedroom. Pete had what seemed like only a minute to take in the expensive surroundings before she returned, wearing a snug fitting tank top and low-slung sweatpants.

The detective briefly wondered what her reaction might be if he said "Sorry ma'am, still too sexy, try again", and then regained control of his thoughts and turned to the business at hand.

"Mrs. Wainwright, you're a friend of Jill Sherman's, is that right?"

"Well, yes, actually we're very close." Nicki responded cheerfully, "Why?' Before Webster could continue, a sudden realization prompted her to interrupt. "You're a friend of Jack Ferris, aren't you? I saw you last night, at the bar, remember?"

"Yes, Jack and I go way back" he said, returning her smile.

"What a coincidence! He was just here a couple of hours ago, estimating a decorating job for us."

"Really? Well, Jackie does a nice job, you'll be happy with his work. Great guy."

Nicki noticed a change in Webster's demeanor as he paused, a signal that the time for small talk had ended. She was about to learn the purpose of his visit, and felt her heart rate increase slightly.

"Mrs. Wainwright, I'm afraid I have some bad news." Another pause. "Is there anyone here with you?"

Nicki's face had turned pale at the mention of "bad news." Her voice quivered as she answered the question. "No, I'm alone, my husband has town council meetings today."

Unable to contain her growing panic any longer, her eyes already filling with tears, she nearly shouted "Detective, what happened? Did something happen to Jill?"

Not wishing to prolong the apprehension, Webster knew it was time to state the cold facts. "There was an accident last night. Mrs. Sherman's vehicle went off the road near the Silver Creek Bridge, out on Powers."

Nicki sprung to her feet, as if she were about to rush to her friend's aid. "Oh God, is she alright? Where is she, which hospital?"

"Ma'am, I'm so sorry to have to tell you this — she was pronounced dead at the scene."

For a few seconds Nicki's only reaction was an incredulous stare, as if her mind was unable to process what she had just heard. Tears streamed down her cheeks as she lifted both hands to cover her mouth, preventing a scream of agony from escaping. When she moved her hands aside to speak, Webster could see that her lips were quivering; in fact, her entire body was shaking. He rose to offer whatever little comfort he could provide, and gently guided Nicki back into her chair.

"Are you sure?" she sobbed, hoping desperately that there was some doubt in the identification of the victim. "You're sure it was Jill? What would she be doing out there? She lives in Heron Ridge!"

Spotting a tissue holder on a nearby table, Webster picked it up and handed it to Nicki. "Yes, we're sure it was Mrs. Sherman. I was at the scene myself. She was driving the white Jaguar."

Her hands muffled Nicki's response as she leaned forward and covered her face, crying painfully in a manner Pete had seen many times before when a loved one had been lost. He gave her a few minutes to recover, and then pulled a notebook from the breast pocket of his jacket. He had broken the news, and now it was time to obtain whatever information he could from the shattered friend of the deceased.

Nicki suddenly looked up at him, revealing the swollen features and reddened eyes that would be her visage for days to come. "Oh God, Tim is out of town! He doesn't even know!"

"Actually, Mrs. Wainwright, I spoke to him before I came here. He's on his way home."

"How horrible, to have to hear about this over the phone."

"Well, for what it's worth, we informed the Dallas PD and they went to his hotel to break the news. They gave him my number, and he called to get more information from us."

Nicki cradled her head with both hands, shaking her head side to side in disbelief.

"Mrs. Wainwright, you were with her last night, isn't that right?"

Sitting up and looking her interrogator in the eye, Nicki's answer was almost defiant. "You know I was, detective. We saw each other at Woody's. You do remember that, don't you?"

Webster felt his cheeks flush at this subtle implication that he may not recall everything that had happened the previous night. "Yes ma'am, I'm afraid you saw me at the end of a very long day."

"Oh, I didn't mean it that way", Nicki lied, adding in a more convincing tone "Certainly you're entitled to relax when you're off duty. I just meant, well, you and Jack — Mr. Ferris — probably remember seeing me and Jill there."

Webster struggled to regain control of what should have been a routine questioning. "And then you and Mrs. Sherman went to the Barton house for dinner?"

"Yes, a group of us had dinner, and then went to the bar for a drink. Jill and myself, my husband Jim, Joe Garrity, and Alan Kaplan. Joe and Alan are business associates of Jim's."

"Did the entire group leave together? When did you last see Mrs. Sherman, can you recall the time?"

Nicki's attempt to reply was lost in another burst of sobs. To her credit, she managed to recover, staring blankly at the floor as if visualizing the scene.

"Jill and I were at the bar, discussing the price of condo's with two men we had just met. They were both professional men, attorneys who had recently relocated to Grove Park, and they were interested in the local housing market."

"Do you know their names?" Pete asked, looking up from his notebook.

"No, one of them was Gary something — I have their cards, though, do you want me to get them?"

"Before I leave, yes. Please continue."

Nicki was almost calm now, as she recited the details and recounted her final memories of Jill.

"My husband was suddenly in a hurry to leave — he's so unpredictable — and we sort of rushed out. It was around eleven, I think." Fresh tears began to run as Nicki voiced the thought that would haunt her. "I never thought to offer her a ride home. We said a quick goodbye, and just — left her there."

Now the pain returned, and Pete remained silent until the tortured woman could regain some semblance of composure. He was about to ask a series of delicate questions.

"Mrs. Wainwright, what was Jill Sherman drinking last night?"

Nicki gave him a surprised look, and a different type of hurt was reflected in her eyes. In her present state she hadn't seen this line of questioning coming, but now realized that it was inevitable that the subject of alcohol intake would be discussed.

"At Woody's, Jill was drinking Diet Pepsi. At dinner, she had a Cosmopolitan."

"How many drinks would you say she had before you left?"

"Same as me, three. But I'm sure she wouldn't have stayed long after we left, our group had broken up for the night."

Pete knew better than to challenge that statement, knowing that he could check it out later. The last thing he wanted to do was to seem offensive or judgmental, and lose the cooperation of the victim's best friend. Still, his questions needed answers.

"Mrs. Wainwright, did you see Mrs. Sherman indulge in anything else that might have altered her mood?"

Glancing at Webster's notepad, Nicki was suddenly aware that her comments would be included in a formal report at some point. "I don't know what you mean, Detective," she stalled.

"I mean did she take any type of drug? Prescription or recreational?"

Nicki again studied the sculpted carpeting as she considered her response. The room was silent except for a mantel clock that ticked off the seconds. She didn't want to answer, but it wasn't in her to lie.

"I have no comment on that, Detective."

Pete decided to leave it at that, at least for now. The physical evidence collected at the scene and the medical examiner's findings would provide the answer, and Nicki Wainwright's reluctance to reveal the truth was, for the moment, understandable. "One last thing, and I'll be on my way. How would you describe Mrs. Sherman's state of mind in recent days, and specifically last night?"

"I'd describe her as happy, contented. We were very close, and I didn't see any sign of problems." After a moment's hesitation she added, "of course, one can never know another person completely, but Jill didn't seem troubled at all, if that's what you mean."

She began weeping, quietly this time, and Webster rose to signal an end to the interview.

"Thank you for your help, and again, I'm sorry to have to bring you this news. Now, if I could trouble you for those business cards, I'll be on my way."

When he had gone, Nicki slowly closed the door and leaned against it for support. She hadn't felt so empty and alone for years, and felt drained of all energy. Slumping to the floor, she wrapped her arms around her stomach as if to contain the grief, crying and repeating Jill's name over and over.

CHAPTER 17

JIM WAINWRIGHT CLIMBED into BIGJIM1 and headed for the comfort of home, looking forward to a warm seat in front of the fireplace and a perfect Manhattan. As he left the parking lot, his cell phone buzzed and for the first time that day he chose to answer rather than let the call go to his voice mail. He picked it up and studied the display, but without his glasses the incoming number was impossible for him to read.

"Hi!", he began cheerfully, fully expecting to hear his wife's voice respond.

"Jim", a distinctly non-female voice answered, and Wainwright instantly recognized the caller as his longtime friend, advocate and political ally, Al Kaplan.

"Jesus Al, we just said goodbye 10 minutes ago. You miss me already?"

"Sorry to bother you Jim, I know it's been a long morning."

"Ah, I'm just kidding, you know that. What's on your mind?"

"Jim, have you spoken to Nicki today?"

"Not yet, no", Wainwright replied, feeling a pang of guilt. "I was just about to call her to let her know the meeting was over", he added, although that wasn't really the case. He was hoping that Nicki had her own agenda for the day, so he could relax at home without rehashing the morning's events for her. He knew she'd wonder why the project was so important to him, and that wasn't a conversation he was ready to have.

"So, you haven't heard — Jim, I have some very bad news, and maybe something good."

Wainwright knew that Kaplan wouldn't make such a call without good reason, and he sat up a bit, picking up on the degree of gravity in his friend's voice. Al was a trusted advisor who had always looked out for Wainwright's interests, and possessed two attributes that made him invaluable in light of recent events — loyalty and greed. If Wainwright was to pull off the Harmon deal, he would need Al Kaplan's assistance.

"Dammit," Jim sighed, "why is there always a tradeoff? Okay Al, gimme the bad news first."

There was momentary silence at the other end, and just when Wainwright doubted the connection, Al replied. "It's about your friend Jill Sherman."

Wainwright felt the urge to remark that Jill was Nicki's friend, not his, but something about Al's tone stopped him from doing so. "What is it?"

"Jim, she's been killed in a car accident. It seems that her car went off the road last night. Went down an embankment and hit a tree."

"Oh, my god!" Wainwright gasped. His thoughts immediately turned to Nicki, wondering if she knew, and if so why hadn't she called him? He listened wordlessly as Al related the few details that he knew, after which they exchanged remarks that expressed the proper level of shock and concern at the death of Jill Sherman.

When the moment was right, Wainwright inquired as to the good news Al had mentioned.

"Jim, this is going to sound a bit callous — more than a bit, actually."

"Go ahead, I need to hear something positive, Al."

"The accident happened on Powers Road, at the bridge over Silver Creek. The one we're proposing to have rebuilt as part of the project."

"Really," Wainwright remarked, as he began to see the significance of Al's point. Unsure that the Supervisor had grasped his meaning, Kaplan continued to lay it out for him.

"Jim, we can use this. I know that sounds cold, but it's a fact. This accident highlights the danger of that area to motorists, and draws the media's attention to it. It should be repaired whether the development is approved or not, before any more lives are lost there. Jill Sherman had a lot of influential friends in this town, and this could move some of them over to our side. After all, nothing promotes activism like the loss of a loved one."

For the moment the tragic death of his wife's best friend was put aside as Wainwright began to see light at the end of a tunnel. He loved this guy!

"Al, you're a genius! Let's run with this. Make a list of the Shermans' closest friends at the club, then get over there and feel them out. See if you can inspire them to take some type of action in support of the bridge repair, especially the wives. You know what to say — 'Jill Sherman must not die in vain, and this tragedy could result in the expedited approval for an immediate reconstruction that saves the lives of others.' That kind of thing. Can you do that?"

"Of course, Jim, I'm on it. We needed this."

"Yeah, after the way things went today, we need every edge we can find. Man, Harmon was pissed. That woman took him to the woodshed."

"That's his fault, not ours, Jim. He showed up unprepared, and without an engineer to back him up. And the information New Century submitted was half-assed, they should know better than to take approval for granted. It makes our job more difficult."

"You're right, and when I speak to him I'll be sure to mention that. Not right away, I mean after he calms down." The Supervisor chuckled at the thought of Harmon being skewered by Brenda Jackson.

"Listen, I gotta call Nicki, if she's heard about Jill she must be devastated. I'll try to call you later to brainstorm this thing some more. Thanks for letting me know, Al." Wainwright breathed a sigh of exasperation as he ended the call.

"What a shitty weekend" he muttered to himself, and tapped on the phone to call his wife.

CHAPTER 18

THAT EVENING PETE and Jack met up at their favorite watering hole. Woody's bar area was crowded and noisy, so they claimed a table against the back wall where it would be possible to have a conversation without shouting to each other.

Pete plucked a Buffalo wing from the steaming platter that had been set before him, unable to resist for another second the inviting smell of butter and hot sauce that rose to his nostrils. He had been in the middle of his description of the accident scene, at least those details that he felt comfortable revealing, but for now the case had taken a back seat to his hunger. After dipping a carefully selected wing into a bowl of blue cheese dressing, Pete stripped the meat from one side with his teeth, feeling Woody's infamous Nuclear hot sauce biting at the corners of his mouth, and savored the moment. That first wing was always the best one, especially when it was followed by a long swig of cold beer. Having fully experienced what he considered one of life's greatest culinary pleasures, he returned to his explanation of events, which now was reduced to a series of brief statements between bites.

Jack was busy with his own less deliberate wing-eating technique, but he listened intently as his friend related the facts, sounding as if he was reciting his report from memory.

"So," Pete said, sitting back and wiping his face with a paper napkin, "it's pretty clear what happened, she lost control of the car in exactly the wrong place. Anywhere else within a half-mile and she'd probably be alive today. There are a couple questions I have, but we may never know the answers."

"What questions, Pete?"

"Well, for one, what was she doing so far out of town, way past Heron Ridge?"

"The weather was bad, I can tell you first-hand that driving conditions sucked last night. She could have just missed her turnoff and not realized it. Add the effects of a few drinks, and — ".

Pete interrupted. "I didn't say anything about blood alcohol content, Jack. What makes you think she was drunk?"

"Pete, we saw them right at that bar, and from here they headed for Barton House! Do ya think they might have had a drink or two, detective?" He cocked his head and raised an eyebrow, trying hard to seem objective. Jack was feeling guilty about what he wasn't telling Pete. What had happened between he and Nicki would remain their secret, since it wasn't police business and had no relevance to the case. Still, it was deceptive to act as if he hadn't any personal interest in the case. Thankfully, the detective was more than ready to change the topic of conversation.

"By the way, Marti was asking about you today" he offered, pausing to hear his friend's reaction.

"Asking about me? Like, asking how I've been?"

"No, I mean she wanted to know what I thought of you. What kind of guy you are, do you have a girlfriend, that kind of stuff. She seemed pretty interested." He smiled, letting the implication of those questions sink in.

"That's weird" Jack mused, as he grabbed the last wing from his plate. He dipped it, and then paused to complete his thought. "I mean, we talk at the gym sometimes, just small talk. I ran into her at the Crouching Lion one night and we had a few beers together. Nothing more ever happened, I guess neither of us felt any chemistry, you know?" He was downplaying the event, and the subject seemed to make him uncomfortable.

"Oh, I didn't know that. I don't know, maybe it was idle conversation, just thought I'd mention it in case you find her attractive. I mean, if there's any interest on your part."

Jack chuckled and replied "Pete Webster, matchmaker! No thanks, man. She's a nice person, but I just never thought of her that way."

"Uh huh" Pete said, as if Jack's reply had been precisely what he had expected. He looked Jack in the eye and said, "Let me guess. You're more interested in Nicki Wainwright."

Caught off guard by the accuracy of Pete's statement, Jack was speechless. He felt himself blush, and his blank expression was Pete's confirmation that he had struck a nerve. Jack tried to read Pete's poker face, but couldn't yet be sure what his friend the detective actually knew.

"Jackie, take some advice from an old friend, be careful there. I mean, I can understand the attraction, the challenge, whatever. But think at least twice before you fool around with Mrs. Town Supervisor."

"Thanks Pete, really, but I'm a big boy. I can take care of myself." Jack was uncomfortable, unsure whether Pete was speaking as buddy or cop.

"Look, I realize that you're a grownup, and a pretty sensible one most of the time. Except for that annoying habit of trying to stretch every single into a double — how many times did you get nailed at second base last year?" He was referring to their beer-league softball games.

Jack laughed, and drained his glass. How did Pete know about his thing with Nicki, had he seen Jack's van in the Wainwright driveway?

"Seriously, tread lightly around these rich people. They have their own little society, some of them are very well connected. They're not like us."

"Not like us?" Jack repeated, obviously insulted. "What, she's out of my league, Pete?" unwittingly continuing the baseball analogy. "Am I some lower form of life because I work with my hands?"

"No, no, I didn't mean that at all, come on! You have a nice thing going, you're starting to get work from a certain clientele, don't screw that up."

Jack was indignant, and somewhat amused. "Okay big brother, thanks for the advice. You sound a little paranoid, though."

"You know me Jack, I've been a cop in this town for a long time. I see things you don't see."

"Like what? What do you know about the Wainwrights that I don't?" Jack challenged, hoping for some inside information.

"I'm not talking about the Wainwrights now, I'm speaking in general terms" Pete said, lowering his voice and checking to see if anyone sat near enough to hear their conversation. Satisfied that they weren't being overheard, he leaned forward to emphasize the importance of his point. "You've lived here a long time too, but you only know what you can see, the top layer of things. Cops are different, they know things that aren't discussed with the public, not even with their closest friends. There's a deeper layer of knowledge that we have, whether we want it or not. The darker side of life in the perfect town."

Jack was looking at Pete as if seeing him for the first time.

"Jesus, you make it sound like danger lurks around every corner. How many beers have you had?"

Pete tried not to be insulted by the remark. "It's hard to explain, but a lot of people aren't what they seem to be, at least that isn't all they are. You see a respected doctor, I might see a desperate guy who is suspected of selling prescriptions. You see a successful businessman, I see a possible money launderer. A Little League treasurer who steals the money from fundraising to support a gambling habit — I could go on, but do you see my point? Most people are good citizens, but we have to realize that some are not what we think."

"Okay, I get it. I just don't see how that concerns me, I'm not any part of that kind of thing."

Pete looked frustrated. "You're right, sorry, I'm just rambling. Spending too much time at work, I guess. Seriously though, keep your nose clean and watch where you play, that's all I'm saying. Don't piss off the wrong people. End of speech, now let's play some nine-ball for a beer."

Jack was relieved to be finished with the lesson Pete was so intent on teaching. His buddy was trying to warn him without embarrassing him, and for that Jack was grateful. He wasn't about to abandon Nicki, but it wouldn't hurt to be careful.

"I'll flip you for the break. Call it."

CHAPTER 19

JACK FERRIS LEANED closer to the windshield, trying to get a clear look at the road in front of him as the Cherokee's worn wiper blades sloshed furiously back and forth. The maroon 2008 Jeep was his second and, supposedly, more reliable vehicle, but it was showing one of the effects of being poorly maintained. He had been meaning to change the blades for weeks, but hadn't gotten around to it, and now they smeared the raindrops into a watery glaze that lent all the clarity of a glass block window. A warm front had moved into the region, bringing a steady downpour that was quickly melting the recent snowfall and would soon cause flooding in the usual low lying areas of town. Spotting a parking space within sight of the Reynolds funeral home he pulled to the curb, shut the engine down and slumped back into the seat with a sigh of resignation. Like most people, Jack dreaded having to take part in wakes or funerals, but he was compelled to come here and pay his respects. He had not known the Shermans well, but would have felt somehow guilty had he not attended.

Finally exiting and stepping into the puddled street, he paused momentarily to collect himself before approaching the house of grief. A thin layer of fog hung close to the ground, lending an eerie presence to the gabled building. A few mourners stood on the covered front porch, studying their phones or grabbing a smoke, and Jack made his way past them to the open doors. The crowd already had filled the parlor and much of the entrance hall, and it was a struggle for Jack just to sidle through and hang up his coat. He slowly worked his way towards the front of the viewing room and stopped there, looking around in vain for a familiar face. As he waited for an opportunity to approach the casket and kneel before the deceased to offer his personal prayers, Jack couldn't help overhearing two male voices engaged in conversation nearby. Without turning to look, he immediately identified the self-important baritone of Jim Wainwright.

"No, sadly I won't be able to make the funeral, I have to fly to New York tomorrow. Unavoidable."

"What is it, the Power Authority thing?"

"No, the other thing. I gotta meet with the top dog."

Wainwright's acquaintance seemed to lower his voice, but Jack was tuned in now.

"Why in New York? His office is here."

"I don't know, but he was very insistent. Even had the ticket delivered to my office. I'm sure Harmon gave them an earful about the meeting, they're probably getting nervous."

Jack had no interest in the Supervisor's business or political life, but one facet of the conversation interested him. After the next day's funeral and the breakfast gathering that was to be held immediately after, Nicki would be alone at home. He was convinced that Nicki would welcome a visit with him, or even just a phone call, and she was surely in need of whatever comfort he could offer.

Finally, it was Jack's turn to kneel before the sleeping beauty and offer his prayers. He had not known what to expect, and thought that Jill Sherman looked surprisingly natural, considering the circumstances of her death. Her face remained lovely, although heavily caked with makeup as if she had been prepared to take a part in a play on some distant stage.

Jack rose from the kneeler and was met by the truly stricken countenance of Ted Sherman, and his heart went out to him. They had only spoken a few times before, but Jack knew the man to be extremely friendly and down to earth. It was upsetting to see the depth of his despair, and Jack knew that his own poorly worded condolences could not make a difference. He simply expressed his sorrow as he shook Ted's hand, and then moved aside in deference to the others who were waiting to perform the same ritual. Jack was glad to have come, but it would be a relief to leave these mournful surroundings.

The close quarters and suffocating anguish in the room were nearly claustrophobic, and Jack turned to make his way out. As he did so his eyes swept the room for a glimpse of Nicki, but she didn't seem to be there. He managed to reach the entry hall, and began searching for his overcoat on a rack that had far exceeded its intended capacity. Sensing a presence at his side, Jack turned his head and found himself looking directly into Nicki's sad green eyes, still remarkably beautiful in spite of the absence of any makeup. She managed a sweet flicker of a smile for him, and then spoke to him as if they were no more than casual acquaintances.

"Nice to see you Mr. Ferris, thanks so much for coming." She took his hand, covering it with both of hers, and slipped a piece of paper into his palm. Before Jack could respond, Nicki had left him to return to the visiting room.

At last he located his overcoat and began to make his way toward the exit. As he did so he took one more look into the room filled with the bereaved, and caught a glimpse of Nicki at her husband's side. Stopping briefly to steal a glance at the note she had passed to him, he read its simple, but powerful message. "I'll be at home tomorrow afternoon."

CHAPTER 20

JIM WAINWRIGHT TAPPED his fingers impatiently against the gleaming surface of the Waldorf-Astoria bar as a fresh cocktail was placed in front of him. The first Manhattan had been a proper blend of bourbon and sweet vermouth, but hadn't yet achieved the desired effect of dampening his jangled nerves. Glancing at his watch for the fourth time in the last two minutes, he hoped there was time for the second round to accomplish that mission before the impending meeting.

In different circumstances a stay at a landmark New York hotel would have been a welcome diversion from the 'enormous responsibilities of business and government', as he would describe them, but this was not a pleasure trip. Wainwright wished that Nicki were here with him, sharing a carefree weekend getaway like in the old days, and then dismissed the thought and reminded himself to focus on the matter at hand.

Wainwright had been summoned to this unusual meeting place by Victor Harmon. Although Harmon had declined to reveal any details other than the appointed time and place, Wainwright could easily guess the agenda. He would be asked to explain why he had so far been unable to deliver on certain promises that had been made, and that he was beginning to regret. Big Jim was smart enough to know that refusing to attend this meeting would send the wrong message to his new associates, so he agreed to fly to New York for an afternoon meeting at Sir Harry's Bar, inside the Waldorf. He planned to employ his considerable communication skills to smooth things over and buy more time, and then fly home the next morning.

A tap on his left shoulder interrupted Wainwright's contemplation of recent events. Momentarily startled, he turned to find himself looking into the tanned, smiling face of Victor Harmon.

"Mr. Supervisor, how are you? Thank you for coming."

Harmon was, as usual, impeccably attired in what appeared to be a custom-tailored suit. His black hair was stylishly moussed and mussed, and he exuded the air of a rising young star of Wall Street.

"Victor, it's great to see you again!" Wainwright lied.

"My employer would like you to join him at his table." Harmon stretched out an arm to direct Wainwright's attention to one of the small round tables that lined the perimeter of the bar. Each table was decorated with an inlaid checkerboard and illuminated by the glow of a small shaded lamp, and Wainwright could see that one table was occupied by a man who chose to remain in the dark.

Looking to Harmon for confirmation, Wainwright received a nod of assent and slid from his barstool perch, drink in hand. He made his way towards the designated table, followed closely by Harmon, and as they drew closer Wainwright realized that the man he was about to meet was not Kevin Cochran. Although the two had never met, he had seen Cochran at the Grove Park country club, and this portly gentleman bore no resemblance to him. He appeared to be around sixty years old, bald with a rough dark complexion, and wore an off-the-rack suit with a black shirt that was open at the neck, revealing a gold chain.

As they reached the table, Wainwright set his drink down and was about to introduce himself, but stopped short when he saw a hand signal from the stranger, indicating that he should wait a moment. The man then glanced at Harmon, who leaned closer to Wainwright and discreetly moved a hand up and down his back. He was holding some type of electronic device, about the size of a disposable lighter, and deftly switched it into his other hand to lightly sweep it across Wainwright's chest. Apparently satisfied, he motioned for Wainwright to be seated.

"Mr. Wainwright, this is my employer, Mr. Gotts. Please, have a seat."

Harmon pulled out a chair for the perplexed Supervisor, who sat down without a word. He was shocked that these men considered it necessary to check him for wires. They wanted to be sure that he wasn't recording their conversation or, worse yet, transmitting to officers of the law. Gotts had made no attempt at a greeting or a friendly handshake, and seemed to be intently studying Wainwright, sizing him up.

As Harmon dragged a chair from an unoccupied table and sat between them, Wainwright managed to form a weak smile before speaking. "Excuse me, but I'm a bit confused. I thought I would be meeting with Mr. Cochran today."

Gotts raised his bushy eyebrows at this and finally spoke, revealing a gravelly voice. "Vic, did you tell him that?"

Harmon, who had positioned his chair slightly away from the table as if he wouldn't be involved in the conversation, shook his head. "No sir, I indicated that Mr. Wainwright would be meeting with my employer."

"Ah, so that was it," Gotts replied, turning to face Wainwright. "You thought Vic worked directly for New Century."

"Well, yes, I assumed that — "

"Mr. Cochran is not personally involved in this matter, and we won't mention his name again. Are you familiar with the term 'out-sourcing', Mr. Wainwright?"

"Of course. Please, call me Jim." It was annoying, the way this man deliberately pronounced "Wainwright" as if he thought the name was amusing. It was the same feeling he had when Harmon called him "Supervisor."

"Well Jim, think of Victor and I as suppliers. We've been contracted to provide a service, one that New Century is not staffed to handle. You deal directly with us, and discuss this matter with no one else, understand?" He finished the statement without a smile, and leveled a steely gaze at Wainwright to determine whether he had sufficiently made his point.

"Certainly." was all Wainwright could manage. His mouth was suddenly dry, prompting him to lift the glass to his lips. He took a sip, but tasted nothing more than melting ice cubes at the top of the glass, and continued with two large gulps that brought a satisfying burn to his throat.

Gotts watched him drink, obviously enjoying Wainwright's discomfort, and leaned closer. "Mr. Wainwright, you know the reason for this meeting, don't you?"

"Mr. Gotts, sir — look, I want to assure you that the situation is under control. I have an understanding with several influential members of the Town Council and the Planning Board, and we're going to get this project approved. But you have to understand, these things take time."

Paulie Gotts was unmoved by Wainwright's clichéd assurances. He had dealt with scores of Jim Wainwrights in his time, and to him they were all the same. Arrogant, over-confident and greedy, these small-time politicians never seemed to fully appreciate what they were getting into. It was part of Paulie's job to enlighten them.

"I understand that the Planning Board met with your town council, and our proposal wasn't very well received. You don't find that disturbing?"

"That was unfortunate, I agree, especially because of the media coverage. But it wasn't an unusual initial reaction to those of us who are familiar with Grove Park. There are some well-established groups who believe it's their civic duty to protect the town, the environment, and — you know — their way of life. This was an opportunity to raise their voices in public dissent, and they took advantage of it.

"The fact is, they will lose this battle. Eventually another one will present itself, and the do-gooders will move on. Those of us who support the development are fully capable of handling a few preservationists. We'll get our support from the business community and from influential members of the Town Council. The editor of our local newspaper, The Citizen, is ready to endorse the plan in print. It's a small-time operation, but that paper carries a lot of weight in our town."

Wainwright was on a roll, the liquor having relaxed him and loosened his tongue. He wanted to exude complete confidence in what he was saying, assuaging any fears that he was not in command of the situation. After pausing to drain his glass, Wainwright added "Mr. Gotts, you can rest assured that Jim Wainwright will not let you down."

Paulie Gotts was, unlike Wainwright, a man of few words, and they were chosen carefully. The momentary silence that preceded his reply was too much for the Supervisor to bear, and he continued with a statement that he immediately regretted.

"'course, it wouldn't hurt to spread a little money around. Grease the skids, so to speak." He chuckled as if kidding, but it was obvious that he hoped Gotts would agree.

Vic Harmon had been quietly listening but withholding comment in deference to his superior. Now, however, he was compelled to place a hand firmly on Wainwright's arm, a signal that he had said enough.

It was clear that Gotts felt that Wainwright had said too much. Once again he leaned towards Wainwright, even closer this time, his tight-lipped face turning brick red. Gotts was visibly shaking as he attempted to control his rage.

"Listen to me carefully, you putz, and try to remember who you're dealing with. You will do what you were contracted to do, and the deadline is thirty days from today. That's a very generous time frame, but we are aware of the difficulty of the task. There will be no further changes to our arrangement, and you will never again speak of it publicly or privately, not to anyone.

"Do you understand the word '*dead*line', Mr. Wainwright?"

Wiping perspiration from his upper lip, Wainwright glanced at Harmon hoping to find support, but found none. The false bravado had evaporated, and he finally managed to stammer a careful reply.

"Yes sir, I think I do."

Gotts sat back, unclenching his hands, and appeared to relax somewhat. The anger had dissipated, but the smile he flashed at Wainwright lacked any trace of warmth.

"Good. We understand each other. A few months from now this will be over, and you and your lovely wife can enjoy a nice vacation, eh?"

The mention of his wife was unexpected, and Wainwright perceived it as an added threat. He was still digesting the comment when Gotts rose to his feet, and Harmon quickly followed suit.

"Good bye, Mr. Wainwright" he said, and they walked away, leaving a shaken Jim Wainwright still seated, holding an empty glass.

CHAPTER 21

NICKI OPENED THE door and meant to meet Jack with a smile, but couldn't manage it. She saw the look of genuine empathy on his face, and before either one could speak she burst into tears.

Without thinking, Jack stepped inside and put his arms around her, whispering "I'm so sorry", and her only response was to place her arms around his neck and hold tightly to him as she wept.

Regaining her composure enough to break away and close the door, Nicki looked at Jack and mouthed a barely audible "thank you".

"I didn't know Jill, but I know that you two were very close." Jack offered, as Nicki bit her trembling bottom lip and nodded. "I just had to tell you how sorry I am, and if there's anything I can do, anything at all — "

"Thank you, Jack, that's so sweet" she interrupted, truly touched by his sincerity. "I wanted — " she seemed too embarrassed to finish her thought, and for a moment Jack had doubts about his decision to come here. "I needed to see you again, Jack, you've been on my mind so much lately. Besides, I still have your sample book and I thought you might need it."

"No, no, I wanted you to take your time with that. Actually, I know this must have been a tough day for you, and, uh — " stammering now as Nicki's eyes held his in a gaze he couldn't look away from, "I mean, I know you're alone here, and I just wanted to make sure you were okay." The last statement had a definite air of "there, I said it", as if Jack had unburdened himself. She placed both hands on his face and kissed him, and for that moment Jack was gratified to know that coming here had been the right thing to do, after all.

The shrill electronic ring of the nearby portable phone once again broke the spell. Nicki managed to ignore the first two rings, then gently broke away to pick it up.

"Hello? Oh, Jim, where are you?" She paused as her husband replied, and then the words burst from her along with fresh tears. "Jim, I still can't believe this happened!" Nicki listened for a while and then looked at Jack as she said "so what time will you be home?"

Jack recognized the question as his cue, and knew that it was time to exit. Nicki was still listening to her husband but her eyes were trained on Jack as he walked over, squeezed her hand, and silently kissed her on the cheek. As he turned to leave, Nicki grabbed his arm to hold him there.

"Okay then, I'll see you tomorrow. Call me before you board — bye." She placed the phone in its cradle and returned her attention to Jack, smiling fully for the first time in days.

"Can you stay a while? Let's just have a glass of wine and talk for a while. I want to know all about you."

Jack's instincts told him that leaving might be the sensible thing to do, but he couldn't say no to her. After all, that was what he had been hoping Nicki would say.

"Yeah, I'd like that, if you're sure."

"I'm sure. And I don't worry about what the neighbors might think, if that's what you mean. Now have a seat, I'll get the wine."

*

Curled up on a large cushioned chair across from him, Nicki sipped her wine and fixed her gaze on Jack. "Tell me about yourself, Jack. What led you into the decorating business?"

Jack shrugged, inwardly wincing at the "decorator" label. He papered and painted interior walls, and sometimes offered suggestions on furnishings if asked, but did not consider himself a decorator.

"Not too much to tell really. I'm a pretty unremarkable guy."

Nicki smiled at his modesty and waited for him to continue.

"I grew up in the area, went to school here in town. When I was a kid, the only thing I really got into was sports. My goal was to be a professional baseball player, and I was sure it would happen. Didn't really have a backup plan." He blushed slightly and looked away, apparently dismissing the train of thought, but Nicki was genuinely interested.

"What happened? Did you lose interest in baseball when you discovered girls?" She was about to laugh, but was stopped short by the serious look on Jack's face. He looked past her, as if the subject was deeply personal for him, perhaps painful.

"No, it wasn't that. Things were going great for me. I was a junior in high school, and the papers were calling me one of the top players in the state. I pitched, played outfield and hit for power, just what the scouts were looking for. They were calling my dad all the time, feeling him out."

"About what?" Nicki refilled their glasses, eager to hear more.

"We had a big decision to make. After my senior year, I could accept a full ride to play college ball, or sign a pro contract and play for a minor-league team." He stopped there for a moment, as if to savor the memory.

"What did you decide to do?"

"Well, as it turned out, neither one. The last game of my junior year, I was pitching. There was a ground ball hit to my left, and I ran over to cover first — I'm sorry, do you know about baseball, or am I boring you?"

Nicki could tell that this memory was important to Jack, a defining moment in his life, and she wanted him to share it with her.

"No, not at all, I know exactly what you mean. I watched a lot of baseball with my dad. Go on."

"Okay. Well, I ran over to cover first, and Jerry Blackman, our first baseman, tossed the ball to me. Routine play, just catch it and step on the bag, right?"

Nicki nodded, sensing that the play he was describing would turn out to be anything but routine.

"As I caught the ball, my foot came down wrong, like the base wasn't exactly where I expected it to be. I felt my knee sort of hyperextend, and just then the runner crashed into my leg. He was coming hard, trying to beat the throw, and I guess he just stumbled and kind of lunged forward out of control. The next thing I knew I was rolling on the ground in pain.

It felt like I'd been shot in the knee. Turned out, the ligaments were all torn or severed. That was the end of the baseball dream."

"That had to be hard, especially for a teenager."

Jack responded with a wry smile, realizing that no one could grasp just how devastated he had been.

"It took a long time to get past it. Way too long. I sort of dropped out afterwards — stayed away from my friends, since most of them were teammates. I just didn't feel like I fit in anywhere. My dad died about a year later, that made things worse."

He paused and shrugged his shoulders, trying for the millionth time to put these painful memories aside.

"Eventually, I had to find a job. I went to work for my uncle Wes, he did painting and general contracting. I settled on the painting part, mostly because I could work alone and take some pride in the end result."

Jack grinned, embarrassed to have been so unexpectedly open about a twenty-year-old heartbreak. "Sounds like a bad country song, huh?"

"I'm sure there's a lot more to tell about your life since then, Jack. Have you ever been married?" She knew that she was boldly prying, but was encouraged by his initial willingness to share himself.

"I was engaged once, but things didn't quite work out the way we planned. Had my share of female friends since then, but none that I wanted to settle down with. The last few years I've been pretty busy with work, trying to make enough money to finish the house."

"You're remodeling a house?" she asked, skipping right over the mention of an engagement.

"No. I built a log cabin on some land I bought, up on Emery Road. Do you know where that is?'

"Yes, I do, actually. A log cabin?"

He chuckled. "Not like the one Lincoln grew up in, Nicki. It's a lot more ambitious than that. You might even be impressed."

"I'm sure I would. I'd love to see it sometime, could I?"

"Sure, I'd be proud to show it to you, maybe you could appraise it for me. I'm still working on the interior, but as a whole I'd say it's eighty percent completed."

Before Nicki could respond with her next question, Jack had one of his own. " I have to ask you something now, as long as we're sharing."

"Okay," she said, a bit uneasy about what he might ask.

"What are we doing here, Nicki? I mean, where is this going? I'm starting to have some pretty strong feelings towards a married woman, and that's never happened to me before."

"All right, that's fair. I've been wondering what you must think of me, a married woman carrying on as if she's single." She set her glass down, half expecting him to protest her characterization, but Jack was all ears.

"To be honest with you, my marriage is pretty much an empty shell, and has been for a long time. I'm starting to think that I don't really know who my husband is, maybe I never did.

Up until a few months ago, I'd been in a period of self-indulgence, something I'm not very proud of. I was trying to escape, or find myself, or maybe find someone else. I won't go into detail, I'll just say that one day I took a hard look at how I was living my life, and made a decision to re-dedicate myself to my marriage. But it hasn't worked, in fact things seem to have gotten worse."

She blinked away the tears that were building, and looked straight into his eyes.

"And then, I met you. There was something special about you, I don't know how to explain it. I was drawn to you. I sensed that you might feel the same way towards me, and I had to find out. I don't know where it's going, Jack, I only know that I'd like to know you better. My marriage is over, but I'm not divorced, not really free. I couldn't blame you if you didn't want to get involved with me."

Jack realized that her words were exactly what he'd been hoping to hear. "Your instinct is right, I do feel the same way. I'm not going to walk away, unless you tell me to. Just one question, and I won't press any further. What do you mean, you don't know him?"

Nicki shook her head slowly, rolling her eyes as if she didn't know where to begin.

"I've had doubts for a long time, for so many reasons. Jim was always somewhat secretive, lately more than ever, and I suppose I've been naïve to put up with it. Maybe I just didn't want to know what was going on, or I was afraid of what I might find out. For a while I was convinced that he was having an affair, but now I think it's something much more than that."

Jack was too intrigued to keep his earlier promise.

"What do you mean by 'something much more'?"

Nicki wasn't put off by his follow up at all, she seemed relieved to be able to confide in him.

"The first time you were here, when I showed you around the house, there was one room we didn't go into."

"Right, I remember one door being closed, I assumed it was another bedroom."

"That's Jim's home office. He keeps the door locked. Like I said, he's strangely secretive. But a few weeks ago, I had a chance to see what was in there."

She lifted her glass and took a long drink, as if preparing herself to go on.

"Jim was working in his office one night, and I heard him calling for me. He sounded scared, he was really shouting. I ran in there and found him doubled over in pain, holding his stomach. He kind of collapsed to the floor, and I called the rescue squad. It turned out that he had kidney stones, and they had moved into his urinary tract. They kept him over-night in the hospital, and when I finally came home to get some sleep it was late, about 2 in the morning. I couldn't sleep, and I started poking around in his office, the inner sanctum that he keeps so private. There's a wall safe in there, in the closet, and Jim must have opened it at some point before the pain started. It was still open, and I took the opportunity to see what was in there."

"And?" Jack was on the edge of his seat.

"I won't tell you everything I saw in the safe, but among other things there was an old Iowa driver's license with a picture of Jim on it, a very young Jim. But the name on the license wasn't Wainwright, it was James Wright."

It was obvious from Jack's demeanor that he didn't find the name dif-ference to be as disturbing as Nicki had.

"Could be his old fake proof, from the years before he was old enough to drink legally. Or maybe he really did change his name, for perfectly innocent reasons. I suppose asking him would be out of the question."

"I don't want him to know I'm suspicious, Jack! Besides, the other things in the safe were confusing, and kind of frightened me. Trinkets, old costume jewelry that I didn't recognize – and money, a lot more cash than a person would normally have on hand. I want to know who I'm married to, and what he's up to. The anxiety was getting to me, so I hired a private investigator to look into Jim's background. I had made a copy of the driver's license, and I gave it to him."

"Really. Has he found anything?"

"I don't know yet, I haven't heard from him. I've been meaning to call him, but with everything that's happened — "

"I understand. Well, maybe this P.I. will find some answers for you, and hopefully it won't be anything criminal. In the meantime, be careful, huh? I mean, until you know more about what's going on."

She looked down at her glass, idly running a finger around its rim. "Oh, I'm careful, trust me. But it's an awful way to live."

Jack stood up and reached down for her hand, and Nicki rose to meet him.

"Nicki, I think I should go. Thanks for having me here, I enjoyed it."

"I'm so glad you came, Jack."

He pulled her close to him and their lips met, and this time it was Nicki who managed to break away.

"I want to see you again Jack, and soon — and I want to see that wonderful home you've built."

"I'd like that."

Minutes later he had gone, and each of them was already missing the other.

CHAPTER 22

I T HAD BEEN a long Monday, and Jim Wainwright was still in his town hall office at 6 PM, waiting for his cell phone to ring. The section of Town Hall that housed his office was deserted, as the only other people in the building at that hour were working the evening shift in the police department wing. He usually enjoyed this quiet time at the end of the work day, when he could set aside the endless details and demands of town politics and concentrate on his more urgent personal matters. Lately, he had been given a lot to think about. In addition to the Cedar Ridge development proposal there was this distressing new problem to deal with, one that threatened to destroy the life he had built in Grove Park.

The phone call from Mitch Goren had been a virtual lightning bolt, completely unexpected and thoroughly terrifying. Jim hadn't seen Mitch for over two decades, since he had abandoned the Midwest and relocated to New York. The pairing of Goren and Wright had a history in Iowa that, as far as Wainwright was concerned, would best be left there. Their shared interests in hunting, fishing, and partying were memories that Wainwright sometimes allowed himself. He mentally locked away their darker exploits, those that only the two of them were aware of, because those secret acts were outside of the law, and some were outside the boundaries of human decency. At some point the relationship had soured, and each man found reasons to avoid the other. In the end, James Wright disappeared from Iowa completely, ignoring a significant debt that was owed to Goren, and had rarely thought of him in the intervening years. He hated the thought of becoming reacquainted with this thug, and with his own past.

Earlier that day Goren had initiated contact a second time, leaving a message on Wainwright's cell phone. Repeatedly addressing him as "good buddy", he had demanded a face-to-face meeting that night. Jim was to wait in his office for Goren's next call, advising him of the meeting location.

Good buddy, Wainwright muttered to himself in disgust. This guy sounded like the same malevolent hick that he had left behind years ago, and although it was disturbing to hear from him, there was no reason to think Goren couldn't be manipulated again.

Wainwright retrieved his bottle of Jack Daniels from the bottom desk drawer and was pouring himself a generous drink when his cell phone chimed. He set the bottle down, hesitated for a second, and then lifted the glass and stiffened his resolve with a satisfying gulp before answering the call.

"Wainwright".

He heard Goren's chuckle at the other end. "You know, I don't think I'll ever get used to that name, Jimbo. You'll always be Mr. Wright to me." He chuckled again at his little joke, and waited for a response.

"Mitch, you don't need to get used to anything. Just tell me what it is that you want."

"Aw Jimbo, don't get all pissed off! I was just kiddin'. But you're right, there is something you can do for me. You should know what it is, but maybe you forgot by now, what with this new life you made for yourself. Let's meet and grab a bite, and we can talk about it."

"Where and when?" Something told Jim that Goren already had a plan. He was keeping his responses brief, hoping that his manner wouldn't betray the fact that he was very nervous. As he suspected, Goren was ready with a suggestion.

"There's a place just off the interstate, a few exits from town, a truck stop called Merle's. Big sign with a cowboy on it, you know the place?"

"Sure, I know it" Wainwright answered. He didn't like the idea of being seen with Goren but if they had to meet in public, Merle's wasn't a bad choice. The chances of being seen by someone who knew him would be slim, and the home cooked fare was said to be very good. The situation was unnerving, but his appetite was unaffected. "What time will you be there?"

"I'm on my way, get going." Goren commanded, and abruptly disconnected.

*

It was after seven when Jim Wainwright reached the entrance to Merle's Diner. The familiar neon sign blazed into the night from its 50-foot perch, trolling the nearby interstate highway for potential customers. It was a figure of a bow-legged cowboy wearing an oversize Stetson, tossing a lariat with a loop that flashed on and off in sequence, adding the illusion of a circular motion.

He pulled the Hummer in and passed by a row of cars that were parked in front of the diner, none of which displayed out of state plates. A half dozen big rigs were parked in the large stone paved lot to the rear, some with their diesel engines left rumbling at idle speed while the drivers grabbed a quick meal. Wainwright decided that this would be the best place to leave the truck, lessening the possibility that a Grove Park resident might stop by and recognize the Supervisor's vehicle. For the first time, he regretted his purchase of vanity license plates.

Wearing a baseball cap and Carhart barn jacket in a lame attempt to blend with the clientele, Wainwright entered the restaurant and paused to look around. The lighting was subdued, and the low murmur of conversation was punctuated by the clatter of dinnerware being dropped into the bus trays as tables were cleared. The sound of George Jones crooning in the background enhanced the country feel of the place, as did the table legs covered in denim, each with a mini cowboy boot at the bottom.

He surveyed the counter and dining area, wondering if he would be able to recognize a man who had become such a faint visual memory, when a nearby waitress approached him.

"One?" she inquired routinely as she worked her wad of chewing gum.

Just then Wainwright spotted the familiar face, older and weathered now but unmistakably Goren, at a booth in the far corner. The battle scar was as prominent as ever, almost pink against the tanned skin that surrounded it. If Mitch the Stitch had seen Wainwright come in, it wasn't evident as he concentrated on his meal.

"I'll be joining that gentleman," he said, pointing to Goren.

Walking slowly towards the booth, Wainwright stopped next to the vacant bench and waited to be acknowledged. Finally, exhibiting an incredible calm and lack of curiosity, Goren looked up from his plate and met Wainwright's gaze.

"Hello Jimbo," he said in a voice devoid of emotion, "Set down."

Wainwright seated himself as the hovering waitress placed a menu in front of him.

"Coffee?"

"Yes, just black, please."

When she had gone, it was Goren who broke the ice. "Kinda strange seein' each other after all this time, ain't it?"

"Yes, you could say that."

Goren smiled, sensing that he was much more at ease than his counterpart. "You've done real good for yourself, Jimbo. I always knew you would."

"I've worked hard, been a little lucky. Made a good life here. What's keeping you busy these days?"

Goren laughed at the unintended irony of the question, just as the waitress returned. She set a steaming mug in front of Wainwright and automatically topped off Goren's cup.

"Ready?" she asked, continuing her habit of communicating in one-word queries.

Before he could respond, Goren chimed in. "Why don't you bring him the special, Ginny?" He pointed to his plate of meat loaf and mashed potatoes, drowned in gravy. "It's real good eatin', Jimbo".

Avoiding any further discussion, Ginny nodded in agreement and scurried off, leaving Wainwright to wonder about Goren's apparent familiarity with her. Had he made her acquaintance just this evening and simply read her nametag, or had he been a regular here of late?

There was another silent standoff as each man waited for the other to begin the conversation that had brought them here. Goren resumed eating as Willie Nelson took a turn at providing the musical accompaniment.

Wainwright studied his former friend, noticing for the first time the knuckle tattoos on Goren's hands. He had the words "love" and "hate", one on each hand, crudely inscribed. The tattoos reminded Wainwright of the villain in a movie he had seen years ago, although Mitch was certainly no Robert De Niro. It was the sort of thing a bored prisoner might have done in an attempt to look tough and fit in, and it was quite possible that Goren had done some hard time.

Neither man looked up when Ginny returned with Wainwright's meal, and instinct told her to skip the usual offer of further service. When she had left, Wainwright could wait no longer. He got right to the point.

"So what is it, Mitch? Tell me why you're here."

Goren raised his eyebrows in mock surprise and sat back as if wounded. "That's it, good buddy? No catchin' up? No small talk about the good old days? Just cut to the chase, huh?"

"We can chat about the old days later." Jim replied as his fork cut into a slab of meat loaf. "First I want to know your intentions."

Goren's animosity rose to the surface.

"Okay, I guess you're going to play dumb, so here it is — twenty-seven years ago, when we were *real* close friends, we made a deal. A damned important one, as you'll recall. I held up my end of the bargain, but you disappeared without doing your part. There's no friggin way you could have forgotten that."

Wainwright stopped eating, but didn't respond.

"You promised to pay me ten grand, as soon as things settled down and the life insurance check cleared. But you never intended to pay me, didja, good buddy? No, you ran out on me, disappeared without a word. Well, now I'm here and I mean to collect what I'm owed — with interest. Otherwise, the good people of your cute little town will find out who the hell you really are."

Goren had leaned even closer as he spoke, his hoarse whisper reflecting the anger he felt as he growled those last words over the table. Wainwright knew that this was not the moment to engage in an argument, or any sort of denial, but his pride would not allow him to be threatened without a response.

"What would they find out, Mitch? That I changed my name, left the past behind? So what? A lot of people do that, for completely legitimate reasons."

"Do a lot of people pay to have their old lady murdered?"

The blunt question hit Wainwright like a punch to the stomach. He dropped his fork and took a furtive glance behind him to see if it might have been overheard. Satisfied that his secret remained safe, at least for now, he returned his attention to Goren.

"You have no proof of that" Wainwright hissed, "and keep your voice down!"

Goren seemed to collect himself, and sat back again before resuming his passive aggression. "Tell me Jimbo, do you still have that set of Medalist golf clubs? The ones you had custom made?"

Wainwright was puzzled at the abrupt change of subject, and surprised that Mitch would mention a specific manufacturer. He wouldn't have been caught dead on a golf course in their younger days, and had always mocked Jim for taking up the game just to rub elbows with clients.

"I think they're in storage or in the basement somewhere, I haven't used them in years. They're old technology, no one uses those little blade irons anymore. Did you look me up just to borrow my old golf clubs?"

"No. I have the one I want. What would you say if I told you I still had a club from that set? Those custom-made sets were all serialized, the number's engraved on each club. I even called Medalist and gave them the number, and your name was still on file there. Imagine that."

"What the hell are you getting at, Mitch?"

"The nine iron has the number on it, proving you owned it. It also has Kim's blood and tissue on it, and probably your fingerprints, or DNA even. No prints of mine, I was smart enough to wear gloves. When I tell the cops that I was remodeling your old house, and found it hidden in the wall, do you think that would get their interest? Hell, they might even re-open the case, huh?"

"Remodeling? You never did any remodeling in that house. You're not making sense, Mitch." Wainwright was doing his best to hide his discomfort, without success.

"Well, I was gonna tell you, but you didn't give me a chance. I own that house now."

"What? You're kidding!" was all Wainwright could say. At this point he couldn't separate fact from fiction.

"A nice young family moved in some years back. You see, I was away for a while and when I got back I wanted to buy the place but they outbid me. Eventually they heard about the deaths that had taken place there, and that must have rattled them a bit.

Then someone broke into the place while they were on vacation, pretty much trashed it. Lucky for me, they put it up for sale, and I took it off their hands real cheap." His satisfied grin made it obvious that he had been responsible for the break-in.

Wainwright was interested now, and pushed the reminder of his dinner aside. Mitch's story sounded plausible, and it was time to put this thing to rest.

"Alright, let's assume that what you say is true, and you go to the cops. It's your word against mine, and they probably wouldn't have enough to nail either one of us. I think you know that. Of course, you also know that I don't want to have to deal with the questions it would raise, and the media attention. So, I'm asking you again, Mitch, what do you want?"

He was attempting to exude defiance and confidence in the face of this intimidating foe, but Wainwright had a familiar tell. As he struggled to control his emotions, the wine stain above his right eyebrow became more prominent. Goren recognized it as proof that his former friend's heart was beating like a drum in response to his very presence here, and saw an opportunity to raise the stakes.

Goren leaned close again, to emphasize the importance of his words. "I want twenty-five grand, Jimbo. That's less than a thousand for each year I've waited. Cash, small bills, untraceable. And I don't aim to negotiate with you."

This last was said with such conviction, it had the effect of a threat. Wainwright didn't immediately answer, he simply tapped his fingers nervously on the formica tabletop, staring into space as if he were processing Goren's demand. He had twice that amount in just those denominations hidden at home, courtesy of Victor Harmon. Wainwright could get Goren out of his life, hopefully forever, and still have twenty-five thousand for himself, but he wanted to give the impression that coming up with that much cash would be a difficult task.

"Mitch, that's a lot of money, it may take some time to get it for you. Surely you can understand that."

"One week." Goren felt that he was in complete control of the situation, and could afford to pressure his former partner in crime. "I'll call you one week from tonight and tell you where to meet me. No excuses, no games."

Inwardly shaken, Wainwright nodded in agreement, and Goren slid out of the booth and stood up as if to end the meeting.

"I guess we'll skip the heart to heart talk about old times, huh Jimbo? I'll be in touch."

He pulled a twenty from his wallet and tossed it onto the table, then walked away without a backward glance.

CHAPTER 23

PETE WEBSTER HAD known for months that he would have to find the resolve to change his lifestyle, or he might disappear forever.

It had been three years since he had buried his beloved Mary, and Pete still felt lost without the light of her presence. Thankfully, people had finally stopped greeting him with that grave, sympathetic look that made him so uncomfortable. In fact, Pete sometimes felt that everyone had forgotten about Mary a bit too easily. They evidently assumed that Pete had successfully moved on with his life, or that he should be spared the pain that any mention of Mary's name would surely bring.

The truth was that Pete still felt the acute sense of loss every day, and had found only one effective antidote. At first he had decided that his work was the answer, and surprised his co-workers by returning to his job the day after the funeral. Friends understood that he needed to occupy his thoughts with something other than memories and sorrow, and it seemed to them that Pete was doing as well as could be expected.

It wasn't long before Pete came to the realization that police work would never crowd the unwanted thoughts from his mind, at least not the cases he normally dealt with. They were the everyday transgressions that took place in any small town; vandalism, domestic disputes, shoplifting, and every so often a theft or break-in. The work was necessary, and important to those involved, but it wasn't enough.

In the end, Pete found solace at only one place, Woody's bar. He became a regular there, usually arriving at happy hour and often staying until the late local newscast showed up on the television above the bar.

On the nights when he planned to stay at home and take a break from the Woody's routine, solitude and sheer loneliness drove Pete from his home. At this point, it would be unusual to walk into Woody's and not see Pete Webster sitting at the bar half in the bag, unable to help himself even though he knew this was the wrong answer to his problem. The question Pete was forced to ask himself was, where would he go from here? The obvious answer frightened him, and he could easily picture his regression into an alcoholic haze, and into oblivion.

So tonight, once again, Pete would attempt to turn things around. He had left home intending to seek comfort at Woody's, hating himself and his weakness even as he drove that familiar route. Then, as he neared his destination, something inside of him made him change course. Some combination of self-loathing and determination had convinced Pete to test his will to change, hoping that he could muster the strength to stay away from the bar for just one night.

He drove to the police station and trudged toward his desk, once again relying on his work to occupy his mind long enough to save him from himself. The night shift cops greeted him as he passed by, but they were occupied with their duties and didn't have time for conversation. That was fine with Pete, he needed time to organize his desk and his thoughts.

Finding a place to set down his large cup of Tim Horton's coffee was no easy task, as documents and scribbled pages covered the entire surface of his desk. Pete silently surveyed the mess, and felt a pang of regret as he realized what a shoddy job he had been doing of late. Maybe this was the night that things would begin to change.

He set to work organizing the papers by date, and then by case number. Many of the pages were his handwritten notes from a variety of interviews and crime scenes, awaiting further attention. In better times Pete would have translated the hard copies into word documents and filed them on his computer in dedicated folders. That way they were easily accessible and could be posted to the department's network, to be shared with other interested parties on a read-only basis.

Lately, however, Pete had lost interest in that type of efficiency. He had started scanning his notes into the computer rather than typing them, even though his personal shorthand was difficult for others to interpret.

After a while, he had simply allowed the pages to pile up on his desk. Tonight he would have to make up for weeks of cutting corners and early exits.

After two long hours of typing, scanning, and electronic filing, Pete became bored with his own caseload and logged on to the departmental network. He entered the shared drive where information on active investigations could be viewed by those with the required security clearance. Pete sometimes browsed the cases, to stay in touch with what had been keeping the other officers busy.

This time Pete was not actually browsing, he had a particular event in mind. After reviewing and typing his notes on the Sherman accident, Pete was curious to read the report filed by the Accident Investigation Unit. He located the proper folder, but for some reason no documentation had been posted to it. That was unusual, considering the time frame, and he wondered what could account for the delay.

Having seen Eric Bronski at his desk on the way in, Pete decided to walk down the hall and ask him about it. He needed to stretch his legs anyway, with the added benefit of passing some more time.

Bronski had seen Pete enter the building earlier, but pretended to be surprised as he approached.

"Pete, what the hell are you doing here? Did Woody's burn down?"

Pete tried not to be over-sensitive in his reaction to the remark, although it confirmed his suspicion that he was becoming a departmental joke.

"Ha ha, real funny, junior. Actually, I came in to check up on you. You know, evaluate your performance."

Bronski laughed, but his facial expression became one of uncertainty. He was up for a promotion and didn't want to seem disrespectful. "What's up?" seemed like a safe comment.

Pete pulled a chair over to Bronski's desk and sat down.

"No big deal, kid, take it easy. I was just in the system looking for your findings on the Sherman fatality, but I couldn't find anything. Is it filed?"

Bronski frowned as he reached into a nearby file cabinet and pulled out a green folder. A completed report would be placed into a tan folder and forwarded to the records building, where each page would be scanned into the departmental database. The green folder was an indication that Bronski's investigation was ongoing.

"Been meaning to close this one out, I just haven't gotten to it yet."

Knowing Eric, Pete felt there was more to this story.

"What's keeping you from closing it? Something bothering you?"

"Ah, it's probably nothing, just me being anal. You know how sometimes a detail doesn't quite fit, you can't explain it? It bugs you."

"That's what makes a good investigator, right? Not letting those things go unexplained. So, what is it?"

Bronski's reluctance evaporated and he leaned forward, eager to share his thoughts with an interested colleague.

"I was talking to Randy over at Rowland's body shop, on Cooley Road. I just happened to mention the Sherman's Jaguar, and what had happened. Turns out, Randy did some of the restoration on the car. The last thing he did was pull off the bumpers and have them rechromed. He reinstalled them a few months ago."

Bronski stopped as if expecting a question from Pete, but none came. He simply nodded, wishing that Eric would get to the point.

"Well, I remembered seeing damage to the rear bumper when we were at the scene, and taking a picture of it. Now, that car hit a tree head-on and folded up like an accordion. How would the rear bumper get damaged?"

"Maybe it was scraped somehow as the car road up the guard rail."

"No, this was impact damage. Like from another vehicle. So, I assumed that it was there before this accident. It could have happened anytime in the last three months."

"But you're not totally sold on that."

Bronski shrugged. "I don't know. It's a reasonable assumption, but there are limits to it. This car wasn't driven much at all, and there are no accident reports or insurance claims. No one recalls seeing any damage to that bumper, and this car gets attention wherever it's parked. And Randy says Tim Sherman was so meticulous about the car, he wouldn't let anything go unrepaired."

"So, Sherman told you the car was undamaged before that night?"

"Well, as far as he knows. He can't be a hundred percent sure, since he's been out of town a lot, and they keep a cover on the car when it's in the garage."

"Is that it, or are there other things that don't add up?"

"No, just the bumper thing. Everything else points to an accident that was the result of slippery conditions, poor visibility, and a driver who was under the influence."

"What was her blood alcohol level?"

"At the time of the crash, no way to tell. Too much time had passed before the body was processed. The screen showed traces of cocaine, though."

Having listened to Eric's commentary, Pete failed to see any reason to spend even another minute on the case, and was inclined to say so. But he decided to let him down easy.

"Okay, look — the coroner ruled that death was caused by head and chest trauma, that won't change under any circumstances. If it makes you feel better, keep the file active for a while longer, until you're satisfied."

"Right. I didn't know where I'd go from here, anyway. I'll just hold onto it for now."

Pete rose from his chair. "Why don't you send the files and digital images to me, I want to take one more look."

"Sure, no problem, Pete."

Webster turned, fighting his sudden urge to run out and get a drink. He planned to force himself to return to his desk and review the Sherman information, and eventually head for home. One night away from Woody's was tougher than he would have imagined, but he had done it. Tomorrow night would be an even bigger challenge.

CHAPTER 24

"THERE'S A LINE of windmills at a farm out on Briggs Road. You know the place?" Goren was all business, and seemed know the Grove Park area surprisingly well.

"Yeah. I know where that is."

"Good. A gravel road runs down the line. Meet me at the end of the road, under the last windmill. Nine o'clock sharp. I'll be watching, Jimbo. Make sure you don't bring anybody with you."

"I understand, and I told you no one else knows you're here. Who the hell would I bring?"

"I don't know, I guess I just don't trust you. Now, what do you suppose would cause that?"

Wainwright didn't respond.

"You got the money, right?"

"Yes, I have it, small bills, nothing over a fifty."

"Good man. See you there, Jimbo." There was a click, ending the conversation.

*

At 8:55 Wainwright turned off of Briggs Road, onto the seasonal road that accessed the windmills. Although he had driven past the spot many times, he had seldom seen the blades turning, and thought that the owner must have blown a lot of money and saved very little in energy costs. On this night, however, a steady wind had brought the windmills to life. Wainwright braked the Hummer to a stop beneath the last of the gawky towers, and decided to shut down the engine and leave the headlights on as he stepped out to look around. There was a shed at the base of the tower, probably housing some type of electrical equipment related to the wind turbines. It was the only possible place of concealment in the area, and Wainwright felt safer keeping it illuminated.

Raising the collar of his jacket and turning his back to the biting wind, he managed to light a cigarette and stood next to the halogen beams, listening to the low-pitched whirring sound that emanated from the blades above his head. He estimated that the hulking white tower was over 100 feet tall, topped by a set of three twenty-foot long blades. There must have been some heavy guy wires supporting the structure, but they were hidden by the night. It was pitch black, the overcast sky preventing any moonlight from assisting as he looked for detail in the surroundings.

As he waited somewhat nervously for his nemesis to arrive, Wainwright had no idea that he was being watched. Goren was studying the scene from the edge of a wooded area some fifty yards away. He had carefully chosen this site for their meeting, and now his patience was being rewarded. The elevation had allowed him to watch Wainwright's approach without revealing himself and, best of all, he had discovered another access road nearby, where he could safely leave his car and make his way through a strip of woods to his present location. Wainwright would be totally surprised, expecting him to come driving down the road that paralleled the windmill line. Satisfied that they were alone in this rather desolate spot, Goren left his position and quietly approached his unsuspecting target.

The sounds of the wind and humming turbines rendered Goren's movement inaudible until he was a mere twenty feet away, and Wainwright looked frightened as he whirled to face some perceived danger. He seemed relieved to find that it was Goren, or at least Wainwright thought it was. Where had he come from?

"Mitch? Is that you?"

"Hey Jimbo." The now-familiar voice could barely be heard above the gusts. Goren looked past his former friend, silently chewing a toothpick as he checked the road again for any unwanted company. Assured that they were alone, he stepped closer.

"Where is the money?"

"In the truck. Did you bring something to put it in? I want to keep the briefcase, it was a gift from my wife."

Goren found the request to be humorous, given the circumstances.

"Aw, that's sweet, man. She'll have to buy you another one though, I didn't think to bring a bag. Hope it wasn't too expensive."

Wainwright felt a vibration in his coat pocket, and instinctively reached for it. Seeing the movement, Goren stepped back and reached behind him, whipping a handgun from the waistband of his jeans and pointing it at Goren.

"Hey! Jesus, I was reaching for my phone, put that thing away!"

"No calls, Jimbo! I think you should start taking this a little more seriously before you get hurt." His tone was more hostile than Wainwright had expected, and he knew that the situation was not just delicate, but very dangerous.

"Is the briefcase on the front seat?"

Wainwright nodded, hoping that Goren wouldn't get it himself.

"All right, I want you to move real slow, keep your hands in sight, and get it for me. Do it!"

Moving towards the Hummer, Wainwright made a decision to at least try and get some information before the exchange was completed. He turned towards Goren, hands out at his sides, and took notice of the gun that was still pointed at his chest.

"Mitch, can I ask you just one thing before we get this over with?"

Goren was in no mood to be friendly, in fact he appeared to be fighting his own nerves. "You can ask". He replied, not promising to answer.

"I need to know how you found me. Even though I believe you when you say this is all you want, there could be others who come after me the same way."

Goren spit his toothpick out and shook his head. "I don't think that'll happen, don't worry about it. Now open that door and get the briefcase."

Wainwright knew he was pressing his luck, but he persisted. "How do you know that?"

Goren's patience had worn thin, but he took a few seconds to look around before replying. He concluded that there was no harm in telling part of the story and besides, he enjoyed gloating.

"A guy showed up at my house one day, said he was a private investigator from some little town in New York. He showed me a copy of an old driver's license, and asked if the picture on the license looked familiar. I looked at it and there you were, staring back at me from twenty-some years ago.

"Seeing that picture set me back for a second, but I acted like I hardly remembered the guy. I said it had been a long time and all, but this dick had done his homework. He knew that we were good buddies at one time, and I think he had talked to the cops and found out about Kim."

Wainwright's lips tightened at the thought of his first wife, and the thought of being investigated. "Did this guy say who hired him?"

"No, not at first. Not willingly. It wasn't hard to find out where he was staying, though. I paid him a visit that night, and sorta persuaded him to tell me what was going on."

"Who was it? Who hired him?"

"I never got that part from him. As soon as he told me where to find you, and what name you were using, I had what I wanted. But don't worry, he won't be filing a report. I made sure of that."

Before Wainwright could speak again, Goren barked at him.

"Now open that friggin door!"

Wainwright did so, and reached across to the passenger seat. He had brought his small .38 Ruger and placed it under the briefcase, and if he intended to use it this would be the moment. Grabbing the briefcase handle, he looked back to see how Goren was positioned. There was no way to pull out the gun without being seen, and possibly killed. Still, this was a lot of money to give up so easily.

He straightened up and turned to exit the car just as the eager Goren took a step forward. As Wainwright exited and stood up he swung the briefcase hard, hitting the extortionist squarely on the jaw and sending him backwards. Goren's gun flew from his hand, and Wainwright dove back across the seat to grab his own weapon. By the time he turned back, Goren was at the Hummer door, enraged, pointing his revolver at Wainwright's head.

"You bastard, you're gonna pay for that. Get out here and kneel down!"

Shaking uncontrollably and babbling apologies, Wainwright dropped to his knees. He saw Goren pick up the briefcase and move behind him. A few minutes passed as Goren unlatched the case and tried to estimate the amount that it contained without benefit of sufficient light. Wainwright heard the case snap shut and then felt the gun barrel at the back of his head.

"Please don't. Please don't, Mitch, I'm sorry!" He closed his eyes, wondering if he would hear the shot before the bullet tore through his brain, but nothing happened.

"Who's that? Who is that?" Goren shouted.

Wainwright opened his eyes, and saw headlights approaching, about a hundred yards out.

"This ain't over, Jimbo!" Goren shouted, and took off running, disappearing into the darkness.

CHAPTER 25

WAINWRIGHT MANAGED TO regain his feet as the blinding headlights drew closer, until the pickup skidded to a halt next to the Hummer. His brush with death had made his legs unsteady, and he thought he may have wet himself.

The truck's doors opened and two men jumped out, neither of whom Wainwright had ever seen. They were young grimfaced kids, probably in their twenties, both dressed in what looked to be some kind of military camouflage apparel. The one from the passenger side was holding a shotgun at hip level, aimed in Wainwright's direction.

"Stay right there, and put your hands on your head!" the driver barked, as they cautiously came forward.

"Okay, put the gun down, I'm unarmed!" Wainwright protested. He couldn't recall where his gun had been left after the scuffle, and hoped they wouldn't find it.

"Who are you, and what are you doing here?" the driver asked.

"I can explain. Really, there's no problem."

Now the passenger, clearly an angry young man, pointed the weapon at him from three feet away. "Answer him, what are you doing here? Did you see all those signs that said 'no trespassing'? This is private property!"

Wainwright had always been a skillful liar, and his brain raced to concoct a story on a moment's notice, hopefully one that would make sense to these strangers.

"I'm Supervisor Jim Wainwright. You've heard the name?"

"Supervisor of what?" sneered the driver. His mouth worked a sizable chew as he looked Wainwright up and down.

"I'm the Town Supervisor of Grove Park. Put that gun down, please. I've been through enough."

"A politician, huh? Big deal, I hate politicians. I'll ask one more time, what are you doing on our property?"

"I was on my way home, and I picked up a hitchhiker, a young kid. Stupid of me, I know, I guess I'm a little too trusting. He pulled a gun on me and told me to turn down this road, and then told me to get out and leave the truck running. I think he meant to rob me and take the truck, but I scuffled with him. He got the best of me, and had the gun at my head when you guys showed up. You saved my life!"

"Yeah, right" shotgun said. "He wanted to steal this bright yellow piece of crap, huh?"

"I swear that's what happened. What else would I be doing here, for God's sake?"

"You never know. Some people think these wind turbines are ugly, they want us to take 'em down. Doesn't matter to them that we power three homes from here, and that if more people did the same we'd be less dependent on foreigners for oil. They already tried to sabotage us a couple times."

Wainwright had no idea who these guys were, possibly some kind of rural survivalist group, but he didn't really care. He only wanted to extricate himself from this nightmare. "Look, I don't know anything about that. I told you what happened, and I'm grateful that you guys showed up when you did. I just want to go home, no need to bother the police with this."

The driver appeared to be in charge, and he took over possession of the shotgun, keeping it trained on the intruder.

"Go check the shed."

As his partner obeyed the order, the driver spit a stream of tobacco juice on the ground at Wainwright's feet.

"I wasn't about to call anybody. What happens here is our business, I don't trust cops."

There was silence until the shed inspector returned, with a nodded assurance that all was in order.

"Okay, bud, I'm gonna let you go. But don't come back here, you hear?

And just for the record, I don't buy that bullshit story you told us. If I catch you here again it's your ass. Now get in your truck."

"Thank you. You won't see me here again, I promise you."

He returned to his truck and climbed in, thankful to see the glint of gunmetal on the floor as he did so. Covering the gun with his left foot, Wainwright started the engine and backed around the pickup, then slammed it into drive and headed up the road, feeling drained but glad to be alive.

He turned onto Briggs and headed for the safety of Grove Park, wondering where Goren was at that moment, and hoping that he would be satisfied to take the money and run. Even if he was safe from Goren, Wainwright knew he still had a problem. Someone close to him, at least close enough to have suspicions, was having his background investigated. He would have to tread carefully around everyone, including his wife, until he could identify this new adversary.

CHAPTER 26

"JUMP IN, I'LL drive."

Jack was stopped in his tracks by Nicki's words. The idea seemed rather foolhardy in light of their recent agreement to keep their relationship a secret, at least until there was some sort of commitment between them.

It had taken three days for Jack to complete his work in the Wainwright home, and some of those hours were spent in increasingly personal conversation with the lady of the house. Since then Nicki had said they were soul mates, a term Jack considered to be vastly overused, but he shared her sentiment. They had been meeting discreetly for over three weeks now, becoming increasingly intimate, if not in the purely physical sense then at least in mind and spirit.

Nicki had told Jack that she would call him right after his Saturday workout, so they could spend a full day together for the first time, but decided instead to drive to the Strong's gym and wait in the parking lot.

She had only been there a few minutes when Jack appeared, shading his eyes from the sunlight that had bathed the area for days. Unseasonably warm temperatures portended an early spring, and for the time being memories of a rather harsh winter had melted away with the snow. It wasn't until he reached his van that Jack noticed the yellow Hummer nearby, and heard Nicki's stunning invitation. He was undeniably glad to see her, but reluctant to take a step they might later regret.

"Nicki, why are you driving this school bus?"

She laughed at his description of the Hummer. "Jim had to drive to

Rochester for some sort of seminar, he asked if he could borrow my car. It's more comfortable for long trips, you know, and much better on gas. So, we are goin' four wheelin'!"

"Nick, are you sure? I mean, someone is bound to see us."

She smiled at him and shrugged her shoulders in a "so what?" mannerism, and playfully asked "What's wrong Jack, are you embarrassed to be seen with me?"

Knowing full well he was being needled, Jack returned her grin as he tossed his gym bag into the van and grabbed a jacket from the front seat. After adding a pair of sunglasses, he walked to the passenger side and climbed in.

"You know better than that, right? I was just being sensitive to your situation."

"You let me worry about that, sweetie. Besides, these windows are so darkly tinted they're illegal."

They chuckled as she turned the key in the ignition, bringing the powerful engine to life, and as Jack relaxed and settled back into the seat he realized that he had no idea what their destination was.

"So where are we headed?"

Nicki was beaming, obviously happy to reveal her plan.

"I know a perfect spot for a picnic. It's a little way out of town, just off of Davis Road. It's a great spot, overlooking Shale Creek. You've heard of the Eternal Flame, right? It's near there."

"Oh yeah, I've heard people talk about that, I guess it's a natural gas flame behind a little waterfall. Sounds cool, but I've never seen it."

"I brought a bottle of wine and some cheese, we'll sit in the sun for a while and then hike down to the flame, okay? It's a pretty easy hike, there are trail markers now."

Jack was enjoying his stint as a passenger, watching Nicki handle the man-size truck and listening to her enthused explanation. She continued to drive away from the village to the east for about five minutes as Jack tried to keep his eyes focused on the roadside scenery. They enjoyed the ride mostly in silence, and Jack would occasionally glance over at her, feeling increasingly comfortable with the situation.

Nicki turned onto a short gravel road which ended in a small clearing, a parking area that would accommodate several vehicles, although at present the Hummer was its only occupant.

"Jack, would you take the basket? I'll get the blanket. The trails start here and eventually lead down into the ravine, along the creek bed. That one goes left to the flame, but we're going to the right. Careful, there are exposed roots everywhere that will trip you up."

"You lead, I'll follow, Captain." They laughed and started out.

Ten minutes later they reached a series of large flat stones that, as promised, overlooked the creek some thirty feet below.

"What do you think? I love it here; the view, the sound of the water. It's so peaceful, don't you think?"

Jack answered her with a kiss. "It's great."

"Glad you like it. Let's have some wine, I brought a nice red with a convenient screw top."

They spread the blanket to sit on and as Jack poured Nicki turned to him with a serious look, and surprised him with an uncharacteristically revealing statement.

"Jack, I want to be honest with you, always. So I want you to know I've been here before with someone else, but that's been over for a while now. It was a mistake, nothing like what we have. I only want to share this place with you now."

He appreciated her honesty, and it was clear that Nicki had wrestled with the decision to tell him.

"You don't need to explain anything to me, Nicki, let's just enjoy the day."

"No, I want you to know — I want us to really know each other, and not hide anything."

She hesitated, and then looked straight at him as if to gauge his reaction as she said, "it was a woman."

Jack's face seemed to convey understanding, even sympathy, as he imagined a woman, possibly Jill Sherman, sitting in his place.

"Look," he said, taking her hand," it's okay, I get it. I'm not the first person to share this special place with you. I'm just happy we're here now, so let's lighten up and enjoy this day."

Before long they were once again completely relaxed and comfortable with each other, enjoying the freedom that their surroundings provided. A cool breeze whispered through the trees, over bare branches that would soon display their newly minted leaves. Even the cardinals and jays had gone quiet as Nicki took Jack's face in her hands and kissed him tenderly. He reclined onto the blanket and she leaned into him, kissing him again and staying with it as if she meant business.

Just then they heard a noise from the woods behind them, twigs snapping as if they were being stepped on in a hasty retreat. They listened for a while, Nicki frozen in her position on top of Jack. Finally she laughed and stood up, embarrassed to have been so startled by what had probably been the sound of a deer that had picked up their scent. She was about to remark that it must have been a jealous buck, when they heard the distant sound of an engine starting.

"What the hell?" Jack said, jumping up to look around.

Nicki shrugged. "I don't know. I think a lot more people come here lately to see the flame, even during the cold weather."

Jack had had enough of the outdoors for one day. "Look, Nick, it's not as warm as I thought it would be out here, let's hike down to the flame some other time. Why don't we go to my place? Drop me at the gym to pick up the Jeep, and then meet me there, okay?"

"I thought you'd never ask!" she immediately replied, delight showing in her face. "You must have read my mind, let's go!"

CHAPTER 27

JIM WAINWRIGHT EXITED the elevator of the Rochester Carlton Arms Hotel and proceeded to room 322 as he had been instructed. Through Victor Harmon, he had been summoned to a second meeting with the repugnant Paul Gotts. This wasn't a confrontation he was looking forward to, but Wainwright felt better prepared this time. At the very least, he knew who he would be dealing with.

Wainwright's knock went unanswered for a minute, leaving him to stand uncomfortably in the corridor as a few of the hotel's guests passed by. He was about to rap on the door more forcefully when Victor Harmon opened it, dressed casually but looking somewhat tense.

"Jim, good to see you, come on in" he said, extending a hand. Wainwright wondered why Harmon would be so formal, considering they spoke to each other on an almost daily basis. Apparently, he wasn't the only one who was on edge in Gotts' presence.

The suite was spacious, with a sitting area that featured a large wall-mounted flat screen television. It was tuned to a basketball game, but the sound was muted. Gotts was seated in a plush leather chair, resting his stocking feet on the glass-topped coffee table. He made no move to greet the newcomer, and didn't bother to acknowledge Wainwright's presence until a beer commercial filled the screen.

"Friggin' Curry. Nobody can stop him. I'll never bet against him again."

Harmon took a seat on a couch across from his boss, and Wainwright joined him. There was silence as Harmon busied himself by pouring three drinks from a bottle of Wild Turkey, waiting for Gotts to begin the conversation.

"So, Mr. Wainwright" Gotts began, with an exasperated sigh. "I was hoping we wouldn't need to see each other again, but I'm concerned about the reports I'm getting from Victor. He seems to be unsure about how things are going, so I thought we should meet again."

Wainwright shot Harmon a perplexed look. Once again Harmon had misgivings that he hadn't conveyed, and thought it would help to call in the heavy.

"I'm confused, Mr. Gotts. Vic and I speak to each other quite often, and I've told him repeatedly that the proposal will be accepted."

"Yeah, that's what Victor told me" Gotts replied, reaching for his drink, "but that's not enough, is it? This is an important deal for Victor, and he needs to close it successfully. I'd hate to see him fail. Tell me what you've done since that last board meeting to strengthen our position."

"We've reached out to some of the dissenting members of the Planning Board and the Council, and I know that we've swayed some votes to our side. We're also working closely with a citizen's group that supports the project's bridge reconstruction aspect, and they've been very vocal. Things are falling into place."

As usual, Gotts was unmoved. He looked to Harmon, as if giving him permission to speak.

"Here's the thing, Jim. I get the feeling that you're being way too casual about the situation, and have been from the start. You don't seem to be taking any action, I don't see you getting as involved as we expected. Have you personally spoken to any of the planning board members?"

"Well no, not personally, I have good people around me to handle that. I have to delegate these things, I can't do it all myself."

Gotts interjected. "What about this ballbuster, Brenda Jackson? She's the real problem, from what Victor tells me. Have you tried to get to her?"

Wainwright was unsure how to respond to Gotts' phrasing. He was irritated that Harmon had deemed it necessary to get Gotts involved, and was tired of being pressured. He drained his glass and returned it to the table, striking it with more force than he had intended, as his frustration boiled over.

"Listen, you people came to me with a proposal, and I accepted. You had a problem, I agreed to solve it. Now, I keep telling you that I have things under control, and all you do is badger me! Why don't you let me do what I was paid to do and stop wasting my time?"

Wainwright knew he was getting in deep, but now he was on one of his patented rolls.

"I have a lot going on right now besides this goddamned project of yours, you have no idea what it's been like. I can't always be available to hold Victor's hand!"

Harmon was shocked at the outburst, staring at Wainwright in disbelief. Amazingly, Gotts showed no anger in the face of this blatant disrespect. If anything, he seemed intrigued by what he had just heard. He picked up the bottle and poured Wainwright another drink.

"Now we're getting somewhere" he said, adopting a fatherly tone. "You have other problems that are distracting you, is that it?"

Wainwright took a drink, resolving to tread carefully lest he reveal too much.

"Yes, like I said, it's been a rough time for me, but I'll get through it." His words lacked conviction, and Gotts could tell that this man was in over his head despite his protests to the contrary.

"Maybe you want to return the money and walk away, is that it?"

"No, that's not an option."

Gotts played his next card as planned. "Why don't you tell us what these other problems are. We might be able to help clear them up, and you can return your full attention to our project. I know a lot of people, we have resources available to us."

Wainwright had never considered that possibility, but welcomed the offer of help. In a strange way, these were the only people he could trust with the sordid details of his past, and how it had come back to haunt him. Going to the police was certainly not an option, and he didn't want even his closest friends to know what was going on. In that instant, he made a desperate decision.

"All right. I don't know what you could possibly do, but I have nowhere else to turn, so why not? Maybe you can give me some advice, if nothing else. But what I'm going to tell you stays between us. If the wrong people were to find out, I may as well be dead."

Gotts and Harmon exchanged glances, trying to remain expressionless. Who was this guy, and what was the big secret? They couldn't wait to find out.

"You have our word on that, of course."

This time Wainwright helped himself to the bourbon, preparing to unburden himself.

"Well, the problem you already know about is Brenda Jackson. The truth is, we can't even approach her about Cedar Ridge anymore, she's so adamantly opposed. It's like a crusade with her, she won't listen to reason. The Council can approve the project against her recommendation, but that's not acceptable to us. It would leave the appearance of impropriety, and the press would smell a rat. So, we need to somehow convince her to change her position. The other problems are more complicated."

Wainwright launched into the story of his relationship with Mitch Goren, taking care to avoid any specifics about their crimes. He told them about Goren's unexpected appearance in Grove Park, including the payoff and his fortuitous rescue by the landowners. Harmon and Gotts interrupted frequently, pressing him for details, and Harmon even jotted down some notes. They were particularly interested in Goren's present location, but Wainwright had no idea where he had gone.

"He'll be back for more" Gotts predicted, an opinion that Wainwright shared.

It was Harmon who posed the question that Wainwright had been asking himself for days.

"Who do you think hired the P.I.? Any ideas?"

"No, none," Wainwright lied, shaking his head and looking into his glass. He wasn't about to suggest the most likely possibility, that Nicki had hired him.

"Really?" Gotts asked, "no idea at all?"

"None."

They were out of questions and the bottle was nearly empty, and Gotts was eager to speak to Victor in private. Wainwright wasn't about to share the secret that was worth $25,000, at least not yet.

"Okay, let us look into it and see what we can do."

"That's it?" Wainwright had expected some advice from these men, some suggestions as to how to proceed.

Gotts chuckled. "You've laid quite a story on us. Let us discuss this and see what we can come up with to help. Meanwhile, you focus on the Cedar Ridge vote. It's coming up pretty soon, right?"

"In a couple of weeks, I'm sure you know that. Like I said, that's the least of my problems. Maybe you can see that now."

Wainwright rose to leave. He had quite a buzz on, and he knew of a good strip joint nearby. That always took his mind off of his troubles.

Harmon shook his hand again at the door, an earnest look on his face as if they had bonded somehow. Gotts had returned his attention to the television. Without looking up he said, "We'll be in touch."

Take your time, thought Wainwright as he closed the door behind him. He hoped he had seen the last of Paulie Gotts.

CHAPTER 28

"JACK, I JUST can't get over how adorable this place is! You must be so proud to be able to say you built it yourself."

Jack grinned at Nicki's choice of adjectives. "Actually, I was going for manly and rustic, but thanks."

"Oh, it is, of course!" she gushed, "but to a woman it's adorable, too."

Nicki had first seen the house a week earlier, when they had met there for lunch. Once again, she marveled at Jack's workmanship and attention to detail, and was doubly impressed.

It had been five years since Jack purchased the wooded five-acre tract that fronted on Emery Road. In his mind it was the perfect lot, offering the privacy of a rural setting and also reasonable access to the necessary utilities. The entire first summer was spent clearing trees to create what was now a crushed stone driveway, rising to a slightly higher elevation where the construction had taken place. His choice of a log home design was the culmination of years of research and daydreaming, and purchase of the materials took almost every cent of his savings. Each log was pre-cut to specific dimensions and numbered to match the architectural drawings that were provided. With more than a little difficulty, Jack and his part-time crew of neighbors and friends completed the outer structure and floor joists that were provided by the Wisconsin manufacturer. After that he was largely on his own to buy materials locally, as he could afford them, to complete the interior. Almost two years passed before the house was far enough along for Jack to move in, and it had taken him another two to bring it to its present state, which he estimated at eighty to ninety percent complete.

The plan featured a large garage and workshop at the ground level, with the main living space on the second floor and a lofted bedroom area above. There was a large stone fireplace and a railed deck around three sides, just as he had always imagined. Jack had succeeded in building his dream home, but it had felt somehow empty until now. To his surprise, Nicki's presence seemed to fill the void.

"Nic, are you hungry? I could make something for us."

"Oh no, don't go to all that trouble. I'll just cut up the rest of this cheese, while you put some music on."

They kissed, and then separated to accomplish their assigned tasks, hoping to rekindle the mood that had been interrupted earlier. As Jack browsed through his collection for something that would provide just the right mood, he heard a yelp of pain from the kitchen.

"Ouch!! Oh, shoot! How stupid."

Jack ran to the kitchen to find Nicki cradling one hand in the other, a rivulet of bright red running down to her wrist.

She looked at him almost apologetically, as if not knowing what to do next. "The knife got away from me."

Jack snatched a dishtowel from a nearby wall rack and wrapped it around her fingers, guiding her to the bathroom. Once there, he turned the cold water on and removed the towel, holding her hand under the flow before inspecting the wound.

"Okay, that's not too bad. The bleeding is nearly stopped already. Let me put a butterfly on it and wrap it in some gauze." He noticed that Nicki was trembling a bit, her face paled by the sight of her blood.

"Do you think I need stitches?"

"No, I don't think so, it isn't very deep. See how it looks tomorrow, and if you're not sure about it see a doctor, alright?"

He gently applied a small bandage around her fingertip, holding the small flap of skin in place.

"Thanks sweetie, I feel better now. I guess I overreacted when I saw the blood."

Jack reassured her with a hug. "Don't worry about it. Just stay away from sharp objects for a while."

Later, as they sat together in the living room listening to Tim McGraw, Nicki once again turned pensive.

"What are you thinking about, Nic?"

She returned to the moment, snuggling closer to him. "Nothing."

She smiled wryly at her answer, and restated. "Everything."

Jack made the assumption that she was thinking about the background check of her husband.

"Have you heard anything from Hartman?"

"No, not a word. I wish I'd never hired him."

"You mean because he's a stiff, or because you don't want an investigation at all?"

"Both, I guess." she replied, with a shrug.

Nicki adjusted her position on the couch, sitting sideways so she could look into Jack's eyes, as if to emphasize the importance of her next thought.

"Jack, I've made a decision."

In the seconds that followed, Jack's mind raced through the possibilities. What had she decided? Was Nicki about to tell him that she was leaving her husband? He should have been pleased at the thought, even elated, but instead of those emotions he felt panicked.

"I decided not to wait for Hartman's report. I'm going to confront Jim myself, and tell him what I saw. I'm going to be honest and direct, and demand an explanation. That's what I should have done before, instead of over-reacting and going around him."

Jack's immediate reaction was to inwardly chastise himself for jumping to his own misguided conclusions, but his concern for Nicki quickly replaced it.

"Are you sure? I mean, the things you found really upset you, it seemed as if you were afraid of what they might mean. Can you trust your husband enough to believe his explanation?"

"I don't know, but I have to hear it. I think I'll be able to tell whether he's being truthful or not, and I didn't mean that I was afraid of being physically harmed. Jim is all bluster, he would never hurt anyone, especially me."

She smiled and sat in his lap, putting her arms around his neck.

"Don't worry, it's the right thing to do. I have to do it before I can move on."

Nicki's lips were tantalizingly close to his, but Jack wasn't quite ready to end the conversation. "One more thing, and then we'll change the subject. What about the hang-up phone calls you mentioned last week, have they stopped?"

"Oh baby, that's nothing to worry about. I don't think it's at all related to my situation with Jim."

"Really. So, you know who it is?"

"Maybe. I told you, it's nothing to be concerned about. Now, about that change of subject." She pressed her lips to his, putting all of herself into the kiss so her feelings for him would be conveyed with certainty. Jack responded in kind, trying to ignore the unanswered questions that seemed to hover over them.

He was crazy about Nicki, but was beginning to feel that he knew very little about her. He had so far assumed the role of the understanding lover, telling Nicki that there was no need to explain a troubled past to him, that they would be a fresh start for each other. Now he was beginning to wonder if that had been the best course of action.

CHAPTER 29

"I'M SORRY, I just can't decide — do you have something a shade darker?"

Smiling sweetly from behind the glass display case, the elderly sales clerk submitted yet another small bottle of nail polish for her customer's examination. "This one is a bit darker dear, but it's very close to the color you're wearing."

Brenda Jackson took the bottle and held it next to the glossy nails of her free hand for comparison, and was shocked at the similarity.

"Oh my god, am I in such a rut that I can't break out to choose a different color for my nails?"

She placed the offending bottle firmly on the counter alongside a dozen others that had failed to win her approval. Without any further hesitation, she snatched a bright shade of pink from the collection.

"I'll take this one" she announced to her advisor, pleased with herself for having been so decisive. The clerk smiled again, recognizing that her customer had finally chosen the very first color she had seen, ten minutes earlier.

"Do you like the color I picked, honey?" Brenda asked her daughter, aware that the six-year old had been quietly patient during the selection process. She placed a debit card on the glass and turned to show off her purchase.

"Kiana, do you like — "

Brenda stopped in mid-sentence as she found herself speaking to the spot where had her daughter had been standing just minutes before. Kiana wasn't there.

"Kiana?" She scanned the area around her, quickly covering a twenty-foot radius, and did not see her child. Her stomach tightened involuntarily.

"Kiana!" louder this time, sharp enough to turn the heads of nearby customers.

"Did you see where my daughter went?" she asked the sales lady, who looked up from her computer screen in confusion.

"Why no, I — it's so busy today, I hadn't really noticed her." Her voice was still droning on in the background as Brenda's eyes continued to roam the store. She was in one of the smaller boutiques on the Galleria Mall's second level, and Kiana's absence must mean she had left the store. The exit to the main mall area was in sight, but she couldn't bring herself to go out there. She wanted to stay put so Kiana could find her when she became bored with whatever had caused her to wander away. Two teenage girls had been peering into the glass display case to her left, admiring the gold necklaces.

"Did you see my daughter? Did you see where she went?" Brenda's tone was panicked now, desperate, as if she wanted to grab them by the shoulders and shake the information from them.

Looking guilty for not having been more observant, they mumbled "Um, no" almost in unison, and automatically began looking around for the child they hadn't even seen.

Brenda turned to the clerk. "Look, could you watch for her for a few minutes? Her name is Kiana. She's six years old, wearing a red jacket and tan slacks. If she comes back here, tell her to wait here for me!" It was more of a command than a request. Without waiting for an answer, she rushed away towards the mall crowd that was slowly filing past the storefronts.

Brenda moved quickly as she looked for her missing daughter, not quite running but causing enough commotion to catch the attention of those she passed. She continued to call Kiana's name, until a number of people had stopped moving, staring at this woman who was so obviously distressed.

The sudden trauma of her situation hit Brenda hard, and she appealed to the growing crowd of onlookers. "Please, has anyone seen my little girl? She's six years old, wearing a red jacket and tan slacks, and Dora sneakers. Anyone?"

They looked at her with sorrowful eyes, wishing they could ease her pain and feeling helpless. Brenda's heart was pounding, and she felt nauseous. She turned her back to them and put both hands on the railing for support. Looking down onto the first-floor concourse at a sea of people, her eyes searched desperately for some sign of Kiana.

A patch of red caught her attention through the crowd, and Brenda struggled to focus on the spot as bodies passed by, intermittently blocking her vision. Then it was there again, a flickering red that could be the fabric of Kiana's coat. She worked her way along the railing to improve her line of sight, and eventually a gap in the foot traffic allowed her a clear look. Her heart leapt to her throat as she saw her little girl, seated alone on a marble bench, calmly watching the passing crowd.

"Kiana!" she shrieked, waving her arms over her head. The huge empty space between them swallowed most of the sound, and Kiana didn't react to her mother's cry. Brenda ran to the nearest stairway, and flew down the spiraling steps two at a time. Reaching the bottom, she made a beeline for the bench where she had seen Kiana.

She was still there, and as Brenda came closer she felt complete relief, as if her world had returned to normal after a brief nightmare. She also felt a touch of anger at the way her little girl had wandered off, after being instructed otherwise so many times in her short life.

When she reached her daughter, Brenda had no immediate thought of scolding her. She was sobbing, and emotionally exhausted, able to do nothing more than put her arms around her beautiful baby and hold her tightly. After a few moments she leaned back to look at Kiana, to determine the depth of her trauma at having been lost, but the child's face was remarkably unperturbed. If anything, Kiana appeared puzzled at her mother's disheveled state.

"Kiana! Why did you leave me? You know Mommy always tells you not to wander off, to stay at my side! Why did you do that?"

"The man said he was taking me to Daddy, to play a video game."

Brenda was becoming upset all over again. She put her hands on Kiana's shoulders, commanding her total focus and attention.

"What man? Where?"

"At the store with the nail polish. He was by the door, waving to me.

Like this." She put a hand out and drew it back towards her, mimicking the motion that meant "come here," or "come closer."

"And you just went right over to him, without telling me what you saw?"

"You were busy."

Brenda's guilt came flooding back. It was, after all, her fault. She was the responsible adult, who had been too distracted with nail polish to protect her daughter.

"Kiana, what did the man say?"

"He said he was Daddy's friend, and Daddy wanted me to come to the arcade and play a game. He was taking me there, but then he told me to wait here for you instead. Can I get some popcorn, Mommy?"

Brenda was still wiping tears from her face, trying to collect herself and regain control of her thoughts. Her child had been abducted, and then left behind for some reason. Had someone become suspicious, and scared him off? She wanted to ask Kiana a few more questions, and then notify the police.

With trembling hands, she reached into her purse for her cell phone without taking her eyes off of Kiana, and at that moment the phone's ringtone sounded. Holding her child's hand to keep her near, she raised it to her ear.

"Hello?"

A male voice, one that Brenda didn't recognize, answered her.

"You had quite a scare, didn't you?"

"Who is this?" she replied, her tone sounding shaken rather than demanding.

"Next time it could be worse. Support the Cedar Ridge proposal, and you won't have to worry." The line went silent.

"Who is it Mommy? Is it Daddy? Is he still at the arcade?"

Brenda felt dazed, still attempting to process the horrific events of the previous fifteen minutes. One thing was very clear to her, however. Her opposition of the development proposal had angered someone, and she now had a very evil enemy.

Looking around as if she expected her tormentor to be watching from a safe distance, Brenda gripped her daughter's hand tightly and quickly led her out of the mall.

CHAPTER 30

THE WORKDAY BEHIND him, Pete Webster climbed into his car for the ride home. It was unlike him to drive so slowly and deliberately, except on those occasions when he had stayed too long at Woody's. On those nights, he navigated the back roads carefully, avoiding traffic and law enforcement, and he had always arrived home without incident. If he was really tanked, one of his mates would arrange for a cab to drive Pete home, or Woody might make a call to the station and ask if a patrol car might be able to swing by and pick him up.

On this day, Pete had a different reason for taking his time, although the root cause was the same. He was delaying that moment when he would have to enter a house that was empty and quiet, offering only the sound of the television to keep him company. It was something he had gradually become accustomed to, but today was different simply because of the date. Today, if given the chance, the memories of Mary would fill every room in the house and every corner of his idle mind.

Valentine's Day had always been more than just a Hallmark holiday to Pete and Mary. She had accepted his proposal of marriage on that day in 2002, and each anniversary of that event had been a celebration of their commitment to each other. Some years it was a romantic overnight stay in a hotel room that overlooked Niagara Falls, other years they stayed at home and Mary cooked a special dinner for them. Usually they both took the day off from work, and exchanged inexpensive, but treasured, gifts. And they always made love passionately, reaffirming the sense of unity that had marked their ten years of marriage.

Pete was determined not to spiral into despair when he finally arrived at home, and immediately threw himself into the task of making his dinner. He broiled a strip steak and baked a huge potato, and added a salad with Italian dressing. This was much more elaborate than his usual evening meal, which was normally obtained from the frozen food aisle at the supermarket or the drive-through window of a fast food chain.

Having satisfied his appetite, Pete cleaned up the kitchen and sat down to watch the local news. He soon found his mind wandering and became restless, deciding that it might be a good time to straighten up the rest of the house. When that was done he considered doing some laundry, but in his heart Pete realized that only one thing would help him get through this night. As much as he cherished his memories of Mary and their time together, at times like this it was really too painful to re-live them. He decided to make an exception to his recent abstinence, and go to Woody's to tie one on.

It was still early evening, so there would be time to stop at the station before heading to the bar. He could spend an hour clearing open items from his desk, and leave a message that he might be coming in late the following day. Fifteen minutes later, Pete was on his way.

Entering the station, Pete headed directly for the office he shared with two other detectives, Hank Rowan and Manny Furillo. Manny had been on disability leave for two months due to a back injury suffered on the job, and wasn't expected back anytime soon. Rowan was at his desk, tapping his computer keyboard with one finger of each hand as he entered some type of report. He seemed glad to see Pete, as if he needed a break from the drudgery.

"Petey, what brings you back here? Something going on?"

"Naw, just catching up on some things. I thought you'd be gone home by now, didn't you say it was Gracie's birthday?"

Hank was in his early fifties, a crusty veteran who seemed to enjoy the "bad cop" reputation he had built. He was known for being tough on anyone who broke the law, disregarding circumstances of age or social status. Hank was gruff, but Pete knew that when it came to family he was a softie. His granddaughter had been born the year before, and Hank was a different man when her name was mentioned.

"Yeah, I'm headed there now, I just had to finish this thing up. We caught that purse snatcher today."

"The one who's been working the mall?" Pete was familiar with the case, having interviewed one of several victimized women.

"Yep. Daryl Swanson, 22. Friggin' heroin addict, big surprise. These kids will do anything for cash, and we're gonna see a lot more of 'em out here in paradise."

"I guess so. People feel safe around here, they're not as careful as they should be. That'll change." They were returning to a theme that had recently become common in their conversations, and Pete warmed to it.

"Crime doesn't stop at the city limits. People somehow assume that criminal activity is confined to the metro area, north of us, as if there's some invisible barrier keeping it from reaching Grove Park. They've got their heads in the sand. "

Hank chuckled at Pete's phrasing, even though he agreed with the premise. "You mean you don't think we're enough of a barrier?"

Webster smiled, shaking his head wistfully, and ignored the question as Rowan rose from his chair for his final comment.

"Actually, this kid is from a good home, his daddy's a doctor. He must have gotten tired of giving the kid money, knowing where it was going. Damned shame, what drugs can do to these families." He raked a hand through his curly grey hair. "Well, I gotta run. Take care, Petey. Don't do anything I wouldn't do."

Pete was becoming increasingly anxious for that first beer, but he wanted to at least look at his messages before leaving. When Hank had gone, he pulled three adhesive notes from the edges of his computer monitor, where the civilian office assistant had left them. Two were from the same person, the victim of a recent burglary who wanted to know the status of the investigation. Pete had spoken to him the day before, and nothing had changed since then. He knew the guy would call again, since it was now a daily occurrence.

The other note was from someone named Sally Raines, who wanted Pete to call her back. The name was unfamiliar and the message didn't indicate any urgency, making it an easy call to put that one off for a day.

"Hell, for all I know it could be one of those unsolicited 'customer service'

calls for a credit card company", he thought, but he knew that was the voice of his building desire for alcohol. His sense of duty won out, and he reached for the phone.

Pete dialed the number and got an answer on the first ring, a female voice. "Hello?"

"This is Detective Webster of the Grove Park P.D. Am I speaking to Ms. Raines?"

"Yes, you are. Pete, it's Sally Hartman."

"Sally?" Pete realized why the voice sounded so familiar, and was momentarily taken back by it. Sally was the wife — now ex-wife, he deduced — of Steve Hartman, an old friend from Pete's days on the Buffalo police force. It seemed a century ago that he and Steve had gone through the police academy together, and had been partnered in a patrol car. At one time the two cops and their wives had been very close, eventually losing touch after Pete joined the GPPD. Steve had quit the Buffalo force long ago to become a private investigator, and Pete seldom heard from him. All Pete knew about Steve's current situation was that he had an office in Buffalo, and a drinking problem that had hurt his business and, most likely, his marriage.

Pete couldn't recall his last conversation with Steve, but he knew that he had last seen Sally at Mary's funeral.

"Steve and I divorced a few years ago, and I went back to my family name. Sorry, I should have known you wouldn't recognize the name Raines. Thanks for returning my call, Pete."

"Sally, of course! I thought the voice was familiar. How are you?" He felt odd speaking formally to a woman he had once known so well. As much as it now pained Pete to admit it, there had been a time when he and Sally had been strongly attracted to each other. They had never acted on those emotions, and Mary never gave him any indication that she noticed, but Pete was sure that his wife must have known. The Websters' move to Grove Park shouldn't have meant the end of such a close friendship, but both couples seemed satisfied to slowly drift apart. Eventually, their communication had been reduced to nothing more than the cards they sent each other at Christmas.

"I'm doing fine, Pete, thank you, but there's something that's got me worried. It's about Steve."

An ingrained reaction prompted Pete to grab a pen and prepare to take notes as they spoke.

"What is it, Sally?"

"Well, as I said, Steve and I are divorced. I don't see him very much anymore, except when he comes to pick up Jonathan for the weekend, which isn't very often."

"So, Jonathan lives with you." Pete thought their son must be about ten years old now.

"Yes. The first year or so after we split Steve used to visit him all the time, and then things changed. He started showing up drunk and begging to be a family again, it was very sad. And sometimes, very ugly. For a while I had a restraining order placed against him, and his visits were limited. I hated to do that to him, but I had to protect Jonathan. Unfortunately, Steve became more and more bitter, and for the past year we've hardly seen him."

"I guess that's understandable, to a degree."

"To some degree, yes, but Jonathan can't understand why his dad gets so mad sometimes, and why he doesn't come to see him anymore. I can't explain that to him, and Steve and I argue about it all the time. About that, and the support payments that he stopped sending."

"I'm sorry to hear that, Sally. It's tough for a kid to be caught in the middle that way." He wondered where this story was going, since it was certain that Sally hadn't called him for his expertise in family counseling.

"Exactly! Jonathan shouldn't have to suffer for our mistakes. I don't really care about the money, we're fine without it, but Steve should pay more attention to his son. In a way, that's why I called you."

Pete was growing impatient. "Sally, are you saying you want me to have a talk with Steve? That would be pretty weird, we really aren't close anymore."

"Oh no, Pete, that's not it. I'm sorry, I'll get to the point.

Steve called me last month late at night, he said he was out of town on a case. He was feeling bad about the way he's been acting towards Jonathan lately, and we had this long conversation about putting our own feelings aside and doing what's best for our son. He may have had a few drinks, Pete, but he knew what he was saying, it was sincere. Sometimes it takes a little alcohol to break down his tough-guy act, so he can express his true feelings. Jonathan was asleep, but Steve insisted that I wake him so they could talk. He promised him that he'd be at his birthday party, and that they'd go camping together real soon." Sally paused, to maintain her composure.

"He never showed up, Pete. No phone call, nothing. I was so mad, I couldn't wait for him to show his face here just so I could slap him. Jonathan was devastated, it broke my heart to see him that way."

"Did Steve have an explanation?"

"That's just it, I still haven't heard from him. That phone call from Iowa was the last time we spoke. I thought it was strange that he would make a phone call like that and then not call again at all before Jon's birthday. Then, when he didn't show for the party, I was so furious I couldn't even call him because I knew I'd end up screaming at him over the phone. But now it's two weeks later, and I can't find anyone else who has seen him, either. Something's wrong, Pete, I should have realized it sooner. Steve has disappeared for a few days at a time before, you know that, losing himself in a bottle, but this is different."

"That night when he said he was out of town, do you know the exact date?"

"It was early January, the fourth, I think."

"So, over a month ago. You said Iowa, did you get the name of the town?"

"Yes, I think he said Carthage. I remembered it because it made me think of Hannibal."

Pete was confused. "Hannibal Lechter?" It was the only "Hannibal" he could come up with on short notice.

Sally laughed out loud, in spite of the serious tone of the preceding conversation. "No, Hannibal! The one who used elephants to get his army over the mountains, remember? The Alps, I think. Anyway, he was from Carthage."

"Oh, that Hannibal" Pete replied, trying to act as if he was familiar with the story. "Carthage, Iowa, huh? I'll make a call to the local P.D.

there, see if Steve contacted them at all. We can also check the phone records to find out exactly where he called you from. There are some other things we can do to track him down, but that's for me to worry about. You just keep trying family, friends, anyone you can think of, and let me know if anyone has seen Steve since January seventh."

"Alright Pete, I'll call you if I have anything new. If not, I'll wait to hear from you."

"Sounds good. Sally, one more thing. Think about that phone call from Iowa. Did Steve mention anything about what he was working on, or who he was working for?"

"Oh, Pete, I've wracked my brain trying to remember everything Steve said. But I'm sure he didn't mention anything like that."

Pete wasn't surprised at her answer, it wasn't something he would expect Steve to share with her, but he would need that information. He'd have to visit Steve's office and see what could be uncovered.

"Okay Sally, give me a little time and I'll see what I can find out."

"Thank you so much, Pete. I knew I could count on you, even after all this time. Goodbye now."

As Pete said goodbye he was already at his keyboard, searching a database that would yield the phone number of the police headquarters in Carthage, Iowa. He dialed the number and was connected with a dispatcher, who told Pete that both of the on-duty officers were out on calls. The chief of the five-man force was literally "gone fishin'", and she was hesitant to give out his cell number. Pete requested that the dispatcher give his number to the first available officer, or to the chief if he happened to call in. As the call ended, Pete abruptly rose from his chair, surveyed his desktop, and decided to call it a night. He was rather proud of himself for holding out as long as he had, and the Steve Hartman story had given him something to think about over those first few beers. There were only a few hours of Valentine's Day left to kill.

CHAPTER 31

I T WAS AFTER ten when Pete Webster looked away from the big screen above the bar and saw Jack Ferris heading towards him.

"Jackie, where the hell have you been?"

Jack smiled and hung his jacket over the bar stool next to Pete.

"I was going to ask you the same thing. I've been here at least three times without seeing you, that's a record."

"I haven't been here, except for bowling night. Been taking better care of this fine body of mine. So, what have you been doing lately? Gettin' any?"

Ordinarily that would have been a throwaway remark between them, just something guys say to each other, but it made Jack a bit uncomfortable. He knew Pete suspected that he and Nicki had become further involved, but Pete had never come right out and asked, and Jack hadn't volunteered the information.

"Nope. Why, did you have someone in mind for me?"

"I have enough trouble taking care of myself" Pete laughed, then stopped as he remembered something. He poked his finger at Jack's shoulder and added, "Hey, maybe I do! Marti asked about you again. I really think you'd get along with each other, Jackie."

Jack didn't want to dismiss the remark and leave the impression that he was seeing anyone else. "Did she ask you to fix us up, or what? I mean, what the hell does she ask about?"

Pete was distracted by the big screen again, checking the score of the hockey game that was in progress. "Oh, I don't know. Just how are you doing, general small talk. Always asks if you're seeing anyone. Stuff like that."

"Well, don't talk me up too much, Pete. I like Marti, but I'm not into her that way, you know?"

"No problem there, dude. I didn't recommend you that highly anyway."

They laughed, clicked their brown bottles in recognition of a good shot, and drained them. Pete had the look of a very thirsty man.

"Woodmeister, two more, boss!" he shouted, and as Woody opened the bottles he made a mental note to ask Pete for his car keys before serving him another round.

Before he could pick up the bottle that Woody slid in front of him, Pete's cell phone summoned him. He left the bar area as he pulled it out of his pocket, and walked to a relatively quiet corner near the seldom-used pay phone.

"Pete Webster."

"Detective Webster? This is Officer Pearson, Carthage P.D. Our dispatcher said you had an urgent matter to discuss."

Pete explained the situation, and asked if Pearson could recall Steve Hartman coming in to the station.

"Well sir, I didn't recognize that name, but I do remember an ex-cop from New York stopping in to see the chief about a month back. In fact, I think he spent a couple days here in town. I don't really know what he was after, but Chief Jennings would be able to tell you more."

"Right," Pete sighed, knowing what was coming next. "But the Chief went fishing and doesn't want to be bothered unless the town is burning down."

An embarrassed Officer Pearson chuckled at the thought of how Mayberry that must sound to the New Yorker. "Yes sir, he's been working long hours, and he's been looking forward to this trip for quite some time. But I assure you, he will get your message and phone number."

"All right Officer, I appreciate your help. And believe me, I totally understand the need for some down time once in a while. I'll wait for a call from your boss."

Pete shoved his phone into a pocket and headed back to the bar, wondering if Officer Pearson had detected any trace of inebriation in his speech. In any case, it was fortunate the call hadn't come a couple of hours later, because Pete was eager to finish what he'd started.

CHAPTER 32

I T WAS TOO early for lunch, but Jim Wainwright was famished. That wasn't unusual for him, but in recent weeks he had lapsed into old habits. Instead of resolving to fight his prodigious appetite by eating a healthy snack of raw veggies, he looked for the nearest fast food sign and pulled in. As he was about to swing the Hummer into the drive-thru lane of Burger Barn his cell phone vibrated, and he rerouted to an empty parking space. No need to share his combo-meal preference with whoever might be calling, especially if it was his wife.

"Yeah." Wainwright often used such a no-nonsense opener to give his caller the impression that he was very busy at that moment, although it was seldom the case.

"Mr. Wainwright, I hope I'm not calling at a bad time. Do you have a minute to talk?"

The gravelly voice, combined with a distinctive Bronx accent, unmistakably identified the caller as Paulie Gotts. Wainwright scowled at his mental image of the man, cursing himself for not letting the call go to voicemail. There was something about being in Gotts' presence that made his skin crawl, and even a telephone conversation with him was strangely uncomfortable.

Wainwright couldn't recall anyone having had this effect on him since he was a teenager. His father was the Gotts of his youth, constantly prodding, badgering, and intimidating his only son. Living with him was pure hell until the day young Jimmy stood up for himself and put an end to it. That was the day he became a free man, although the manner in which he gained liberation was a secret that couldn't be shared with anyone. If he could handle that situation so well, this one should be no different. Steeling his nerves, he was able to respond in a casual voice.

"Sure, I've got a few minutes, what's on your mind?" For some reason Wainwright stopped short of speaking Gotts' name over the telephone. It just didn't seem like a good idea.

"Well, I been thinking about our last meeting. I relayed some of your concerns to certain others, and they suggested that I provide assistance wherever I can. After all, we don't want you distracted from the task at hand with the vote only a few days away. The meeting is Friday, am I right?"

"Yeah, the seventeenth, that's right. In fact, I'm working on that situation full-time, right up until the meeting. But I'm a bit confused now, what is it that you're offering to do?"

Gotts chuckled, as if he found it humorous that Wainwright expected him to provide details over the phone.

"I have a few ideas, but don't worry about me. The point is, we realize that you need to concentrate on getting the result we all need. Clear your mind of all other concerns, let me worry about those for now. As a wise man once said, 'Reap the rewards of your actions, not the consequences of your inaction', *kapish?*"

Wainwright doubted that a wise man, or any other, had ever used that phrase. He was now visualizing Gotts as a reptilian figure, reclined in a leather chair as he sucked on a huge cigar and croaked into the phone.

"Consequences?" was Wainwright's weak reply. He wouldn't be talked down to, and Gotts' implication that there would be a price to pay for failure was exactly the type of heavy-handed threat that infuriated him.

"Listen, just relax," Gotts attempted a soothing tone. "All I'm saying is that we're gonna make your life a little easier, so that you can do the same for us. This call is just a reminder, to make sure that you're giving this matter the attention it deserves. I'll let you get back to it, Mr. Wainwright. Have a good day."

The call was disconnected, leaving Wainwright staring at the display for a few seconds. Gotts had never called him before, and he wondered what had compelled him to do so today. Normally, all communication would be through Victor Harmon. Gotts must be under pressure from his employer, or perhaps from someone higher in the chain of command, and he was responding by turning the screws on Wainwright.

What had he meant by "providing assistance"? The last thing Wainwright wanted was further involvement with these people, and now it seemed there was no getting away from them. He had meant to fend them off by explaining some of the other problems he had been dealing with, and they had interpreted his explanation as a cry for help. In retrospect, maybe his meeting with Gotts and Harmon had been exactly that.

He backed the Hummer out and then guided its width carefully into the ordering lane, having decided to take Gotts' advice. His immediate course of action would be to drive around aimlessly while he downed a double burger, and give the situation some serious thought.

CHAPTER 33

PETE WEBSTER LAY motionless, gathering the strength to roll out of bed and deal with the throbbing headache that would surely increase in intensity when he stood up. He had gotten thoroughly wasted the night before and was tempted to call in for a sick day, but thoughts of the Steve Hartman case wouldn't allow him to rest. Eventually he threw the sheet aside and slowly rose to his feet, taking a few moments to allow the dancing white spots to clear from his vision before shuffling into the kitchen. Once the coffee maker was brewing and he had downed three aspirin, Pete began to feel functional. It was almost nine, and he figured he could be at the station by ten, no questions asked.

He was trying to recall where he had left his cell phone when it came to life, revealing its' location in a pocket of the jacket he had worn the night before.

Pete was sure it would be somebody from the department wondering when, or if, he might be inclined to get his ass in there. In the months following Mary's death he had often been too hung over to go to work, and the call had always come. It became embarrassingly obvious that the chief had given orders to place a call to Pete whenever he was late, for fear he might harm himself while in the throes of depression. Pete appreciated the concern, but the routine had long ago gotten old.

"Yeah, Webster here."

"Detective Webster? This is Chief Jennings in Carthage."

The call was not at all what Pete had expected, but he had the presence of mind to grab a pen and note pad as he replied.

"Chief, thanks for calling back. I take it Officer Pearson relayed my message?"

"Call me Harlon, and yes, he did. You wanted to know about the P.I. who was in here about a month ago, the guy from New York. Hartman, right?"

"That's right, Steve Hartman. He called his ex-wife from your town in early January, and as far as she knows he hasn't been seen since. I plan to run that down today, but I wanted to talk to you first. Can you tell me what Steve was asking about?"

"Well, I don't remember the details, but he was asking about a former resident, a guy who left here about twenty, mebbe twenty-five years ago. Jim Wright's his name, they used to call him Jimbo."

"You knew this man?"

"Oh yeah, I remember him, alright. We used to frequent the same bars and poker games about a hundred years ago, when we were young. He disappeared from here in the early nineties, I'd say, after his wife died. Hadn't heard another thing about him until this Hartman showed up."

"And did Steve say why he was looking for this man?"

"Well, I didn't get the feeling he was looking for him, really. More like he was doing a background check. 'least that's how I took it."

"So, he didn't give any indication of who had hired him, or why?"

"No, not really. Truth be told, I was in the middle of a few things, and I didn't give him a lot of time. Just rattled off the names of a few of his old boys who still live around town, and he went on his way. Never gave it another thought until yesterday. So, he's gone missing, has he?"

"Well, his ex thinks so. He's a former partner of mine, so like I said I'm going to see what I can find out."

There was a pause, and Pete could hear someone speaking to the chief about a car wreck on Route something or other.

"Detective, I'll have to get back to you. Duty calls, you know?"

"Sure Harlon, I understand, maybe we can continue this later."

"Tell you what, Pete. I'll have Marilyn fax a copy of the information the P.I. left here, I think I still have it somewhere." Pete could hear papers shuffling and pictured Harlon Jennings behind a desk piled high with old paperwork, much like his own.

"I'd appreciate that, and I'll talk to you later."

"Hold for Marilyn."

After a short pause during which Pete feared they had been disconnected, she was back. "Okay sir, can I have that fax number?"

"Marilyn, do you have a scanner there? You could scan the information and e-mail it to me."

"Well sir, I'm not really up on how to use the scanner thing and Officer Pearson is out right now. I don't think the scanner works anyway, just the printer. Don't fret over it, I'll be sure to fax it for you as soon as the Chief finds whatever it is you're looking for."

After making sure the dispatcher had the right fax number for the Grove Park station, Pete drank his coffee and gave the situation some thought. Calls to Steve's office had brought no reply, so he must not have employed even a part-time office assistant. After checking in at the station, the next logical move would be to go there and see what he could find out.

Pete recognized the possibility that the whole thing could be a misunderstanding and that Steve could be on a vacation somewhere with a woman his ex had never met, but somehow it didn't feel that way. He decided to keep things to himself for now while carrying out his unofficial investigation, and see where it took him.

CHAPTER 34

THE ONE THING about painting that had always appealed to Jack was that it was so easy for him, so effortless, and yet somehow satisfying. He found the task to be completely enjoyable, even when it lacked any truly creative element.

If someone were to describe his vocation as mindless, Jack would have been deeply insulted, but in fact he thought of it just that way. The process of taping, edging, cutting in and rolling demanded precision and care, but they now came to him so naturally that he seemed to accomplish them as if on autopilot. As he worked, his mind typically wandered to any number of subjects, ranging from the dangers of ozone layer depletion to the unfinished hardwood floor in his kitchen.

In recent days, however, his thoughts consistently centered on his relationship with Nicki Wainwright. Jack was falling in love with her, and she with him. It was not a situation he was completely comfortable with, in light of Nicki's marital status, but it wasn't one that he was about to run from. He wanted to spend more time with her, to explore the depth of their feelings for each other, and let events play out in spite of the consequences. His initial reaction to the increasing signs of her affection was apprehension, the fear that he would have to slow things down before they spun out of control. Eventually that trepidation had passed, and Jack decided to make an unspoken commitment to overcome the obstacles that faced them, so they could build a life together.

The owner of this home was a prominent local doctor whose wife had greeted Jack warmly, started a pot of coffee for him, and dashed off to begin a day of antiquing with friends. She left Jack alone with his tools and his thoughts and asked only that he lock up before leaving.

All of the prep work had been accomplished the previous day, and Jack looked forward to the easy part of the job. As he applied a soothing sage green to the largest wall, he was calculating the number of days since he had last spoken to Nicki. He had expected to hear from her before Valentine's Day, and when he didn't he thought it best not to call lest he appear too clinging. He wondered if they were in some sort of silly unintentional stalemate, with neither party willing to be the first to reach out. After all, it was entirely possible that Nicki shared his distaste for the appearance of being needy.

Eventually Jack's inner self produced a clear thought, which he whispered aloud to himself. *"Jesus, just call the woman. She's probably wondering why you haven't, so be the man in the relationship and take charge!"*

It was early in the workday, but Jack had reached a good temporary stopping point. The first coat had been applied, and he could wait for it to dry completely before beginning the second. He was pleased with the color, and with the way this brand of paint covered the white primer coat. Jack wasn't sure that a second coat was even necessary, but the client had already paid for it and the custom-blended color was not returnable for a refund.

He wiped his hands and picked up his phone, which was already unintentionally decorated with traces of color from his previous fifty or so jobs. Nicki had once commented on the unique design of Jack's cell phone, thinking that the colors were a cool skin offered by the manufacturer.

Jack had expected Nicki to answer, and felt unprepared when the call went to voicemail. Where was that damned inner voice when he needed it?

"Nicki, it's me. I, uh, I haven't heard from you, and then I thought maybe you were waiting for me to call, I mean I hope you were, and so — well it's early and I just realized that you might be out running. I'll give you a call later, I really want to talk to you about some things, in person. Or maybe I'll just show up and surprise you. See you later, I hope. Bye."

Maybe I'll just show up and surprise you? Jack was already kicking himself for that one. What if Nicki wasn't really into being 'surprised' in public by her secret lover? On second thought, wasn't she the one who had made a big show of being unafraid, when she whisked him off in the Hummer? He had to stop walking on eggs and second-guessing her, before he was drove himself crazy.

CHAPTER 35

B Y NOON PETE Webster had made his appearance at the station, staying just long enough to make his presence known and to make a phone call to Sally Hartman. In Pete's mind her last name would always be Hartman, as much as he tried he just couldn't get used to her maiden name.

Sally seemed grateful that Pete was fulfilling his promise to look into Steve's possible disappearance, but also was frustrated at the lack of useful information.

"Pete, I collected every old key I could find in my house, and one of them might be the key to Steve's office. He gave me one a long time ago, and I never thought to return it. Even if I have the right key, he may have changed the locks since then, but I think we should go over there and try it."

Pete preferred working alone, especially without help from a civilian, but the offer of a key, and the opportunity to see Sally in person, was too much to pass up. He agreed to meet her at 1900 Genesee Street in Buffalo, the office of Steve Hartman Enterprises.

Arriving there an hour later, Pete spotted a tall slim female standing in front of the ancient brick two-story, staring up at the second-floor window of Steve's office. She was wearing a dark calf-length raincoat as protection against the chilling drizzle that was falling. Despite the collar that was raised around her face, Pete recognized Sally immediately, and his heart seemed to skip a beat with an old, familiar excitement. He wondered what Sally was feeling, and was amazed at how guilty the thought made him feel in spite of his widower status. He pulled to the curb and parked behind a silver Ford Focus that he assumed to be hers. Sally walked up to meet him, managing to smile through her worry, and they hugged briefly.

"Hi Petey. Thanks for coming, I knew I could count on you."

"No problem, hon. You look wonderful."

Sally was as beautiful as ever, still wearing her hair straight and long. She was very tan, the result of either a recent vacation trip or a series of visits to a tanning salon. Whatever the source, it had brought out the freckles that Pete had always found attractive. She wore very little makeup, only enough to accent her almond eyes.

"Aw, thanks. You too, Pete. It's been a long time, huh?"

Pete wondered what Sally was really thinking, and supposed that she had noticed lines and wrinkles that confirmed how rough his last few years had been.

Resisting the urge to gush, he simply offered, "Yes, it has. Too long."

They were no longer smiling, just staring into each other's eyes, letting their thoughts wander to another time, and then Sally made a move to snap them into the present.

"So, I have two keys that might fit, let's try them."

The lower floor of the building was vacant, its windows covered with plywood. This formerly pleasant neighborhood was now rather seedy, featuring mostly empty storefronts with a few taverns and pizzerias sprinkled among them. The surrounding side streets featured long rows of old wood frame houses that had been built in the thirties and forties, mostly owned by absentee landlords who rented to low income families. Pete didn't remember it as a high crime area, but he hadn't worked the city for decades and knew that his opinion was outdated. This building couldn't have been what Steve had in mind when he struck out on his own, it simply reflected what he could afford.

He took Sally's arm and they walked to the rear entrance. Surprisingly that door was unlocked, and they started up the dark, narrow staircase that led to a landing and the office door. Before Sally could hand Pete the keys she had brought, he caught her attention and put a finger to his lips, signaling her to be silent. She instinctively backed against the far wall, wondering what danger Pete had sensed, and then spotted the cause of his concern. This door was not only unlocked, it was slightly open. The wood frame was shattered where someone had forced it open with a crowbar or a well-placed shoulder, and Pete was gently pushing the door open to get a better look before entering.

Satisfied that the intruders were no longer present, Pete stepped in and flipped a light switch, revealing exactly what he had expected.

"Oh my god!" Sally whispered, before covering her mouth as if she were suppressing a shriek, or a sob.

The office had been crudely tossed, the floor littered with papers and empty drawers. File cabinets and two desks had been emptied and turned on their side, and one wall was scorched from a fire that had been intentionally started but hadn't caught on as planned. The place reeked of kerosene, and Pete wondered if turning on the lights had been a good idea, considering the fumes.

"Sally, why don't you wait out there while I take a look around?" She didn't need to be asked twice to leave such an upsetting scene, and stepped back without a word.

Pete took a pair of latex gloves from his pocket and pulled them on as he surveyed the room. He ticked through the usual motives for an act of this type, and came up with three. The first was random vandalism, the act of some bored neighborhood kids or, more likely, junkies who knew the place could be accessed with minimal risk. They would know that Steve hadn't been around, and probably would hope to find items that could be easily turned into cash on the street; maybe a computer, or a camera. If they were lucky, there could be a gun or a small safe. For all Pete knew, maybe there had been.

The other two possibilities were more disturbing, and Steve's line of work made them just as likely as the first. The ransacking could have been a search for information that Steve was collecting, and the subject had sent someone to retrieve it.

Number three, Steve could have made an enemy of the wrong person, and this was an attempt to gain a clue to his location so they could track him down.

As he walked through the small office space, Pete began to dismiss the idea that this had been the work of treasure-hunting teens. There were no piles of paperwork tossed onto the floor by the handful. It seemed that each one had been dropped there individually, after a quick viewing to discern the subject matter. The walls were bare, stripped of any framed pictures or licenses that had been hung there.

Pete sifted through the remaining papers, which were old case files and copies of invoices, a few cancelled checks and other uninteresting items. He found nothing that had a date more recent than 2015, although one of the file drawers was labeled "2016".

There was a desktop printer lying broken in one corner of the room, and cables strewn around the desks, but no computer or disks. The only thing to be gained here was a confirmation that Steve Hartman was very likely in some sort of trouble, something Sally had realized at first glance. He wouldn't mention it to Sally, but Pete was relieved that he hadn't found any blood. He walked out to the hall, where she stood waiting, ashen faced and trembling.

"What does this mean, Pete?"

"I don't know yet, but it's time to make this official. I'll contact the Buffalo PD about the break-in, and I'd like you to come in and file a missing person report. After that's done, I'll talk to the chief and see if I can get myself assigned to it. Now, you try to stay calm and drive home carefully. Got that? We'll meet at the station later. Let's go, hon."

Pete guided her down the stairs and outside, aware that Sally was eager to head south, away from the mean streets. She wanted to be back home with Jonathan in the relative safety of Grove Park.

CHAPTER 36

JIM WAINWRIGHT STOOD outside the door of George McClure's office, just down the hall from his own, gathering the courage to walk in and tell his story. Wainwright knew that he was about to bring unwanted scrutiny to his closely guarded personal life, but he could think of no other course of action.

The Supervisor walked in to find McClure at his desk, leafing through computer printouts. As Chief of the Grove Park Police Department, he was responsible for compiling data that would justify his recent request for an increase in manpower. McClure was an institution in the GPPD, having worked his way up through the ranks over a span of thirty years. He was now six months from retirement, and looked forward to putting as much distance as possible between himself and the collection of egos that currently headed the town's government. To him, today's administrators were all about dollars and cents, making decisions from the business point of view rather than considering the public welfare. McClure preferred more of a common-sense approach, and he thought it should be obvious to those in power that the police department was badly understaffed. The force had not been sufficiently expanded to keep pace with the increase in population Grove Park had experienced over the last ten years, leading to an increase in crime and slower response times when answering calls and complaints. The man standing before him, Town Supervisor James Wainwright, had thus far refused to take part in any discussion that involved an increase in the town's payroll, to the frustration of Chief McClure.

"George, can I interrupt you?"

McClure's face showed surprise at the presence of the Supervisor in his office, since the two had not yet been able to form a relationship as friends or teammates, but he recovered quickly.

"Jim, good morning! Of course, come on in. Rescue me from this pile of paperwork." He motioned to the visitor's chair that was positioned next to his desk. "Have a seat. I just made some hazelnut coffee, want a cup?"

Wainwright declined, and waited for McClure to be reseated before continuing.

"George, I have a problem, and I need your advice."

McClure leaned his elbows on the desk, hands folded, giving Wainwright his complete attention. He sported a grey handlebar moustache that he had originally grown for his role in a community theater production, and Wainwright knew that the Chief would soon be twirling the ends as was his habit. "All right, I'll do what I can. Tell me what's on your mind, Jim."

"It's about my wife, Nicki. She's —" he stopped, unwilling or unable to say the word that came to mind, and groped for a more acceptable phrasing. "I haven't seen or heard from her in over twenty-four hours, and I'm worried. I just don't know where she could be George, and I need your help to find out."

Having expected the subject to be related to town business, McClure was caught totally off guard. There was an awkward silence as Wainwright tried to maintain his composure, his lip quivering.

"My god! Of course I'll help, Jim, that's what we're here for. Let's not overreact, though. Usually these things are easily solved, some sort of misunderstanding, crossed signals, that type of thing. Mrs. Wainwright is probably fine. Until we know that for sure, this department will do all we can to find the answer."

"All right, so where do we start? Is there a form to fill out, a missing person report that has to be filed?"

"Give me one minute, I'm going to have Detective Hank Rowan join us. He's an experienced investigator, and he'll take your statement and get the wheels into motion. I'm going to listen in, and decide what resources we'll need."

Wainwright appreciated McClure's words, but had the distinct impression that if he were not the Town Supervisor it might have been at least another twenty-four hours before any action would be taken.

Within a few minutes, Wainwright had been introduced to Hank Rowan, who explained that their conversation would be recorded, since his handwritten notes often turned out to be difficult for even Rowan to decipher. Wainwright did not protest, and the detective started a small digital recorder.

"Interview with James Wainwright regarding missing person Nicole Wainwright, Wednesday, February 15th, 2016, 9:36 AM."

Mr. Wainwright, when did you last see your wife?"

"I last saw her yesterday, early in the morning, about 7:30 or 8. Nicki's an early riser, something we don't have in common. I had just gotten out of bed and was heading downstairs for coffee when I heard the door close. I went to the window, the bay window in our parlor, and looked out. She was heading out on her morning run, which she does three or four times a week."

"Does she always follow the same route when she runs?"

"Yes, as far as I know. She runs up our street, Amelia, to Robinson Road and goes north. Then she takes a left on Kingston, that would be west, until she reaches Route 19. She comes back to Amelia, turns left again, and she's home. It's about five miles, and it normally takes her close to an hour."

Rowan was silent as he finished his crude diagram of the route Wainwright had described. His first act following the statement would be to check for recent accident reports involving pedestrians, and a team would be sent to drive the route and inspect the roadside areas.

"And you didn't see or hear from your wife after that?"

"No, we both have full schedules and I had meetings all day. I didn't have a chance to call her, and she didn't call me."

"What about after your workday, when you arrived home?"

Wainwright squirmed a bit, as if the answer was somehow embarrassing. "Well, as I said, I had meetings the entire day, into the evening. I arrived home about 8, exhausted. Nicki wasn't there, which wasn't unusual, she often has a late appointment. I assumed it was either that, or she had gone out with friends. She doesn't usually answer her phone, so I texted her a couple times, didn't get a reply. I had a drink, laid down on the couch to watch television while I waited, and fell asleep. I slept there all night, and when I woke up this morning she still wasn't around."

"Could she have been out running again? You said she did that three or four times a week."

"She almost never runs on consecutive days anymore, but I thought that might be it. Then I looked around the house, everything still looked undisturbed. I went into the kitchen to make some coffee, and that's when I noticed her purse and cell phone on a chair. Must have been there the night before, but I didn't see it. Everything in the house looked undisturbed since I had left yesterday. Dishes, newspaper, everything was the same. Nicki would have straightened up the house if she had been home since then. Her running shoes and the wind suit she was wearing are not in the house, either, I looked everywhere."

Rowan sat back and stared at his notes, formulating his next few questions.

"You didn't notice that last night?"

"No, as I said, I didn't do much except have a drink and lay on the couch, and then I went out like a light."

"Was her car at home?"

"I didn't think so at the time, but it must have been. I found it parked in the garage this morning."

Rowan raised his eyebrows. "You didn't see it there last night?"

"No, because I didn't pull into the garage last night. I parked in the driveway and went in the front door, so I didn't see her car, but it's in the garage now so it must have been there last night. That's another thing that alarmed me."

For the first time since he had begun to tell his story Wainwright felt challenged, as if he had to defend his lack of awareness. It occurred to him that it would be a good idea to have counsel on hand, and he decided to call Al Kaplan at the first opportunity. Rowan seemed concerned and professional, but there was an underlying skepticism that Wainwright found unnerving.

"Mr. Wainwright, is there anything else that was a red flag for you, something that convinced you that your wife might be in jeopardy?"

"Well, I've already told you, Detective. Nicki's gone, but her car, her purse, keys, phone, all her personal items are home, just as she left them yesterday when she went running. I haven't heard from her, and I haven't found anyone else who has."

"So you made some calls this morning, trying to find out if anyone had seen her?" Wainwright nodded emphatically even as Rowan asked the question.

"Yes, I called the office first, our real estate office. No one had seen her today, or yesterday. I called a couple of her friends, no luck there, either."

"All right. I'll need the names of the people you spoke to, and any others you can think of."

"Certainly. To be honest with you, I don't know who Nicki's closest friend would be right now. She's been spending a lot of time with Jill Sherman, but —" his voice trailed off.

"Oh, yeah, that was a terrible thing."

"Nicki took it very hard."

Rowan slid a sheet of paper in front of Wainwright, and stood up. "Okay sir, you get started on that list of friends and family. I'm going to get a couple of our guys out on a preliminary search, then I'll start running down your list to see if anyone has a lead for us."

Wainwright was relieved that some type of plan was taking shape, and that their session was coming to an end.

"Do you mind if I do this in my office? I'd be more comfortable there, and George could have his office back."

McClure had been an interested, albeit silent, listener as Rowan had conducted the interview. "Of course, Jim. Write down anyone you can think of, and include places that your wife visits frequently. Stores, dry cleaners, favorite restaurants, anyplace she might have been recently."

"Right. Thanks again, I'll be right down the hall." Wainwright left the room and headed to the sanctity of his office, noticing that Rowan had stayed behind with McClure. He wondered what the cops would have to say to each other once he was out of earshot.

He fully intended to do his part by compiling a list of people that the police could contact for information, but Wainwright knew that his first priority was to contact Al Kaplan. He hit number six on the speed dial and was connected with Al's office.

"Mr. Kaplan, please. This is Jim Wainwright, tell him it's urgent."

After a minute of classical music, Al came on the line.

"Jim? Kerry said it was urgent, what's going on?"

"Al, I'm at the office and I need you to get here as soon as you can. Can you get away?"

"Sure I can, is it about the council meeting? I thought we were going to meet this afternoon."

"No, it isn't that, I've got something else going on here. Al, I just reported Nicki missing. Get over here, and I'll explain everything. I've already gone through it with the police, and I could use your advice."

Al was stunned by his friend's words, and was about to ask the first of a flood of questions that came to mind, but thought better of it. "I'll be right there, Jim. Sit tight."

They hung up without any further conversation, and Wainwright sat back, breathed a heavy sigh, and buried his face in his hands.

CHAPTER 37

AFTER LISTENING TO the Town Supervisor's unexpected revelation, George McClure took a few minutes to speak with Hank Rowan in private.

"What the hell do you make of this, Hank? Any reason we shouldn't take him seriously?"

Rowan was a born cynic who had taken countless statements in his career, from victims and the accused. He had gotten used to the fabrications and exaggerations that came with that territory, and took great pride in being able to separate fact from fiction. This time, however, he hadn't heard anything that led him to believe that Jim Wainwright was anything but a worried husband.

"I don't see any reason to doubt him. Not yet, anyway. If it were someone else reporting a missing spouse, I'd probably tell him to give it another 24 and get back to me if she still hasn't shown up. But Jesus, George, this is the wife of the Town Supervisor. I think we should get on it, don't you?"

McClure knew that his detective was right.

"Yeah, of course we will. I just wanted your gut feeling, that's all."

"My gut tells me that this guy isn't my favorite person, and I've always considered him kind of a phony prick, but this woman may be in trouble. Let's start looking, and keep talking to him, and see where it leads."

McClure nodded approval. "You start with whatever list of names he comes up with, I'll get Pete to start canvassing their neighborhood. Where is he, anyway?"

"He's in the interview room with an old friend, Mrs. Long Legs. Take a guess what the complaint is."

"Her husband hit her?"

"Nope. It's her *ex*-husband, and he didn't hit her. He's missing."

"Christ, we haven't had one of these in years, and now two in one day! I'll go in and get him, you get started. We'll need some copies of that jogging route."

McClure rapped his knuckles twice on the door of the interview room, and without waiting for a reply let himself in.

He had expected to find Pete Webster taking notes or assisting with the report forms, but it looked like that part of the session had been completed. The detective was seated across from a woman who looked to be on the younger side of forty, holding her hand in his as he offered words of comfort and encouragement.

They both sat up straight in their chairs as the chief burst in, pulling their hands apart like two teens who had been caught groping when they were supposed to be studying. For a moment the embarrassment on Pete's face made McClure regret his abrupt entrance, but he recovered quickly.

"Pete, sorry to interrupt, I need to speak to you."

Pete stood, and gestured towards the woman.

"Chief, Sally Hartman." Catching himself, he added, "Sally Raines, I'm sorry. Sally, this is Police Chief McClure.

There was no reaction from McClure, so Pete continued. "Sally and I go way back. Her husband, Steve, was my first partner in the city."

McClure realized that Rowan was right; this lady was wearing a skirt that made it impossible to miss those long, shapely legs.

"Ma'am" was all he could manage, accompanied by a quick nod in her direction. Before he could go on, Webster took the lead.

"Chief, Sally is here to file a report that concerns Steve Hartman. It seems no one has seen him for weeks, at least no one we know of. The last time he and Sally spoke, Steve was in Iowa on a job. He's a private investigator."

McClure was eager to get to his intended conversation with Pete, and wanted to tactfully put an end to this story.

"I see. And Mr. Hartman is a Grove Park resident?"

"No, he lives over in Glenwood but like I said, he's a friend, so I told Sally to come in and file it here. I know it's out of jurisdiction, so if necessary I thought I'd take a day or two of personal time and see what I can turn up. Maybe go out to that town in Iowa, talk to the locals."

McClure's frown didn't hide his discomfort at Pete's request. "Mrs. Hartman, ordinarily I'd be glad to let Pete go for a couple of days, but this is not an ordinary day. We can get you in touch with the Glenwood P.D. and the county sheriff. I hope any fears you have are unfounded."

Sally felt the urge to repeat her proper surname, but decided to let it go. The chief had made it clear that she was being dismissed, despite his statement of concern.

Webster persisted. "George, you haven't heard everything. I really need to find out what's going on, I owe Steve that much."

McClure glanced at Sally as if he was holding back, not wanting to discuss the matter any further in her presence.

"Ma'am, could you excuse us for a minute? Just have a seat outside, this won't take long."

"Certainly" was all her anger allowed her to say. She rose and left the room, doing her best to put a chill in the air as she huffed past the chief.

"George, why are you so tight? What's going on?"

"Sit down, and I'll explain. I'm sorry Pete, I hate to be rude, but I can't let you go anywhere right now, I need you here. We'll have to let someone else look for your friend, and maybe you can help out next week. Right now we have a similar case, closer to home."

"Similar? Do I have another old friend who disappeared?"

McClure ignored the sarcasm and continued. "About an hour ago, Jim Wainwright walked into my office and reported his wife missing. He said it's been over 24 hours, and he can't find anyone who has seen her since early yesterday, when she set out for her morning run."

"Nicki Wainwright is missing?" Webster's demeanor changed to a level of concern that McClure hadn't expected.

"You know her, Pete?"

"No, not really. I mean, not personally, but I know of her. She's pretty hard to miss in this town — real estate queen, wife of the Town Supervisor, good-looking socialite. That qualifies as high-profile in Grove Park."

"Exactly. I'm hoping that she just got pissed at the old man and took off for a day, letting him worry a little bit to teach him a lesson. So far there's nothing to back that up. We need to do this right, Pete, that's why I need you to get involved."

Pete agreed that this took precedence over his personal interest in the Steve Hartman case, and was already planning how he would explain that to Sally without offering specifics.

"I'll make a call to Glenwood P.D. about Steve, I know a couple guys over there. How do you want me to start on this?"

"Well, Hank is on it already, he's getting a list of contacts from Wainwright. He'll run those down, see if anyone has seen or heard from her.

"I want you to take a couple of uniforms and cover her usual running path, you can get that from Hank. Knock on every door that has a line of sight to the roads she would have been on, try to get a last known location."

"We should get the dogs out there, too."

McClure stood up stiffly and massaged his lower back. The unexpected pressure of the day was making him feel his age.

"I'm waiting for the sheriff to get back to me about providing some county resources, including their dog team. I already told Wainwright that we'll want to take a look around his house. If he agrees, I want a county forensic team in there."

"Good. But it's only been 24 hours. Couldn't we be accused of over reacting?"

McClure shook his head emphatically.

"Not as far as I'm concerned. Remember Jose Ortiz?"

Pete recalled the Ortiz case, and nodded assent. Jose Ortiz was fifteen years old when he went missing in August of 2007. His parents were Mexican illegals who had traveled north to find work picking strawberries, endive, and anything else that demanded cheap human labor. They reported him missing in the nearby town of Edinboro, where the local cops took a report but failed to actively search for him until three full days had passed. Even then, they made only a token effort to find him and gave up on the fifth day. Jose's mutilated body was found in a wooded area two weeks later by hikers, and the case was never solved.

A media firestorm ensued, centered on the Edinboro police departments' blatant disinterest in the disappearance of the boy and the lack of respect for the plight of his parents. It became obvious that the family's lack of social status had everything to do with the police force's failure to act promptly and effectively, not only in the search effort but also in pursuit of the killer. Although the circumstances in the Wainwright case were much different, McClure's point was well made. It was proper to assume the worst, do the work up front, and hope for the best outcome.

"All right, Pete. Get to work, and keep me posted. No time off until further notice. If she doesn't turn up, we'll meet here tonight for a briefing."

Pete watched him leave, and began to prioritize his immediate tasks. First, get with Hank before he left, to get the exact route that Nicki Wainwright would have taken. Then deal with Sally and establish the Glenwood contact. At some point after he left the station, he planned to make a phone call that wouldn't be mentioned to anyone else.

Pete would have to call Jack Ferris, and ask him the question he had been avoiding for weeks.

CHAPTER 38

"OKAY, I'M GOING to take a ride over there just to familiarize myself with the route she would have taken. Talk to you later, Hank."

Pete folded the rough sketch and stuffed it into his back pocket. As he walked to his truck, the bitterly cold wind whipping around him made Pete wish he had a winter hat to pull down over his ears, and he silently cursed the area's unpredictable weather patterns. He brought the engine to a fast idle and belted himself in, then decided to make a phone call before pulling out.

Pete needed an answer to a question that had gone unasked for too long. Friendship aside, circumstances demanded that he confront Jack Ferris about the depth of his friendship with Nicole Wainwright.

"Yello" was Jack's usual corny greeting when he was in an up mood.

"Jackie, it's Pete. Listen, something came up today that you should know about."

"Hi Pete, what's going on?"

"Just between us for now, okay?"

"Uh, okay. Is it a secret?"

"It's about a woman who's been reported missing. It isn't public knowledge yet, we're just starting to look into it."

Something in Pete's voice put a chill into Jack's spine. "Is it someone I know?"

"It's Nicole Wainwright. She went out for a run early yesterday, no sign of her since then." He paused intentionally, waiting to gauge Jack's reaction. The shaken response didn't give Pete much to analyze.

"Nicki's missing?"

"Yeah, her husband reported it this morning. You know why I'm calling, don't you?"

"Well, I don't know where she is, if that's what you mean."

"It's a little more than that, buddy. I need to know whether you're involved with Nicole Wainwright, and be honest with me."

Jack's exasperated sigh was clearly audible. "All right. Yes, we've been seeing each other, and we've become close friends. I haven't spoken to her for a few days, though."

"When did you last speak to her?"

"Last Saturday, at the gym. We were going to hook up this week but it didn't happen, I had Valentine's Day dinner with you, remember? Pete, are you saying something's happened to Nicki?"

"I don't know yet, it's still early. She could turn up safe and sound, but we're starting to investigate."

"Jesus, can I do anything?"

"You can let me know if she contacts you, or if you think of anything that might give us a lead. Other than that, stay near the phone. If she doesn't show up soon, we'll have more questions for you."

The tenor of the conversation wasn't lost on Jack. This was Pete the detective speaking, not the drinking buddy.

"Of course. Pete, call me if you find anything. This is all pretty shocking, you know?"

"Yeah, I will. Talk to you later, Jackie."

As Pete ended the brief, awkward conversation, he cursed Jack for not having the good sense to avoid involvement with a married woman. Heading toward Amelia Drive, he had the feeling that his best friend had gotten in way over his head this time.

CHAPTER 39

THE FIRST THING Al Kaplan noticed upon entering Jim Wainwright's office was the startling change in his friend's appearance. Over the years Kaplan had sometimes seen Wainwright depressed, and lately he appeared to be under considerable stress, but he had never looked so pale and haggard. It was as if Wainwright was already convinced that some terrible harm had befallen his wife.

"Jim, are you alright?"

Wainwright sank back into his leather swivel chair and shrugged his shoulders resignedly.

"I'm worried, Al. I don't know where she is, and it scares me to death."

Kaplan could see that his client needed a rest, but he could only provide assistance if he knew the details of the situation.

"Tell me everything that's happened, Jim, exactly what you've told the police. Do you want some coffee before we get started?"

"No, I'm fine. The facts are, I haven't seen or heard from Nicki in well over 24 hours, since she went out for her early morning run yesterday, about 7:30. No one I've spoken to has seen her. I don't think she ever came back from that run."

"My god, Jim, I don't know what to say, other than it's much too early to give up hope. There's no reason to think the worst."

"Al, we can discuss the details later, but first I have something to tell you, in confidence. Privileged, okay?"

"Of course Jim, as always. Attorney and client."

Wainwright took a long pause, collecting his thoughts before beginning.

"We go back a long way, don't we, Al?"

"Almost twenty-five years, I'd say. They went by quickly."

"But we didn't grow up together. I know very little about what happened in your life before we met, and you know even less about mine."

"I guess that's true, yes." Kaplan saw a man who wanted to bare his soul, and wasn't sure he wanted to hear that. "What are you getting at, Jim?"

"I'll just say this for now — if this thing goes on much longer, if Nicki isn't found safe and unharmed, the police will begin to assume foul play. Unless there is good reason to suspect someone else, the husband becomes their 'person of interest', am I right?"

Kaplan raised both hands as if to dismiss the thought from any further consideration. "Jim, please, you're getting way ahead of the events here, aren't you?"

"I'm saying that if the police have reason to investigate my background, they'll come up with some things from my past that might cause further suspicion."

Kaplan was momentarily without words.

"Oh, don't get me wrong Al, I'm not a fugitive from justice. I'm just a guy who left a bad situation behind and started over. Anyway, here's my point; the police will look into my past, my personal life. They've already asked permission to search my home."

"Did you agree to that?"

"Not yet, but do I really have a choice? Why on earth wouldn't I agree to it, if I have nothing to hide?"

Al was silent, unsure at this point whether his client had something to hide or not.

"You'll be receiving a large package from UPS. It's a box of my private papers and such, things I don't want the police to look through. I know that you're not obligated to tell them about it unless you're specifically asked. Trust me, this stuff is not relevant to Nicki's disappearance. All I want you to do is keep the box for me until this thing is over. Can you do that for me, Al? Ethically, I mean."

Al was loyal to a fault. His faith in Wainwright had taken a hit, but he wouldn't let it show.

"Yes, I can do that. Jim, are you sure you want to allow the search? We could insist on a warrant, limit the search somehow to protect you."

"No, no warrant is necessary. Let them do their job, maybe they'll find something that leads to Nicki. At the least they may be convinced that I'm telling the truth."

"All right, but I'll make sure I'm there to observe. Anything else? Should we try to postpone the vote?"

"Absolutely not. But there is one thing we need to do."

Wainwright leaned over and, with great effort, opened the bottom desk drawer and pulled out the bottle of Jack. He set it on the desk between them.

"Let's have a drink."

CHAPTER 40

A S PETE WEBSTER, Hank Rowan, and Chief McClure gathered in the station's interview room for an update, Nicki Wainwright had been missing approximately 36 hours. McClure was already aware that no significant leads had been uncovered, but he wanted a recorded summary of events.

"All right, gentlemen, it's been a long day and it isn't over. Sooner or later I'll have to make some sort of statement to the press. They've gotten wind of the door-to-door investigation, and they smell a good story. Tell me what you've got so far. Hank?"

Rowan began to flip through the pages of his notebook.

"Well, we contacted almost everyone on the list Wainwright gave us. There were twenty-some names, about half of them relatives. None of Mrs. Wainwright's family lives in the area, they last saw her almost a year ago at her brother's fiftieth birthday party. Mother's in a nursing home in Pennsylvania, where her brother lives. Another brother died from cancer about ten years ago.

"Only one of the friends I spoke to struck me as really close, the sort of person Mrs. Wainwright might confide in, that was Mrs. Victoria Raymond. They had lunch at the country club on Monday, and so far, that's the last sighting we have.

"Mrs. Raymond told me she hadn't seen much of Mrs. Wainwright for a few months. She gave me some background, though. According to her, Mrs. Wainwright was introduced to the real estate business by a Vivian Lane, who treated her as the daughter she never had. She was single, known as Nicole Moore back then. Eventually Mrs. Lane took her as a partner in her brokerage, and when she died suddenly a couple of years later the business was left to Nicole Moore. Sometime after that James Wainwright became a friend and sort of a mentor, and that became a romantic relationship. They were married in 2012, I checked the date.

"Mrs. Raymond claims that Mrs. Wainwright considered it a huge mistake to have married and given control of the firm to her husband, and had told her as much before their friendship cooled off. Lately Mrs. Wainwright has been tight with Jill Sherman. I get the idea that Mrs. Raymond disapproves of something about her former friend's recent life-style, although she claims that Mrs. Wainwright seemed quite happy at this Monday lunch. She told Mrs. Raymond that she was getting involved in the business again, started back into her running routine, etcetera. So we have some fact, some opinion, some conjecture from her. From what I can tell, there's no reason to think Mrs. Wainwright might harm herself.

"Aside from that interview, we showed Mrs. Wainwright's picture at local stores, dry cleaners, and other places in town where she might have been seen recently. I went to her office and the gym she belongs to, and that Monday lunch was the most recent sighting. At her office, they said she hasn't been in much for the last few weeks. Pete?" He turned to a clean page to write down any new facts that Pete might have.

"I didn't get much more. We knocked on every door in the neighbor-hood and along the jogging route, and didn't find anyone who could posi-tively say they saw her yesterday. A couple of neighbors on Amelia see her run by regularly, but they couldn't be sure if they had last seen her Mon-day or Tuesday. They described her outfit as light colored; her husband said she was wearing light blue."

"I spent some time with the county guys, too. They had two dogs over there, and Wainwright supplied a shirt to provide a scent. Both dogs seemed to hit the trail pretty strong and led us down Amelia in the direc-tion she would have taken, but they completely lost the trail after we turned onto Robinson, about a mile from the house."

We're planning a more complete search of the fields along that stretch, but that won't happen until tomorrow morning."

Pete sat back and flipped his notebook closed.

"That's about all I have. Did Wainwright sign the consent to search?"

McClure rubbed both hands up and down his face as if to wipe away the weariness he felt. "Yeah, he signed it. The forensics team should be there right now. Maybe one of you should go over there."

Pete wasn't ready to leave just yet.

"I saw Wainwright in his office, has he been here all day?"

McClure shrugged his shoulders and nodded. "In and out."

"I think Hank and I should talk to him again."

"I don't know, Pete, his lawyer is at the house, observing the search."

Rowan chimed in, eager to ask some questions that he had regretfully avoided in his initial interview. "Why does he need his lawyer? We're not accusing him of anything, we're just trying to find his wife, for Christ's sake."

McClure's reply was interrupted by a triple knock, and Jim Wainwright entered the room without waiting for an invitation. He looked drawn, and somewhat irritated.

"I heard there was a meeting going on. Have you found something? Why isn't anyone keeping me informed?"

McClure motioned for Wainwright to take a seat at the unoccupied end of the table. "We're just finishing up, Jim, I was about to come and see you myself."

"What have you come up with?"

McClure shook his head somberly, and spoke in a compassionate voice. "Not much, so far. She had lunch with a friend, Mrs. Raymond, on Monday, no one has seen her since then except you and possibly a neighbor as she started out on her run. We're continuing to show her picture around, and I intend to make a statement on local television and ask for any relevant information people might have. Are you okay with that?"

Wainwright was surprised by the notion of sharing his plight with the general public, but seemed resigned to it.

"If that's what you think is best, go ahead. Most people will recognize her, Nicki's picture is in the HouseFinder section of the Buffalo paper every weekend. Did Victoria notice anything different about Nicki, did she say anything seemed odd that day?"

"No Jim, she said your wife seemed fine, nothing remarkable about the conversation."

Pete decided to seize the moment. "Mr. Wainwright, would you mind providing some deeper background information? It might help us to focus the investigation more effectively."

McClure saw Wainwright hesitate, and jumped in.

"Jim, this is Detective Pete Webster, have you two met?"

"Yes, sure, I think we've crossed paths. Detective, I'm sure you know that I answered questions this morning. What else do you need to know?"

"Well, we have to consider all the possibilities. We contacted relatives and friends without any results, so it's time to look in other directions. We need some kind of a lead."

Wainwright didn't say a word, but it was obvious that Pete had his full attention.

"Was there anyone in Mrs. Wainwright's life who would be considered an enemy?"

Now Wainwright had an immediate response, folding his arms defensively as he said "Not a soul. Everyone loves Nicki."

Pete was patient, having expected Wainwright's initial reaction. "No business differences, legal squabbles, disputes with a neighbor, anything like that? Think about it."

"Really, Detective, nothing at all."

"How about you?"

Wainwright stiffened, interpreting the question as an accusation.

"What do you mean?"

"I mean, is there anyone out there who might want to harm you, either directly or through your family?"

"Oh, that. Look, of course I've had disagreements with a lot of people, business and politics will do that, but nothing that would make someone my mortal enemy. I can't think of anyone who would do whatever you're suggesting, to get back at me."

Pete allowed Wainwright to dismiss the idea for now, and embarked on another line of questioning that was common in such a case.

"How about your marriage? Any problems there?"

Wainwright was indignant, and looked to McClure for assistance.

"George, is this really the best way to find Nicki? By asking these deeply personal questions?"

"Actually yes, Jim, it's part of the process. When a spouse goes missing we have to cover this ground. Of course, you're free to have representation present, but we need to know everything if we're going to solve this."

The Supervisor heaved a sigh of exasperation, and took a few seconds to loosen his tie and regain his composure.

"No, I don't need anyone here. I'm just frustrated, you know?"

Wainwright was getting to the point where his ingrained defenses were down, his usual self-importance seemed to have faded. This was the point where a witness might begin to provide meaningful insight into a case, or at least further personalize the subject. Hank recognized that, and picked up the thread.

"How would you describe the state of your marriage, Mr. Wainwright?"

"To be honest, my marriage is a rather hollow one these days," he wistfully admitted. "We haven't been getting along for quite some time. We don't argue, or scream at each other. We just don't talk to each other much at all anymore, at least not about anything meaningful. We each go our own way, but we still sleep in the same bed, we still go out together to social functions. I don't think most people would be able to tell, but we have some problems to work out."

Hank didn't allow an emotional pause, knowing that the clock was running and Wainwright was speaking candidly.

"Any reason to think that your wife might be having an affair?"

Wainwright frowned and knitted his eyebrows, looking down at the tabletop. He didn't seem outraged, or even insulted, by the question, sending the message that he had considered the possibility himself.

"I haven't seen any proof of that, no, but I'd be lying if I said I hadn't suspected it."

Rowan sat forward, sensing that some useful information might lie below the surface of Wainwright's statement.

"Is there anyone specific that you might suspect of having an affair with her?"

Pete had been scribbling notes but stopped when he heard the question, his pen poised above the paper. He hoped no one noticed that he held his breath as they waited for the answer, never looking up from his notes.

"No, I don't have one particular person in mind. I just have a feeling. She's out on her own day and night, who knows what goes on. Maybe I don't want to know."

If the answer was intended to evoke sympathy, the detectives were immune. Pete jumped in, true to form. "And you?"

"No, detective, I don't have a girlfriend, if that's what you mean. Pete was inclined to ask what else the question could possibly mean, but didn't want to appear combative when Wainwright was cooperating so fully. He accepted the answer and moved on.

"Has Mrs. Wainwright ever gone off for a few days without warning? After an argument, anything like that?"

The look on Wainwright's face indicated confirmation even before the words were out.

"Well, yes, once, about a year ago. She called me on the second day, from the Bahamas. I was considering reporting her missing that time, too, I was starting to panic, but then she called."

"What was your wife's explanation?"

"She said she just became desperate to get away, she was 'stressed out' and need to get away." Wainwright accentuated the phrase "stressed out" with finger quotes, as if he disdained the term. "She was very apologetic, and I was relieved that she was alright. She really did need a vacation, but there was no excuse for going off without telling me."

"Was she alone there?"

Wainwright pursed his lips at the question he had anticipated.

"No, she was with a close friend, Jill Sherman."

All three cops exchanged glances, verifying that they recognized the name. Pete was ready to resume his part in the interview.

"That was an awful thing, the way she died."

"Yes, she was a beautiful woman, a shame that she was taken so suddenly. Nicki was devastated by that." Wainwright appeared to be uncomfortable with the mention of Jill Sherman.

"Did you approve of their friendship?"

Wainwright was puzzled by the question. "Why would I object to my wife having a friend?"

"They spent a lot of time together, while you and Mrs. Wainwright grew apart. A lot of men would resent that."

"Well, not me. Jill was a little too flirty for my taste, but Nicki enjoyed her company. At least she wasn't out with some guy, right?"

Pete was out of questions, and he could see that Wainwright was becoming increasingly irritated with the probing of such a sensitive topic. He stood up as if to bring the meeting to a conclusion.

"That's all I have for now, sir. We'll let you know if there's anything new."

"Please do, I'll be in my office for a while. There's a town council meeting tomorrow, I need to do some preparation for that." He shook his head, as if in disbelief of the situation. "Life goes on, you know?"

He stood and left the room, not realizing how callous his final comment had sounded.

McClure made no mention of it, his thoughts preoccupied with the search of Wainwright's home. "Hank, you'd better get over to that house and see if anything interesting turns up. Pete, check out Wainwright's alibi for yesterday. Be discreet, but find out where he was all day, and even the previous night. And keep digging into the wife's personal life, maybe there was a love interest that her hubby didn't know about. We'll meet back here in the morning, before the search."

They parted ways before Pete had an opportunity to speak with Hank in private. He had withheld the information that Jack had given him out of loyalty to his friend, but Pete knew it was a mistake. He still hoped that Nicki Wainwright would be found safe, and Jack's name would never come up in the investigation, but that seemed less likely with each passing hour.

He resolved to tell Hank what he knew about Jack and Nicki the next morning, before his deception landed him in more trouble than he was already envisioning.

CHAPTER 41

DARKNESS HAD FALLEN by the time Hank Rowan arrived at 55 Amelia Lane. A white van bearing the Erie County Sheriff logo, its rear doors opened wide, was backed up to within a few feet of the front step. A police cruiser was parked across the apron of the driveway, and an officer was stationed there to make sure any curious neighbors kept their distance.

Hank pulled over in front of the house and parked behind a black Infiniti FX that he knew to be the property of Al Kaplan. He flashed his badge at the young deputy as he walked past, and crossed the lawn to the front entrance. Kaplan was outside having a cigarette, and he acknowledged Hank with a nod, smoke escaping through his nostrils in a kind of old school way.

It looked as if every light had been turned on inside and outside the house and garage, and the front doors were left open for easier access to the van. Hank stopped at the door and pulled a pair of paper booties over his shoes before entering.

He stood in the entrance looking into the parlor, where a large tool-box lay open in the middle of the room. After a few seconds a woman came into sight, and noticed Hank's presence. She was dressed in the "bunny suit" commonly worn by forensic technicians as they worked a crime scene, and held a clipboard in one hand.

"Can I help you?" she asked as she approached.

Hank showed his badge and introduced himself.

"Donna Mackey" she said matter of factly, pulling off a latex glove to shake Hank's extended hand. "I'm the team leader here tonight."

"What have you got so far?"

"Pretty standard stuff. We took video and still shots in every room before anything was disturbed. Didn't see anything obvious like signs of a struggle or blood, and no evidence that any kind of a mess had been cleaned up.

"We found her cell phone in the purse, our guy is checking it out right now. We're told that the laptop is hers, and there's two desktop PC's to be looked at. We'll do that at the lab."

"Mind if I look around?"

"Knock yourself out. Wear gloves though, we're just starting the detailed sweep."

"So, everything looks pretty normal so far."

Mackey stopped and raised a finger as she remembered something else. "Oh, one other thing. There was a package on the step when we arrived, addressed to Mr. Wainwright. Not addressed, actually, just his name. The lawyer was pissed that we opened the box, but he got over it."

"What was in it?"

Mackey shrugged. "A golf club." She held up the clipboard and read from it. "Medalist 9 iron. One of our guys said it's pretty old, but he thinks each set was custom made, very expensive back in the day."

Pete was unimpressed. "Maybe he bought it on EBay, or had it regripped."

Mackey seemed amused, and for a moment Hank thought she might even smile. His instinct turned out to be wrong.

"Mmm — no. The packaging had no shipping label or postage and, like I said, no address. And the grip looks worn."

Hank was too embarrassed to offer any further speculation.

"We documented it and took pictures. Should we leave it here?"

"For now, yeah, as long as it's on the record."

A technician called Mackey to the rear of the room and showed her an envelope that had been placed into a transparent evidence bag. They spoke briefly before Mackey sent him off to rejoin the hunt.

"He found an envelope in the glove box of the Volvo. A Valentine card, signed "love, Nicki", nothing else written on the card."

Hank was finally hearing something that could be significant, and began thinking out loud.

"So, she never had a chance to give it to her husband, which makes sense if she left so early in the morning. Or maybe she disappeared even earlier than he says."

Mackey had been saving the best for last. "She wrote a name on the envelope. 'Jack'."

"Jack, are you sure? Not James, or Jim?"

"Jack. She has very nice handwriting."

Pete felt another twinge of regret at his failure to speak to Rowan about Jack Ferris. Mackey was studying him, as if waiting for some further comment. He took a few steps towards the rear of the house, avoiding eye contact.

"That's a good start. I'll let you get back to work."

CHAPTER 42

JACK FERRIS NORMALLY spent a lot of time in front of his Sony 65" Smart TV, watching sporting events and a wide variety of cable series. At times he found himself on the couch, remote in hand, not staying very long with any one program but instead switching idly from one channel to the next until hours had passed.

At the moment he was more focused, nervously awaiting the start of the late news broadcast on channel 5.

Jack normally avoided the local news like an electronic plague. He wasn't interested in convenience-store holdups, house fires, or the cute human-interest stories that were used, and repeated, to fill the ninety-minute time slot. He didn't consider himself cold-hearted, just more interested in a broader view of the world.

The local weather forecasters were particularly irritating to him. Each station had a meteorologist whose predictions carried a fifty percent accuracy rating at best, and every subtle change in the atmospheric conditions was treated as a momentous and extremely complicated event. This year's winter had turned mild quite early, bringing above average temperatures and a rate of precipitation that was more typical to Seattle than it was to western New York. This had prompted the talking heads to drone on endlessly about flood watches, The Farmer's Almanac, and the evidence of global warming. And if Jack hadn't already heard their theories, the regulars at Woody's could always be counted on to bring him up to date.

Becoming impatient with the amusement park jingle that was blaring from the surround sound, he pressed the button to switch to another local channel. Even though he was looking for any news of Nicki's disappearance, it was shocking to see her smiling face fill the screen. The picture was not a recent one, her hair was longer and darker than he had ever seen it, and her face appeared fuller. Still, the sight of her brought tears to Jack's eyes.

"If anyone has seen her they are asked to call the number on your screen. Nicole Wainwright is thirty-eight years old, five feet six inches tall, weighs approximately 120 pounds and was wearing a light blue jogging suit when last seen."

Jack's stomach turned as the gravity of the situation hit home. Without being conscious of it, he had moved closer to the screen and knelt there, staring up at Nicki's image.

"Once again, anyone with information on Mrs. Wainwright's whereabouts is urged to call the number below. A search of the area where she was last seen will begin tomorrow morning, according to Chief McClure."

The anchor smoothly segued to the next story, and Jack squeezed the remote to catch another broadcast. Ten minutes passed before he realized that there was nothing more to be seen, indicating that all of the local channels had slotted the search as their lead story.

Anxious to know what possible clues, if any, had been discovered, Jack decided to call Pete on his cell. It went straight to voicemail, where a generic recorded voice told him that Pete Webster was presently on the phone, and instructed him to leave a message after the tone.

Jack began haltingly, unsure of how he should word his message. "Pete, it's Jack. Uh — I just saw it on the news, the story about Nicki. I was wondering what you've found out so far, is there anything new that you can tell me? They said there's going to be a search tomorrow, and something about needing volunteers. Should I help, or just stay out of it for now?"

The request felt somehow inappropriate, and he was unable to come up with anything more.

"Call me if you get a chance. Thanks, buddy."

CHAPTER 43

THE CALL FROM Sally was a welcome interruption to the tedious search of the Wainwright home, and Pete asked her to hold on while he made his way outdoors to a more private setting.

"Sally, I apologize for not calling, but it's been a hectic day. How did the Glenwood people treat you? I made a call to try and convince them that it's a credible report."

Sally sounded surprisingly calm, and Pete wondered if she had taken something to settle her nerves.

"Yes, everything went well, they seemed to take it seriously. They had me write out a statement, which took forever, and I was assured that someone would look into it right away. We'll see."

Contrary to her words, Sally sounded less than encouraged.

"I'm sorry I couldn't do more for you. As soon as I get some time, I'm on it.

"I know Pete, don't apologize. You've been wonderful."

There was silence for a few seconds as Pete groped for words, until Sally bailed him out by continuing her train of thought.

"I didn't call to make you feel guilty, Pete. And I didn't call just to thank you, although I hope you can tell how grateful I am for all of your help. What I really wanted to say was that it's been so great to see you again, after all this time. I think I forced myself a long time ago to forget how it felt to be around you, to put you out of my mind. But these last few days have brought it all back, and I wanted you to know that."

Pete was thrilled with Sally's emotional response to their reunion, although her candor was a bit startling.

"Sally, I'm glad to hear that. I feel the same way, but I didn't have the courage to say it. It didn't seem like the right time, you know?"

"I know, but you didn't have to say anything. I could feel it, just like always. I'm not sure what happens next, Pete, I just didn't want to go to sleep without telling you."

"I'll call you tomorrow, maybe we can get together for lunch, or dinner, something."

"I'd like that. Now I'll let you get back to work. I saw that woman on the news, I hope she's okay."

"Me too, hon, me too." Pete was astonished at the ease with which the term of affection had slipped out.

"I'll talk to you soon Sally, sleep well."

"You too, Pete. Good night."

Pete closed his phone and returned to the house, shaking his head in wonder at the unexpected events that were impacting his life.

CHAPTER 44

RESIDENTS OF ROBINSON Road had viewed similar scenes before, but always from the comfort of a favorite easy chair while tuned in to CNN or Fox News. They were unprepared for the disturbing noise and growing commotion that was taking place literally in their own backyards.

Helicopters operated by the county and state police forces were already making low passes over the open fields and sparsely wooded areas that paralleled the eastern side of the two-lane roadway, the unmistakable sound of their spinning rotors providing a dramatic background to the events taking place on the ground below.

Police officers and search personnel struggled to communicate, their voices overwhelmed by the pounding reverberation each time a chopper passed overhead. The volunteer group consisted of firemen from nearby towns and a civilian group based in Buffalo, numbering close to 150 in all. Onlookers and a growing media contingent had been relegated to a vantage point away from the possible crime scene, at the intersection of Robinson and Amelia Lane.

Pete Webster wasn't assigned to be part of the ground search effort, but he had gone there to lend support in whatever capacity was required. He knew that searches such as this were difficult to organize and execute effectively, especially when coverage of a large grid demanded the assistance of non-professionals.

Pete had a secondary motivation to be on hand, one that he considered essential to his peace of mind. He intended to meet Hank Rowan there and to disclose his knowledge of Jack Ferris' relationship with the subject of the search. Pete remained convinced that his friend had nothing to do with Nicki Wainwright's disappearance, but he knew that he had withheld the information far too long already. He wondered how Hank would react to the purposely delayed disclosure.

As he approached the site, Pete was impressed with Chief McClure's management of the operation. Robinson Road had been closed to traffic for a length of two miles, running north from Amelia. Uniformed officers manned the barricades at each end, sipping coffee and barking instructions to drivers who had found their intended route unavailable and now sat dumbfounded, taking in the sight while deciding on an alternate route to their destination.

Heavy gray clouds formed a low ceiling, occasionally showering cold rain onto the participants, and a stiff breeze contributed to a wind chill that drove the effective temperature well below fifty degrees.

A large tent covered the road near the Amelia barricade, where search volunteers signed in and donned bright orange rain ponchos. They had already been divided into small groups and were receiving instructions from uniformed team leaders. McClure walked among the volunteers, reinforcing what they had just heard by reminding them to avoid touching any possible evidence, encouraging his increasingly chilled reinforcements to immediately call for a uniformed officer if they spotted anything at all.

A group of vehicles owned by Grove Park and Erie County law enforcement had been parked further down Robinson Road, including a large motor home that served as administrative headquarters. After addressing the troops, McClure made his way there to confer with the Sheriff's representative. Once again, Pete was impressed by the Chief's hands-on approach and leadership skills. Age may have slowed him down physically, but George was certainly proving that he was still capable of directing the force.

Pete hung his I.D. tag around his neck and stopped in at the volunteer tent, helping himself to a steaming hot cup of disappointingly weak coffee. He wandered toward the command center, keeping to himself as he scanned the crowd in hope of finding Hank Rowan among them. He was disgustedly tossing the contents of his cup to the ground when a meaty hand clasped his shoulder.

"Mornin', Sunshine." It was Hank, holding a Tim Horton's cup as he grinned at Pete's apparently foul mood.

"I wish there was some goddamned sunshine," Pete growled. "Could it be any gloomier out here?"

"Yeah, I know," Hank offered as he looked across the road. "Let's hope it doesn't get more depressing."

Pete nodded in agreement, joining his friend in hoping that no body would be discovered. Before he could speak, Hank turned to face him.

"So, did you see anything interesting at the Wainwright place? I looked over the evidence list this morning, it seemed pretty thin."

"Nah, they're still checking the computers, though. We turned the place back over to him." Pete shoved his hands into his jacket pockets and shrugged, preparing to launch into his embarrassing confession of the undisclosed information.

"Actually, there is something I need to tell you about that. Did you notice the Valentine card that was listed?"

Just then an electronic version of the William Tell overture sounded from Hank's phone, precluding his answer.

"Sorry, Pete. Give me a minute." He lifted the phone to his ear and walked away, as if he expected to find a spot that would be immune to the racket emanating from the helicopter passing overhead. Pete waited impatiently, his irritation at the delay tempered only by his amusement at Hank's choice of ring tone.

After a few minutes Hank returned, frowning as if he had found the phone call to be disturbing. Without any mention of that brief conversation, he turned to Pete as if it hadn't happened at all.

"So, tell me about the card."

Pete decided to forego his needle about the ring tone, sensing that Hank was not in the mood for joking. "It was found in the glove box of her car, in an envelope that was addressed to someone named Jack. Just the usual sappy greeting card, signed 'with love, Nicki.' Nothing else written on it."

Hank shrugged. "So, who's Jack?" Something in his manner made it clear that he already knew the answer.

"Well, that's what we need to talk about. I think 'Jack' could be a good friend of mine, Jack Ferris."

Hank nodded knowingly, briefly staring into space beyond Pete as if trying to call up a memory. "Jack Ferris. I've met him, haven't I?"

"I've probably introduced him to you at Woody's, yeah."

"Uh huh. And did you suspect that he was tapping the Supervisor's wife?"

Pete chewed the inside of his lip and looked away, embarrassed at what he was about to reveal.

"I suspected that, yes, but I didn't know for sure until Wednesday night. I called Jack and asked him straight out if he was romantically involved with Nicki Wainwright, and he admitted that he was." Pete paused and waited for Hank's reaction.

"Jesus Pete, you never mentioned that to anyone, even after we questioned Wainwright about the possibility of his wife having an affair? What the hell is going on?"

"Listen Hank, I know now that I screwed up, I honestly don't know what I was thinking. I guess I was hoping that she'd turn up quickly, unharmed, and Jack could be kept out of it. That was stupid, and I know it looks bad, but the guy is my closest friend."

Hank was unmoved. "That's no excuse, dammit! Look at what's going on around us, Pete. We're not playing games here!"

"I know, you're right. I fucked up, Hank."

Rowan held out his phone for Pete to see. "That phone call was from a guy named Riordan, he works at Strong's gym. He heard that I was over there asking questions about Nicki Wainwright, and then he caught the story on the news broadcast. Riordan claims he saw her and Jack Ferris together on several occasions, including last Saturday. He's sure that they were more than just friends."

Pete didn't comment, simply nodding to acknowledge the confirmation of his earlier statement.

Hank continued, softening a bit. "Well, I'm glad for one thing. I gave you a chance to come out with it before I told you about Riordan, and you did. How you explain this to McClure is your problem. Good luck with that."

"I'll tell him as soon as I can get him alone."

"Good idea. Have you heard from Ferris since he told you that he was screwing around with her?"

Now it was Pete's turn to hold up his phone. He worked through the menu until Jack's unanswered message was queued up and handed the phone to Hank so he could hear it for himself. Rowan listened intently, cupping his hand over his left ear to block out the noise that surrounded them.

"What did you tell him to do?" he asked, handing the phone back to Pete.

"Nothing. I haven't returned the call. I didn't want to have any further communication with him until we had this conversation. Should I call him and tell him to come in?"

Hank shook his head as if Pete's idea was out of the question. "No. Call him and tell him to stay at home. Tell him *I'm* coming to talk to him", he ordered, tapping his chest emphatically. "I wanna talk to this guy right away."

Pete opened his phone and scrolled to Jack's cell number.

"And", Hank added," make sure McClure knows what's been going on before you leave here." His voice and visage made it clear that he now saw Pete in a different light, as if a basic element of trust had been violated. Pete hoped that it was a temporary state of affairs and not an end to their working relationship.

"I will." Pete hit the send button, relieved to have everything out in the open. Still, as he waited for Jack Ferris to answer, he felt an acute sense of betrayal in his gut.

CHAPTER 45

"MR. WAINWRIGHT, PAUL Gotts here. I heard about what's been going on there. How are you holding up?"

Wainwright had been expecting this call, but he knew that Gotts' primary concern was not Nicki's safety. The town council and planning board were scheduled to meet in less than eight hours, and the Cedar Ridge proposal would be the first item on the agenda.

"I'm managing, Mr. Gotts, thanks for asking." Wainwright was actually glad to have the chance to ask a few questions of his own, when the moment was right.

"I won't take up much of your time, Mr. Wainwright, I know you've got your hands full there. I've spoken to Victor, and he's concerned that your dealings with the police might keep you from attending tonight's meeting. That greatly concerns my employers, so they asked me to speak to you personally. In spite of the situation, we need you to see this thing through. After the project is approved we'll help all we can with the other, uh, problem. Can you do that?"

Once again Wainwright was amused at Gotts' attempt to sound like a man of some educational background. He wasn't a stupid man, but his Bronx accent and self-taught phrasing couldn't hide the fact that he had grown up on the tough streets of New York, with men like himself as role models.

Wainwright didn't miss a beat, having planned his response in advance.

"You can assure your employer that I'll be there, and tell them that the approval is in the bag. Is that what you wanted to hear?"

Gotts disliked Wainwright's tone, but it was, in fact, exactly what he wanted to hear.

"Yes, it was, thank you for being so direct. So, your sources are confident that you have the votes for approval?"

"Absolutely. We have the council majority, and the planners can only make a recommendation before our vote. Anyway, there won't be a problem. My people tell me that even Brenda Jackson has gone quiet on the subject."

"Really?" Gotts managed to sound genuinely surprised. " What do you think changed her mind?" He smiled to himself, anticipating Wainwright's self-serving reply.

"I've been telling you all along, you people underestimate my influence in this town. You should remember why you came to me in the first place."

"Yes, I guess you're right. Victor seems to share your opinion. I hope you're both right."

Gotts could have added "for your sake", but he didn't need to. It was understood. The Supervisor decided that a change of topic was in order.

"Gotts, I received an unusual package recently, it contained something that I hadn't seen in years. Does it mean what I think it means?"

"Well," Gotts began, choosing his electronically transmitted words carefully as was his habit, "I trust that it was comforting to see it again. Problem solved, no?"

Wainwright had wanted to dispose of the golf club, but he was aware that the police had seen it. He had tossed it into the back of the Hummer that morning with the intent of taking it to his rented storage space, where the set of vintage irons would once again be complete.

"Yes, it appears to be. And the situation with Nicki, do you know something about that?"

Wainwright listened carefully, trying to gauge Gotts' reaction to the insinuation.

"Mr. Wainwright, you need to control your emotions right now, and listen to what I'm about to tell you. Take care of the vote, and make sure it goes our way. As soon as that is resolved, we can turn our attention to your wife's disappearance."

"What does that mean, Gotts? Do you know something? I told you, the vote is in the bag!" Wainwright was shouting into the phone, his volume rising in concert with his blood pressure.

Gotts was unfazed. "Mr. Wainwright, try to calm down. I'll see you tonight, after the meeting.

"You're here? In Grove Park?"

"Not far away. I'm feeling lucky, and there's a craps table calling my name. I'll get back to you tonight."

In spite of all that was going on, Wainwright was keeping his eye on the ball. "I assume you'll be ready to complete our deal. Or do I see Victor about that?"

There was no response. After a few seconds, Wainwright realized that, once again, the conversation had already come to an end.

CHAPTER 46

WHEN PETE WEBSTER finally caught up with George McClure, the search operation had been underway for nearly an hour. Up to that point nothing of any consequence had been discovered, and there were still no solid leads in the investigation of Nicki Wainwright's disappearance. Pete found the Chief chasing a persistent television crew back to the designated media zone. It was unusual to see McClure lose his temper, but the pressure of the day's events was getting to him. Expletives were flying as he ranted at the local anchorwoman and videographer, who continued their attempts at an interview even as they retreated. Dropping one last f-bomb as he turned away, the red-faced McClure found himself face to face with his detective.

"Who the hell does she think she is, Katie Couric?" he groused, to no one in particular.

Pete could hardly have chosen a worse moment to initiate this conversation, but he had little choice.

"Chief, I know there's a lot going on here, but I need your attention for a minute."

Realizing that he needed to calm down and collect himself, McClure took a deep breath and focused on Webster with all the attention he could muster. "Make it quick."

Pete did his best, telling the story the same way he had explained it to Hank Rowan. Having unburdened himself a second time, Pete braced himself for McClure's reaction. Considering the circumstances, the old man let him off easy.

"All right, Webster, I don't understand what the hell you were thinking, but I'm glad you told me about this. And I'd love to rip you a new one right now but, as you may have noticed, I'm kinda busy! We'll have to address all this later, and believe me we will address it. I'm not going to let this slide."

Pete was contrite, and eager to move on.

"I know that, George, and I'm sorry to hit you with this, especially now."

"Sorry doesn't cut it. Get back to work, and find out if Ferris could have something to do with all this. And try to conduct yourself like an objective professional!"

The Chief brushed past Pete and stalked away, shaking his head in disgust.

CHAPTER 47

JACK FERRIS WAS on his elliptical machine, nearing the end of his customary 45-minute program, when he received the disturbing phone call. Pete's tone had been decidedly more formal than Jack would have expected, tersely informing him that the search was underway and that, so far, there had been no discovery of evidence related to Nicki's disappearance.

Jack was about to ask for a more detailed description of the search activity when Pete cut him off.

"Look, Jack, that's all I'm at liberty to say about the investigation, anything else is strictly police business. But there is something you need to know, so listen carefully."

Jack pulled the phone away from his ear for a moment as he toweled the sweat from his head and neck, and took a deep breath in an attempt to lessen his heart rate.

"Okay, Pete, I'm listening."

"Hank Rowan got a call from someone who saw you and Nicki Wainwright together several times. Rowan wants to talk to you."

Jack threw the towel aside, switching the phone to his other ear.

"Who was it? Who said that?"

"That doesn't matter, does it, Jack? The fact is, you and Nicki were involved. You told me that yourself, and I had to share that information with Hank."

Jack took a moment to process Pete's last statement.

"You told him what I said about me and Nicki? About a private conversation between friends?"

"Jack, we've been friends forever, but I'm a cop. I'm not your lawyer, it isn't covered by any kind of confidentiality. You confirmed what I had already suspected, and I kept it to myself as long as I could. Too long, really. But now things are getting pretty intense, and I had no other choice. Jack, you're my best friend, but I couldn't keep you out of this any longer."

Pete's manner had turned impatient, almost angry, a result of the conflict he was feeling. He was ticked off that Jack had refused to take his advice to stay away from Nicki Wainwright, and more disturbed that it had now come between them.

"Right. You're right, Pete, I guess I've put you in a bad position, I can't expect special treatment. What happens now?"

This time Pete sounded less matter-of-fact, as if he truly sympathized. He knew that Jack wasn't prepared for the scrutiny that he was about to experience.

"You know who Hank Rowan is. He'll be there shortly to ask you some questions. He may even want to take you in to the station."

"Jesus, Pete, do I need a lawyer?"

"I don't know, Jack, that's your call. My advice would be this; if at some point the tone of the questioning makes you uncomfortable, tell them you want counsel present before going any further. Up until that time, just cooperate and be straight about things."

"Pete, I'm already a long way past uncomfortable."

"Who would you call? Do you have anyone in mind?"

"I did some work for a guy named Battaglia last year, got to know him a little, played cards together a few times. Maybe I should call him."

Pete's eyebrows shot up at the immediate mention of Ray Battaglia. He was one of the top defense attorneys in the city of Buffalo. Clearly Jack wasn't totally unprepared for this turn of events, something that Pete found at once comforting and somehow unsettling.

"Yeah, he's good. Jack, I gotta go. Stay put until Hank gets there, and keep your cool. If he takes you to the station, I'll probably see you there later."

Jack had gotten the message. They were close, but in this matter Pete had to be a neutral party.

"Okay, later, boss."

*

Stones crunched beneath the tires as Hank Rowan slowly approached the Ferris residence. He exited the car and stood beside it for a minute, studying the secluded surroundings and admiring the attractive A-frame structure. As he approached the front door, it was swung open by the owner and now person of interest, Jack Ferris.

Jack had not changed out of his workout clothes, hoping to appear relaxed and congenial, but he couldn't quite manage a smile. He pushed the storm door open. "Detective Rowan?"

"That's right, Mr. Ferris. I take it you've spoken to Pete Webster."

"Yeah, Pete called and told me — told me to expect you. Come on in."

Rowan entered and took a look around, trying to get a glimpse into the Jack Ferris persona by studying his home field. What he saw was a neat, tastefully furnished living space that reflected a quiet lifestyle. As they sat down, Jack tried to break the ice.

"I think we've met before, right? Pete introduced us, at Woody's"

"Yeah, he mentioned that." Rowan's reply was void of any emotion or interest, dismissing any notion of small talk between the two.

"Mr. Ferris, I'm here as part of the investigation into the disappearance of Nicole Wainwright. I have information that the two of you are friends." It wasn't a question, but Rowan obviously expected a response.

Jack began his reply, but was stopped short by uncooperative vocal cords. He cleared his throat and continued.

"Yes, that's true." He had already decided to take Pete's advice. He planned to answer Rowan's questions respectfully, but without offering more information than was required. If the interview became too uncomfortable, he would refuse to go on without an attorney present.

"Mr. Ferris, I have a lot of questions for you, but I'm going to start with the most important ones. Mrs. Wainwright has been missing for over 48 hours, and we have no solid leads as to her whereabouts. Do you have any idea where she might be?"

"No sir, I wish I could help you, but I don't know where she could be."

"When did you last see her?"

"I saw her last weekend, at Strong's gym. I work out there every Saturday. As I was leaving, Nicki — Mrs. Wainwright — was in the parking lot, and we had a conversation about the work I had done at her house. That was the last time I saw her."

"So that was Saturday, the eleventh."

"Uh, I guess so, yeah. Saturday."

Rowan was outwardly skeptical. "That's all you talked about? Nothing more personal?"

"Not really. Just small talk." Jack was already slipping into deceit, trying to guess how much Rowan knew before he answered fully. To his relief, Rowan seemed satisfied with the reply.

"And you haven't seen her since then?"

"No sir."

Rowan noted something in his pad and abruptly changed the course of the interview.

"Let's talk about you, Mr. Ferris. How long have you been a resident of Grove Park?"

"I've lived in the area all my life, sir. I thought you knew that. Pete Webster and I grew up together, we were classmates all the way through high school."

"I see." Once again Rowan ignored the reference to Ferris' friendship with his fellow officer.

"How long in this residence?"

"I bought the lot in 2011, spent a year clearing it and another two on the construction. Moved in permanently about three years ago. It still isn't finished, but I'm getting there." Jack looked around at his source of pride, and a brief smile crossed his face as he remembered how impressed Nicki had been.

"Well, you did a hell of a job. Me, I can barely hammer a nail without banging a thumb."

Jack grinned. "I can relate to that. Thank god for nail guns. Makes things a lot easier, especially all these hardwood floors and moldings."

"I'll bet it does. So, what do you do for a living, Jack?"

Jack was sure Rowan already knew the answer, causing him to wonder how many of these queries were mere verification of what the detective knew to be true.

"I do mostly interior painting, wall coverings, some trim work. That kind of thing."

"Ever been married?"

"No sir."

Rowan awaited further comment, but Jack offered nothing more.

"Never met the right person?"

"I guess not."

"Tell me how you came to know Mrs. Wainwright. Where did you first meet?"

Jack's lips tightened as he looked at the floor and took a long inhale, expanding his chest and exhaling audibly. The action struck Rowan as somehow theatrical rather than genuine. If Ferris had been romantically involved with Nicole Wainwright to any real depth, he would certainly remember their first meeting without difficulty.

"Actually, it was at Woody's. The same place I met you, Woody's Pub. I had stopped in after work for a beer, and I ran into Pete. He may not remember it though, he was pretty shitfaced by the time I got there." Jack appeared to be amused at the thought of Pete's overindulgence. Rowan didn't see the humor, having been in the position of covering for a hung-over Pete Webster far too often.

"Anyone else who might recall that meeting?"

"Well, Mrs. Wainwright was with a friend, but — "

"What?"

"Her friend Jill was there, but she died in a car wreck later that night."

"Jill Sherman. So that was well over a month ago."

"Sounds about right."

"What was the conversation between you and Mrs. Wainwright?"

"Oh, she introduced herself and said she had seen my work in some of her friend's houses, including the Sherman's. She wanted an estimate, some ideas, that kind of thing. Gave me her card."

"That was it, no one else was there?"

Jack paused as if considering his answer, then plunged ahead.

"Her husband was there. He seemed kind of pissed that the ladies had left their little group, and came over to break things up. He said it was time for them to leave, they had a dinner reservation across the street."

Rowan's interest was piqued at the mention of Jim Wainwright.

"You and Mr. Wainwright know each other?"

"No, not at all. I mean, we were never introduced, but I knew who he was, Town Supervisor and all. When I did the work at their house he was never around, so I'm not even sure he knows who I am."

Rowan let those words lie there for a moment, writing something more as Jack fidgeted.

"This meeting at Woody's, you never met Mrs. Wainwright before that?"

"No, I — well, I had seen her before quite a few times. Like I said, we go to the same gym – Strong's gym — to work out."

Jack could feel the perspiration on his forehead and the palms of his hands. It was all he could do to resist the urge to wipe away the telltale sign of nerves, thereby drawing attention to it.

"I see. So, you already knew each other before the night at Woody's."

"No, no. We were — aware of each other, but we hadn't spoken before."

Rowan had visions of the lustful, furtive glances that must have been exchanged inside Strong's Gym.

"Okay. At some point you became romantically involved with Mrs. Wainwright. Is that correct?"

Beads of sweat combined and sent a trickle down the side of Jack's face. He pointed to the machine in the far corner of the room.

"Mind if I grab my towel?" He was on his feet before Rowan could answer.

"Are you alright, Mr. Ferris?"

"Oh yeah, it's just that I was in the middle of a workout when you got here, so I'm still sweating, sorry."

"I was asking if you and Mrs. Wainwright had an affair."

"Well yes, I thought Pete told you that." Rowan accepted the confirmation of an affair without acknowledging the reference to Webster.

"Has she been here recently, Mr. Ferris?"

Jack desperately wanted this to be over. He needed a chance to calm down, reduce his heart rate, and stop perspiring. The cop had rattled him, and Jack knew he was doing a great impression of a man who had something to hide.

In fact, Rowan had that exact impression as he awaited the answer. The grandfather clock ticked seconds off in the background, reminding Jack that he was taking too long to consider his reply.

"Yes, she was here a couple of weeks ago. She'd been asking to see the place. Nicki was in real estate, you know, and I wanted her opinion on the market value of it."

"She was here on an appraisal." Rowan sounded like a sarcastic prosecutor ridiculing a response from the witness.

Pen scratched on paper for a full minute before Rowan looked up. He put his hands on his knees and looked Jack up and down, as if his opinion of him had not been fully formed. Then, much to Jack's relief, he pocketed the notebook and slowly rose to his feet.

"Is that it, Detective?"

Rowan gave him a wry smile, finding a touch of humor in the optimistic delivery of the question.

"No Mr. Ferris, we've only gotten the broad strokes down. I have a lot more questions for you, but I'll ask those down at the station."

"Do I have a choice? Am I being arrested for something?"

"Yes, and no, in that order. I assumed that you'd want to cooperate fully, in the interest of finding Mrs. Wainwright."

Jack's head was spinning.

"Of course, I want to help. I'm going crazy wondering where she could be." Jack dismissed the notion of calling a lawyer, at least for now.

"Can I change into some sweats first?"

"Sure, go ahead. I'll wait right here." Rowan had no intention of letting this guy get too far from his sight.

CHAPTER 48

GROVE PARK TOWN hall stood in the heart of the village, a two-story structure covered in 19th-century brick that had been reclaimed after the demolition of several local buildings. Successfully designed to be large enough to provide for most of the town's governmental needs while still melding with the quaint surroundings, it featured thick glass entrance doors opening to a large vestibule from which visitors gained access to the town's official functions.

The center portion of the ground floor housed the courtroom, behind which the Town Attorney, assistants, and town judges had offices. The adjoining wing was home to police headquarters, including a dispatch area that utilized the latest tracking and communications technology. The town council met in chambers located on the opposite side of the court-room, behind an impressive set of large oak doors. The room featured theater-style tiered seating for guests and those local citizens who wished to attend the meetings, either to speak out on current issues or simply observe their elected officials in action. The council table was located front and center, with a leather swivel chair and microphone for each member.

The second floor of town hall was divided into offices that were home to the town clerk, building inspectors and other minor officials, with cubicles for administrative assistants that had become a jungle of computer terminals and stacks of paperwork. The largest office, with a window that offered a view of Main Street, was reserved for the Town Supervisor.

Supervisor Wainwright stared out the window as he groused. "Why aren't there any cops out there? Christ, we've got protestors in the crowd, they should be moved away from the front entrance. What the hell is McClure doing?"

Al Kaplan didn't need to answer, they both knew what was occupying the police chief at that moment. The pressure of the events of the last two days, along with this upcoming vote on New Century's development application, was becoming too much for his friend to handle.

"Jim, are you sure you want to do this? I can chair the vote, it's a slam dunk."

Wainwright turned from the window to face Kaplan, pointing a finger at him.

"Don't baby me, Al — of all people, you should know I can get this done. Just make sure you have my back covered down there. Let's go."

*

"That's it, Jen. My equipment's catching too much rain, I'm going back to the van and have a smoke. He might already be in there, anyway."

Jennifer Banks hated to give up the chance to get a few seconds of filler video as James Wainwright arrived for the Grove Park town council meeting, but she had to admit that the persistent downpour had become a showstopper. She watched helplessly as Danny retreated to the WKBG mobile unit to dry out, and to fire up what she suspected would be something more mellowing than a Marlboro Light.

Small groups of locals milled about, holding signs that stated their opposition to "out of control development" and support of some sort of bridge reconstruction. Jennifer wasn't familiar with those issues, nor was she interested. The City & Region reporter would cover that, she was here for the larger story.

They had been in the field for eight hours already and, despite Danny's eagerness to wrap things up and start the weekend, Jennifer had insisted on staying in Grove Park a couple of hours longer. The story of a woman gone missing, the beautiful wife of the Supervisor of this seemingly idyllic town, was already stirring interest outside the region.

Jennifer had received a call from her producer informing her that CNN would be including the story on their Current Headlines news breaks, and Jennifer might be asked to tape a 30-second report for their exclusive use.

CNN!! Ten years of hard work covering the news in and around Buffalo was about to pay off, and Jennifer refused to be deterred by a little precipitation. They had already transmitted a solid summary of events from the search site, with rain dripping from Jennifer's raven hair as she described the activity in the background of the shot. Her makeup had washed away by then, but Danny had assured her that the conditions merely made for more compelling television. Jennifer would be sure to call her Mom after the six o'clock news had run, to get her opinion.

For now, she decided to join the local citizens who were gathering in the vestibule. It was a chance to get a feel for their mood, and possibly garner some interesting rumors, through casual conversation and eavesdropping. And if her hair had a chance to dry, even better.

After that she intended to move to the other side of the building to get a comment from the Grove Park police chief. They had met earlier that day on Robinson Road when the chief personally chased Jen and Danny back to the media corral, cursing them all the way in what Jennifer considered a very unprofessional display. Danny had the whole incident on tape, and the chief must have been made aware of that. He eventually came by and apologized, and asked them not to use the footage that would portray him as an overwhelmed small-town cop. In return, he promised to give Jennifer an exclusive interview, what he termed "a couple of minutes at the end of the day" that could run on the late news show. Since then Jennifer had been mentally preparing the question she would lead with, and formulating her comments for the final shot.

They had missed Wainwright, but that was just going to be icing on the cake, anyway. She decided to leave the coverage of the town council's affairs to others, and concentrate on the police wing.

At precisely five o'clock the doors of the council chambers were opened to the public. A group of at least fifty Grove Park residents shuffled in from the vestibule, some of them still shaking raindrops from their coats and umbrellas.

Those who were attending their first council meeting were impressed with the surroundings that their tax dollars had funded, and stopped to take in the view of the expansive curved table where the council members would be seated and large flat screens on each side where presentation material could be displayed.

Cameras were placed at the rear of the auditorium and at each side, recording the proceedings for delayed broadcast on the local public-access cable channel, but those who turned out that night weren't satisfied to view this meeting from their living room at some later date. They had come to be heard, or to lend support to others who would step to the microphone and express heartfelt opinions to their representatives on the council.

Fifteen minutes later the council members had all taken their seats, and the Supervisor allowed ample time for them to adjust microphones and self-consciously shuffle papers as their constituents looked on. As the idle conversation of the hundred or so attendees dropped to an expectant murmur, Supervisor Wainwright struck his gavel against its rosewood sound block and brought the session to order.

From her seat at the far-left end of the council table, administrative assistant Janice Morgan used her laptop to send the meeting agenda to the twin screens. She then introduced the first order of business, a proposal to approve the expenditure of $5,000 for the purchase of replacement recycling bins. A discussion ensued as to the reasons that so many of the supposedly durable plastic bins required replacement after only one year of service in Grove Park's recycling program. A seemingly straightforward decision was then delayed twenty minutes as council members took turns alternately blaming and defending the employees of the town's waste management contractor.

Councilman Luke Brady was convinced that the damage was caused when the bins were emptied and then tossed carelessly onto streets and driveways, particularly during cold weather. When he referred to those responsible as "garbage men", council member Anna Fronczak quickly asked to be recognized.

"Mr. Brady, my son is one of the employees that you are demeaning, and I strongly object to your characterization of these men. They are up early and work long hours, frequently in inclement weather, performing a job that we all take for granted. They aren't paid all that much, and they're worth every penny."

A few giggles from the crowd made Fronczak wish she could reword her last statement, but she opted to remain silent and try to hide her embarrassment. Eventually the measure was approved, as were a handful of other non-controversial items. The engine of town government was running smoothly once again.

As the final agenda item was announced, Wainwright cleared his throat and took a sip of water, anticipating a personal triumph. He felt confident, and fully in his element presiding over the approval of the Cedar Ridge Development application. Scanning the faces before him, the Supervisor spoke in a calm, controlled timbre.

"We have one hour scheduled for the public comment session. Speakers, please limit your remarks to five minutes maximum. There will be no response, agreement or rebuttal from the members of this council, as this is your time to express your concerns and we want to hear from as many of you as possible. Ms. Morgan will handle the order of speakers. Please begin with your name and address."

With that, Wainwright relaxed into the back of his chair and turned to the guest lectern.

A matronly woman of about sixty was already in place, and nervously introduced herself as Ruth Warren, a teacher and village resident.

"Mr. Supervisor, members of the council, thank you for this opportunity to speak. My main concern is the development's impact on Grove Park schools, particularly the North Elementary district which is nearest the proposed site. I teach third grade there, and class sizes are already causing undue stress to the staff. I think that any increase in class sizes would be detrimental to the school and to the learning process, and I wonder if the increase in tax revenue will be sufficient to cover the cost of so many additional students. On behalf of the teacher's union, I recommend that any new residential development be discouraged at this time. Thank you."

Wainwright had anticipated such critical remarks from the public, and was not rattled. In his experience, the degree of protest they had just heard was nothing out of the ordinary. The majority of speakers on any proposal would be negative, as those opposed would be more passionate and eager to share their views. Hopefully there were a few motivated proponents on hand as well.

Over the allotted hour sixteen people stepped to the microphone to share their opinions, and generally voiced ideas that the council members had expected to hear.

The head of a local environmental group was the most eloquent, and one of the few who used the full five minutes to make his case. He was strongly opposed to Cedar Ridge, citing its detrimental effect on wetlands and the natural drainage of the area. He criticized the environmental impact studies submitted by New Century as superficial and sub-standard, and employed his background as a civil engineer to make his case in terms that were easily understood. He left the distinct impression that he knew much more about environmental impact than did the writers of the studies, and when he finished there was a smattering of applause.

Several residents who would become neighbors of the new mansion dwellers were firmly opposed for a number of reasons, increased traffic and noise being the most frequently mentioned. Simply put, they were happy with their secluded lives and saw enough new faces when they ventured into the village proper.

There were encouraging comments from a few village inhabitants who had their own interests at heart. One was a well-spoken construction laborer who had been out of work for months and was experienced in the framing of new houses.

Another was in favor of the project because it included the reconstruction of the Powers Road Bridge that had been the scene of so many tragic accidents in recent years. She described the flowers of remembrance that relatives of the victims placed at the scene of their heartbreak, and again there was a light ripple of applause and a few tears wiped away as the speaker returned to her seat.

The final speaker was Howard Randall, a well-respected local businessman who Wainwright knew to be a good friend of Al Kaplan. Randall urged the community to embrace growth and to welcome the infusion of fresh blood to the town citizenry. He added that, if the development was allowed to go forward, he intended to become a resident of Cedar Ridge.

Wainwright wasn't sure how it had been arranged, but Randall's position as the final speaker was a stroke of genius. From the front row, Victor Harmon made eye contact with Wainwright and nodded approvingly.

"Thank you. I'd like to thank all of you for sharing your thoughts with us in preparation for this important vote, and to that end we will now hear from the Grove Park planning board."

He sat back as Janice Morgan made the introduction. "The recommendation of the Planning Board will be presented by the board's coordinator, Brenda Jackson."

CHAPTER 49

AT GROVE PARK police headquarters, Assistant District Attorney David Greco entered the small conference room and was greeted by the unmistakable smell of raw onions. McClure, Webster and Rowan were seated around a table that held an assortment of submarine sandwiches and several cans of soda.

"David, you're just in time, have a seat. We ordered subs, so we'll have dinner while we review. Ham, turkey, or roast beef?"

"Anything that doesn't have onions on it."

McClure chuckled. "Roast beef, then." He grabbed a tightly wrapped package marked "RB" and slid it across the table in Greco's direction.

The short, stocky, sharply dressed ADA was not particularly chummy with the police chief or the detectives, nor did he wish to be. It was their job to provide him with enough evidence to win in court, and if Greco was dissatisfied with what was provided he could be very confrontational.

"Thanks, Chief. Hank, Pete, good to see you guys again. What have we got?"

There was a loud pop as Rowan jerked the tab of his Sprite, moving the can away from his lap as it threatened to bubble over.

"So far, not much. We ran a pretty exhaustive search today along Robinson Road, where she would have been running, and came up empty."

Greco unwrapped his sandwich and sat back in his chair. A question begged to be asked, and he wanted to pose it to McClure without sounding overly negative.

"Chief, are you having any regrets about orchestrating such a costly search at this early stage of the investigation? I mean, we have no evidence of foul play, no reason to suspect any ill will toward Mrs. Wainwright. No offense, but it seems that you could have waited a little longer before attracting so much attention from the media, to say nothing of the taxpayers."

McClure was amazingly calm in the face of Greco's second-guessing. He was prepared for the question because he knew that it would be asked by the press at some point, and he answered with conviction.

"How can we find the evidence if we don't look for it? We have a prominent citizen, the wife of the Town Supervisor, who goes out for a run and hasn't been seen for two days. We canvassed the entire neighborhood, contacted friends and family, anyone we can think of, and no one has seen her.

"Why wait any longer to conduct a search? If we had found evidence of a crime out there you wouldn't be asking why I organized such a costly operation, you might even be commending the police for moving so quickly to solve this case. The fact that we came up empty doesn't mean we did the wrong thing. Tell that to the media and the taxpayers."

Greco was satisfied with the answer and appreciated McClure's non-combative manner, although he had sounded a bit testy towards the end of his speech.

"Fair enough. Just for the record, you know. Devil's advocate and all that."

McClure looked to Webster, who was washing down his meal by draining a can of Mountain Dew. "Pete, you've been running down leads from the tip line all day, anything useful?"

Pete flipped a steno pad open, regretting that the copious notes did not contain much useful information.

"I spoke to fifteen or twenty people who claimed to have seen Mrs. Wainwright. Some of them were credible, but the time of their sighting was before the morning of her disappearance, not after. Most of the others were too vague in their description of the person they saw to be useful, and a few seemed like they just wanted a little attention. One woman was more definite, though.

"Cheryl Boorman lives four houses from the Wainwrights, but she wasn't home when we did our first canvass of the neighborhood. She saw Mrs. Wainwright starting out on her run that morning, still on Amelia. Boorman says she leaves for work at 7:40 every day, and claims she drove right past her. She accurately described the sweat suit that the subject was wearing, also her sunglasses. She says they even waved to each other. Right now, Mrs. Boorman seems to be the last person to have seen Nicole Wainwright, and makes it definite that she was out running."

McClure glanced over at Greco, knowing that Pete's report had further justified that morning's search effort. "That's it, nothing else?"

"I'm afraid that's it, nothing else worth mentioning."

"Okay. Hank, we've already discussed Ferris, but go over it again so David can hear it."

Rowan picked up his notebook and lifted his reading glasses into place, glancing at Pete as he began to speak. It was a quick moment of eye contact, probably unnoticed by the other attendees, as if Hank wanted to be sure that Pete was prepared for what he was about to hear.

"This morning at about 9:30, just as the search was getting underway, I received a call from a guy named Paul Riordan. He's an assistant manager at Strong's Gym, where Mrs. Wainwright was a member. He heard that I'd been there yesterday asking about her, and thought he should give me a call.

Basically, Riordan told me that Mrs. Wainwright had a *special friend* at the gym." Hank's raised eyebrows served to italicize the term used by Riordan.

"He told me that the guy's name was Jack Ferris, also a regular at the gym. He'd seen them leave together several times, and had witnessed some goodbye kisses that made it obvious that they were more than just workout buddies."

Hank removed his glasses and put his notes aside.

"It turns out that Jack Ferris is a close friend of Detective Webster's. When I spoke to Pete, he confirmed that Ferris had already admitted to being involved with Nicole Wainwright. Pete called Ferris at home to verify his location, and I went there to interview him. When I arrived — ,"

"Whoa, wait a minute, I'm confused." Greco extended his palms towards Hank, signaling him to slow down his rapid-fire explanation. "When did Ferris make this admission?"

All eyes were trained on Pete. He had known this was coming, and the only option was to be straightforward and take the heat.

"He told me on Wednesday. Actually, I had called Jack to let him know that Mrs. Wainwright was missing, because I had suspected for a while that they had been seeing each other. Like Hank said, Jack and I are tight, and he had brought up her name a few times. I asked him directly and he said that he had been romantically involved with Mrs. Wainwright."

Greco dropped his pen to the table to accentuate the shock he felt.

"Detective Webster" he began, addressing Pete with a renewed sense of formality, "did you share this information with anyone?"

"I did, but not until this morning."

"What took so long, Detective?"

McClure remained silent, waiting to see how Pete's reasoning would play with Greco.

"I thought — I was hoping that Mrs. Wainwright would reappear under innocent circumstances, so I gave it a little time before bringing up Jack's name. I told Hank about it this morning."

Greco was adamant. "He just said he found out from Riordan."

Hank saw fit to intervene. "Pete was in the middle of telling me about Ferris when Riordan called."

Greco suspected that Pete gave up the information only because he knew it was about to come out, but didn't verbalize the thought. "Chief, did you know about this?"

"Yes. Pete told me about it himself, and I intend to address the issue when time allows. I need him on this case, but I made it clear that he stays away from Ferris. Now, let's hear about this guy."

Greco was disturbed by McClure's lenient attitude, but he decided to drop the issue for now. He shot Webster a withering look as Rowan continued.

"Okay, so we know Wainwright and Ferris were having an affair. Pete also told me about this Valentine's card that turned up in the search of the Wainwright home. They found it in the glove box of her car. It was made out to 'Jack' and signed 'Nicki', nothing else except for whatever was printed on it by the manufacturer."

"She didn't get a chance to give it to him? So she didn't see Ferris on Valentine's Day, Tuesday. And she was last seen that morning." Greco added to his roughly sketched timeline.

"Right, she never gave it to him, but at the very least it's further evidence of their relationship. As I started to say, I went to the Ferris residence to have a talk with him. He readily admitted that he knew Nicole Wainwright, and that they had been romantically involved. He said he had last seen her on Saturday, the eleventh, when they had a conversation in the parking lot of Strong's Gym. According to Ferris, she'd been at his place only once, to get a look at the house he'd built and appraise its value. He was cooperative, but seemed really nervous, edgy. When I requested that he come in and provide more detail, he agreed. Eventually, his story changed quite a bit."

Hank's delivery lent a suggestive tone to his last statement, and Pete was anxious to know exactly what Jack had said. He hadn't seen his friend, nor had he been involved in the interrogation, on orders from McClure. The Chief brought an end to Rowan's dramatic pause.

"What was the change in his statement, Hank?"

"He originally told me that the affair had been going on for about a month, since he'd done some work at the Wainwright house. Apparently, he did the painting while she hung around and flirted with him. They continued to meet after the job was finished, but he claimed they had never closed the deal — never had sex. Like I told you, he said she'd only been to his place the one time, and that was more of a business thing.

"Later, he admitted that things had gotten more serious than what he first described to me. He said that he met her outside of Strong's gym on Saturday, February 4th, and by then things were already getting serious. She picked him up in the Supervisor's Hummer, that yellow one, and they wound up at his house. They spent the entire day there and, according to him, became intimate for the first time. That evening she drove him back to the gym and dropped him off at his car, and supposedly they both went home from there. Ferris says he last saw her at the same gym this past

Saturday, the 11th, and they talked for a while but didn't leave together. Says he hasn't seen her since."

Greco stopped his notation and sat back in his chair.

"So, he's in here answering questions without a lawyer? Did you make him aware that he had the right to counsel?"

"Yeah, of course. A little while ago he made a call to Ray Battaglia's office. Battaglia wasn't in, but they said he would be here as soon as possible. I stopped the interview immediately, and we're still waiting for him to show up."

The D.A. wanted assurance that Ferris' civil rights hadn't been violated. "What made him change his story? You just wore him down?"

"At one point, an hour or so after we got here, I reviewed the facts for him, showed him how things looked. Missing woman, he'd been involved with her, a card addressed to him found in her car, cell phone records that would show that they communicated frequently, all of it."

"I'm a little nervous about Ferris answering questions for so long without representation. Good job, though, sounds like you went by the book. Interesting that Ferris retained a heavy hitter like Battaglia. Are you planning to resume when he gets here?"

"Maybe. I definitely want to keep him here a while longer. We need a warrant to search this guy's home before he has a chance to clean anything up. I think he finally told me about the day they spent at his place because he knows we might find evidence that proves she was there recently."

Greco closed his book with a loud snap and looked at McClure.

"I'm on it. Under the circumstances, Ferris' admissions should be enough to justify a quick warrant from any reasonable judge."

McClure saw the disturbed look on Pete's face. "Webster, anything you want to add? I know it's tough, this guy being your friend and all."

Pete shrugged. "I just want the truth, same as you. But since you ask, I'd like to remind everyone to remain open minded here. Focus on Jack, but continue to pursue other leads. Am I the only one in this room who thinks James Wainwright is holding something back? That he doesn't show the concern you might expect from the husband of a missing woman?"

McClure seemed to discount Pete's concerns.

"Pete, he's still the Town Supervisor and he still has a business to run, he can't be here every minute waiting for us to tell him something new."

"No, but he could be out there looking for his wife, or at least show up at the site while we search for her body."

For the first time, Pete had given voice to the notion that a woman who had been missing for two or three days might well be dead. McClure's stance was unaffected.

"They had some important vote tonight, that's why the media and the crowd were out front. I guess he had to be there."

Greco was eager to obtain the warrant that would permit a search of the Ferris property. As he stood to leave there was a rap on the door, and as it opened a female officer timidly looked in without entering. She was rather cute, even without any trace of makeup, and her sandy hair was cropped into a very short style.

"Sorry to interrupt, Chief, I have something for Detective Webster."

"Don't apologize, officer, this room could use a pretty face." McClure cringed inwardly, realizing that his remark was blatantly sexist, and was relieved when Webster bailed him out.

"Marti, come on in."

As she approached, he saw that her left arm was wrapped in an elastic bandage, and was supported by a sling that matched the dark blue of her uniform.

"What happened to your arm?"

Officer Lucas frowned, and her cheeks turned pink with embarrassment.

"Oh, nothing serious. I answered a vandalism call at the high school, and caught up with one of the kids. He was trying to pull away, and we both went down, and something popped in my elbow. The kid got away, and I got two weeks of light duty."

"Hm. Well, at least you got a good look at him, right? You're bound to run into him again. So, what's up?"

Marti's good hand held a manila folder, which she handed to Webster. "I was going through the incoming faxes, and I came across this one from the Carthage, Iowa P.D. Your name's on the cover sheet, and — well, I thought you might not realize it was there. It looks like something you should see."

Pete accepted the folder and placed it on the table, planning to look at the contents after the meeting had ended, but Marti stood fast as if waiting for his reaction. Sensing that everyone in the room was now mildly curious, Pete opened the folder and slid the cover sheet aside. The second sheet was an enlarged image of a driver's license, and he turned it ninety degrees to get a better look.

"Son of a bitch." He picked up the page and continued to study it.

Marti leaned closer, her voice barely more than a whisper. "Is that who I think it is?"

Pete didn't look up at her, his gaze remained on the faxed page as he said "Thanks, Marti. Would you excuse us, please? Dave, don't go anywhere yet."

Without a word, Officer Lucas straightened up and obediently turned to leave, closing the door softly behind her. When she had gone, Rowan took the fax from Pete and stared at it, and Greco moved behind him to get a look.

"What the hell is this?"

CHAPTER 50

BRENDA JACKSON WALKED to the lectern and carefully placed a few pages of notes beneath the task light. She was dressed in a beige business suit, perfectly tailored as always, her appearance exuding a confidence that was far from what she actually felt. She knew that one of the men in this room could be her anonymous tormentor, or he could be stationed somewhere near her home at that moment, waiting for his instructions to be determined by her actions.

Brenda wondered if those seated nearby noticed how her hands trembled as she put on her reading glasses, and hoped to God that her voice would not join in the betrayal.

"On behalf of the planning board, I would like to thank the council for taking the time to hear our final recommendation on the New Century application." She still had managed to make only the briefest eye contact with the council members, and continued to look down at her notes as she began her remarks.

"Five weeks ago, our board met with this council and with representatives of New Century to discuss their application for rezoning, and for the subsequent construction of a housing development to be called Cedar Ridge. At that time the planning board raised serious concerns on several fronts, some of them the same concerns that we heard earlier tonight from members of this community. I'd like to review the action items that were assigned to the applicants at that first meeting, and New Century's response to those items.

"The board contended that questions of environmental impact had not been adequately studied, and that forms submitted were incomplete and did not outline an acceptable plan. New Century agreed to perform a second series of soil tests and to submit a revised plan to our engineering consultants.

"The board specifically questioned the drainage model, and pointed out that additional replacement wetlands were required by state law. Again, New Century agreed to address these shortcomings in a revised plan."

Janice Morgan had crept forward to place a cup of water on the lectern, and Brenda paused to take a sip before continuing. She was halfway home. She had only to add a few remarks about the satisfactory response from New Century, a lukewarm recommendation of approval, and afterwards a brief explanation of her change of heart for the other planners. Gripping the sides of the lectern, she summoned all her strength and forged ahead.

"A week ago the board received the second iteration of the Cedar Ridge engineering documents, and a second submission of the required forms." Another pause, a second sip of water, and Brenda knew that every set of eyes in the room was trained on her. In that moment she knew what must be done.

"Having studied the revised plans, this board and our consultants are shocked at New Century's arrogant and cavalier attitude in this process. The newly submitted plans fail to adequately address any of the concerns we have expressed, the same concerns you heard from our citizens during the public session."

Brenda's voice was firm now, and she raised the volume to an inspirational level.

"Our engineers found only minimal changes to the plan, so slight that they constitute a revision in name only. Most of the forms we received are nearly identical to the originals, the only difference being the recorded date of submission. This conduct by an applicant is unheard of, and displays a curious air of entitlement and lack of respect not only for this board, but for our entire community."

There were whispers of approval among the crowd, and a few hoots of encouragement. A shocked Wainwright rapped his gavel to quiet things down, but wasn't sure how else to react. As he looked to Kaplan for help, Jackson was just hitting her stride.

"Putting aside for a moment the logistics of the New Century proposal, there are other underlying questions to be answered. After making campaign promises to institute a moratorium on further development, why would members of this council, and more specifically the Town Supervisor, strongly support this project so soon after their election? Why are we told that the only way to fund the replacement of an antiquated bridge and straighten the road leading into it is to include the project with the Cedar Ridge proposal? Lives are being lost there, and if the town cannot afford to fix it, we should be appealing to the county and the state to help us. That's what elected officials do!"

Now it was the council members who avoided all eye contact, and the applause was allowed without a warning report from the gavel.

"Thank you, Mrs. Jackson. The council will take — "

"Mr. Supervisor, I have something more to say! On a personal note —"

Now the gavel interrupted her statement as Wainwright made a desperate attempt to control the damage. "Mrs. Jackson, you are here to speak on behalf of the planning board, your personal opinion should have been heard in the public comment session."

Anna Fronczak interjected. "Mr. Supervisor, I, for one, would like to hear her out."

Other council members agreed, and Wainwright felt the situation slip from his control.

"The council will hear your remarks, Mrs. Jackson." Then, through gritted teeth, "Please continue."

"On a personal note, I would add this. If you insist on entertaining thoughts of further development in Grove Park, I urge you to find new partners. I question the integrity and ethics of New Century Limited, and have personally been a victim of intimidation tactics that were meant to secure my public approval of this project."

Gasps of surprise and groans of sympathy and outrage could be heard.

"Just recently, threats were made against my family. To my horror, I was subjected to a demonstration of just how easily a child can be taken from an unsuspecting parent."

Al Kaplan had been silent, a fact that was not lost on Wainwright, but now he shouted his objection as if there were no microphone in front of him.

"Mrs. Jackson, this is not the proper forum for any such allegations! In fact, your remarks could be construed as slanderous. Have you reported these threats to the police?"

"It happened, Mr. Kaplan, and the person responsible made it clear that Cedar Ridge was the reason. To be honest with you, it worked. I came here tonight prepared to change my recommendation in order to protect my children." Tears rolled down her cheeks, but Brenda Jackson remained defiant. "It was only when I began to speak that I found the courage to say what was on my mind. This board emphatically recommends that the application be denied."

Wainwright had heard more than enough.

"Mrs. Jackson, the council thanks you for your candor. I suggest you take up this matter with the proper authorities as soon as possible."

Still shaking with emotion, Jackson collected her papers and turned away from the microphone to return to her seat. Wainwright hesitated, trying to think of some way to recover from her attack, and then made what he felt was a command decision from the burning decks. Without asking for approval from the other council members, he pointed to Victor Harmon.

"I call on Victor Harmon, representing the New Century Corporation. Mr. Harmon, before this council makes a decision on the Cedar Ridge proposal, would you like to make a statement?"

Make it good, Harmon, he thought to himself, as council members looked at each other but made no objection.

Harmon stood, buttoning the coat of his Armani suit as he did so, and turned to face the transfixed onlookers.

"Yes, Mr. Wainwright, thank you," he began smoothly, hiding his discomfort behind a dazzling smile. He spoke without the benefit of electronic amplification. "On behalf of New Century Limited, I would like to assure you that our organization had absolutely nothing to do with the incident Mrs. Jackson has described, nor would we ever condone such actions by our supporters in the community of Grove Park. I'm sorry she has had to experience such a traumatic event, and I hope the authorities find the person or persons responsible."

Turning back to the six who would vote, he continued in his most earnest manner. "I urge the town council to approve our application for rezoning and construction, so that we can become partners in creating a development that will be the pride of the community and a testament to the wisdom of managed growth." He seated himself rather stiffly, doubtful that his words would be sufficient to regain the momentum they needed for a positive result.

Wainwright had hoped for something more galvanizing, but under the circumstances, Harmon's brief declaration would have to do. The council had committed to making a decision at this meeting, and there would be no opportunity for a private discussion among the council members before the vote.

Councilmen Howard McGregor and Gerald Fremont had never voiced a strong opinion for or against Cedar Ridge, and had nothing to gain from approval. Realizing that there may be something to gain politically by distancing himself from the project, McGregor leaned towards his mike and made a strong move.

"Mr. Supervisor, over the course of the last four or five weeks we have studied this matter in great detail, as has the town planning board. I believe we have all the input we require to make our decision, and I call for an immediate vote on this matter."

Fremont immediately seconded the motion.

Wainwright was sure that there would be resistance to the motion.

"Opposed?"

Once again he had overestimated his allies, and the question was met with silence. There was nothing to do but act on the motion, and he banged his gavel once, with authority.

"Very well. You have in front of you document number 27290, requesting rezoning of the tract described therein from agricultural to residential, applicant New Century Ltd. All in favor?"

Wainwright raised a hand, and heard the lone "ay" from Al Kaplan.

He felt his blood pressure rise, and the birthmark on his forehead became more noticeable. If rezoning was denied, the Cedar Ridge project was dead in the water.

"Opposed?"

"Opposed." Four voices spoke in unison.

Cheers and applause burst from the spectators, many of who were now standing to shake hands or high-five. The Supervisor felt lightheaded, out of body, but had the presence of mind to verify the results. He hammered the gavel loudly until order had been restored.

"I'll now poll the council. Mr. Kaplan?"

"Approve."

"Mr. Brady?"

"Opposed."

"Fronczak?"

"Opposed."

And so it went, until the vote was verified. The application was denied by a vote of four to two. Wainwright could do nothing more, and there were other urgent matters to attend to.

"Ladies and gentlemen, please forgive me, I must now leave to attend to a personal matter." He was well aware that his wife's disappearance was common knowledge, and no one could blame him for abandoning the meeting. "Mr. Kaplan will take charge of the formal conclusion of the meeting."

He stood and left the table, unsure of where he was headed.

CHAPTER 51

PETE STUDIED THE facial expressions of Dave Greco and Hank Rowan as they took a close look at the faxed driver's license.

"Does this guy look familiar? Picture him about twenty-five or thirty years older."

Rowan's eyes were suddenly wide with recognition.

"Wainwright?"

"Sure looks like him, doesn't it?"

"This guy's name is James Wright" Greco thought aloud as the combination of familiar features and the name hit home.

Finally, even McClure left his chair to get a look at the page.

"Pete, what's this all about?"

"I'm not sure yet, but I'll tell you what I know so far. Remember when you first told me that Nicole Wainwright was missing? I was in a meeting with a woman named Sally Raines."

McClure had an excellent memory for details, and often displayed it to prove that he hadn't lost anything over the years.

"You said she was the wife of the guy you partnered with on the Buffalo force."

"Right. Steve Hartman, he's a P.I. now. He and Sally are divorced."

"Good looking woman." Once again McClure regretted that his response had been somewhat unprofessional, but the others smiled as Pete nodded a firm agreement.

"That she is. I hadn't seen either one of them in years, but Sally called me because she was worried about Steve. He missed their son's birthday party after promising to be there, and she can't find anyone who has seen him in the past six weeks."

The others had returned to their seats, and Greco resumed his note taking as Pete continued.

"Steve last called Sally from Iowa, a town named Carthage, where he had gone as part of a background check. He didn't say who he was working for or who the subject was, just the name of the town. As a favor to Sally, I agreed to look into it."

McClure stared at his detective, wondering what else he didn't know about Pete's recent activities.

"I called the Carthage P.D., and asked if Steve had been there recently looking for information. Turns out, the Chief of Police there remembered him stopping in to ask questions about a former resident. He said Steve had left some kind of documentation there, and he thought it might be still lying around the office somewhere. He said if he found it, he'd have a copy faxed to me. That's what you're looking at."

McClure was finally able to process the implications of Pete's story.

"So you think this James Wright that your buddy was investigating is our James Wainwright?"

"Well, I didn't until I saw this. I mean, who would make the leap from James Wright to James Wainwright without a solid reason? But that sure looks like him."

Rowan picked up the fax for another look. "Same hair, same face, and that birth mark on his forehead. Of course, we can't be sure, but it's very possible."

Greco wanted to know if Pete had developed a theory that he hadn't yet shared. "Let's say we make the leap, that Wright and Wainwright are the same person. What's the significance of that?"

Pete had exercised restraint, but felt that it was time to make his point.

"It means someone was checking into James Wainwright's past, and the person that was hired to do the investigation hasn't been seen for six weeks. And now, Mrs. Wainwright is missing."

Rowan was right with him.

"She could have hired the P.I."

"Exactly." Pete hated to drop another previously undisclosed detail to the group, but it had to be done. "And there's something else. Sally and I went to Steve's office to see if we could find out anything about who might have hired him. The place had been broken into and trashed. It didn't strike me as a random break-in by crack heads, it looked like someone else had been there looking for something. I shared that with the Glenwood P.D. when I made the reach-out call."

Greco had never been involved in a case even remotely as intriguing as this one, and was still trying to get his arms around it. "Detective Webster, your friends seem to be all over this thing. How do you explain that?" His delivery was almost accusatory.

"I can't explain it, Dave. I know how it looks, now that we know these events are related and two of the players are friends of mine, but it's all a mystery to me just as it is for you."

Greco appeared to accept that, at least for the time being.

"Well, I have to move on that search warrant." He looked to McClure. "What's the plan?"

"I want Hank to stay with the Ferris investigation, and find out everything he can. Pete, you stay with the Wainwright lead, find out if he used to be James Wright from Iowa. See if you can find out what Hartman was looking for."

Greco was already at the door, and stopped with his hand on the knob.

"Chief, I recommend calling the Sheriff on this. You're going to need more resources, and the county can provide that,"

McClure was already resigned to the fact, but wanted to remain in control as long as possible.

"I have to make some kind of statement to the media. I'm sure I'll be speaking with the Sheriff shortly after that. Let me know when the warrant is in hand, and I'll request the county forensic team again."

A few minutes later McClure was the only one in the room, left to ponder the case and wonder where it might lead.

CHAPTER 52

A THROATY ROAR SOUNDED from the Hummer's dual exhaust, imparting a satisfying sense of power as James Wainwright hit the open road on his way out of the village, with no specific destination in mind. He had planned to check in with McClure right after the council vote to find out what was being done to find Nicki, but in the wake of the shocking result he needed solitude to think things through. He had fled without even speaking to Victor Harmon, who was talking to a couple of strangers in dark suits when Wainwright had last seen him.

He ignored the insistent ring of his cell as long as possible, guessing that it would be Harmon calling to berate or perhaps threaten him, but it wasn't Wainwright's style to avoid confrontation. Picking it up to look at the incoming i.d., he was startled to learn that the caller was not Harmon, but his boss.

"Hey, Mr. Wainwright! Is the meeting over?"

Amazingly, Paulie Gotts was not yet aware of the bad news.

"Mr. Gotts. Yes, the meeting ended about ten minutes ago."

"Where the hell is Victor? He didn't even call me. It passed, right?"

"Gotts, I can barely hear you, are you at a casino?" There was no mistaking the din of hundreds of slot machines in the background, and Wainwright took the opportunity to deflect Gotts' question with one of his own.

"Yeah, I'm just cashing out. I been on a hell of a hot streak, man. Unbelievable, I never rolled 'em like that before, never! Must be my lucky night." Gotts sounded more than a little drunk, and then for a moment the signal was lost.

"Gotts, can you hear me?"

There was silence, and then something from Gotts that was too garbled to be understood.

"Hello, Gotts, are you there?"

"..ckin' phone. Meet me ... ed lant ....280. ight?"

"Meet you at the Red Lantern, is that what you said?"

There was nothing further, and Wainwright was forced to make a series of assumptions. For some reason Harmon hadn't yet been in touch with his boss, and Gotts assumed that the vote had gone well. He was telling Wainwright to meet him at his hotel room, presumably for the payoff, and Wainwright was fairly certain that Gotts had mentioned the Red Lantern Motor Inn which was located about halfway between Grove Park and the Arrowhead Casino.

Wainwright surmised that Gotts had chosen the outdated Red Lantern for its convenient location, in spite of the decided lack of amenities. Gotts would be able to conduct their wrap-up meeting without running the risk of being seen, and possibly remembered, in Grove Park. Any local would have told him that the Lantern was a base of operations for transient drug dealers and hookers, especially since the casino had opened, but Gotts probably felt comfortable there. He was no stranger to the seedy side of life.

The Inn was about five miles away on Route 19 in the direction Wainwright was headed, and the casino ten miles further. Wainwright knew he would be there before Gotts arrived.

*

Ten minutes later he had backed the Hummer into a spot in a shadowy corner of the Red Lantern parking lot, facing the front of the motel. There was a lower level consisting of about a dozen rooms, with a small lobby in the center. Iron stairways at each end led to the balcony that fronted a second tier of rooms, each with a molded plastic chair next to the door. Not surprisingly, no one was taking the opportunity to sit outside and enjoy the view of the traffic whizzing past on route 19.

It was fully dark, and a thick layer of low-hanging clouds prevented the moon from shedding any light onto the landscape. Gotts had mentioned room 280, which would be one of the last rooms on the right side of the upper tier. Each room had an entrance door that faced the lot, allowing occupants, as well as visitors, to come and go without passing through the lobby. All things considered, this was a good place to rendezvous without attracting unwanted attention, as long as the other guests were behaving.

It was easy to spot Paulie Gotts as he pulled into the parking lot of the Red Lantern with the slow, deliberate actions of a driver under the influence. He drove right past the Hummer without a glance, and pulled into a parking space at the end of the row, next to a large moving van. Wainwright exited the Hummer and gently pushed the door closed. He walked along the row and approached the black SUV from the rear with all the stealth he could manage, and arrived just as Gotts' was struggling to extract his bulky frame from the rented Navigator.

"Hey, you're here!" Gotts had never before been so amiable in Wainwright's presence, the alcohol having temporarily erased his tough guy demeanor. His brow was lifted in an almost comical effort to raise his droopy eyelids, as he tried to focus on the item Wainwright was holding across his body. Recognizing the nine iron, his squat face broke out into a grin of amusement.

"Oh, I see you brought my little present, huh? Iss a little too dark to play golf though, ain't it?" He let out a throaty chuckle that turned into a violent cough and caused him to lean against the car for support. "Well, I already told you, you're welcome. I told you we'd help you out. Consider it a bonus." Gotts stopped short of mentioning that he had also recovered most of the cash that Goren had extorted from Wainwright, since he had no intention of returning it.

"And what about Brenda Jackson? That was you, helping me out again?"

Gotts' shrugged and cocked his head to the side, shrugging off any accolades for something that came so easily to him.

"Iss what I do."

Wainwright took a glance around the shadowy parking lot, confirming that no one else was around. The rental van's bulk obstructed any view of them from all but the last few rooms, and he returned his attention to Gotts.

"And what do you know about my wife's disappearance?"

Gotts put his hands to his chest in the manner of the wrongly accused.

"Hey, I had nothing to do with that, Wainwright. Why the hell would you even ask me that?"

Wainwright's contempt for this man was building toward rage, but in his inebriated condition Gotts failed to notice.

"Look, I know you got a lot on you're plate right now, but take it easy." Once again he was leaning back into the car for support. "Come in and have a drink. As soon as I hear from Victor we'll settle up. Come on." Gotts pushed off from the fender and turned away, waving for Wainwright to follow him.

In an instant the carefully crafted persona of James Wainwright, twenty-five years in the making, melted away and was replaced by that of James Wright. Gripping the leather-wrapped shaft tightly with both hands, he lifted the club to strike and hesitated for a second, drinking in the sheer thrill of the moment. As Gotts turned to say something more the club swung downward in a vicious arc, making a sound like the cracking of a thick eggshell as the hosel buried itself in his forehead. He fell onto his back, his widened eyes glazing over as his body twitched a strange dance and then was still.

Wainwright stood over the body, breathing hard with the adrenaline rush. As rational thought returned, he took a look around and felt confident that no one had been watching. Despite the situation, he felt strangely calm as he bent down to check the dead man's pockets.

There was a large roll of bills in one, probably ten grand if the hundreds on the outer layers continued to the center. The other pocket held only a player's rewards card from the casino, which was quickly wiped off and tucked back in. Wainwright regretted not wearing gloves as he opened Gotts' wallet and emptied it, before wiping it clean with his tie and tossing it under the Navigator. A check of the vehicle's interior came up empty, but Wainwright was undaunted.

He pried the room key from Gotts' clenched fist, and then dragged the body a few feet and rolled it until it was under the box of the rental truck. Hopefully it wouldn't be discovered until morning, when some poor sucker would have his relocation delayed, in return for a story that he would tell for years.

Driven by greed, Wainwright decided to push his luck by taking a look at room 280, on the chance that there might be a briefcase filled with payoff cash inside. As he stepped around the cab of the truck, he heard a door open and laughter echoed through the parking lot. A young couple was leaving their room on the lower level, and Wainwright was relieved to see them walk towards a car on the opposite side. He watched the car until it was out of sight, and then walked boldly to the stairway and made his way up. Room 280 was the second door from the end, and his hands trembled with excitement rather than fear as he turned the key.

Wainwright flicked the light switch, and a rather dim bedside lamp revealed a shabbily furnished room that smelled of mildew. There was a queen-size bed covered with a faded maroon spread, a small dresser scarred with burn marks from countless untended cigarettes, and a nightstand.

An overnight bag lay open on the bed, and Wainwright rifled through it to find only a change of clothing and toiletries. Using a thin washcloth as a glove, he opened and closed every drawer in the room, all of which were empty except for a few dead roaches. It was hard to believe that Gotts had intended to spend the night here. No wonder he had gotten shitfaced before returning.

Within a few minutes Wainwright had determined that there was no bundle of cash in the room. Cursing the dead man, he wiped off the interior doorknob and took a look outside before leaving. As he made his way back to ground level, a list of tasks was forming in his head: Get on the road, toss the murder weapon and room key where they won't be found — get safely home, clean up, and head to the police station to resume his role as the pathetic worried husband. Deal with Harmon, who would undoubtedly be looking for him.

Reaching the safety of the dark parking lot, Wainwright fully realized how much more complicated his situation had become. This time, however, he had been the proactive party. He was controlling his own destiny again, and it felt good.

CHAPTER 53

"THIS IS A great house, Sal. I can see you still have a knack for decorating."

The brick-front ranch with its updated open floor plan, set in a development of a hundred or so similar homes, was much smaller than the home that the Hartmans had once owned. Pete now knew that Sally had purchased it three years earlier as a "handyman's special", and had carefully restored it with help from her father.

She appreciated Pete's compliment and knew that it was sincere, but Sally's perception was that he was nervously searching for something to kick-start a conversation. She thought that his feelings for her were genuine, but some lingering guilt was still making him uncomfortable. Sally empathized, realizing that it would take time for him to come to terms with that. She walked up to him, so close that there was body contact, and looked into his eyes as if she could read his thoughts.

"Thanks, Pete. I'm glad you're here." He pulled her into him and they kissed, following with a long, clinging embrace that seemed to verify their emotional attachment.

Sally took Pete's hand and led them into the dining room, stopping along the way to mute the television. Two coffee cups and a carafe were already on the table, and as she poured Sally addressed the second reason for Pete's visit.

"So, you said you had a lot to tell me." Sally sipped her black coffee as Pete added cream and sugar to his, stirring carefully as he considered the best way to begin.

"When we were interrupted at the station the Chief was pretty — abrupt".

She arched her eyebrows at the under-statement. "Not to mention goddamned rude."

"Yes. He wanted me to apologize for him. He was under a lot of pressure at the time, I guess by now you know what he wanted to talk to me about."

Just then Pete heard the front door open and slam closed, and a boy of about ten or eleven ran into the room, stopping short at the sight of the stranger seated in their dining room. His dark hair and eyes were all Sally, but Pete could also see Steve reflected in his son's features. Strange how some kids' faces could remind you of either parent, depending on the moment, he thought.

"Jonathan, this is Detective Webster, an old friend. He used to work with your dad."

Pete initiated a handshake as he was introduced.

"Nice to meet you, Jonathan. Your dad and I used to share a patrol car, we were partners."

A look of renewed hope lit up the young man's face.

"Do you know where my dad is?"

"No, I don't son, I'm sorry. Not yet. But I'm going to try and find out, okay?"

"Oh. Yeah, okay." He was crestfallen, and Sally left her chair to provide a comforting hug.

"Jon, why don't you play outside for a while, I need to speak to Detective Webster in private. Alright, sweetie?"

Jonathan appeared eager to break away from the mothering that was bordering on embarrassment for him. "I'm going back to Liam's, he just got a new Hoverboard!"

"Okay honey, be back in about an hour, or call me -— and be careful!" She returned to her seat and encouraged Pete to continue.

"So, you apologized for the Police Chief's behavior, and I accept. Go on." Her smile conveyed a certain satisfaction, and amusement, that the older cop was somewhat ashamed of his treatment of her.

"I was saying that by now you can guess what Chief McClure wanted to see me about." She nodded knowingly.

"The Supervisor's wife. Another missing person, only this one hit a little closer to home, right?"

"Not for me, Sally. Steve's case is just as important to me, but it was out of our jurisdiction."

Sally waved a hand as if to dismiss Pete's interpretation of her comment. "I understand that Pete, I do. I'm grateful for everything you've done."

"Well, it turns out that I've been assigned to look into Steve's disappearance after all. We've found a connection between the two cases."

"Oh my god Pete, you're kidding! They knew each other?"

Sally left her chair to grab her purse from a nearby sideboard and rummaged through it, pulling out a cigarette case and lighter. "I don't usually smoke in the house, but this is making me nervous."

Pete waited as she lit up and took a deep inhale, as if the smoke would allow her to concentrate.

"Here's what I can tell you. Before Nicki Wainwright disappeared, someone hired Steve to check into her husband's background. That's what he was doing when he called you from Iowa."

"The Supervisor has a sordid past?"

"We don't know much about his past, that's part of what I'm looking into. I can't say much more than that."

"She might have hired Steve to get information about her husband, and now she and Steve are both missing. That can't be a coincidence, Pete."

Although he was impressed by Sally's perception, Pete didn't want to encourage her any further.

"Sally, rule one is 'don't assume anything until you can prove it', so let's not jump to conclusions. We're going to get to the bottom of this, that's why I'm catching a flight to Carthage when I leave here. Well, three flights, actually."

"It takes three flights to get to Carthage?"

"And a rental car."

They traded smiles, and Sally covered his hand with hers.

"I wish I could go with you."

"I'd welcome the company, believe me. You stay here and take care of your son, and I'll be back in a couple of days. We'll stay in touch with each other, right?"

They rose and wrapped their arms around each other to say goodbye when Sally unexpectedly stepped back. She was looking past Pete into the living room, where something on the television screen had caught her attention.

"What did that say?" She hurried over to restore the sound as the camera zoomed in on News Five reporter Jennifer Banks.

"A source close to the investigation tells me that Ferris and Nicole Wainwright were romantically involved and that he is considered to be a person of interest. Police have questioned Ferris, and I'm told that a warrant has been issued to allow a search of his home."

Pete was incredulous. "How the hell did she know that?"

"Didn't you hear? 'A source close to the investigation'. Funny, my source didn't even mention that guy." She stood hands on hips, in mock exasperation.

"I'm sorry Sally, I just can't share everything about the Wainwright side of things. Jack Ferris is a friend of mine, I've already taken crap for not bringing his name up sooner. I have to be careful what I say, even with you."

She understood completely, and once again was warmed by Pete's regard for her feelings.

"I should know that, right? After all, I was married to a cop. Besides, I think I can get better information from Jennifer Banks."

Pete chuckled at her jab. "It looks that way, doesn't it? Just remember, you can't believe everything they say on television."

"Is she right about your friend? Was he 'romantically involved' with the missing woman?"

"Yeah, she was right about that. Sally, I'd better go, I don't know how busy the airport will be."

"Be careful, Peter. And remember to say hi to Hannibal for me."

CHAPTER 54

HAVING CONFERRED WITH his newest client for well over an hour, Ray Battaglia left the interview room to find the detective who had been responsible for questioning Jack Ferris.

Battaglia had a richly deserved reputation as a commanding presence in the courtroom, and his intention was to bring that same aura to the headquarters of this small-town police force. Even at the age of 66, he was an impressive figure; close to six feet tall, tan and fit, with a full head of fashionably styled gray hair. He felt underdressed in his faded jeans and white button-down shirt, with open collar and sleeves rolled back, but if nothing else it underlined the urgency of his appearance.

Battaglia had been on his way to a ski vacation in the central part of the state when he received the call from his office. The schizoid weather had made a mess of the local ski season, and conditions were much better away from Lake Erie. He knew that Jane, his trusted personal assistant of fifteen years, would not have bothered him with a trivial matter. When she described Jack's situation Battaglia turned around at the first available Thruway exit, instructing Jane to relay the message that he would take the case and for Jack to say nothing further until he arrived.

Rowan let the big-shot lawyer stew for a good while before he came out to begin their meeting. He was on the phone with county forensics for about ten minutes, and spent another fifteen sipping coffee in a back room while Battaglia paced back and forth impatiently. Hank didn't plan to let this guy intimidate him, but he would have felt better with someone like Pete Webster backing him up. He rinsed his coffee cup carefully, and went out to meet the opposition.

"Detective, you've held my client here all day and questioned him extensively without providing him the benefit of counsel. How the hell do you explain that?" As expected, the wait had made Battaglia prickly.

"Nice to meet you, Mr. Battaglia, I'm Rowan. You've been in there with your client for quite a while, so I'm sure he told you that he came in voluntarily to provide whatever help he could in locating Mrs. Wainwright. He was free to leave at any time, and still is. When he expressed to me that he wanted to call his attorney before going any further, we ended the interview."

"I'll be discussing that further with the D.A., and with a judge at the appropriate time. Right now there are some things that Mr. Ferris would like to tell you, in light of present circumstances."

Battaglia was now aware that a warrant had been obtained to allow a search of Jack's home, and the detective guessed that this unsolicited offer of further information could be related to evidence that would turn up.

"Something that slipped his mind earlier?" Hank added just a touch of sarcasm to his tone, enough to needle but not enough to be overly adversarial.

"He wanted to consult with me before getting into all the details. I wish he'd thought of that earlier, but so be it."

They returned to the room where Jack was waiting. He was drained as a result of hours of alternately answering questions and sitting idly in an otherwise empty room, but he appeared to be much more relaxed than he had been earlier. Evidently Battaglia's presence had lessened his fear of the situation, possibly because he had been encouraged to reveal something that would make him less of a suspect.

"Mr. Ferris, I understand you have something more to say now that Mr. Battaglia is present. As I advised you earlier, your statement is being recorded."

Jack glanced at the video camera mounted in a corner of the ceiling, and then to his lawyer for a final approval before speaking. At the same time, Rowan was offering silent thanks that their conversation at Ferris' home, with several mentions of his friendship with Pete Webster, was not available on tape.

"It's about something that Nicki told me the first time we were — opening up to each other."

"Okay. And what was it that she told you?"

"We were getting to know each other, and at one point Nicki started talking about her husband. We had kind of avoided the subject up until then, but she wanted to tell me about him. I think she had been keeping it to herself, and just wanted to tell someone."

Jack paused, as if he was anticipating some interest from Rowan.

"Go on" was Hank's only response. He hadn't moved to take any notes.

"She told me about this time when he had to stay overnight in the hospital because of kidney stones, or something like that. I guess he's a pretty secretive guy, even with his wife, and she wasn't even allowed to go into his home office. He always kept the door locked.

"So that night when she was alone in the house, she had a chance to go in there and look around. He had a wall safe, and it was left open. Nicki said she found some things in there that made her nervous, I mean it scared her for some reason."

Now Hank leaned forward slightly, leaning on the table with hands folded. "Well, did Mrs. Wainwright tell you what was in the safe?"

"A lot of cash, and some old jewelry. It didn't sound too mysterious to me, except for one item. It was an old out of state driver's license. From somewhere in the Midwest, I think. It was her husband's picture on the license, but the name was different. It said James Wright, not Wainwright."

Ferris and Battaglia had been counting on Rowan to show more interest in Jack's new information. "So cash and jewelry, and you're sure she didn't say anything else about the contents of that safe, outside of the driver's license?"

"I'm sure, but there was something else. Nicki said she had hired a private investigator to look into it. Then another time, I think it had been like a month, she told me she still hadn't heard from the guy, he wasn't even returning her calls."

"Did she tell you his name?"

"I'm pretty sure his name was Hartman. But then last week she had decided to forget the investigator and just come right out and ask her husband about it. Confront him, was the way she put it. I know Nicki was afraid to tell him she'd been snooping around, but she wanted some answers. She was going to bring it up that night."

"What night was that?" Rowan was writing now.

"It was a Saturday, the 4th."

"Mr. Ferris, did you speak to her after that conversation, to find out how things had gone?"

Ferris sat back in his chair, turning up both palms.

"We spoke this past Saturday at the gym and outside in the parking lot, but not about that. I wish I would have brought it up. I haven't seen her or heard from her since then."

Battaglia had been sure that Jack's revelation would be deemed important, but the detective seemed almost bored.

"Detective, I get the impression that you already knew about this."

Rowan shrugged, never one to tip his hand. "I'd say it's corroboration, it may help confirm some things we have from other sources." He looked at Ferris.

"Was it Iowa?"

Jack's eyes widened with sudden recollection.

"Iowa, right! It was an Iowa driver's license with the name James Wright. How did you know?"

"Is there anything else you remember that might be useful? About what was said that night, or anything else at all?"

Jack pursed his lips thoughtfully, slowly shaking his head.

"No, nothing else I can think of."

Rowan addressed the lawyer.

"As long as we're here, I have something I'd like to ask about. Do you have any objection?"

Battaglia was wary. "Ask your question, and I'll decide whether it's in my client's interests to answer. He's already cooperated quite fully."

Hank had been looking forward to this moment since they had entered the room.

"Mr. Ferris, you've been doing some work inside your house, is that right?"

"I guess you could say that. I built the house myself, it just isn't quite finished yet."

"I noticed that some of the flooring is unfinished."

Jack was always eager to talk about the house he had built. "Yeah, it took me awhile to get the material I wanted. It's butterscotch oak. The real thing, tongue and groove, not that laminate crap that you snap together."

Battaglia was losing patience. "Detective Rowan, I like the DIY channel as much as the next guy, but where is this going?"

Rowan kept his eyes firmly locked on Ferris, choosing not to acknowledge the interruption.

"We found some flooring pieces outside the house, thrown into a barrel with some other scraps."

"Yeah, that's my burn barrel. I throw scrap pieces in there, and mistakes. Haven't had a fire for a couple of weeks, though."

As he finished his reply, a sudden recollection brought a look of dread to Jack's face.

"These particular pieces appear to have been removed from the kitchen and replaced with new ones. Don't ask me how forensics knows that, but they assure me that it's true. They also found bloodstains on those pieces. We won't have specific lab results for a while yet, but it's definitely blood. Care to save me some trouble, and tell me whose blood that is, Mr. Ferris?"

"Don't answer that! Detective, I need some time to speak with Mr. Ferris in private."

Rowan left them alone for exactly three minutes before returning. Their animated conversation stopped as soon as he opened the door, but Hank sat down without offering the benefit of an extension. Battaglia seemed slightly flustered, but managed to collect himself.

"Mr. Ferris would like to address those blood stains. It simply slipped his mind with all that's been going on, but there's a very plausible explanation."

Rowan looked to Ferris, who was obviously shaken and eager to explain.

"The same day I was telling you about, that Saturday, Nicki was cutting up some cheese in the kitchen, and cut her finger. I disinfected the cut and bandaged it for her. She didn't need stitches, but it was bleeding pretty bad for a few minutes.

"I didn't notice that there was blood on the unfinished hardwood until the next day. That floor wasn't stained yet, but it was finish sanded. Instead of trying to spot sand to get the blood out, I just replaced those pieces. Until you mentioned it, I totally forgot that I had thrown them into that barrel."

Rowan was skeptical, to say the least. "So, you forgot to mention that Mrs. Wainwright was bleeding that day, even though I continued to ask if there was anything else I should know."

"Yes, I swear I forgot all about it!"

"Until I told you what we found, then you remembered."

"Yes!"

"Detective, you asked for the truth and my client provided it. What more can he do?"

"Mr. Ferris, did you in fact harm Nicole Wainwright in some way?"

Battaglia made a move to object, but Jack restrained him.

"No! I did not, and would never harm Nicki. Never."

"Maybe it was an unfortunate accident, something you didn't mean to happen."

"No, I told you! She was fine when she left, it was just a cut finger! You'll see, when Nicki shows up you'll see the mark to prove it."

"Are you talking about an autopsy finding?"

Battaglia shot out of his chair, feeling that he had waited far too long to put an end to the badgering of his client.

"Detective, unless you intend to bring charges against Mr. Ferris, we're walking out of here."

Rowan's stare burned holes into Jack's pupils. "You can go. Just let us know exactly where you'll be, Mr. Ferris. We may have some more questions."

To Battaglia's dismay, Jack had more to say before leaving. "You should be questioning her husband. He's the one with some kind of secret, the one who might want to make sure Nicki doesn't tell someone whatever it is!"

Battaglia hustled his client out of the room, leaving Rowan behind to write down some additional thoughts. This guy had the opportunity, but why would he want to harm his lover? Was Ferris right, did Wainwright have a motive to make his wife disappear?

Taking things one wild step further, could Wainwright and Ferris have been co-conspirators for some reason? That was off the wall, but a good cop had to consider every possibility before deciding on his theory of a case.

He hoped that Nicki Wainwright would reappear alive and well, rendering all those questions moot. But it didn't feel as if that was likely.

CHAPTER 55

JAMES WAINWRIGHT CHOSE a circuitous path through Grove Park on his way to Amelia Lane, and then continued past his home and around the block to be sure that he was not being observed. Once inside, he locked the door behind him and stopped in the kitchen to find a plastic trash bag before heading upstairs. He removed his clothing and placed it, shoes and all, inside the bag and twist-tied it, still unsure where he would dispose of it.

After showering, Wainwright turned on the small television in the master bedroom before returning to the adjacent bathroom to shave. As he lathered up, something he heard in the broadcast caught his attention. They were talking about Nicki. Hurrying to the set, he raised the volume, noting that it was too early for this to be the normally scheduled newscast. A local anchor cutie was seated at the news desk, speaking to a live remote that occupied the other half of a split screen.

"Jennifer, what can you tell us about this new suspect, if anything?"

"Christine, his name is Jack Ferris, and he's a local man who works as an interior designer and painter. A source close to the investigation tells me that Ferris is not described as a suspect as this time, but that he is a person of interest in the disappearance of Nicole "Nicki" Wainwright.

"I've learned that Ferris recently did some work in the Wainwright home, and that he and Mrs. Wainwright had been seen together by numerous witnesses in the last few weeks."

Christine arched her eyebrows in a manner that seemed over the top for a serious news anchor, as if she were truly hearing this for the first time. "Is Ferris still being held by the police?"

Banks ignored the form of the question, continuing with the delivery that she had gone over in her head for ten minutes just before the red light went on.

"Police questioned Ferris for most of the day, and a search of his home was conducted this afternoon. The results of that search have not been released to the media, and we are awaiting the announcement of the next scheduled statement by Grove Park Chief of Police George McClure."

"I'm told that Ferris has not been charged, and in fact has now been allowed to leave in the company of his lawyer, Jack Battaglia."

"Thanks, Jennifer, great work. I know you'll be staying on top of –"

Wainwright's open hand slammed into the television, sending it crashing to the floor.

"Ferris! Ferris and Nicki?" he shouted, "I'll kill that bastard!"

*

James Wainwright burst into the police headquarters as if he owned it, his eyes searching the room for George McClure. He spotted him at the coffee station, talking to one of his detectives.

As he crossed the room he barked "George! Where is that sonofabitch, I want to talk to him!"

If McClure was surprised by the Supervisor's sudden appearance, or by the demands being made, he didn't show it.

"Calm down, Jim, please. Let's go into my office."

He turned to lead the way, with the fuming Wainwright only a step behind. "Calm down, my ass! I want to hear what he knows about Nicki, even if I have to beat it out of him myself!"

The threatening remark was delivered at a volume that turned heads throughout the room, just before Wainwright entered the office and slammed the door loudly behind them.

McClure seated himself behind his desk as Wainwright leaned on it from the other side.

"Where have you been, Jim? I thought you'd be checking in with us after the council meeting."

"I went for a drive to clear my head, then stopped home for a hot shower and heard the news report. Don't change the subject, George."

McClure had more questions for Wainwright, but it had been agreed that they would wait for additional information from Webster before confronting him.

"They said you had a suspect, Jack Ferris, and that he and my wife have been screwing around! Is that true?"

"Sit down, Jim, please."

"Is it true?" Wainwright slapped the desk in frustration.

"Some of that is true, yes, although I haven't found out who leaked it to the press." McClure waited for Wainwright to sit before continuing. "First of all, at this time Ferris is not suspected of anything. We still have no evidence that a crime has been committed. We've questioned him at length about his relationship with Mrs. Wainwright, and it appears that they've been seeing each other for a couple of months at least."

"And you just let him walk out of here? Do you even know where he is?"

"Listen to me, Jim. I don't want you going anywhere near Jack Ferris. Let us do our job. Believe me, we're not going to lose track of him."

"How are you going to find Nicki if you don't squeeze the truth out of this guy? He's out there right now with his big-time lawyer, laughing at us!"

McClure stood up to signal that the meeting had reached its end, as had his patience.

"I'm sorry you don't have more confidence in us, Jim, and I understand you're upset after all that's come out today. You should know that we have the full support of the county sheriff, the state police, even the FBI if necessary, to get to the bottom of this. You have to trust us, we'll find her. Go home, Jim, get some sleep. I'll call you personally if anything happens."

Wainwright was still agitated, but the day's events coupled with the news of his wife's indiscretions had left him exhausted. McClure was right, he needed to go home and get some sleep.

"I do trust you, George. I just want you to find my wife, that's all." Without another word, he left the building, wondering what his next move should be.

Back in his office, George McClure was twisting the ends of his moustache and asking himself the same question.

CHAPTER 56

IT WAS PAST three o'clock on Saturday afternoon when Pete Webster finally arrived in Carthage, Iowa. He had managed to doze off a few times on the connecting flights that had taken him to Cedar Rapids by way of Detroit and Madison, but with so little sleep it was all he could do to stay awake as he drove the last twenty miles to his destination.

"Welcome to Carthage, the little town with a big heart". The sign was old and somewhat faded, except for the red heart that had been substituted for the word and had apparently been used for target practice at some point in time. At the bottom, Pete thought that it read "population 976", and as he drove into the town he would have bet that the total hadn't increased in the years since the sign had been posted.

Main Street, as that short stretch of Route 263 was called inside the town boundaries, featured a collection of two-story wood frame storefronts, with a half dozen or so newer buildings intermixed. The main source of activity at that hour seemed to be two low metal structures featuring large block-letter signs that identified them as Tractor Supply and the Horse and Livestock Feed Store. The vehicles parked diagonally along both sides of the street were predominately pickups and SUV's, most of which were muddied but fairly new. This was a typical heartland town, home to many hard-working people who wouldn't think of living anywhere else, and probably to a desperate few who would do anything to get out.

In the center of town an imposing red brick edifice stood out from the rest. Just below its second-floor windows an inset panel of concrete displayed letters in relief that for eighty years had declared this to be the Carthage Town Hall. Pete spotted an empty space right in front and pulled in, hoping that Police Chief Jennings hadn't already left for his favorite fishing hole.

The updated stainless steel doors opened to a large open space filled with desks arranged in neat rows, with no concession to the gray noise-reduction cubicles that were used in most contemporary office settings. The desks and their occupants were separated from the entrance by a counter that ran from wall to wall, interrupted by an ornately carved hardwood half-door in the center. It looked out of place, possibly an original item that had been retained as an accent to the renovated interior. At the rear wall Pete spotted a door with a frosted glass window featuring black stenciled lettering that read "Harlon Jennings, Chief of Police".

As he took in his surroundings a smiling, fiftyish woman approached her side of the counter.

"Good afternoon, can I help you?"

Pete's self-introduction was cut short by her familiarity with local police matters.

"Oh, Detective Webster, of course! Chief Jennings has been expecting you. Had me run out for a sandwich so he could eat lunch in the office. He didn't want to miss you. Come on through!"

This has to be Marilyn, Pete thought as he passed through the heavy, spring-loaded gate.

Two civilian employees and one uniformed officer nodded a hello as he passed by, and Webster had the feeling that they all knew exactly who he was and why he had come to their town. The office grapevine was the same, no matter the setting.

He followed Marilyn into the inner sanctum and was met by the imposing figure of Harlon Jennings, who by Pete's quick estimate was presently carrying at least 300 pounds on his 6'4 frame. His dark, ruddy complexion was topped by a military buzz, complete with whitewalls, and he grinned as if an old friend had just arrived.

"Detective Webster, good to meet you in person!"

Pete endured a handshake that was akin to having his hand squeezed in a vise, and was invited to take a seat. He offered his badge and i.d.

for inspection, and the two men exchanged small talk to break the ice. Whether in Grove Park or Carthage, it seemed that most conversations began with a review of the current weather conditions. It was in the mid-forties and overcast, which Pete noted was pretty close to the weather he had left behind in New York.

Satisfied that he had made his visitor sufficiently comfortable, Jennings leaned back with hands behind his head and got to the point.

"So, as I understand it, Pete, you're here for two reasons. One, to find out where your friend Mr. Hartman might have gone, or at least what he was doing here in Carthage. Two, to ask about the man he was investigating, James Wright."

"That's correct." As Pete opened a small leather-bound notebook Jennings tapped his finger on a sheet of paper that was centered on his desk blotter.

"If it's okay by you, I'd like to start us off with this. I took some time to jot down some pertinent facts, so I don't leave out anything important this time."

"That sounds fine, Harlon, I appreciate you taking the time to do that."

Jennings took a sip of the fresh coffee that Marilyn had brought in for them.

"First, Steve Hartman. He came in to see me on January fourth. I checked the logbook for a couple of calls I remembered from that day, so I'm pretty damned sure of the date.

"He asked about Jim Wright, and I recognized him right away when Hartman showed me a copy of that Iowa driver's license. I told him what I could remember about Wright, which wasn't that much since I haven't seen him since Hector was a pup. We'll get back to him later."

Webster wondered who Hector was, but decided to chalk it up as a Midwestern colloquialism. Maybe he'd ask Sally about that one when he got back.

"I didn't have a lot of time for Hartman that day, but I gave him the names of three local boys that Wright used to run with. Turns out that one of them, Kyle Warren, moved out of state a while back. I spoke to his ex, she thinks he's in California and hopes he stays there. The other two, Tommie Upshaw and Mitch Goren, are still around. Goren's been in and out of jail a few times, he's a druggie and a thief. I locked him up for assault once, and I can tell you he's not a pleasant man.

The other one, Upshaw, is pretty straight. He has a problem with alcohol, but he manages to hold down a job at the shovel factory and has a family.

"When we're finished here, we can look them up and ask some questions about what they might have told Hartman, which probably wasn't much. I can't picture either one confiding in a P.I. from New York, no offense intended."

Pete smiled. "None taken. Is there anything else you can recall about Steve? Did you see him again after that first visit?"

"No, can't say that I did. After you called I checked at the motel where he stayed that night. It wasn't too hard to find, there's only one left in town. Ida Miller runs the place, she told me that Hartman checked in and paid for two nights, but he never showed up to check out. She still has some stuff that he left in the room. Just an overnight bag with clothes and toilet articles, a magazine, that kind of thing."

"No laptop, notebook, anything like that?"

"Nope. I'm afraid that's all I can tell you. He either left here in a hurry, or ran into some trouble."

Pete agreed with Jennings' assessment. "We know that Steve rented a car at the Cedar Rapids airport, a black 2016 Ford Taurus. It was never returned." He let Jennings assume that the information was uncovered by official police sources, when in fact it was Sally who had done the digging on her own. She was determined to find out whatever she could from her home, utilizing telephone and internet connections.

Jennings pursed his lips at the news. "Sorry to say, it doesn't sound good, does it?"

"Not at all. Now, what can you tell me about Wright?"

Jennings slid his notes to Pete's side of the desk.

"That'll give you the basics. His family moved to Carthage when he was a teenager, I believe the dad had passed away shortly before. His mother died a few years later, I don't know the details. After high school he worked a few different construction jobs, then got into selling real estate. Did pretty well at it, from what I can recall."

"How well did you know him, Chief?"

"Not real well, but we frequented some of the same gin mills and I hunted with him and some mutual friends a few times. We played in the same poker game for a while, before I gave up that sort of thing."

"But you eventually lost track of him?"

"I wanted to get into law enforcement, which meant giving up gambling and drinking, and certain acquaintances. Later, I was glad I did."

"Meaning what, exactly?" Webster sensed the most interesting details of Jim Wright's past did not appear on the page he was holding.

Jennings sighed as if he wasn't sure how to begin.

"There's something I didn't tell you on the phone, because I wasn't sure if it was the right thing to do. It isn't anything official, I'm only able to talk about because I've been around here so damned long.

"Jim Wright was married in '87 to a local girl named Kim Jeffries. Real sweet kid, a couple years younger than him. They owned a house out on Route 79, inherited it from Kim's parents.

"On the night of August 15, 1990, Kim Wright was alone in the house, her husband was away on a business trip to Keokuk. That night someone broke into the house and bludgeoned her to death.

"I was new on the force then, so I didn't have much to do with the investigation. No one here did, really, the State boys handled it and it was never solved."

"Jim Wainwright's first wife was murdered?"

"Assuming Wright and Wainwright are the same guy, the answer is yes."

"They're the same guy, you can bet the ranch on that. You said the case was never solved, but you must have had your own theory. Something tells me you liked the husband for it."

Jennings was reluctant, but it was obvious that he wanted to share his thoughts on the case.

"There was no physical evidence against him, and he had a solid alibi. He was out of town on business for a couple of nights, actually discovered the body himself when he got back home. His hotel info checked out, and there were a few people who verified meeting with him. My question is, who else had anything to gain from Kim's death? I just couldn't buy that random crime bullshit. I know that these traveling serial killers exist, and there were some women who went missing in this part of the state in those years, but I just had a bad feeling about him. And as far as I know, Kim Wright was a stay-at-home wife, not likely to be involved with anyone outside of her marriage. In a town this size, we would have heard something about it."

"How did Jim Wright profit from his wife's death?"

"It wasn't a fortune, but there was some life insurance, and the house and property. He put the place up for sale and as soon as the check cleared, he took off. I never gave him much thought after that until your friend showed up asking about him."

Pete was writing furiously, building a profile of James Wright.

"Anything else, Chief?"

"Just a general feeling that the guy couldn't be trusted. He was always loud and obnoxious, and kind of a phony. Had some real shady friends. He was known to brag about cheating on his wife, and how she waited on him hand and foot. Throw in a quick temper, and you've got the makings of a bad guy. Does that sound like your Mr. Wainwright?"

"I don't know him well enough to answer that, Harlon. Is there a case file I can look at?"

"Afraid not. We had a fire a while back, most of the old records were lost. They hadn't been entered into any kind of computer system. If Marilyn couldn't find it, it doesn't exist."

Pete clicked his pen to retract the ballpoint. "Okay. If that's everything, I'd like to look up the two guys that Steve spoke to."

Once again, Jennings hesitated before deciding to speak. "As long as I'm emptying the vault, there are a couple of things that bear mentioning. It might not mean a thing, but there was another death in that same house, maybe two or three years before Kim was killed. Her mother, Melanie Jeffries, took a tumble down the stairs and wasn't found until the next day, dead from a broken neck, I believe."

"So, it was accidental."

"No reason to think it was anything else, at least not at the time.

There was a ladder at the top of the stairs, she may have been changing a light bulb and toppled over. Coroner thought maybe she had a heart problem, too. In any case, that was how Kim and Jim inherited the Jennings place."

"Interesting."

"I'll give you one more interesting fact, then we're out of here." He stood and hitched up his belt. "When we go out to see Mitch Goren, you're going to be at the scene of the crime. I didn't realize it until all of this came up again, but Mitch lives in the old Jennings house. Bought it a couple years ago."

Pete shook his head. "Harlon, you are full of surprises."

"Probably all just coincidence. Like I said, I'm just telling you everything I know about Jim Wright."

Pete believed that he'd gotten full disclosure from Harlon Jennings, but he was sure that there was a lot more to know about James Wright-Wainwright.

CHAPTER 57

"**L**OOKS LIKE WE'RE in luck. That's Tommie's truck, he's at his favorite watering hole. We'll talk to him first."

They had only driven a few blocks from the Town Hall when Jennings spotted the brown Dodge Ram pickup, parked in front of a run-down building with a crude hand-painted sign above the entrance that read "The Dungeon". The windows were painted black from the inside, leaving the name of the establishment as the only clue to the nature of its interior.

Pete pulled open the weighty steel entry door to step inside, and was engulfed by the pulsing sound of death metal, played so loud that he was amazed he hadn't heard it from outside. As the door closed behind Jennings, the room seemed to turn pitch black. He hesitated a few moments before walking any further, giving his senses time to adjust to the minimal lighting and the assault of speed guitar.

Following the Chief a few steps forward, he could make out a dimly lit bar at the back wall, and about a dozen patrons gathered around it. There were no bar stools, only scattered tables and chairs and a few shelves built around the support posts where patrons could rest their drinks, or their elbows, on crowded nights. There were large posters hung randomly on the walls, featuring fluorescent patterns that were illuminated by the black lights mounted above them. The only other source of light was a row of video games to their right, in front of the opaque windows.

Jennings tapped Pete's shoulder and pointed to a lone game player in the far corner.

"That's Tommie. I'll hang outside and have a smoke while you two chat. His meth-head friends would get real nervous if they saw him talking to me, you'll have a better chance on your own. I'll be waiting right outside." He was almost shouting to be heard, and Pete completely understood why Harlon would rather wait outside.

As Jennings left, Pete made his way toward the corner where a solidly built man was battling electronic vampires, or zombies, definitely some type of malevolent beings. At the bar, a few heads were turned to check out the unfamiliar face. It felt as if he were wearing his navy blue windbreaker with POLICE spelled out on the back in huge white letters. Webster stopped at the side of the machine, well inside the range of the man's peripheral vision, but Upshaw's eyes remained riveted to the screen.

"Mr. Upshaw? Tommie Upshaw?"

Upshaw gave the joystick a final thrashing as his alter ego met his demise and was replaced by a bloody script that read "game over". He turned towards Pete and looked him up and down, smirking at the brown leather jacket and Dockers that were so blatantly out of place, given the setting.

"Yeah, that's me, just like the Chief told you."

Upshaw was dressed like the others that Pete could make out through the murky atmosphere of the place; black cutoff tee shirt, dark jeans, wallet chain, heavy boots and a frayed black "Resident Evil" baseball hat. Judging by the gray in his long pony tail this guy had to be pushing fifty, but still seemed right at home among the younger crowd.

Pete introduced himself, discreetly flashing his badge so that only Upshaw could see it. A temporary break in the musical assault allowed conversation at a normal volume.

"Hey, don't bother hiding it. They labeled you for a narc the second you walked in, man."

"That's alright. I'm not working undercover, and I don't care about the local drug trade. I just need a few minutes of your time."

Upshaw displayed his empty beer bottle to a passing waitress whose spiked hair was dyed to glow pure white under the UV bulbs.

"Two?"

"Sure, and have one yourself, Bets. He's buying."

If buying a round was the price of admission, Pete considered it a bargain. As she left Tommie turned to the machine, dropped two quarters into the slot and resumed his quest.

"Let me take a wild-ass guess here. You want to know all about J.W." He lifted a plastic cup to his chin and spit tobacco juice into it without taking his eyes from Pete's.

"If you mean James Wright, that's a good guess, Tommie. I know you were asked about this before, but bear with me."

"What the hell did that boy do, kill somebody?"

"Why would you say that, Tommie?"

"Lots of people askin' about him is all. I told what I know to the cop that was in here last week. Jesus Christ, don't you guys talk to each other?"

Pete was caught off guard by the reference. "Last week? The guy I'm talking about was here in January. A private investigator, Steve Hartman."

Upshaw turned away from his game as their beer was delivered. "Thanks, Betsy."

She handed Pete his Bud Light and favored him with an unexpected smile. Betsy was very young and very cute, despite a penchant for piercing that seemed a bit over the top. "That's six bucks. I didn't have one, but thanks anyway."

Pete handed her a ten. "Keep the change, Betsy." He appreciated the fact that she, at least, hadn't treated him as the enemy.

"Oh, January, yeah! That was the first guy that asked about J.W. I told him we weren't that close, I don't know why Harlon keeps telling people that. We gambled some, sucked beers together at a few titty bars when we were younger, that was about it. I barely remembered him. Just what the hell am I supposed to know?"

"Do you know why he left town?"

Upshaw's disgusted look told Pete that rather than hiding something, he was simply tired of the subject. "Mister, a lot of people have left over the years. Look around, this town ain't exactly a thriving metropolis, now is it? Besides, the man's wife was killed here, right in their own house. Wouldn't you want to leave all that behind and start fresh somewhere?"

Pete had never been in the habit of drinking while on duty, but the bottle he was holding made its way to his lips in a sort of conditioned reflex. Upshaw did the same, thirstily pouring half the bottle down his throat before releasing a long burp.

"How many times did you speak to Steve Hartman?"

"Once." He shrugged. "Why?"

"He's missing, and until we know better you're one of the last people to speak to him."

That seemed to get Tommie's attention.

"Well, I only seen him the one time. I told him he was barking up the wrong tree, it was Mitch Goren who was tight with Jaydub. So he left to look him up, I gave him directions to Mitch's place — Jim's old place."

"Ever speak to Mitch about it afterwards?"

Upshaw rubbed his jaw. "Yeah, he was pissed at me for giving up the directions. Can't blame him, really, I tend to keep talking as long as the other guy's buying." He emptied his bottle with a few strong gulps.

"So who was here last week? You mentioned that someone else asked questions about Wright?"

Tommie was already looking for Betsy.

"A week, more or less. I forget his name. Shorter, stocky guy, sounded like he was from New York. Like you, but with more of a New York City accent, like in the movies."

Pete suppressed a grin of amusement. "What did he ask you?"

"He asked about Jim a little bit, but this guy was more interested in Mitch."

"Did you give him directions, too?"

Upshaw spread his arms in a mea culpa and grinned sheepishly.

"He was buying!"

Pete's chuckle was drowned out by a fresh blast of guitar and growling as the sound of Cannibal Corpse filled the room. He let Upshaw return to his video fantasies and left The Dungeon, stopping briefly to slip Betsy another twenty towards Tommie's tab.

CHAPTER 58

JENNIFER BANKS WAS taking a well-deserved break from the job, enjoying her lunch in the parking lot of Burger Barn, the only fast-food franchise in the village. She had decided to eat in her car rather than inside the building because the urge to call her mom for a critique of her television appearance was irresistible, and she didn't wish to be overheard.

"So, what did you think of my reporting, Mom? Did you catch that news break last night, the live one?"

"Of course I did, Jennifer. You were terrific! Very poised and professional, not even one stumble. We're so proud of you! Everyone's been calling and saying the same thing."

"Thanks Mom, that means a lot to me." She felt an inner glow.

"I was changing channels all night, recording whatever I could. Did you know you were on CNN? Your dad jumped right out of his chair!"

Jennifer smiled, picturing her dad's excitement. "Yeah, I knew they planned to run it. I heard that Fox is pretty interested, too. I have to make my splash before they send their own crews to cover it."

"Honey, I can't believe the attention this is getting. I mean, I think it's just awful that this poor woman is missing, but is it all that unusual these days?"

Although her mom was genuinely happy for Jennifer, she still didn't seem to grasp the potential of the story.

"Mom, this is exactly what the mainstream media thrives on; an attractive, successful woman, who seems to lead this perfect life in small-town

America, suddenly goes missing. Now the details of her private life begin to come out and we all wonder what might have happened to her, and why. Remember the Patterson woman, in Phoenix?"

"Yes, of course, who doesn't? That beautiful pregnant girl, killed by her husband. What a shame that was."

"You almost feel as if you knew her personally, don't you? There were previously unknown reporters who made their reputations reporting that case. It's the reason Lindsey Locke has her own cable show."

Anita Banks had to agree. "Mmhm, you're right, Jen, it's very intriguing. But I hope she turns up soon, alive and well."

"Me too, mom. Whatever happens, I want to be the one to tell the story. People love fiction, but there's nothing like a real-life mystery to get the attention of television viewers. We're all curious about each other's private lives, aren't we? It's my job to report the facts, but the speculation is what keeps them tuned in." Checking her phone for the time, Jennifer saw that only thirty minutes remained before her next meeting. There wasn't time to explain her plan to balance effective reporting with pure titillation.

"How do you get all this information, Jen? Your father and I were wondering about that. You're a step ahead of all the others."

The question surprised Jennifer, and she wasn't about to discuss sources, even with her parents.

"You know how people love to talk, Mom. Everyone wants to tell their friends something new, something they didn't know. I guess it makes them feel important. I just try to be the one they confide in."

Her mother laughed. "In other words, none of my business."

"It's all about trust, mom. They trust me to get the information out without mentioning names, no matter who asks. Even you."

"Okay, okay, I understand. Are you going to be here for dinner?"

"No mom, sorry. Gotta work."

"But, it's Saturday."

"I know, but until Nicole Wainwright is found I'm on this twenty-four seven. I have to run, mom."

"One more thing, Jen, and this is just between the two of us. Do you think the boyfriend did something to her?"

"I honestly don't know, but I intend to find out. Talk to you later."

"Be careful, Jennifer."

"Okay mom, I will." She made the promise while wondering what danger her mother thought was lurking. "See you guys soon. Love you."

CHAPTER 59

"WELL, WHAT DID you think of The Dungeon?" Jennings was leaning against the white unmarked Tahoe that the department leased for him, one of the few perks of his job. A few cigarette butts were scattered at his feet, and he blew out a trace of smoke as he crushed another one under his boot.

Pete squinted and shielded his eyes against the transition to daylight. "Brings a whole new meaning to the term 'American Gothic', doesn't it?"

Jennings was either unfamiliar with the painting or unappreciative of Pete's yankee sense of humor. He continued to look at the New Yorker without comment.

"I mean, it was a little dark in there, but it was worth the visit."

"Used to be a real nice place, back in the day. Had the best dance floor in town. 'Course, it was also a strip club a few years back, so maybe this ain't so bad. What did Tommie have to say?"

Pete was making an entry in his notebook. "He didn't have much to tell me about Steve, but I didn't get the feeling he was hiding anything, either. He said we should talk to Goren."

"That's it? You were in there for a while."

"Well, he did say something that was interesting. He remembered talking to Steve back in January, but Upshaw said that someone else was here just last week, asking questions about Wright. But this guy seemed more interested in Mitch Goren."

They got into the Tahoe and Jennings started the engine.

"I know where Goren's place is. You ready to meet him?"

"Looking forward to it".

Daylight was fading into dusk when they turned into the gravel drive that led to the former home of Kim and James Wright, currently the residence of Mitch Goren.

The two-story farmhouse looked to be every bit of 100 years old, built in the restrained Victorian style that was common to the Midwest in that era. Exterior maintenance had apparently been ignored in recent years, evidenced by missing shutters and by shingles that hadn't seen a fresh coat of white paint in decades.

Jennings leaned over and reached into the glove box, removing a small handgun. He knew full well that the gun was loaded, but out of habit checked the cylinder before handing it to Pete.

"I'll go with you this time. Goren isn't as easygoing as Upshaw, he won't like the idea of the law coming to his door unexpected."

The piece was a Smith & Wesson Chiefs Special .38 with a short barrel, probably older than Pete but in pristine condition. Webster hadn't thought it necessary to bring his own gun on this trip, and was grateful for the security that this one provided. As he tucked it into his belt at the small of his back, Pete wondered if Chief Jennings was always this cautious. What was it about Mitch Goren that made Jennings so nervous?

They exited the truck and advanced onto the front porch, warily scanning their surroundings. Jennings raised a hand to rap on the weathered door, but stopped before his knuckles made contact.

"What?" Pete whispered, and then followed Jennings' eyes to the doorjamb. The wood was cracked and broken as if it had been forced open recently.

They backed away in opposite directions and peered into the windows, trying to see through yellowed window coverings that were no longer sheer. They made eye contact, each man shaking his head to indicate that no movement had been seen.

Jennings pulled a 9mm semi-auto from his shoulder holster and moved alongside the door, reaching out to gently push it open. The ever-widening field of vision was devoid of any activity, and he took a step inside as Pete hung back.

"Mitch Goren? This is Chief Jennings, are you in here?"

When no response was heard, he turned to Pete and waved him in. Pete's first thought upon entering was that some major renovation was underway, still in the demolition stage, but he quickly realized that it was a false impression. They stood in a kitchen that was in total disarray. Cabinet doors hung open, their contents having been spilled out onto the floor and countertops. Stepping gingerly through the debris of shattered dinnerware and overturned chairs, they made their way into the living room.

Furniture cushions had been cut open and thrown to the floor, and large sections of the lath and plaster walls had been torn away in some kind of manic search for objects unknown. Jennings moved to the foot of a stairway and called out again before starting upward, motioning for Pete to stay put. He returned a few minutes later.

"Same thing up there. Looks like someone went crazy in here looking for something. Money, maybe – some kind of stash."

"No sign of Goren? Any blood?"

"Nothing. Let's go out and have a look around, his truck's parked out back."

There was a dilapidated barn behind the house, about a hundred feet back, with an earthen ramp that led to its' tightly closed sliding door. A black Laredo was parked just below the incline.

Verbal communication was unnecessary as the two experienced lawmen became a team, as if they had been partnered for years. Weapons drawn, they moved past the vehicle on opposite sides, stopping briefly to glance inside.

The ramp was crumbled away on Pete's side where the stone retaining wall had failed long ago, making it unlikely that the structure could be used for anything but storage. Jennings was at the door, which was secured with a long cane bolt on the left side. He drew it upwards with some difficulty, rotating the rod back and forth as he pulled. The screech of metal on corroded metal was like fingernails on a chalkboard, and both men were relieved when the bolt was fully disengaged.

Pete grasped the handle and set his feet firmly, giving the door a strong pull to the side as Jennings trained his Glock at the opening and prepared himself for another entry. The wooden slab moved stubbornly along the rusted suspension rail, grinding to a halt after only a few inches. Pete was forced to tuck his firearm away so he could use both hands to pull. His second effort created a four-foot opening, and he re-armed to follow Jennings inside.

The space immediately in front of them was filled with a collection of items piled haphazardly, probably kept for scrap metal value rather than any further practical use. There were car parts, old bicycles, farming implements, and sheets of corrugated aluminum roofing. As Pete took his mental inventory, an assault on his sense of smell momentarily stopped him from venturing further.

"Man, that's ripe" he choked, fighting a sudden gag reflex.

Jennings was already covering his mouth and nose with a handkerchief, something Pete had never seen fit to carry but now wished that he had.

"Yeah, something died in here for sure" came the muffled reply.

Pete turned back toward the doorway to find a light switch, trying desperately to find a breath of fresh air as he flicked it on. The circuit had only one working bulb, illuminating the far end of the building enough to reveal the source of the foul odor.

They moved closer and saw a man's body slumped in a chair, playing host to a horde of buzzing flies, squirming maggots and various other agents of decomposition.

Pete placed a forearm against his nostrils in a failed attempt to block the stench as he approached the corpse. The deceased was bound to the chair with nylon cord around the torso and thighs, and appeared to have been beaten to death, or at the least beaten and left there to die slowly. There were no obvious bullet holes or other wounds that he could see. The ever-prepared Jennings produced a mini flashlight and took a knee to better examine the blackened, distorted facial features.

"Is it Goren?" Pete asked.

Jennings groaned loudly as he straightened up, kneading his lower back with one hand. "Yeah, that's Mitch. Looks like it's been a few days at least, wouldn't you say?"

Pete was amazed at Jennings' ability to ignore the putrid smell that seemed to envelope them.

"I need some air, Harlon."

"Good idea. Let's go call this in, get someone in here to take care of this mess. Looks like instead of answers we got a lot more questions."

CHAPTER 60

"PETE, HI! I thought you'd call sooner, where are you?"

Pete felt his pulse quicken at the sound of Sally's voice, a reminder of his growing feelings for her. He wondered if there was a mutual excitement at her end.

"I'm still in Carthage, I should be back tomorrow night at the latest. How are you, is everything okay?"

"Sure, except for the fact that you're not here." If he had been, Sally would have seen him smile, eyes closed for that moment, as she provided the confirmation he had hoped for. "What did you find out?"

Pete regretted having to break her light-hearted mood, but he couldn't sugar coat what he was about to say.

"I don't have any good news, hon. The Carthage Chief of Police verified that Steve was here in January, the day he called you, asking about James Wright."

"This guy spoke to Steve himself?"

"Yes. Jennings — that's the Chief here, Harlon Jennings — only spent like twenty minutes with Steve, telling him what he remembered about Wright. He didn't tell him everything, though. I'll fill you in on that when I see you."

"Okay, what else?"

"Jennings told me that he gave Steve a couple of names, guys that Wright used to hang with who are still in Carthage. Steve went to look them up, and when Jennings didn't see him after that he assumed Steve had asked his questions and gone home."

"Which I don't believe, because of the rental car not being returned."

"Right. By the way, good work, but you have to stop calling people and impersonating a police officer."

Sally's hearty laugh eased the tension of the exchange for a moment. "I never did that, I just said I was calling on behalf of the Grove Park P.D., which I sort of was."

"Uh huh."

"Really, I should have been a P.I. Did you forget that I took those classes in criminal justice?"

In fact, Pete remembered it well. Early in her marriage, Sally had the idea that she might become a cop, and have a stronger bond with her husband. Steve had been unable to discourage her, and had talked about his misgivings at length as he and Pete cruised the tough east side of Buffalo in their patrol car. Pete didn't know why she had eventually given up the idea, he was simply glad to have his partner free from the distraction.

"No, I didn't forget. That was a long time ago, huh?"

"I guess." Sally didn't want to think about how many years had passed, and returned to the subject at hand. "So tell me about these two guys that Steve interviewed. Did you follow up with them?"

"You do sound like a cop. Actually, I did. The first guy, Upshaw, is kind of a rednecked barfly. He recalled talking to Steve, and said he sent him on to the second guy, Mitch Goren. I didn't find anyone who saw Steve after that, he didn't even check out of his motel. He was paid up, but never turned in the key and some of his personal items were left in the room. I spoke to the lady who runs the place, she can't recall if the bed had been slept in."

"This is scaring me, Pete."

"Yeah, I'm sorry about that. Sally, we can talk about the rest when I get back."

He heard the sound of a thumbwheel scraping on flint, the hiss of propane, and her quick inhale. "No, I'm fine. What's 'the rest'?"

"I hate to pile it on, but it's about the second guy he spoke to, Goren. Jennings drove me out to see him, said he didn't want me to go alone because the guy had kind of a nasty rep."

"Did he tell Steve that?"

It was a good question, one that Pete hadn't thought to ask.

"I don't know."

"Maybe he should have. I'm sorry, go on."

"When we got there we found the house completely trashed, worse than what we saw at the office. Walls broken out, even. We went into the barn to check it out and found Goren's body. He'd been tied to a chair and beaten."

"You mean like tortured, for some kind of information?"

"Maybe. We don't know."

"Come home, Pete, right now. Get the hell away from there and come home safely. We'll talk tomorrow, or whenever you can get here."

"Alright, but I'll have to check in at the station first, it could be pretty late. I don't want to fall asleep on you."

"Don't worry about that, I was hoping you'd stay over. Jon's with my parents for a couple of days."

The offer took Pete by surprise, and he hoped his answer would sound acceptably cool.

"Well, that's an offer I can't refuse." He immediately knew that he had fallen short of the goal.

"You'd better not! Now get going, I'll see you soon. Call me when you get a chance, so I know when to expect you, okay?"

"I will. Bye, hon."

"Bye, sweetie."

Pete tucked his phone away, already fretting over the details of what he hoped would be the first of many nights spent with Sally.

CHAPTER 61

"WHAT'S GOING ON, Hank? Are they taking the case from us?" Detectives Rowan and Webster had been on their way to a briefing with McClure and Greco to recap the state of the investigation and discuss how to proceed. On the way in, the Chief had pulled them aside to mention that they would be joined by representatives of the Erie County Sheriff, New York State police, and the FBI.

Rowan held up a hand to prevent Webster from getting too worked up over unfounded assumptions.

"No, no, I don't think so, but we both know it's a possibility down the road. This thing is getting a lot of attention, everyone's watching to see how George is handling it."

"Why the FBI, though? Do they think it's a possible kidnapping?"

Hank shrugged off the question as they entered the room. There were three men seated in chairs that faced a large whiteboard where Greco had projected a slide featuring a photo of Nicole Wainwright, with her physical description listed beneath the image. The DA sat at a table, laptop at the ready, waiting for a cue from McClure.

Standing in front of the group, next to the visual display, McClure made the introductions. John Chapman, Chief of the Detectives Bureau, represented the Erie County Sheriff Department. He was new to the position, but Hank and Pete had run into him a few times over the years as he worked his way up through the ranks.

Captain Scott Kirsch, a tall, burly trooper from the New York State Police Bureau of Criminal Investigation, stood to shake their hands.

The Federal Bureau of Investigation, Buffalo office, was represented by Special Agent in Charge Brendan Boldt, who remained seated when introduced. He said nothing, simply nodding in their general direction before returning his attention to the makeshift screen.

Eric Bronski came in just long enough to distribute the printed summary that Greco had asked him to make copies of. As he passed by on his way out Pete tapped him on the shoulder, next to the new insignia that had been added to his uniform.

"Congratulations, Sergeant Bronski. I guess they don't care who they're promoting these days."

Bronski grinned, knowing that Webster was proud of him in spite of the smartass remark. "Thanks, Pete."

The Chief cleared his throat loudly, anxious to get started, and Bronski closed the door behind him.

McClure ran through the basic known facts of Nicole Wainwright's disappearance, and then called on Rowan to explain Jack Ferris' relevance to the case.

"John Philip Ferris, age 38, a lifetime resident of the area. Single, never been married, lives in a home that he pretty much built by himself up on Emery Road.

"Ferris is self-employed, he does interior painting and papering and such. He must be good at it, judging from the list of past clients that he rattled off. "

Greco's presentation moved to a photo of Jack Ferris, also accompanied by a physical description.

"Ferris did some work in the Wainwright home about a month ago, and got to know Mrs. Wainwright quite well. By his own admission, they've been seeing each other frequently since then.

"Ferris told me that he last saw Mrs. Wainwright on the 11th, three days before she was last seen. He says he hasn't seen or spoken to her since then, and couldn't make inquiries for obvious reasons.

"Cell phone records show that Ferris called Mrs. Wainwright's cell phone the morning she went missing, at 8:17 AM. The call went to voice mail, the message was never accessed. He guessed that she was out running, and commented that he might go out looking for her. He says he didn't, he stayed at the job site, but he was there alone."

Hank licked a thumb and turned to the next page of his notes.

"A search of the Ferris home was conducted by the county forensic team. Their most significant discovery was the hardwood flooring, three pieces, found in a burn barrel at the back of the property. They had been removed from the kitchen floor and replaced, and all three tested positive for bloodstains. We know that the blood type, A positive, matches Nicole Wainwright's. It'll be a few days before DNA results are known."

Boldt shook his head slightly, inferring that The Bureau could have helped expedite the DNA testing if only someone had requested it.

Pete knew that he should tread carefully where Jack was concerned, but he had a legitimate question. "Did you confront Ferris with that finding?"

"Yes, after I made sure he had every opportunity to bring it up himself. You can see that on the tape of the interview. He never said a word about the victim cutting her finger with a kitchen knife until I told him what had been found, then he miraculously remembered it in detail."

The characterization of Nicole Wainwright as "the victim" went unchallenged, a clear indication that all parties had resigned themselves to the probability of foul play.

McClure had been briefed by Rowan prior to the meeting, and was anxious to bring out another piece of the puzzle.

"Hank, is there anything in Ferris' background that might indicate violent tendencies?"

Rowan glanced at Pete, then back to his notes. "A few fights in his high school years, and one other notable incident. He never married, but Ferris was engaged at one time. I tracked down the ex-fiancée and asked why they called it quits before the wedding. She said that they had an argument, and Ferris had choked her until she passed out. She never reported it."

Pete was familiar with the woman, but he restrained the urge to attack her credibility. He wanted to wait until he could speak to Hank in private.

Rowan looked pleased with himself, and decided to wrap things up with a personal commentary.

"Ferris was cooperative for the most part, even though he changed his story somewhat from our first interview, but I'm sure he knows more than he's told us. We should keep an eye on him until we find a reason to bring him in again. I don't trust the guy, and I think he'll crack under pressure."

McClure gave Hank a nod, fully satisfied with his presentation.

"Duly noted. Before we get into that, Detective Webster will tell us more about the husband, Supervisor James Wainwright. Anyone care for coffee or a Pepsi before he begins?"

CHAPTER 62

MARILYN KNEW SOMETHING about fishing, and she was impressed. "You made this yourself, Harlon?"

"Yep. The hook setup is from an old Rapala, but I whittled the body myself. It has a double joint, so it wiggles through the water."

Jennings couldn't hide his pride in the workmanship that had gone into the bass-killing lure.

"Once I got the colors right, no largemouth could resist it. Best jerk-bait I ever used. I'm gonna stop at my spot on Bear Lake on the way home, see if I can catch Big Ben."

Marilyn couldn't help laughing.

"You sound just like my daddy. Every good-sized bass that slipped off the hook became an obsession with him."

"Well go ahead and laugh, but I know the shelf where that big boy hangs out, and — " Jennings' guarantee of success was cut short by the by the radio receiver on his desk.

"Car 4 to Base. You there, Chief?"

Marilyn was officially off duty for the day, but her protective instincts kicked in.

"Want me to handle that? I can tell him you just left."

Jennings considered the offer for a moment, then decided that Big Ben could wait a little while longer. He leaned toward the microphone.

"This had better be important, Pearson."

"Hey, Chief. I think it qualifies."

"Whatcha got?"

"I'm out at the old quarry. Had a report of gunshots, but it was just some kids shooting at pigeons."

"Tell me there's more."

"These kids told me about an abandoned car they ran onto in a gully out here, so I checked it out. It's a black Taurus. No plates, but I'm betting it's the one we're looking for."

Jennings checked his watch.

"Stay put, I can be there in a half hour."

"One more thing, Chief."

"Go."

"Remember what you told me about Mitch Goren? How the smell drove that New York cop right out of the barn before he could get a good look?"

"Pearson —"

"Well I ain't popped the trunk yet, but my nose tells me this guy Hartman might be in there."

CHAPTER 63

WHEN THE BRIEFING resumed, an image of James Wainwright was being displayed. It was the picture that had been used on his campaign literature, depicting a dignified Wainwright staring off into space as he considered the weighty issues faced by the town of Grove Park.

Pete regretted not taking the time to reorganize and type a synopsis of his notes, but he was confident that they were legible enough to get through this.

"I'll start with what we knew about Wainwright before this investigation." That phrasing seemed to get the full attention of all participants, even Special Agent Boldt, who had looked rather bored until now.

"James Wainwright has lived in Grove Park since the early to mid-90's, after relocating from Iowa. He worked for a few local real estate brokerages and eventually opened an office of his own. He became very successful, selling both residential and commercial property.

"Sometime around 2008 he met Nicole Moore, also a successful broker, and they eventually became a couple. They were married in August of 2012, despite a considerable age difference."

Pete was aware that his last remark may seem petty to some, but in this room it would be filed away as a possible factor in marital discord.

"Last year Wainwright entered the race for Town Supervisor, and was elected by a wide margin, getting over sixty percent of the vote. He caused a recent controversy by backing a plan for a new housing development called Cedar Ridge, but that proposal was voted down by the town council."

Pete stopped to allow an opportunity for comment, but the others seemed to be waiting for something more interesting.

"Now tell us what we didn't know." McClure prompted him to get on with it as Greco clicked his mouse to bring up another page. It was the scanned image of the Iowa driver's license, next to the previous photo of Wainwright.

"This is an Iowa license issued in 1983 to James Wright. We're sure that it's the man we now know as James Wainwright, but so far we haven't found any official record of the name change. We believe that Nicole Wainwright found this item and hired a private investigator to look into her husband's background. That investigator, Steven Hartman, was last seen in Carthage, Iowa, in January. He had been asking questions about Wright, and visited two of Wright's former friends.

"I went to Carthage myself to follow up, and found that one of those old friends, Mitchell Goren, had been beaten to death just a week ago. This wasn't a bar fight; the guy's body was found tied to a chair.

"No sign of Steve Hartman yet, it's looking like he never left Carthage." He closed his notebook and sat back in his chair. "That's where we are, trying to tie some of this together before we confront Wainwright with it."

The County Sheriffs and the State boys were accustomed to this scenario, a small-town force with limited capacity asking for help when a major investigation was required. The county regularly assisted with forensic teams and laboratory resources. When it came to investigative manpower, the state would often provide the services of experienced plainclothes detectives to partner with the locals.

Chapman was the first to comment.

"Sounds like a lot of loose ends to run down. George, you provide the requisitions and I'll make sure you get whatever is needed."

Kirsch made a similar offer, without asking for any further details of the case. These were administrative officers who managed the force, they weren't expected to become involved with the details of specific cases.

When it was Boldt's turn to speak, he took a different attitude.

"Detectives, we haven't heard a word concerning your theories in this case. What are your gut feelings about this disappearance? Did Mrs. Wainwright simply run off on her own, no pun intended, or has there been a crime committed here?"

Rowan was quick to respond, probably too quick in Boldt's judgment. "I think there's been a crime committed, and I think we have identified a possible suspect. We need to find the — we need to find her, that's priority one."

They looked to Pete for his opinion.

"I understand why Hank feels that way. We haven't found anyone who can give us the break we're looking for, the one that leads us to Mrs. Wainwright. We haven't given up on finding her unharmed, but the searches for physical evidence have come up empty, and every tip we've received has been a dead end. We know that she had at least two men in her life, but we still don't know what motives they may have had to take part in her disappearance. It's frustrating, and we need to keep grinding and collect all the information we can before reaching any conclusions."

McClure nodded in full agreement. "Well said, Pete. Let's consider every possibility, including the chance that Nicole Wainwright is out there, in trouble, waiting to be found before it's too late. That's exactly why we need the assistance of other agencies."

Chapman and Kirsch reiterated their promises of full cooperation and rose from the table.

"Gentlemen, good luck, I hope you get the result we're all hoping for." His counterpart from the Sheriff's office echoed the trooper's sentiments, and they left the room.

Special Agent Boldt remained seated, allowing Pete the opportunity to pose a question of his own.

"Agent Boldt, what's the FBI's actual interest in this? We don't have anything that points to kidnapping, no ransom demand or anything like that. Don't get me wrong, we can use the help, it just seems early for the feds to get involved."

Boldt smiled as if he'd been expecting the question.

"First and foremost, we can provide services that expedite the investigation, resources that a small jurisdiction doesn't normally require. We'll have a computer tech here tomorrow, and with access to our databases you'll be amazed at the amount of personal background information that becomes available.

"If you need evidence processed cleanly and quickly, especially DNA evidence, our lab services can help. If it's surveillance technology that's required, we have some great new toys.

"As you pointed out, there's no reason to treat this as a kidnapping, but our profilers can assist with possible scenarios based on similar cases. In the event a ransom message is received, we can move a team on site.

"For now, the extent of our involvement is up to Chief McClure."

The remark appeared to make the Chief uncomfortable, and he looked at Boldt as if something had been left unsaid.

"That being said, there is another reason for our presence here. Your case may have a bearing on something else that we've been working on, to what extent we're not sure. Please understand, I can't discuss the details of our case with you until I'm authorized to do so. Does the name Paul Gotts mean anything to either of you?"

Pete didn't recognize the name, but Hank jumped in.

"The guy that was found in the Lantern parking lot?"

"That's the one."

Pete was making note of the name. "I've been out of town, I guess I missed that one."

Hank jumped on the chance to fill in the blanks. "I heard from the Sheriffs that he was from New York City. He won a bundle at the casino, they figure he was followed and cracked on the head for the cash. Are they right?"

Boldt's wry smile was a bit smug for Pete's taste.

"I'm sorry, like I said it's too early to share details. Let me just say one more thing, though. Even if Ferris turns out to be your guy, I'm interested in anything you uncover concerning Wainwright. When the time is right, you'll be fully informed, you have my word. Until that time I hope we can work together."

Rowan and Webster knew that the Bureau's idea of cooperation could be a one-way street, but they were in no position to refuse the help. This case was far from over, and it became more complex with every passing day.

CHAPTER 64

PETE WEBSTER HAD received the call from Chief Jennings shortly after leaving the briefing room. As he walked toward Sally's front door, his excitement at the prospect of seeing her was tempered by the weight of the bad news he carried with him. He knew that Sally had been preparing for the worst concerning Steve, but how could a mother be prepared to tell her young son that his father was gone forever?

Pete had delivered such news to the families of victims many times, usually the result of accidents rather than homicides, but this would be more difficult. This time there was a personal connection that wouldn't allow him the insulation of professional detachment, and he intended to be there to help Sally through her time of sorrow.

She opened the door before he could ring the bell, looking radiant and youthful in a snug pair of faded jeans and a pink tank top. The circumstances that had brought them together were regrettable, but Pete once again felt the elation of having Sally in his life.

"Hi babe!"

"Hi Petey. Get in here!" Her smile was beautiful, and the thought of what he was about to say broke Pete's heart. He brushed against her as he entered, just as Sally had intended, and the brief contact felt like a charge of static electricity.

When the door was closed, Sally leaned back against it, pulling Pete into her for a kiss so passionate that a full minute passed before they paused to look into each other's eyes. Even then, Pete had only stopped because he wasn't sure they were alone in the house.

"Where's the big guy?"

Sally tugged her top into place, looking a bit embarrassed by her wanton display, and grinned as she led him further into the living room.

"He's still with my dad. They can't get enough of each other these days. Jonathan is the only grandson he has, not that dad doesn't completely adore my brothers' little girls. They're just not interested in farming, baseball, that kind of thing. Jon wanted me to say hi for him, though."

Now Pete had a turn to be embarrassed, realizing he had poured water on what should have been a spectacular bonfire. He stayed with the small talk, buying time. "Does your dad still have the place out on 19?"

"Yep. Jonathan loves to go out there." Then, not to be deterred, she continued with her initial train of thought. "So should I go upstairs and light some candles? We have some catching up to do."

Pete couldn't return her smile, knowing that he had to postpone a wonderful experience to make time for a dreaded conversation.

"What's wrong, Pete?"

"Sally, there's nothing in the world I would rather do than go up there with you right now. But first we have to talk. It can't wait."

She brought a hand to her mouth, eyes widening as she understood the implication.

"Oh my god, is it Steve? What is it, Pete?"

"I received a call from Carthage earlier, Sally. They found Steve's body. I'm so sorry."

He moved toward her as she slowly crumbled to her knees, burying her face in her hands to muffle her sobs. Pete knelt next to her, and Sally clung to him as she allowed her grief to take control.

When the first wave of shock had subsided, Pete helped her to the couch and brought her tissues and a glass of water.

"Tell me all of it, Pete. What happened to Steve?"

There was no way to soften it, so Pete didn't try.

"He was shot. Jennings said they retrieved a gun from Mitch Goren's place, same caliber. They're doing ballistics tests now."

"So, this guy Goren killed Steve?"

"He may have, or it could have been someone else using his gun, if the sequence of events supports that, we're not sure. It could turn out that the bullet that — the bullet that was taken from Steve's body was fired from a different gun. We don't have those answers yet."

A minute passed in silence, save for the muted sound of Sally's weeping, as Pete waited to hear any other questions she might have.

"What about Jack Ferris, Pete? He's your friend, do you think he could be any part of this?"

The change of subject seemed abrupt, but not out of line.

"I think Jack fell in love with Nicole Wainwright. I don't think he harmed her, but I admit there are things about his private life that I wasn't aware of."

"Like the thing with his fiancée?"

Now Pete was truly surprised.

"How do you know about that?"

"It was on television just before you pulled up, they had a news break on channel five."

Pete had been questioning his objectivity concerning that story and was still trying to sort out his true feelings on the subject.

"As Jack's friend, and having known Janet pretty well, I would take what she said with a grain of salt, an exaggeration at the least. As a cop, I give it consideration as to the viability of Jack as a suspect."

"I see. I know you're in a tough spot, trying to be impartial. I probably shouldn't have asked."

Pete shrugged, his half-smile dismissing her concerns.

"The questions are legitimate, all I can do is tread carefully where Jack is concerned. He's my friend, and I believe that he would never have hurt Nicole Wainwright or anyone else. I just can't say that around other cops."

He sat next to Sally and took her in his arms.

"I think we should light those candles some other night. Is there anyone you can call, so you won't be alone tonight?"

She pulled away slightly, and when their eyes met Pete could see that she was hurt. "You're leaving already?"

"I'm sorry hon, but this case — I have so much to do, I can't think of anything else. We're pretty close to bringing Wainwright in for further questioning, I want to be ready for that."

"Oh, okay. I understand. I'll call my parents after you leave, to tell them about Steve. They'll have to bring Jonathan home and help me try to explain this to him. My mom will probably stay overnight."

"I'll call you in the morning." They shared a long hug as Sally struggled to hold back the convulsive sobs that were about to return, until Pete was able to tear himself away and head for the door.

CHAPTER 65

JACK FERRIS WAS beyond feeling like a suspect, he was beginning to feel like a prisoner. Relegated to residence in a cheap motel room, he could only pass time in front of the blurry 19" television until the police allowed him to return to the familiar comfort of his home.

Jack had stopped venturing out in public unless it was an absolute necessity, unwilling to endure the stares of strangers and the awkward exchanges of small talk with friends, most of whom now seemed uncomfortable in his presence. He had gotten the impression that anything he said would be repeated endlessly at Grove Park water coolers and bars like Woody's, and possibly to the first tabloid journalist who came along. That morning he had been followed by a small group of men with shoulder-mount video cameras, an escalation of attention that had spooked him back to his room.

He was lounging on the double bed, can of Labatt Blue in one hand and remote control in the other, desperately surfing through the cable channels in search of something to distract him from the misery of Nicki's disappearance and his own situation. As he passed through the gauntlet of news networks, Jack heard her name mentioned by the hostess of the wildly popular Locke Report on CNN.

Lindsey Locke was a former prosecutor from New Orleans who had risen to celebrity status during her coverage of the Lisa Patterson case. Patterson was a 28-year old expectant mother who had vanished without a trace from her Phoenix home in December of 2014. Within days it was reported that her husband, David Patterson, was considered by police to be a person of interest in the investigation. The media coverage quickly escalated into a frenzy of reports concerning David Patterson's odd and suspicious behavior in the days before and immediately after the disappearance. When it was revealed that Patterson had been having an affair, presenting himself as a sympathetic character and continuing the charade as search efforts and candlelight vigils went on around him, Locke had been relentless in her vicious assaults on his character and credibility.

Three months later Lisa's remains were found in the desert, and within a week police charged David Patterson with murder. By the time he was convicted and sent to death row, Locke's attack-dog style had won her a dedicated following and the Locke Report was firmly entrenched near the top of the cable news ratings.

Viewers were fascinated by her aggressive grilling of defense attorneys and her shoot-from-the-hip suspicion of any poor soul who caught the interest of the investigative reporters vying for a spot on her show. Locke's teased blonde hair, darkly shaded eyes, and hint of a southern drawl made her a favorite with men, while women appreciated her staunch advocacy of victim's rights. Locke now seemed to specialize in cases that centered on missing females such as Nicole Wainwright, looking for another story that could intrigue viewers with nightly reports for weeks, or even months, as had the Patterson saga.

The Locke Report always featured a wide array of guest commentators and legal analysts, some who were experts and others who apparently were chosen for their bizarre appearance or outlandish opinions. Selected viewer phone calls were aired, and the production made liberal use of split-screen techniques and informational graphics providing a steady stream of background information.

Locke was always in command as the ringmaster, swiftly and skillfully moving from one guest to another and injecting her personal opinion at will, frequently talking over, or down to, the other players. Jack had tuned in somewhat regularly during the Patterson case, and the full awareness of what could be in store for him made him queasy.

Locke was speaking to a female correspondent whose headshot occupied one half of the screen, identified by the crawler as Jennifer Banks of News Five WKBG, Buffalo, N.Y. Jack hardly recognized Banks in her new hair style, still long but also wavy and full.

"Jennifer, what's the story on this Ferris character, was he prominent in Nicole's life or was this just a one night stand, a fling?"

Banks didn't miss a beat, having been advised just minutes earlier of what would be asked.

"Lindsey, it seems the two have been seeing each other for a couple of months, since Ferris was hired to do some painting in the Wainwright home. Ferris has admitted the affair, and I've personally spoken to several witnesses who had seen them together during that time. I can't comment on the intimacy of the relationship, but it appears to have been quite serious."

"So it wasn't a case of this man stalking his former employer, as we've heard from other sources? It was a love affair, or at least a sexual attraction?"

"No, this was definitely not a stalking, they had an affectionate ongoing relationship."

Locke seemed somewhat unsatisfied with the characterization, but moved on.

"Tell us what you know about the search of the Ferris home, you've reported that traces of Nicole's blood were found there, but the police have so far refused to comment."

"Lindsey, sources close to the investigation tell me that bloodstained pieces of hardwood flooring were found outside the house. It appears that they had been removed from a floor in the house and replaced, but had not yet been disposed of. The stains are being tested to determine whether the blood came from Nicole."

Locke nodded knowingly. "Now there's a smoking gun if ever there was one! What does Ferris have to say, Jennifer?"

"Jack Ferris has not spoken to the media since he was released from a full day of questioning by the Grove Park police. He has retained the services of Raymond Battaglia, a prominent Buffalo-based attorney who has defended the accused in several high-profile cases in western New York."

"The Jog Path Rapist was one, wasn't it, Jennifer?"

"Yes Lindsey, as well as Richard Boorman, who bludgeoned a nun to death for the contents of a church "poor box".

"Thanks, Jennifer." Locke quickly dismissed the young reporter and went full frame, once again directing her viewer's attention to the center ring. "We spoke to Mr. Battaglia earlier, here is a portion of that interview."

Jack was mesmerized by what was taking place on the television screen. He had been rendered virtually motionless as he tried to comprehend the surrealistic events that were unfolding, as Lindsey Locke transformed him from a person of interest to a likely suspect in a crime that was not yet known, but must surely be horrific.

He came out of his trance long enough to finish off the twelve-ouncer just as a dapper, almost dashing, Ray Battaglia took his turn on the right side of the frame. He was wearing his best Brioni suit for the occasion, a black pinstripe, looking every bit the successful attorney.

"Mr. Battaglia, thank you for coming on, what's this about Nicole Wainwright's blood being found at your client's home?"

Battaglia smoothed his tie and cleared his throat, seemingly caught off guard by the question. Not every guest was afforded the advantage of being prepped by Lindsey's staff.

"I can't comment directly on that, but I will say that any evidence of Nicole Wainwright's presence in my client's home can be reasonably explained. He has admitted that they were seeing each other, that they had spent time together there. It's no shocking revelation that her DNA would be present in the Ferris residence."

Locke pounced like a cat, one that had toyed with such prey many times before.

"Sir, you're saying that it's *reasonable* for a missing woman's blood to be found all over your client's house? How is that reasonable by any stretch of the imagination?"

Battaglia shifted in his chair, his body language conveying a decidedly lesser degree of self-assurance.

"Well, of course I wasn't speaking specifically of blood evidence, as I said I can't comment on that at this time. You could certainly expect to find hair, perhaps a toothbrush she used, that type of DNA evidence, in light of the fact that she had spent time in the house."

"Just for the record, has your client told police that he had absolutely nothing to do with Mrs. Wainwright's disappearance?"

"Yes, Mr. Ferris has cooperated fully with the police task force that is investigating this. His sole interest is the welfare of Mrs. Wainwright, and he hopes to be helpful in locating her and in her safe return."

"Right, right." Locke's reply dripped with sarcasm that would once have been considered unprofessional.

The remainder of their exchange was a series of questions about Jack's background and personal history, and to Battaglia's credit he was adamant in supporting his client and deflecting Locke's insinuations that Jack was hiding some dark secret concerning Nicki's fate.

Stunned by the realization that he was being portrayed as a villain on a national, even global scale, Jack found himself staring at a commercial for the Ab Builder.

"Christ" he mumbled to himself, pressing both palms to his forehead in despair. "What next?"

A grim-faced Locke returned for a satellite roundtable discussion of the case with several talking heads, some of whom Jack recognized as regular participants on the Report. He snapped the television off, snatching up his phone from the nightstand. Battaglia had given Jack his private cell number, with permission to use it any time he wanted to talk, day or night. This seemed like a good time to use it.

"Battaglia here."

"Mr. Battaglia, it's Jack Ferris." Jack stopped short, unsure whether he was calling to complain or to seek advice in the face of his sudden notoriety.

"Yes, Jack, how are you holding up?"

"I guess I was holding up pretty well until I saw the Lindsey Locke show. She's making it look as if I'm guilty of something just because I was close to Nicki. I guess it doesn't matter that I love her. Why would I want to hurt her?"

"I know, Jack, and that's exactly why I felt obligated to appear on the show and put an end to that type of speculation. I hope you were satisfied with my responses. They didn't actually show much of the interview, but I think it went well."

Jack wasn't prepared to endorse that opinion, and he wasn't about to critique his lawyer's performance for him.

"I'm going crazy being cooped up in this room. When can I get back into my house?"

"I'm on it, Jack, they have assured me that it should be very soon." Battaglia knew that a confirmation that the blood evidence matched Nicole would assure a "crime scene" designation, keeping Jack out indefinitely, but he wasn't willing to share that upsetting possibility.

"There are people following me, did you know that? They might be outside right now, I don't know. They're trashing me on national television! This is way out of control, Ray."

"You have to stay calm, Jack. The case is getting a lot of attention right now, but that will fade when Mrs. Wainwright is found."

"Really? What makes you think that it won't increase?" Jack was unnerved, and his comment showed it.

"I mean that when she is found alive and unharmed, as we believe she will be, this will all go away. Are you with me Jack?"

"Yes, right, I know. Sorry, this is just so freaking crazy for me. I don't like being famous, not this way."

"Try to relax without watching the news, Jack. I'll be here if you need me."

Jack wasn't quite ready to hang up.

"How the hell do they get all this information, anyway? Who are the 'sources close to the investigation' they talk about?"

"I wish I knew. I've complained to McClure, but he doesn't seem able to stop the leaks."

"I want to know what's going on over there, what they've found out about Nicki. Maybe I should make a call, I have friends there."

"Absolutely not, Jack! Stay put, and don't talk to the police without me being present. Detective Webster is not you're ally in this, I don't care how close you two have been."

"Yeah, okay, I'm not going to call Pete. I'm just venting. Don't worry about me, Ray, we'll talk tomorrow."

"Alright. Get some sleep, Jack."

"Yeah. Bye."

Jack had already opened another beer. He intended to finish the eight-pack while it was still chilled, and try to forget his problems for the night.

CHAPTER 66

"WHAT'S ON YOUR mind, Joey? I'm with the Supervisor, we're on our way into a meeting with the cops. Hopefully they'll have something new to tell us."

As the other attendees filed past on their way into the conference room, Al Kaplan had been waiting impatiently for his client to return from a last-minute trip to the men's room. The last thing Al needed was an inconsequential call from Joey Garrity.

"I just wondered how things are going, Al. Jim hasn't talked to me since the vote, is there any news about Nicki?"

"No, like I said we're about to get an update. Anyway, you'd probably hear about it on television before these cops announced anything."

"Yeah, really, they have a hell of a leak down there. Like the thing about Nicki screwing around with the house painter."

"Joey, is there anything else? I gotta run."

"No, I was just checking in. I was wondering though, is it just Ferris or are there other guys?

"What do you mean?"

"I mean do they think Nicki was involved with any other guys, or just him?"

"Christ, Joey, find something to do besides gossip, will you? I'm busy here!"

"Listen to me for a second, Al! Here's the thing – I may have gotten drunk one night and bragged to a few buddies that I was involved with

Nicki. Well, it was bullshit, I was just trying to impress them. So, if it should ever come up —"

Kaplan was disgusted and somewhat angered by his young colleague's admission, and didn't wish to hear anything more. "Goodbye, Joey!"

Wainwright appeared just as an annoyed Kaplan ended the call.

"Who was that?"

"No one. Joey, 'just checking in', whatever that means. Come on, let's find out what these people have to say."

They entered the conference room located at the rear of courtroom 1, joining four other participants who were already seated around the polished oak table. David Greco rose to greet them, and took charge of the introductions.

"Gentlemen, thanks for coming in. Chief McClure regrets that he couldn't be here, and you already know Detectives Rowan and Webster. I'd like you to meet Special Agent Boldt of the FBI."

The table's expansive width made handshakes impractical, leaving all parties to exchange various forms of "glad to meet you", accompanied by nodding heads.

The unexpected FBI presence had gotten Wainwright's attention. "Glad to have the FBI on board, Agent Boldt. Are you a specialist in missing persons, a profiler, something like that?"

Greco intervened before Boldt could respond. "Before we get into that, Mr. Supervisor, with all due respect, we have some questions for you. Further background, if you will, to help us better understand some facts that have come to light. Detective Webster, will you begin, please?"

Wainwright and Kaplan traded glances, silently reaffirming their shared opinion of Greco as a pompous pain in the ass.

"Good afternoon, Mr. Wainwright". Pete squinted down at his notes, then looked up as if to ask a question that didn't appear there, but had just come into his head.

"Mr. Wainwright, I was wondering, what's the origin of your last name? Kind of an interest of mine, finding out where names come from."

Wainwright thought the question was strangely off topic, but wanted to appear relaxed.

"It's a British name, is about all I know," There was a silence, as if more of an answer may be forthcoming, but no further explanation was offered.

"So, your dad's family was from England?"

Wainwright's face reflected annoyance at Webster's interest in such an irrelevant subject, or perhaps at the mention of his father.

"At some point in history, I guess, yeah. My father was born in Iowa and spent his entire miserable life there. Is all of this important?"

Webster continued to write in his notebook as he replied. "Well, you never know what might turn out to be important." Then, looking Wainwright in the eye, "Were you born in Iowa, sir?"

"Yes I was, in Crawford. It's a very small town about 60 miles east of Ames, smack in the middle of the state." He didn't mention the move to Carthage as a teen, hoping it wouldn't come up.

Webster pressed on. "At what age did you leave Iowa?"

Kaplan had heard enough about Iowa, and was exasperated.

"Detective! What are you doing? Really, how on earth does any of this help us to locate Mrs. Wainwright? I mean, taking some background information is one thing, but this childhood history seems like overkill."

Greco saw a chance to apply a needle to Kaplan's ballooning arrogance. He had been challenged before by prestigious, self- important attorneys. Like Kaplan, they saw his youthful, rather studious persona as a sign that he could be easily intimidated.

"Mr. Kaplan, we've just gotten started here. Surely you're not advising your client not to cooperate."

Wainwright remained silent, looking from one attorney to the other as if he were watching a tennis match. The ball seemed to be in Kaplan's court.

"I'm saying that your questions are extraneous, and time is passing by. Mr. Wainwright is completely willing to cooperate in anything that will help solve the mystery of where his wife has gone." Kaplan sat back and smoothed his tie as if giving his permission for Webster to continue.

"Mr. Wainwright — "

"Jim, please" Wainwright interrupted with a smile. Being addressed formally made him feel like he was suspected of something.

"Alright then, Jim." Webster's smile was equally forced. "I'm confused sir, when you were growing up in Iowa you were known as James Wright, isn't that true?"

The question hung in the air, causing Wainwright to seize up for a few seconds, after which he looked at the knowing faces around the table and realized he had been trapped in a hopeless lie, or a withholding of information at the least. Kaplan was the only one present who appeared to be at a loss, and looked to his friend for an explanation.

"Jim?"

Wainwright sneered at his lawyer, angered by the lack of support he had received. "Yes, that's true. My name was Wright, same as my father's. I changed it to Wainwright after I left Carthage. There are legal documents available to back that up."

Detective Rowan wanted more of an explanation.

"If you don't mind, Jim, why the change?"

"I wanted to start fresh in a new place, and the name change seemed like a good idea. I was still grieving the death of my first wife, Kim, and — well, like I said, I wanted to put the past to rest and start over."

Webster resumed his role of lead interrogator.

"Do you know a man named Mitch Goren?"

Wainwright's face went blank, and he looked to the ceiling, avoiding eye contact as he seemed to be calling up some distant memory.

"Mitch Goren? Well yes, I had a friend by that name back in Iowa. Haven't seen him since I left there." Appearing perplexed, he looked to Kaplan, who felt compelled to run interference by asking a question.

"Is this Goren involved in Nicki's disappearance somehow?" Kaplan asked.

Greco continued with his plan to handle Kaplan himself, allowing Webster to concentrate on Wainwright. "We don't know yet, Mr. Kaplan, but he's someone that we're interested in." He nodded to Webster, anticipating the detective's next question.

"Mr. Wainwright" Webster began, not feeling comfortable with the first-name basis after all, "when did you last speak to Mitch Goren?"

Wainwright turned his palms up as if the answer would be a wild guess. "Good God, I don't know, gotta be close to twenty-five years ago. He could be dead for all I know."

The offhand comment brought eye contact between Webster and Greco. The Grove Park detectives had wanted to squeeze Wainwright hard in this meeting, but as a team they had decided against that. The plan was to reveal only a part of what they had learned, enough to shake Wainwright and unnerve him. He would then be carefully observed until they had a better idea of how he was connected to the series of sordid events. It was possible that James Wainwright was the common thread, and when that could be proven he would be pressured at length for more details.

Special Agent Boldt was his usual stoic self, acutely interested in the responses but not showing any emotion as he took notes. He was impressed with the way these local guys could handle an interview.

"Were you aware that your wife had hired a private investigator to check into your background, sir?"

Wainwright was unmoved. "Bullshit."

"It's true, sir. Are you saying that you've never heard of a man named Steve Hartman?"

"No. Should I have?"

"He's the P.I. who went to Carthage to look into your past. Any idea why Mrs. Wainwright would have thought it necessary to have you investigated?"

"No, and I still don't believe she did."

"It's a fact. It's also a fact that Mr. Hartman has been murdered. As it turns out, he never left Carthage."

Kaplan saw his client in jeopardy, and realized that Wainwright hadn't been completely honest with him. "Gentlemen, before he answers any more questions I would like to confer with Mr. Wainwright in private. We should probably return at another time to pick up on this."

Now it was Special Agent Boldt's turn to rattle the Supervisor's cage.

"Just one thing before you leave, Mr. Wainwright. What is your relationship with Victor Harmon?"

"Well, Mr. Harmon has been representing New Century Limited in their development proposal. Of course that's all over now, so we have no relationship."

"I see. And Paul Gotts?"

"Paul Gotts?" Wainwright repeated the name, buying a few seconds to calculate the odds that they might have already checked his phone records. He concluded that it was a strong possibility.

"I've met Mr. Gotts through Victor, yes. I heard about what happened to him, it's a damned shame. Nobody's safe anymore."

It was not the most endearing comment to make in the presence of law officers, but that thought never occurred to Wainwright.

Boldt persisted. "Sir, where were you this past Friday evening?"

Wainwright felt a brief moment of panic, but managed to subdue it.

"Well, as you probably know, I was presiding over a council meeting that night."

"What about after the meeting, where were you the rest of the night?"

"There was a vote against a proposal that I felt strongly in favor of, and I was a bit frustrated. I went for a long drive to cool off, and to think about where else I could look for Nicki. The radio was on, and I heard the news about Jack Ferris being questioned by the police. I drove home to change and shower, and then I went to the police headquarters to speak to George McClure about the search for my wife, and the Ferris thing."

"Anybody see you or speak with you during this drive that you took?"

Now Wainwright was becoming visibly upset, and turned to Kaplan for rescue.

"Look, that's quite enough for now. This fishing expedition has gone on too long. My client came here in good faith, to assist in the search for his wife. We had the impression that some new leads had turned up. If that isn't the case, we're out of here."

Greco noticed with some delight that both Wainwright and Kaplan were sweating. "Mr. Kaplan, I assure you that these questions are relevant. I think your client knows that, even if you don't."

"Is my client being charged with something?"

Greco was quick to reply, and unwilling to share any more of the results of the investigation. "Not at this time. We're simply trying to determine who, if anyone, had a motive to harm Mrs. Wainwright. But we'll need to talk further, so please remain available."

Kaplan stood, as did a relieved Wainwright, and they hurriedly left the room. Boldt immediately made a call on his cell.

"Is everything in place?"

He listened to a long reply that was apparently not what he had hoped to hear.

"All right. Locate the vehicle and get it done." He ended the call and explained the conversation to the others.

"We have a signal from the Hummer but not the Volvo, for some reason. Wainwright drove here with Kaplan but the Hummer is his usual ride, so we're okay. Still, we need to locate the car and get a LoJack on it as soon as possible."

*

Neither man spoke until they had reached the safety of Kaplan's Mercedes. He started the engine but left the car in park, waiting for his friend and client's comment on what had just taken place. Sensing that none was forthcoming, he began to pull out of the lot toward his home.

"No, go left, Al. Drop me off at home, I'll be over to pick up the car tomorrow."

The attorney had expected more of an unburdening, but felt a growing reluctance to become involved any further.

"Sure, Jim. You're under a lot of stress right now, we can talk about this when you've had some rest."

"One more thing, Al. Take that box I sent to you and put it in the car for me, will you?"

Kaplan was more curious than ever about the contents of the box.

"What's in that thing, Jim? Can you trust me enough to at least share that much?"

Wainwright continued to look straight ahead. "They're personal papers. I want to find those documents from the name change, to support what I said. I don't know what the big deal is, it's no crime to change names unless you're some kind of fugitive. It's all legal."

Kaplan withheld comment, wondering how well he really knew this man.

"Take me around the block, those frigging parasites are probably camped out in front. I'll walk through the yard from the back side."

Kaplan was about to float his idea of bringing in another attorney, someone more experienced with criminal affairs, but decided against it. He didn't want to be perceived as abandoning his friend.

"I'll leave the garage door unlocked, in case I'm not there when you stop over. Get some rest, Jim."

Wainwright exited the car and closed the door without another word, and made his way between houses toward his own backyard. Kaplan watched him meld into the darkness, and drove away.

CHAPTER 67

"RONNIE, HOW MUCH farther is it? I think I might need to take a break, dude."

Ronnie Blake glanced back and saw his hiking partner bent over, hands on his knees, trying to catch his breath. He was only 23, but Mike Rifenburg was woefully out of shape. His sporting activities were normally confined to computer video games, but Ronnie had convinced Mike that the short hike to the cache would be enjoyable. To Mike's dismay, he had wrongly equated the word "enjoyable" with "leisurely".

"I told you two minutes ago, it's at the top of the next hill. That's the high point of the area, it drops off from there to the farm."

"I could swear you said that on the last hill, but whatever." Mike straightened up and trudged upward. "This is fun, though. Exhilarating, really."

They came to a plateau and made their way across a shallow ravine to the final rise. Ronnie pointed out a rough pyramid of rocks about three feet high.

"That's it."

Sweating profusely, Mike took his coat off and tossed it over a fallen tree trunk. He took a long look at the surroundings, feeling the satisfaction of having persevered and reached their destination without having his heart explode from his chest.

Ronnie was removing rocks from the pile, uncovering a metal ammunition box that he had hidden there. He opened it and began to carefully examine the contents, sometimes pausing to make annotations in the journal he had brought.

"So what's in there, Ronnie?"

"Some guys from Pittsburgh were here a few weeks ago, and someone from Syracuse. They left a Powerbar, you want half?"

"Sure, I could use some power."

As he ate Mike gazed to the west, where the trees thinned out enough to allow a wider field of view.

"What did you say is down there, Shale Creek?"

"Yeah, it's a pretty deep ravine. If you go upstream from here, staying up on top, you can see the eternal flame grotto without climbing all the way down to the creek bed."

"Seriously? That's cool, I'm going over to take a look."

"Alright. Don't get lost, Mike, it's easy to get turned around when you're climbing over deadfalls and going around the thick stuff. And be careful going near the edge, that ravine is really steep."

Mike was offended by Ronnie's lack of confidence in his ability. "You said I could see it from up here though, right?"

"Yep."

Ronnie resumed his work, and only a few minutes later he heard what sounded like a distant shout. He stopped writing and listened intently, and this time he was sure that Mike was calling to him, although he couldn't make out the words.

"Mike?"

Ronnie headed toward the sound, and heard Mike shout to him again in a voice that was clearly panicked. Twigs slashed at Ronnie's face as he rushed toward the sound, and he finally spotted his friend some fifty feet ahead, on all fours.

"Mike, what's up?"

Mike didn't answer, and Ronnie could see that he was coughing and vomiting. Ronnie's first thought was that the Powerbar must be the cause, and was glad he hadn't eaten his half. He put a hand on Mike's back, not knowing what else to do to help him.

"Mike, are you okay, man?"

"Ronnie, we gotta call 911!"

"Are you sick? Do you think the Powerbar was poisoned or something?"

Mike wiped a hand across his mouth and spit, trying to rid himself of the taste of bile.

"No, it isn't me." He pointed to a spot at the bottom of a slight downhill grade twenty yards away, where a patch of light blue contrasted against the dull brown earth and dead leaves.

"There's a body down there. A woman, I think. Call 911!"

CHAPTER 68

GEORGE MCCLURE HAD been addressing the core of the task force, twelve people who were immersed full time in the search for information that would lead them to Nicole Wainwright. Rowan and Webster were present, as were four detectives who had been assigned to them by agencies outside of the Grove Park police department. David Greco and Special Agent Boldt were on hand, as well as several uniformed officers.

"You've heard a recap of the case as it now stands from the lead detectives, so we're all on the same page. I'd like to thank all of you for the terrific effort being put forth. I don't want you to think the long hours have gone unnoticed or unappreciated. Without your help, we couldn't possibly follow every lead and organize all the information the way you have. Now we're going to put that knowledge to work. I'm going to let Dave Greco take it from here."

Greco took his place at the front of the room, next to an easel that held a poster-size pad of paper in portrait orientation.

"Gentlemen, I'd like to start by asking for your help in solving a problem that has become not only an embarrassment, but possibly a hindrance to our investigation. There's been entirely too much information reaching the media before we're prepared to announce it. This has to stop! With all due respect to you as professionals, I'm not pointing fingers here, I have no idea where the leaks originated. I'm just making sure that everyone involved will be more aware than ever about keeping information within our circle and out of the press until we're ready to release it."

The room was dead silent, causing Greco to wonder whether those present felt insulted by his words. Having made his point, he moved on.

"For the purpose of this meeting I want to make an assumption, one that we won't discuss outside of this room. We'll assume that some sort of foul play has befallen Nicole Wainwright, that a crime has been committed. We will focus our attention on two persons of interest in the case, the only viable suspects based on what we know at this time.

"If in fact Mrs. Wainwright is the victim of a homicide, what motive might James Wainwright or Jack Ferris have had? Let's brainstorm this thing, and use your experience and imagination. Toss out whatever ideas come to mind, no matter how much of a stretch it might be. We'll start with Ferris. Anyone?"

Three voices answered immediately, with variations of a common theme.

"Lover's quarrel."

"Fit of rage."

"Jealousy? Maybe she was involved with someone else."

At the easel, Greco hurriedly listed their comments as the conversation gained steam.

Rocky Showles, a detective on loan from the State Police, was convinced that Ferris was responsible for Nicki's disappearance and had been telling such to anyone who would listen.

"Her blood was found in his house, the DNA matches. They were involved sexually, and something happened to set him off. End of story."

Greco turned to face Showles, holding up a hand to slow him down. "Okay, we've discussed the evidence, let's stay on motive for now."

Rocco Showles was well known and widely respected in upstate New York, having closed dozens of homicide cases, including some that had been thought dead because of a lack of evidence.

"All due respect, Dave, most D.A.'s want evidence and more evidence. Motive isn't usually the tough part of the burden of proof, it's the physical evidence that connect the dots for a jury."

Greco didn't seem the least bit exasperated by the challenge to his agenda. "Absolutely true. All I'm asking is for you to bear with me as we build the best possible theory of this case, assuming that a crime has been committed. If we all understand the most likely scenario, I believe we can better focus our efforts."

Showles shrugged indifferently.

"Sure, I'm open minded." There were a few muted chuckles as Greco continued.

"Now, let's move on to the husband of the missing woman." He tore the top sheet from the oversize tablet and taped it to the wall next to the door, where it could only be seen by the occupants of the room. Returning to the easel, Greco warmed to what he considered to be the more challenging task.

"James Wainwright. Any ideas on motive here? Hands, please, so I can capture everyone's comments." Several hands were raised, and within a few minutes Greco's rather shaky script had filled the entire page. He paused to review what had been recorded.

"'Jealousy.' He found out that she was having an affair.

"She discovered some dark secret from his past.

"Something she discovered about his present-day activities.

"Money. She was pretty heavily insured, and had built her own wealth before they married.

"He hired Ferris to do it" was Hank Rowan's contribution, an idea from left field that Greco loved because it represented the true "think outside the box" spirit of brainstorming.

Like a bidder at Sotheby's, Boldt raised a hand in a subtle, nearly imperceptible motion.

"Yes, Agent Boldt."

"I think it's time we discussed the connection between Wainwright and Victor Harmon, now that Harmon is beginning to talk to us."

Webster sat straight up in his metal chair, which had begun to assert itself as an instrument of torture over the previous twenty minutes. Finally, he would hear the information that the Bureau had been holding back.

A sharp rap on the door interrupted them before Greco could respond. McClure had been standing nearby, and opened it to have a short, murmured conversation with Eric Bronski. McClure turned to motion Webster and Rowan to follow him outside.

"We just took a 911 call. A body's been found in a wooded area off of Davis, a few miles out of town. It could be Nicole Wainwright. There's a patrol unit responding, and I want you two to get out there and make sure the scene is protected. I don't want anyone tramping around in there before the crime scene team arrives."

CHAPTER 69

FIVE MILES PAST the Grove Park village limits Webster and Rowan spotted the flashing light bar of a county sheriff's cruiser that was parked on the narrow shoulder, intentionally blocking a gravel road that cut off to the right. Craning his neck to get a look, Pete could see that it led to a rather dilapidated barn surrounded by outdated earthmoving equipment.

He pulled up to parallel the patrol car while Rowan, from the shotgun seat, lowered his window and flashed his badge as he addressed the burly deputy.

"CSU get here yet?"

"They just drove in a few minutes ago. I'll move up so you can pull in. Bear to the left before the barn, you'll see a dirt road leading back toward the woods. That's where the action is."

"Alright, thanks. Listen, keep everyone out, including the local volunteers, and especially the news creeps, okay?"

"Will do. There's a couple of Grove Park uniforms up there already."

Webster drove in and followed the jolting path that had been charitably described as a road, until it ended at a narrow open field where the other responding vehicles were parked.

Pete was glad to be wearing rough-soled work boots as they made their way on foot over the slick, muddy terrain, up a slight grade toward the tree line where forensic technicians could be seen combing the area. Camera strobes flashed in rapid fire as the scene was recorded in painstaking detail. Hank was having difficulty keeping his leather-soled loafers beneath him, and Webster was sure that his partner was about to go down face-first at any moment. Both men were inwardly thankful when they had made their way to the active area without mishap.

Jerry Roberts, a rather short, muscular Grove Park patrolman familiar to both detectives, walked up to meet them with his partner in tow. Rich Narron was a rookie with only a few months on the force, and was the physical opposite of Roberts. He was tall and thin, with a short crop of bright red hair and a freckled face. He was twenty-eight, but to Rowan the kid looked like he might be a high school senior.

"What have we got, boys?"

Roberts flipped open a note pad, but didn't bother to refer to it just yet as he launched into his report.

"Those two guys over there called it in, they were hiking through here and found the body." Now he glanced down to the pad, as if assuring them that the information he passed on would be accurate and complete. "It's a female, maybe 5'6, medium build, wearing a light blue wind suit and running shoes. She's been out here a while, so visual identification is going to be impossible. You'll see what I mean."

Webster gestured toward the two men, who appeared to be in their early twenties. They stood ten yards away with their shoulders hunched and hands firmly in their coat pockets, shifting their weight from side to side and looking chilled to the bone.

"So they were hiking up here, and just stumbled onto the body?"

"Yes, sir." Narron felt better now that he had contributed to the conversation.

Hank looked at Pete as he jerked a thumb toward the pair. "I'll have a talk with these guys, you go ahead and check with the crime scene unit."

Pete approached to within ten steps of the body, which was now surrounded by a team of forensic scientists dressed in protective Tyvek suits whose specialty it was to discover and collect even the most minute evidence from the site. One of them stood up and turned to him, holding up a hand as a stop sign. She pulled down her mask with a gloved hand.

"Give us some time before you enter the field, cowboy." It was the now-familiar face of team leader Donna Mackey, looking all business.

"Certainly, Officer Mackey. We have to stop meeting like this."

She cracked a smile. "One of the hazards of the job, Detective. Seriously, just five minutes more and you'll be able to get a closer look, I'll tell you where to step. Try to disturb as little as possible, or Marvin will be pissed. He trusts our team to start without him, but you guys are a different story."

Marvin Worley, the county Medical Examiner, was meticulous and accurate, commendable traits which could also make him difficult to work with. In his defense, there was a strict crime scene protocol to be followed, and this case would put his actions under a microscope.

The M.E. would perform his basic examination of the body only after the initial recording of the undisturbed site. Under his direction, the body could then be moved to determine preliminary cause of death and to possibly uncover evidence that might lie beneath it. When the M.E. gave his permission, other law enforcement personnel would be allowed to examine the scene under the direction of the Crime Scene Unit, headed by Mackey, as they completed their exhaustive search of the area. Upon the completion of those efforts, the body would be transported to the county morgue for a more explorative examination, formal identification, and autopsy.

"Will do. We're not trying to rush you, and we know better than to contaminate the scene. We may be small town cops, but this ain't our first rodeo. What did you find, was there any i.d. on her?"

"We can't really move her yet to check for hidden pockets, but her running shoe has a little gold tag tied into the laces with the name 'Nicki' engraved on it. She's wearing the light blue outfit, too."

Pete looked down at what they both knew were the remains of Nicole Wainwright, and tried to picture how naturally beautiful she had looked the day he informed her of Jill Sherman's death. He wondered what dangerous information she could possibly have possessed, or who she had wronged, that might have led to such a violent death.

"What's your guess as to how long the body's been out here?"

Mackey removed her hair net and shook out her curly brown locks.

"I'd say close to two weeks, plus or minus a few days. The M.E. will be more accurate after the autopsy."

"That would fit, assuming she was killed the same day she disappeared."

Two technicians carrying small evidence envelopes passed by on their way to the van, one of them nodding to Mackey to convey that they had completed the initial search for forensic clues around the body.

"Okay, let's go. Put these booties and gloves on, and we'll approach from behind her."

Pete saw that several markers had been laid out, establishing the required north-west datums and a scale that would provide accurate perspective for viewers of the photographs and video. A few numbered marker flags had been placed in the ground near the body. As they reached the corpse, Mackey pointed to the head. "There's not much flesh left on the exposed areas, the face and hands. Between normal decomp, wet weather, and scavengers, it's pretty well gone."

The body was lying on its back, looking more skeletal than Pete had expected. The limbs were splayed away from the torso at unnatural angles, as if they had been pulled at, and the clothing was torn away around the hands and feet.

"Scavengers?"

"Rodents, birds, maybe a fox or coyotes. They'll all feed on carrion." She looked at Pete, thinking that her characterization might have sounded offensive. "No disrespect, I mean that's what this is to them, human or not."

Pete crouched down for a closer look at the dark halo of earth around the skull. It was a rusty brown color, having absorbed what must have been a considerable pool of blood.

"No gunshot or stab wound that I can see. Looks like a blow to the back of the head."

"Yes, and we collected samples from the trunk of this tree, probably dried blood and tissue. We haven't found a rock or anything else that might have been used to inflict head trauma, but we're still searching the grid. If she was running from someone, there could be evidence further out. Oh, and we also collected what looked like stomach contents a few yards away. Turns out it belonged to the guy that found the body."

"I guess we won't be sending that in to the lab, huh?"

Webster noted that clear plastic bags had been placed over the hands of the victim, and he could see that only a few fingers remained intact. He recalled Jack's statement, in which he claimed that the blood in his house came from a cut Nicki had suffered from a kitchen knife. It would be impossible to verify such a wound, if it had ever existed at all.

"Any fingernails left to scrape?"

Mackey shrugged. "A few, but with the long exposure to wet weather, I wouldn't count on any foreign DNA remaining."

Pete rose and backed off a few steps, pulling out his phone to call the Chief. An anxious McClure answered on the first ring, and Pete filled him in.

"No positive i.d. at this point, but it looks like we've found Nicole Wainwright, Chief. You should contact the husband, let him know that the body will be available for identification in a couple of hours.

"We're going to need some people to control all possible access routes to the scene, the news trucks are going to be here any minute. I hear a helicopter already, so the word might be out. We'll be here a while, the M.E. hasn't arrived yet."

"You stay right there and help control things, Pete, I'll make the call to Wainwright. Keep me posted."

CHAPTER 70

GEORGE MCCLURE HAD personally checked with the Supervisor's office and, as he had expected, Wainwright was not in. An assistant accessed his schedule through the network calendar and informed the Chief that the Supervisor had a notation of "business meeting" entered for the entire afternoon, with no specific location or contact listed.

Upon returning to his own office, McClure called Wainwright's cell phone and was immediately directed to voice mail. He left a brief message urging Wainwright to call back as soon as possible, and then waited for more information from the scene. By the time Wainwright returned the call some thirty minutes later, McClure had informed the task force of the grim discovery and had taken part in a more detailed discussion of events with Greco and Boldt.

"Jim, where are you?"

"Just came out of a meeting, George, I was on my way to check in at the real estate office" he ad-libbed. His talent for fabricating lies on demand was honed to a keen edge through a lifetime of practice. In truth, Wainwright had spent a couple of hours at a local racino, playing five-dollar video poker.

"What's up?"

"Jim, I'd like you to come in to the station. There's a possibility that we've discovered something important, and I want you to hear about it from us before the press gets involved."

"Discovered something? What?"

McClure hesitated, unsure of how to frame his reply, leaving Wainwright to continue his demands for information.

"George, have you found Nicki? Do you know where she is? If you want me to hear about it from you, start talking."

McClure felt that he owed Wainwright an honest answer. He hated to deliver such news with a phone call, and had avoided specifics when he had left his message earlier, but the victim's husband deserved a straightforward response.

"All right. A body's been found in the woods near Davis Road. No definite identity has been established, but the detectives on the scene think that it may be Nicole. I'm sorry to have to tell you this way, Jim."

The expected stunned silence endured for only a few short seconds.

"Near the search area? How did they miss it before?"

"This isn't actually in the search grid, Jim, it's further out of town, five miles or so. Near that natural gas flame thing."

"Oh my god. Can they tell what happened? How did she — "

McClure heard the faint indications of sobbing that Wainwright was unable to subdue, and was aware that he was unable to speak.

"Jim, let me send a car to pick you up."

"No, no, I'm alright. Off of Davis Road, that's where she is?"

"It's still a tentative i.d., but yes."

"I'm going out there."

"Jim, no, listen to me, there's nothing you can do there. Just come — Jim?" McClure abandoned his plea, realizing that Wainwright had ended the call.

The Supervisor's mind was racing, but he was not frozen by the shocking phone call. The news had shaken him to his core for only a few minutes, until his survival instincts had kicked in. Still holding his phone, he scrolled to Joey Garrity's name and hit the call icon.

Without explanation, he told Joey to meet him outside the real estate office right away, and was there himself within fifteen minutes. Garrity's white Lexus sport coupe was already parked in the small parking lot behind the office. He had been there only a few minutes when the yellow Hummer pulled in, and Big Jim motioned for him to come over to it. Wainwright reached over to open the door and Joey climbed in, wondering why anyone would own a vehicle that required such an effort to enter.

Joey looked at Wainwright and saw that he was highly agitated, as if he were in a hurry and was restraining himself. "Boss, what's up?"

"Joey, something's come up and I need a favor, I mean *really* need it. Can I count on you?"

Whatever was going on, Joey felt that his loyalty had come into question, and he needed to restore Wainwright's faith in him. He was having second thoughts about his confession to Al, but for now he remained confident that Kaplan had kept that to himself.

"Of course you can. As long as I don't have to kill anyone." Joey's eyes widened as he realized his innocent joke might be construed as a dig, or in poor taste at best. "I mean, of course you can count on me, I didn't mean any disrespect."

Wainwright waved off the clumsy apology.

"Joey, I don't have a lot of time to chat here, just listen up! I need you to go with me to Kaplan's place, drop me there and then take my truck to Batavia for an inspection. I'll give you the address and directions on the way to Al's. Can you do that?"

Joey's face reflected the confusion he was feeling.

"Take your truck for an inspection? Now? In Batavia?" *What the hell was wrong with this man?*

"Look, goddammit, it's not some normal state inspection, this guy's a specialist. Trust me on this, it's important. I need it done, and I can't go there myself. Something has come up, an urgent matter that I have to attend to immediately. Now lock up your car, we need to get going!"

Joey grabbed his jacket and phone from the car and chirped the security system on. As they drove away he was still wondering why he had to suddenly give up his evening for such a routine errand.

CHAPTER 71

HANK ROWAN, LOOKING somewhat winded, walked over to confer with Pete.

"Well, I talked to the dynamic duo there, then I sent them with Stretch to warm up in the patrol car. I want to take them to the station and get a written statement."

"What did they have to say?"

"Like Roberts told us, they were hiking through the area playing some kind of game. The heavier one came across the body first, and his buddy called it in."

"What kind of game, like splatball or something?"

Hank held out his notebook to show Webster what he had written at the top of the page.

"Geocaching?" He looked to Hank for an explanation.

"Some internet thing. You hide a treasure box somewhere, that's the cache part. The geo comes in when you post the GPS coordinates on a web site, inviting other nerds to try and find it."

"That sounds too easy."

"Well, I guess the coordinates get you close, but there are clues to help you find the exact spot. The treasures have names, and you try to find as many as you can. Like earning merit badges, I guess."

"Did they say what this one is called?"

"Yeah. Flameout."

Pete was intrigued. He didn't suspect any connection with Nicole

Wainwright's death, but someone would have to verify the internet story to completely rule it out. "Where's this cache located?"

"It's only about a hundred yards away, they showed it to me. Nothing sinister, just a box with some small items in it. Buttons, coins, a book to leave a message in, that kind of junk. I'm having it photographed, then we'll take it with us. Did they find any i.d. on the body?"

"No, nothing in her pockets at all. When they rolled her we found an old MP3 player and earbuds under the body, that was it."

Pete's phone vibrated, and he answered to hear the concerned voice of George McClure.

"Webster, has the M.E. gotten there?"

"He's here and gone, Chief. They're getting ready to remove the body right now."

"Pete, I think Jim Wainwright may be on his way over there. I wanted him to come here, but he insisted on going to see the body. I screwed up, I shouldn't have mentioned Davis Road. He doesn't know exactly where you are, though."

"It won't be hard to spot. I hear there's a horde of media down at the access point, and some trying to get here from the other side, at the Eternal Flame trail head."

"Yeah, so I've heard. Just be advised, he might be showing up."

"Okay, George, we got it covered. Look, I have another call. I'll get back to you."

Pete deftly switched to the incoming caller.

"Webster."

"Hi Pete. Can you talk?" Sally's voice sounded especially sweet, allowing Pete his first thought of anything other than the crime scene in over two hours.

"Sally, hi — listen, I'm right in the middle of something, I don't have much time to talk. What's going on?"

"Oh, nothing important, I won't keep you. I was wondering if I'd see you tonight is all."

"Wild horses couldn't keep me away. Have I ever used that one before?"

"A few times. Sometimes you even show up."

He chuckled, picturing the smile of satisfaction Sally would have after needling him.

"I'll call first, it could be late."

"Great, I'll be up."

"Sally, one more thing. I need you to look for a web site for me. Write this down.

After a short pause to retrieve a pen she was all ears. "Go ahead."

"I don't have a web address, but the key word is geocaching." He spelled it for her, and gave a brief explanation of the game.

"See if you can find a cache near Grove Park called 'Flameout'. Got it?"

"Yep. I'm all over it, sir."

"I'll see you later, but call me if you find anything interesting."

"'kay. See ya later, sweetie."

Hank saw Pete tuck his phone away, and returned from what he had considered a discreet distance.

"You ready, Romeo? Let's wrap this up and make our way through the mob down there. A couple of 'em managed to get pretty close before we kicked their asses out."

"I'm ready. By the way, the Chief thinks Mr. Wainwright may be on his way out here, so keep an eye out for him."

"That's just great. Man, my feet are killing me. I'm getting too old for this boy scout stuff."

CHAPTER 72

JAMES WAINWRIGHT HAD always believed that, even when things seemed to be going well, it was always wise to have a contingency plan. The one he was putting into motion hadn't been thought out in detail, he had only formulated it in a general sense, but so far that mental preparation had paid off.

Since Nicki's disappearance he had been subjected to the unwanted attention of the media, and had become somewhat accustomed to it. In recent days, as the story had become a national sensation, Wainwright had been relentlessly dogged by the growing pack of media hounds who relayed minimal facts and maximum guesswork to a public that was increasingly thirsty for details. Their pedigrees ran the gamut from local reporters such as Jennifer Banks to cable news icons like the mustachioed Geraldo Garza, who had been spotted in Grove Park a day earlier.

Wainwright's yellow vehicle was easy to spot, but early on he became adept at losing his pursuers in the maze of rural roads outside of Grove Park, allowing him to continue freely to his destination without fear of being observed. That sense of freedom dissipated when he became aware of the involvement of the FBI. The possibility that electronic tracking and recording devices could be hidden on his vehicles had prompted him to consult with an old racetrack acquaintance who was somewhat connected in the Buffalo area, and Wainwright was put in touch with a young guy named Billy Osborne.

Osborne owned a small custom audio shop in the town of Batavia, nearly an hour away from Grove Park, where he installed a wide array of electronic sound and GPS systems in top-end vehicles whose owners didn't trust their ride with the retail outlet installation hacks.

In addition, Billy offered a specialty service that wasn't advertised to the general public. He possessed the necessary equipment to scan a vehicle for hidden transmitters and listening devices. An expensive house call by Osborne the previous night had confirmed Wainwright's suspicions. Tracking devices were found on both vehicles, and Billy was instructed by the owner to remove the bug from the Volvo, but to leave the Hummer intact until further notice.

At that moment Joey was thirty minutes into his journey to Batavia, probably grumbling to himself the entire way. If Wainwright's assumption was correct, police would be monitoring the Hummer's location and soon realize that it was not moving in a direction that would lead to Davis Road, or to Grove Park for that matter. They might be satisfied to observe for a while, but before long an order would be issued to intercept the Hummer and determine what Wainwright was up to.

That deception was vital to the Supervisor because it was buying precious time. He was already guiding the Volvo onto the I-90 toward downtown Buffalo, praying that Osborne's handiwork would keep him a step ahead of the authorities. He was making good time without exceeding the speed limit through traffic that was light, even though it was the afternoon drive time. Most of the traffic volume was moving in the opposite direction, as those suburban residents who toiled in the city and the northern suburbs had completed their workday and were returning to their homes south of the city.

In spite of the circumstances, Wainwright smiled as he thought of Joey piloting the Hummer, forced to listen to country CD's. Osborne had disabled the AM, FM, and satellite radio, keeping the interim driver insulated from any news reports of the possible discovery of Nicole Wainwright's remains. With the cops undoubtedly tracking the Hummer, Joey would unwittingly complete his mission simply by leading them in the wrong direction and buying precious time for his boss.

Ignoring the exits that led to local streets, Wainwright looked for the familiar green sign that read "BRIDGE TO CANADA". Part of the beauty of residing in Grove Park was that one could leave the quiet confines of the village and be in the city within twenty minutes, or in another country in forty via the Peace Bridge.

Following the exit as it wound to the bridge plaza, Wainwright paid the $3.00 toll and continued on toward the row of U.S.Customs inspection booths, rolling to a stop in what he hoped would be a rapidly moving line of vehicles. He was comfortingly familiar with the crossing procedure, having been through it many times before. Some of those trips across the border had been romantic weekends in Toronto with Nicki, back in the happy early months of their marriage. On more frequent occasions, he had crossed over with friends for a day of golf, which was invariably followed by a visit to one of the strip clubs that Americans knew as the Canadian Ballet.

At least six cars had moved through the checkpoint in front of him, and Wainwright noticed that none had been diverted to the area where vehicle searches were conducted. He knew that random searches had been lessened as the years since 9-11 passed by, but the possibility was always there. Past experience was not enough to calm his increasingly rapid heartbeat as the border officer waved him up to his window.

The Volvo's plate number had most likely already been typed into a database by the inspector, looking for any registration nonconformance or other alerts, as Wainwright pulled ahead.

"Afternoon" he offered, trying to convince himself that this was just an ordinary passage on his way to the Links at Fort Erie. He held out his New York State Enhanced driver's license as identification, rather than his passport. The agent asked questions as he studied it.

"Place of birth?"

"Ames, Iowa, U.S.A. sir, now a resident of New York." He was trying to sound friendly and relaxed.

"Where you headed, sir?" These border guys were all business.

"I'm on my way to Detroit, to a seminar on local government. I'm doing a presentation there tomorrow." He knew it was too much information, and stopped himself as the officer peered behind him at the back seat.

Crossing into Canada while claiming the American city as his destination would not have seemed unusual to any Peace Bridge employee, since the driving time from Buffalo to Detroit was an hour less along the northern shore of Lake Erie. Driving to Detroit through the states would involve traveling completely around the lake on its southern side through Cleveland, and then traveling north into Michigan. Businessman making the trip from western New York usually preferred the two bridge crossings in and out of Canada to the increased traffic and extra 75 miles that the American route would involve.

"What's in the boxes?"

"That's my presentation, printed copies to hand out."

The boxes had been left in plain sight, uncovered, to give the impression of a man who had nothing to hide, a huge risk considering what was beneath the top few stacks of meaningless paperwork. All of Wainwright's cash and personal documents were there, including several forms of false identification. He felt perspiration forming on his forehead and upper lip, and it was a struggle to resist loosening his tie.

"That's it? Nothing to declare?"

"No sir, just this stuff and my clothes for tomorrow."

He waited for the officer's command to open the trunk, which he felt was sure to come after making such a stupid statement. There were no clothes on the back seat, indicating that there would be a suitcase in the trunk.

"Go ahead."

Wainwright looked at the officer and hesitated for a moment, making sure of his meaning. When he saw him waving the next car in, He let the Volvo glide forward and drove onto the bridge, knowing that there would be one more hurdle before he could breathe easier. He needed to somehow obtain a clean vehicle to complete his identity change.

He merged into the left lane of traffic and carefully drove over the one-mile expanse, occasionally glancing down at the Niagara River as it spilled out of Lake Erie on its way to a spectacular drop at the world-famous waterfall. There was no going back now.

The news that Nicki's body had been found had been the last straw. As strained as their relationship had become, she was the glue that bonded him to his life in Grove Park. With her gone, there was no reason to stay.

In retrospect, killing Gotts had been a huge mistake, one that

Wainwright had thoroughly enjoyed making but a mistake nonetheless. Even if Harmon was ratting on him, the bribery charges could be handled with minimal damage. Still, his days in elected office would be over.

Wainwright had always taken pride in being a survivor. He had started over before, and he could do it again. After all, this time he possessed the advantages of past experience and a bankroll. He had an expensive set of identification with a new name, and it should be easy to unload the Volvo and obtain a dependable SUV if he met the right sort of people.

Western Canada seemed like a perfect place in which to lose himself, and the drive there would be therapeutic. Eventually there might be an opportunity to move into a small town in Alaska, but there was no hurry. After all, a new life took time to evolve.

CHAPTER 73

SIXTEEN-HOUR DAYS WERE taking their toll on many of the task force members, and Pete Webster was no exception. He had never felt quite so driven in all his years in law enforcement, and certainly had never worked on a case as high-profile as this one.

When the search for Nicole Wainwright began, Webster had been compelled to solve the mystery of her disappearance by his sense of duty alone. When Jack's involvement came to light, he felt an additional urgency to prove his friend innocent of any wrongdoing. Pete had already been involved in his personal investigation into the whereabouts of Steve Hartman, and now it seemed that Steve's murder was also related to the Wainwright case in some way.

Now that Nicole Wainwright's lifeless body had been found Pete was determined to find those responsible, and thereby solve the other mysteries that seemed to be spin-offs of the homicide.

He was driven but still merely human, which was the reason he and Hank had agreed to return to their homes for a couple of hours of downtime and meet up at the station afterwards. They needed time to think about something other than the case, or at least to step back and put their thoughts in order, before continuing the investigation with renewed vigor.

Webster had wolfed down a can of his go-to comfort food, Beef-aroni, and was still sitting at the kitchen table poring over his notes and examining a few photos from the Davis Road scene. There was a knock at the door, barely audible through the sound of the GooGoo Dolls' 'Better Days' that filled the small house, and he hurriedly turned the volume down before answering. As he swung the door open, he was once again treated to the thrill of the unanticipated presence of Sally.

"Hey, what a great surprise, come on in", he managed, self-consciously scanning the room to estimate its position on the embarrassment scale. It looked like an acceptable six out of ten, especially considering his bachelor status, and he relaxed a bit. He took Sally's coat from her, and enjoyed the scent of her Obsession as he placed it on one of the hooks of a wall-mounted rack near the door.

"I was just about to call you. I stopped home to grab something to eat and, well, I'm glad you came." Sally didn't say a word as she stepped into him, and their embrace led to a soft, lingering kiss that was a testament to their growing feelings for each other.

"You don't have to explain, Pete, I know you're consumed by this case right now. I just wanted to see you for a few minutes, so you don't forget me." She flashed an impish smile and sat on the couch, curling her legs beneath her. "Besides, I have to complete my assignment by telling you all about the great American sport, geocaching."

He laughed, and sat down next to her, draping an arm on the back of the sofa as he turned to face her. "Fire away, I'm all ears."

"It all centers around global positioning devices. They're so common now, pretty much everyone has an app on their phone. They're easy to use, and a hell of a lot more dependable than a compass reading. So, now that we have these cool little gadgets, I guess it made sense to invent a game that would utilize them. Thus, geocaching was born."

"As I understand it from Professor Rowan, these people play high-tech hide and seek with them."

"No, more like high-tech treasure hunt. They conceal a small container, and post the coordinates on a web site. You know, longitude and latitude."

"Of course. I have all their cd's" he deadpanned. "Okay, so they put little prizes in the box, and clues on where it's hidden, and people that manage to find the box sign in and go off somewhere to celebrate."

"Pretty much. It's a little geeky, but kind of a neat way to get out and explore different places. They seem to do it in pairs, from what I've seen online. Couples, or buddies."

"Very informative, Sally, as always. Thank you. Did you see the Flameout cache listed anywhere?"

"Yep, just as you were told, there's a western New York chapter of some national organization that has its own site."

She pulled a paper from the rear pocket of her jeans and unfolded it, offering it to him. "Here's a printout, with the Flameout listing."

Pete inspected the page, and spotted a familiar name. "This is one of the guys who found her, Ron Blake. Looks like he was telling the truth, he's the keeper of the cache."

He tossed the page onto the coffee table. "Thanks for the help, hon."

"You're welcome, hon." She stood up and stuck her hands in her back pockets, looking around the room. "So, this is your place. Nice, Pete."

"Oh, thanks. I totally forgot, you've never been here before. Let me show you around." He turned to lead her toward the kitchen, but Sally took his hand and held him back. She put her arms around his neck and fixed her soulful eyes on his.

"I was hoping you'd show me the bedroom. Is that too forward?"

"Not at all. I think that's a wonderful idea."

*

An hour later as they lie on their backs in Pete's bed, physically spent and quietly enjoying the moment, Sally considered asking Pete for permission to light up. She decided against it, and instead broke the silence with a different question.

"Pete, do you think your friend Jack is capable of something like this?"

He rolled onto his side to face her, rising onto one elbow so Sally could see straight into his eyes as he answered. "Absolutely not. It's my opinion as his friend, and also as a cop who thinks he is pretty good judge of people's character. That includes knowing what they're capable of, and I know Jack Ferris didn't do this." He rolled onto his back again, staring at the ceiling as he spoke. "That being said, I'd be a lousy cop if I didn't leave room for consideration of the idea. Until we have evidence that proves otherwise, Jack is a suspect."

"Have you spoken to him yet, Pete?"

"No, not at all. It's a conflict of interest thing, it's better if we don't speak to each other right now. I hope he knows I still believe he's innocent, especially now that she's been found."

"I'm sure he does. Hey, do you have time for a cup of coffee before you go back to work?"

He kissed her forehead and sat up. "Sure do. I have to jump in the shower first, though. Be back in a flash."

When he was finished Pete dressed and headed for the kitchen, lured by the smell of fresh coffee and the thought of a kiss from the barista. He found Sally at the table, looking at one of the pictures from the crime scene. He grabbed a mug and began to pour.

"You sure you want to do that? Those pictures are pretty grisly."

Sally looked up almost in surprise, having been absorbed in her own thoughts.

"I'm sorry, Pete, I should know better than to snoop into your case file like this. It's just that something in this picture caught my eye." She held up a full-page image that showed the position of Nicki Wainwright's MP3 player and earbuds after the body had been removed. "This is retro, it's a Yepp MP3 player. I had one exactly like this, I used to listen to it when I went for my morning walk. I haven't used it in years, since I got my Ipod, and then I moved the music to my phone. I'm pretty sure it's still around the house someplace, though."

Pete leaned against the counter and sipped his coffee.

"She was laying on top of it. That was taken right before they bagged it. She left her phone at home, for whatever reason."

As usual, Sally was ready to offer a logical explanation.

"Well, sometimes walking, or running, is a person's escape from the world, just for a little while. I can understand someone who wants to listen to her favorite music without the distraction of texts, phone calls, social media, all of that. Did you have a chance to check it out yet?"

"I haven't but someone will. I don't imagine we'll get any useful clues from her choice of music, though."

"No," she continued, patiently overlooking the tinge of condescension in his reply, "but it has a memo feature on it. That might be worth checking out."

Pete put his cup down, taking the subject more seriously.

"A memo feature? Why wouldn't she use her phone if that's what she wanted?"

"Like I said, no outside communication. Maybe she hadn't used that feature for a while but it's possible she did. Personal reminders, bright ideas, random thoughts, whatever. Maybe she mentioned a name, an appointment, something like that. I only meant that it would be worth looking into."

"It is, and thank you once again, detective Raines. I'll have someone look into it." This time the condescension was absent.

"What happens next, Pete? Will there be an arrest?"

"I don't think so, not yet anyway. We'll work with the evidence tonight, and see where it leads us. There's a task force meeting tomorrow, and probably some sort of statement to the press after that. McClure will be under the lights again, poor bastard."

Sally stood and walked over to him, taking both of his hands in hers. "Thanks for taking some time out to be with me."

He hugged her and kissed her forehead.

"No, thank *you*, Sally. I needed to see you, and it was perfect. I'm sorry that I have to run back to work."

"Oh, it's okay, I want to get back to Jonathan anyway. My father is with him, so he's in good hands, but his dad's death is hitting him pretty hard. He was pleased to hear that you'll be able to attend the memorial service."

"He's a good kid — young man, I should say. He just needs time to deal with it, I'm sure he'll be fine. He's got a great mom to help him out."

"Thanks. My god, we have to stop thanking each other so much, don't you think?" She laughed as she walked away to retrieve her coat from the rack.

"You mean you're ready to move past the polite stage already?"

"Let's just say that we don't have to be so formal, as if we're afraid of stepping on each other's toes. We know each other well enough to be comfortable, don't you think?"

"I'm all for it."

Sally tugged on his shirt, pulling him closer for a goodbye peck. "A man of few words. I like that, especially when you agree with me. I'll see you tomorrow, Petey. Be careful out there."

CHAPTER 74

PETE WEBSTER ARRIVED a few minutes late for the task force briefing, having attended the memorial service for Steve Hartman. He would rather have been there for the brunch afterward to help console Sally and Jonathan, but he was sure they understood the circumstances that kept him away.

Pete took a seat in the back of the room next to Hank Rowan, raising his eyebrows to convey his surprise that the meeting had started precisely on time. Settling into the metal folding chair, he was further surprised to find that John Chapman was handling the review of the case in place of George McClure, which explained the prompt start. The county sheriff's Chief of Detectives was a no-nonsense supervisor who had earned his position through hard work and attention to detail, and possessed organizational skills that more than qualified him for the job at hand.

Pete turned toward Hank and tilted his head in Chapman's direction with a quizzical expression. Rowan wrote something on his notepad and handed it to his confused colleague.

'*Chief needed time to prep for press conf.*'

Pete nodded his understanding and returned his attention to Chapman, who had been describing the condition of Nicole Wainwright's remains.

"Tentative identification of the victim as Nicole Wainwright was based on the size of the body and also clothing and jewelry that matched the description given by her husband of what she had been wearing when last seen. That identification was later verified through dental records and DNA testing.

"The M.E. found cause of death to be head trauma, although there was also evidence of manual strangulation. Our theory is the killer had both hands around her throat and struck her head repeatedly against a tree. That rules out the possibility that she was killed elsewhere and dumped at the Davis Road site."

Webster heard a comment from Rocky, who was seated on the other side of Rowan. "That explains why we didn't find anything in the vehicles." He didn't elaborate, but Pete knew that the plural form referred to both Ferris vehicles, which had been examined for forensic evidence.

"The two men who discovered the body appear to have no other connection to the crime. One of them, Ronald Blake, has provided further information. He claims to have been in that specific area several times before, and on one of those occasions he observed two people lying on a blanket, and also a yellow truck parked nearby. When he was shown an array of photos, Blake picked out Nicole Wainwright and Jack Ferris as the couple he had seen that day. He had difficulty remembering the exact date but he was sure it was a Saturday and finally settled on February 4th."

This was common knowledge to all of the task force detectives, and Chapman was allowed to continue without question or comment from the group.

"Forensics hasn't been able to come up with much in the way of prints, foreign DNA, or transfer evidence. All of the footprints and tire tracks can be attributed to our responding personnel and vehicles. In short, not a lot to go on." Looking up from his notes, Chapman's gaze scanned the room until he spotted Hank.

"Detective Rowan, tell us what turned up on Ferris' cell phone records."

All eyes turned toward the rear of the room as Hank stood up and cleared his throat.

"Detective Showles and I were assigned to revisit Ferris' alibi for February 14th, the day of the murder. As part of that process we obtained his cell phone records for the past three months, which listed calls to, and from, the victim. We were already aware of one particular call. It was placed to Nicole Wainwright's cell number at 8:34 am on February 14th, and lasted about 20 seconds, just long enough to leave a voice mail."

Webster was already aware of these facts, but jotted down the numbers as Hank continued.

"Yesterday we met with the Verizon people, and they were able to provide a recording of the message left by Ferris, which of course was also found on Nicole Wainwright's phone.

"I don't have the exact transcript with me, but Ferris' message indicated that he needed to speak with Mrs. Wainwright and was aware that she was probably out running at that hour. He said he might just surprise her."

Most of the detectives already had considered Jack Ferris as suspect number one, and knowing looks and nods were exchanged all around. Rowan had one additional comment before he was finished.

"I should add that Ferris had admitted early on that he had been trying to reach Mrs. Wainwright by phone, but he had never indicated that he knew where she would be at that specific time of day. He insists that he remained at the painting job until early afternoon, but we can't find anyone to corroborate."

Pete continued to look straight ahead as Hank seated himself. He was stung by the revelation, and by the widespread perception that Jack was indeed a murderer, and also by Hank's reluctance to tell him personally.

"Thank you, Detective Rowan. Stay with it. As most of you know by now, James Wainwright was not available to assist in the identification of his wife's body. He was contacted shortly after the discovery, and was adamant about driving to the site on his own. He never showed up at Davis Road, and hasn't been seen or heard from since that time. What I'm about to say next is highly confidential, not to be shared with anyone outside of this task force."

It was a familiar warning, and those present knew that it invariably preceded something new and important in the case.

"We have confirmation that a red 2015 Volvo registered to James Wainwright crossed into Canada at the Peace Bridge the evening of February 24th. Video shows a male driver resembling James Wainwright. It's grainy, and he's tricked us once before, but we think it's him this time.

There is no record of the vehicle returning to the U.S. at any port of entry. The FBI is already working with the RCMP to locate James Wainwright as a fugitive from justice. Agent Boldt has asked to address this meeting with previously withheld information. Agent Boldt?"

The special agent strode front and center, looking dashing in his elegantly cut charcoal suit. He hadn't exactly sought camaraderie with this group of street detectives, but was respected for his quiet air of confidence and professional manner.

"As many of you are aware by now, the Bureau has had a vested interest in this matter because of its relevance to a more wide-ranging investigation that targeted the New Century Corporation and its president, Kevin Cochran. Today in federal court indictments were handed down charging Cochran and others with racketeering, bribery, fraud, extortion, and tax evasion.

"Through the cooperation of Victor Harmon, an attorney contracted by New Century, we have obtained enough evidence to charge James Wainwright with the acceptance of monetary and other consideration in return for his assurance that the Cedar Ridge development proposal would be accepted by the Grove Park town council. Unfortunately, Mr. Wainwright appears to have fled to the great white north before he could be placed under arrest.

"As you can imagine, the fact that this man was able to slip out of the country when we supposedly had him under surveillance does not sit well with me, or with my superiors. With the cooperation of Canadian law enforcement, we are determined to bring him back, and we will."

He paused long enough for the assemblage of local cops to fully enjoy the sight of a federal agent with egg on his face, then returned to his explanation.

"Once Wainwright is in custody we will have a lot of questions for him, as do you. He is a person of interest in his wife's death, as well as the deaths of his first wife and possibly her mother. Suspicious circumstances seem to follow this guy everywhere, even in the death of his own father.

"Most recently there was the bludgeoning of Paul Gotts, a known mobster with ties to Kevin Cochran and the Cedar Ridge deal. An informant's statement places a man matching Wainwright's description, driving a large yellow SUV, in the parking lot of the Red Lantern motel the same night Gotts was killed.

"The picture that is emerging is one of a very clever sociopath who may have outwitted the law for decades. Until now."

He relaxed and moved to return to his seat, then stopped to impart a final opinion.

"Gentlemen, after all that's happened I'm sure you'll be keeping your eyes on Ferris, but for what it's worth, I'd be willing to bet that Wainwright is your guy."

CHAPTER 75

THE FRONT DOOR of Woody's Pub burst open as a group of laughing patrons exited. The last of them was carrying a large portable video camera in one hand, and used the other to hold the door open as Pete Webster and Hank Rowan entered.

Raucous afternoon crowds had become the norm at Woody's, even on weekdays, as visiting media crews discovered that this independently-owned bar and restaurant was the best pub in Grove Park. The food was delicious and reasonably priced, and the unpretentious atmosphere was perfect for out-of-town workers who wanted to relax just as they would at home. Added to that was the presence of local customers, most of whom were more than willing to share their opinions concerning the Wainwright case and (so they claimed) personal knowledge of those involved.

Hank spotted two men at the bar in the midst of settling their bill, and pulled Pete with him as he took up the vulture position behind them. The seats were still warm as the two detectives smoothly completed the takeover.

Woody's daughter Kristin, sporting a new streak of cardinal red through her long blonde hair, was clearing the dishes from the bar between them. "Hi guys, what can I getcha?"

Pete was first to respond. " I'll have an O'Doul's, Kris, thanks."

Hank disapproved of the choice of beverages.

"Come on, when I said I'd buy us a beer I meant real beer, not some N/A bullshit. Give us a couple of Blues, dear, and a double order of wings, hot, and make 'em crispy."

Pete was amused at the older man's spirit. "Okay, if you insist, but just one. It's early, and we're on duty."

"Hey, we're working so many frigging hours, who knows when we're on and when we're off anymore? Listen, I just don't want any hard feelings between us, Pete, we've been friends too long for that. We might have different opinions about this thing, but we both want to get to the truth, whatever it is."

Pete clinked his bottle against Hank's. "Whatever it is."

They heard the sound of breaking glass from the back of the bar in the pool table area, followed by angry voices. Kristin gave the two cops a look that was a plea for assistance, and Hank was already on his feet.

"I'll get that. Sounds like the kids are growing their beer muscles." Pete wanted to accompany him, but didn't want to imply that the older man needed help dealing with the situation. He looked up at the newly installed sixty-inch HD flat screen, no doubt financed by the recent increase in business, and saw the ever-serious face of Lindsey Locke. The noisy crowd made it impossible to hear what she was saying, but Pete felt safe in assuming that she was in the midst of the latest installment of the Nicole Wainwright story.

As was his habit, Pete's eyes covered the room, assessing the clientele and looking for familiar faces. Hank had already settled the dispute over the rules of nine-ball and was now engaged in conversation with Ed Flanders, who was unusually animated.

Kristin returned and set a steaming platter in front of Pete, and the smell of hot wings made him realize how hungry he was. He resisted the urge to pick one up, hoping that Hank would be able to break away from Flanders and rejoin him. Ed could really hang, especially after a few boilermakers, and Pete knew from experience that it could be difficult to tactfully put an end to his rambling.

Up on the big screen someone was interviewing two scruffy young men dressed in camouflage clothing. The ever-present crawler identified them as 'Garth and Nathan Jenkins, encountered James Wainwright on their property.'

"Who the hell are these guys?" Pete asked himself, pulling out his book to jot the names down. As he continued to watch the camera panned out to a wider shot, revealing rolling farmland and a line of slowly revolving windmills in the distance. Pete recognized the place, having passed by it a few times as he traveled Briggs Road, and he wondered what connection it had to the case, if any.

"Christ, that guy is annoying," Hank moaned as he returned. "How're the wings?"

"I was holding off until you got back. What was Ed carrying on about?"

Hank grimaced and shook his head. "Oh, he's just drunk and incoherent, as usual. Something to do with the Jill Sherman accident, He claims we screwed up, or we're hiding something, I don't know."

"Like we caused the accident, right?" Pete snorted, wiping hot sauce from his burning lips.

"Actually, I think that's what he meant. I finally told him to look me up when he was a little more clear-headed, and that pissed him off."

"Hank, ever see these guys before?" Pete pointed to the screen above them.

"Nope. What's their story? Looks like a Mossy Oak commercial."

Pete laughed. "I don't know, something about seeing Jim Wainwright on their farm, but I can't hear what it's all about."

Lindsey Locke reappeared, with the words BREAKING NEWS flashing at the bottom of the screen in red letters, followed by EXCLUSIVE. Someone at the bar asked Kristin to raise the volume, and the crowd quieted to listen. The image was now split to show rising star Jennifer Banks, reporting live from an unspecified location in Grove Park, New York. Both detectives stopped eating, keenly interested in what she would have to say.

"Lindsey, a source close to the investigation has provided shocking new details in this case, which has now morphed from the search for a missing woman to the search for her killer."

Locke held up a finger to accentuate a point. "Folks, this is the first time I'm hearing this, so I'm going to hold my questions until Jennifer explains. Go ahead, Jen."

Ever the intrepid reporter, Banks allowed wisps of hair to blow across her face unchecked as she held a microphone and papers in her right hand and shielded her earpiece with the other.

"Lindsey," she began, heeding the producer's advice to use the host's name frequently, "the evidence continues to point in the direction of Jack Ferris, the house painter and boyfriend of Nicole Wainwright. In addition to the bloodstained flooring we've heard about previously, I'm told that cell phone records show that he last placed a call to Nicole at almost the exact hour of her disappearance, leaving some type of threatening message. Even more interesting, one of the young men who found Nicole's body now claims to have seen her at that very spot about a month ago, in the company of Jack Ferris."

Twenty seconds of listening without comment were all that Locke could manage.

"Jennifer, you're saying that Ferris was familiar with the place where the body was found, that they had gone there together in the past?"

"Yes, Lindsey, exactly."

"Jennifer, has the word 'suspect' been used by the police in reference to Mr. Ferris?"

"No Lindsey, he continues to be characterized as a 'person of interest', as is the victim's husband, James Wainwright."

"Jennifer, a little voice in my right ear tells me you also have new information regarding the husband. What's going on with him?"

"Lindsey, the fact is that at this moment no one knows what's going on with James Wainwright, not even the FBI. They were about to indict him on charges unrelated to Nicole's death, but now Mr. Wainwright has disappeared. My source tells me that he has possibly left the country, and a search is underway."

"My word, what is going on in that town, does anybody have a handle on this case?"

Pete looked at Hank in disbelief. "Did McClure have his press conference already?"

"Hell no, and even if he had we wouldn't release that stuff to the press! It's like that bitch has a microphone in the damned meeting room."

Up above, Locke was firing questions at her new protégé.

"Can you tell us what was charged in those indictments, or are they sealed?"

"I don't have details on that, but I have it on good authority that a grand jury has seen fit to charge Wainwright with several crimes in connection to a land development scheme."

"And that's what made him leave the country? I think this man is getting some bad advice."

"Lindsey, it may be that Wainwright is running because of something in his past, as well as his present problems. I haven't confirmed this yet, but I'm told that this man is originally from Iowa, and changed his name when he moved east some 25 years ago. He was a young widower then, his first wife having died some sort of violent death."

"This is information that has not yet been released by the police task force? How solid is it?"

"Lindsey, we're still verifying and running down the details, but I can tell you, this is more than rumor or I would not report it."

If Banks had more detailed information, she was saving it for the next newsbreak. She had already provided enough fuel to feed the frenzy for the next day or two.

"Mr. Wainwright's attorney, Alan Kaplan, has refused comment at this time. There has been no official statement from law enforcement, but there is a press conference scheduled for later this evening, no specific time as yet."

"Jennifer, great work! Keep us posted, I want to know what goes on at that press conference!"

Pete was still staring at Lindsey Locke as she introduced her panel of talking heads. He sat back, arms crossed, and shook his head.

"No reporter alive could collect that much info on their own, and save it all for one big splash. She has someone inside, feeding her the latest information. It has to be someone right inside our little task force."

There were a few wings left on the platter, but both men had lost their appetites. Hank stood, dropped some money on the bar, and hitched up his pants. "Well, young man, what now?"

"I think I'm going to find Boldt and pick his brain about the federal case. They might have some leads in Steve's murder, maybe they'll even be able to tell me how it fits into all of this. Then I'm taking Sally out for a nice, romantic dinner."

"Really! You devil, good for you. I'll see what the other guys have got going, maybe something will catch my interest."

"Maybe we should talk to Jennifer Banks, she seems to have the best sources."

CHAPTER 76

LREADY SOMEWHAT UNEASY with the role of messenger, Officer Marti Lucas was becoming even more uncomfortable as she stood at Eric Bronski's desk waiting to be noticed. He was sitting with his back to her, murmuring into the phone in a tone that made it clear that the call was not official business.

"No, I don't know yet. I told you baby, I'll call you as soon as I find out." Fortunately for him, Baby couldn't see his evil grin as he said "Trust me, I don't — " He spun his chair around, stopping in mid-sentence when he saw that he had company.

"Marti! What's up, sweetie?" Bronski now held the phone tightly against his chest, as if some secret might leak out of it.

His greeting made Marti want to slap the smugness out of him, but she chose to ignore it. Still, it made her task less distasteful, even a bit enjoyable.

"Chief McClure wants to see you."

"Right now?"

"More like five minutes ago. He called your extension, but it's been busy."

"Why the jacket? You finished for the day?"

"Yep, vacation's over. I'm cleared for patrol duty, so I'll be back on my regular afternoon shift tomorrow. You'd better get in there, Eric."

"Yeah. Well, we'll miss you around here."

Bronski ended his private call with a terse "gotta go" and tossed the phone onto its cradle. "Any idea what it's about?"

"I don't know, but he's been huddled in there with a bunch of heavy hitters from the task force. I just happened to be nearby, and the Chief told me to find you and send you in."

"Okay. See you later, kid."

Marti watched him hurry off, savoring the brief flicker of discomfort that he hadn't been able to hide.

*

Sergeant Bronski knocked twice, and took a deep breath as he heard McClure's voice invite him in. There were six people in the small office, all with their gaze fixed on him, and he quickly noticed that he would be the only participant without a chair.

Bronski nodded to Chief of Detectives John Chapman from the county sheriffs and State Police captain Scott Kirsch as they were formally introduced. David Greco and Hank Rowan were seated against the back wall, looking decidedly grim, and in the corner sat Special Agent Boldt.

"This is big," thought Bronski, certain that all of his hard work was about to pay off. He felt his confident smile return, and eagerly waited to hear what sort of special assignment they had in mind for him. Was he about to become an official member of the task force?

McClure skipped the pleasantries and got right down to business.

"Sergeant Bronski, we've been in here discussing a matter of great concern related to the Wainwright case, and it's come to our attention that you might be able to help us understand it. Describe your involvement in the investigative process up until now."

It was a strange request coming from his boss, and Bronski read it as an opportunity to blow his own horn. He reminded himself to try to convey an air of humility while doing so.

"Actually sir, my official duty has been to help out by manning the phones, you know, the tip lines. Early on I helped Detective Rowan, contacting people who might have seen Mrs. Wainwright. He provided a list of names for me, but, unfortunately, I didn't come up with much."

There was no reaction from the others, as if they were waiting for a more complete explanation.

"Recently I've helped get things set up for the task force meetings, made copies to hand out, that kind of thing." I've taken lunch orders quite a few times, too." He grinned. "Whatever is needed."

Once again Bronski was met with silence, and felt compelled to continue with a comment he would come to regret.

"Seriously, though, I'm probably as familiar with the details of the case as anyone outside of the task force. I kind of make it my business to keep in touch with the guys who are closely involved, and stay as informed as possible."

Rowan coughed loudly, an obvious message to Bronski that he had said more than enough. In the interest of objectivity, it had been decided that Chapman would control the interview.

"Sergeant, are you aware of the problems we've had with information being leaked to the news media in this case?"

Bronski realized too late that this meeting was not congratulatory.

"I, uh, yes, I've heard about that. Just coffee room conversation, but I'm aware of the importance of confidentiality."

"Good answer. Now, I want you to think carefully before you answer this — have you been meeting regularly with Jennifer Banks of channel 5 news?"

The question sent a sickening wave of fear rippling through Bronski's stomach as he recognized the underlying accusation.

"Sir, we're friends. We've had dinner a couple of times."

"You've been *friends* for how long?" There was disdain in Chapman's tone as he sarcastically accented the word.

"Actually, I met her shortly after Mrs. Wainwright went missing." Bronski felt his feet sinking deeper into the sand, but he was determined to be truthful. "Ms. Banks spent the afternoon here, waiting to see the Chief. We had coffee and got to know each other a little. She left her card with me, and I called her the next day. We never talked about the case, though."

Chapman chose not to argue that point just yet.

"You saw her at least twice for dinner, were there many telephone conversations?"

"We've been speaking pretty much daily, yes."

"When did you last speak with Ms. Banks?"

Bronski didn't want to respond, but he knew how easily phone records could be checked. He wouldn't be surprised if they already knew the answer.

"Just before I came in here, sir."

Rowan looked to the ceiling, wondering how this kid could be so stupid. The answer had brought Chapman to his feet, and he took a step toward Bronski.

"You're talking to a reporter about this case while you're on duty?" Chapman's anger was building, and he was right in Bronski's face now. "You don't value your job very much, do you, son?"

They were about to bump chests when McClure jumped up to separate them. "John, take it easy! We're all professionals here."

"Are we?" Chapman glared at the young sergeant, contempt coloring his face.

"Look, the call was only a few minutes long, and we didn't talk about the murder or any other police matter. I do value my job, sir, and I keep it separate from my personal life."

Bronski knew that the accusation could jeopardize his career, and looked to McClure for advice.

"Chief, I'd like to have an advocate present before we go any further. I have nothing to hide, but this is getting out of control."

Chapman mumbled something and shook his head in disgust.

McClure thought that they could all use a break.

"Go ahead, make the call, but don't go anywhere. I have a press conference to do, we'll continue this discussion after that."

Chapman couldn't resist a final thrust of the dagger.

"Unless you'd like to do the press conference for him, Sergeant Bronski."

CHAPTER 77

JACK FERRIS SHUFFLED through the glass revolving door at the east end of La Galleria Mall and made his way through the herd of shoppers, pausing at several store windows in an attempt to spot anyone who might be following. He looked for faces that might be reflected in the glass, cleverly avoiding an obvious direct look at those behind him, but it turned out to be yet another idea that only seemed to work in the movies.

Giving in to his paranoia, he finally turned to get a clear view of any suspicious bystanders and found none. Still, it would be foolish to think that the police weren't capable of tracking his every move without being spotted.

The phone call had come as he was watching the Locke Report, where 'shocking' new facts related to Nicki's murder had been revealed. A panel of four guests, conferenced live via satellite, was in the midst of a discussion concerning Jack's probable guilt or innocence. As they debated, viewers were shown the same tired 'Jack Ferris' file footage that had been running for weeks. Clips of 'the boyfriend' entering or exiting the motel, leaving the police station after being questioned a second time, or putting his hand over a camera lens as he left the grocery store.

Outside of his lawyer, Jack had never heard anyone defend him on one of these shows, and it seemed that the only thing keeping this group from recommending a lynching was their increased distrust of James Wainwright.

Jack was uncomfortable to be out in public, but hopefully his five-day beard, baseball cap and dark glasses would be effective in avoiding recognition and the dreaded finger-pointing of whispering strangers.

He walked past the mob at the food court and took the spiral stairs to the upper level, ducking into a bookstore. Surreptitiously browsing from a position that would afford him a view of passers by, he spent a few minutes deciding whether it was safe to continue to his destination. A woman walked into the aisle, and seemed to take an unusually long glance at him, then quickly turned and walked out of the store with her small child in tow.

Satisfied that he had taken all reasonable precautions, but unconvinced that they had been sufficient, Jack left the store and walked across a bridge to the opposite side of the mall. He melded into the passing crowd of bored bargain hunters as they slowly filed past the endless storefronts, and then dropped out as he reached the entrance to Grand Slam Sports Collectibles.

Jack hesitated as a man of about sixty walked quickly past him. He was wearing an outdated blue velour sweat suit, apparently a mall walker getting his daily exercise, and Jack was sure he had seen him earlier on the lower level. He watched the man stop at a bench, where a woman of about the same age had been seated. She greeted him warmly and they walked off hand in hand, leaving Jack to chuckle at his own groundless fear as he walked into Grand Slam.

The proprietor was Tony Carbone, one of the few friends who were still in Jack's corner. They had known each other since grade school, and Jack was honored when Tony had asked him to become godfather to his young son a year earlier. In this new world of former friends who had all but abandoned him, Tony was someone who could still be trusted. Jack waited until Tony walked to the back of the store and casually joined him there.

"What can I help you with?" Tony didn't recognize him at first glance, which Jack took as a compliment to his undercover skills.

"Oh, Jack! Sorry, man, I didn't — "

"Don't worry about it, Tony." He removed the glasses and locked his eyes firmly on those of his close friend. "Tony, I need a favor, and I won't blame you if you say no."

Carbone looked understandably confused, and his face reddened as it always did when he was flustered. "Let's go in the back."

He led Jack through a door at the back of the shop, leading to a narrow service corridor that ran the length of the mall. The walls and floor were bare concrete, and fluorescent lights buzzed overhead. A teenager dressed in green coveralls was pushing a bin of flattened cardboard boxes onto an elevator, and Jack waited until he was gone before speaking.

"Tony, I got a phone call that I really need to follow up on. I have a friend on the Grove Park force who wants to meet privately, off the record, but I have to make sure I'm not followed. Can I use your car? I'll be back in a couple of hours, tops."

Tony was known as a friendly guy with a big smile, but right now he was stern-faced and a bit suspicious, rapidly chewing his gum. "Why is this cop helping you, and why is it such a big secret??"

"Look, I can't explain it all to you, but there's history between us. Tony, I'm being framed for a murder, I need to know everything the cops know. Maybe I can prove my innocence, before I'm railroaded."

Carbone wiped a hand across his forehead as he considered the consequences of his decision.

"So, it's nothing illegal. You're just asking to borrow my car."

"Right. Just to get away from the news people for a while, as far as you know."

"You got it." Carbone pulled a ring of keys from his pocket, removing one and handing it to Jack. "Don't let anything happen to my Neon. It's parked near the Sears entrance, B lot."

"Sabres logo on the rear window, right? Thanks, Tony."

"No problem. It's not that great of a ride, but it's the only one I have, you know?"

"Not just for the car. Thanks for believing in me."

They shook hands, and Tony pointed to a nearby stairwell.

"Take the stairs to ground level, there's an outside exit there. Just ignore the sign that says an alarm will sound if it's opened, the smokers disconnected it. I gotta get back in there before the customers steal everything."

"I'll leave the key under the seat, is that okay?"

"Sure. Take care, Jack."

When he was gone, Jack hurried down the stairs as if being chased, and reached the exit door without encountering any mall employees. Remembering what Tony had told him, Jack ignored the red-lettered sign that warned of an alarm. He hit the crash bar and stepped outside in silence, thankful for the ingenuity that a nicotine habit could inspire.

As the steel door slammed closed behind him, Jack was already jogging through the parking lot toward the safety of the Neon.

CHAPTER 78

"PETE, THIS PLACE is everything I'd heard it was! So elegant, and intimate."

It was nearing dusk at The Orchards, and thousands of tiny lights lent an ethereal glow to the exterior of the imposing white mansion and its intricate landscaping. The interior of the restaurant, originally the home of one of Grove Park's founders, was quite dark and very quiet. Decorative wooden railings and dividers separated the first floor into table groupings of two or three, spaced far enough apart to ensure privacy. Candles provided virtually all of the lighting so that, apart from the servers, diners at each table could easily forget that anyone else was in the room.

"I was thinking Applebee's until Jonathan opted out. I hope he's not tired of me already."

"Oh, not at all, Petey. His friend Patrick asked him to spend the night at his house, and I encouraged it. I think it'll be good for him, help him feel that things are getting back to normal."

"Sure it will. I was just kidding, I'm glad you like this place, I didn't realize you'd never been here. It's a little far out of town, but it's worth the drive. That was the best prime rib I've ever had."

"Actually, I was out this way earlier today."

"Really? There's not much out this way, where were you going?"

"I asked Jon to go for a drive with me, just to spend some time together. I was hoping he'd open up about how he's feeling since his dad — since the funeral."

"How did that go? Is he okay?"

She smiled and shrugged her shoulders. "We never got to that subject, but I think he's fine. All he wanted to talk about was this whole Nicole Wainwright thing. I can't blame the kid, it's on television constantly and it's all people seem to talk about anymore."

Pete frowned. "Grove Park's in prime time, that's for sure."

"He agreed to go with me if I would drive past some of the places that they're reporting from."

Pete seemed amused. "I think that's a very popular tour these days. They've had to assign officers to direct traffic in front of the Municipal Building a few times. Did you drive past there?"

"Yes, I couldn't believe the number of trucks and satellite dishes outside! Are they there around the clock?"

"There are always a few, but what you saw today was unusual. The press conference is going to be held outside the building tonight, so they're all jockeying for position."

A waiter arrived with a carafe of coffee, and Pete poured.

"Where else did you go?"

"We drove down Amelia, past the Wainwright house, and then we turned onto Robinson Road. We saw that huge collection of flowers and messages at the side of the road, the one that was on front page of USA Today."

Pete had the wistful look of a hardened professional who couldn't help but be touched by the public outpouring. "That's the spot where our first searches took place. People started leaving flowers and candles that day, and I've watched it grow. Some of that stuff is sent from out of state, even from other countries. It amazes me, the concern from so many people who never met, never even heard of this woman until they saw her picture in the news reports. Turns out she wasn't even found there."

For a minute they sipped coffee in silence, each with their private thoughts, until Pete realized the mood had turned far too somber.

"You said the tour came here, what's the relevance to the Wainwright case?"

Sally cocked her head slightly, and smiled.

"I said I came out this way, not to this restaurant! We were on Emery Road.".

Pete was learning that Sally did not like to be misinterpreted. He set his cup down, intrigued by her statement. "You went by Jack's house?"

"I was surprised there weren't any news people there. Just the red Jeep, parked up near the house."

"You said you drove past, how could you see a car near the house?"

Sally grinned, happy to correct him again.

"No, you said that. We pulled in to turn around, I didn't want to go any further and get lost."

"No barrier at the driveway, not even tape?"

"Nope."

"Hmph. Maybe — " The vibration of his phone interrupted Pete's thought, and he reached for it. "Excuse me."

Sally mouthed the words "Be right back" as she rose to find the ladies' room. Pete watched her leave, admiring the fit of the black dress she was wearing, and then answered the call.

It was Detective Showles, at task force headquarters.

"Yeah, what's up, Rocky?"

"Pete, I need some input. It's no emergency, but the boys tell me that they've lost track of Ferris."

"Lost track of him? How long ago? I can't picture Jack running off somewhere."

"I guess about an hour now. He was at La Galleria. His car is still there, so maybe he's still in the mall somewhere, but his tail doesn't think so. After the Wainwright thing, he thought he'd better call for help."

"Okay, so what can I do?'

"Well, assuming Ferris is still around, where would he go? Where the hell do we look?"

"Start by looking at the mall again. Jack has a good friend who owns a place called Grand Slam, on the upper level. He could have gone there, just to have someone to talk to. I'm out here at The Orchards, I'll get back to the station as soon as I can."

Sally returned, freshly glossed lips shining in the candlelight, as a waiter appeared with the dessert cart. She saw the troubled look on Pete's face and decided to make it easier for him.

"Thanks, but I couldn't eat another thing. Did you want to get going, Pete?"

He looked up at the server. "Just the check, please."

CHAPTER 79

THE CIRCUMSTANCES WERE not what Jack Ferris had hoped for, but it felt good to be returning to his home for the first time in weeks. He had looked forward to the day when he would be exonerated and move back permanently, and wondered if this meeting could be a means to that end. Just as Marti Lucas had promised, there was no sign of the police or the press as he pulled into the driveway. He saw her Jeep Cherokee parked next to the house, and parked the Neon beside it. The front door was ajar and Jack entered cautiously, to be met by the familiar scent of stained pine that still permeated every room. It was comforting, until the rest of the scene hit home. His belongings still lay where they had been scattered and upset by the search teams, and mud had been tracked everywhere. Jack felt violated and angry, forgetting for the moment that he was not alone.

"Hi Jack. Close the door, please, and leave the lights off."

Marti Lucas was standing in the shadows across the room, near the stairs that led to the loft. The A-frame's soaring windows allowed barely enough of the fading daylight for him to see that she was dressed in her police blues.

"Hi Marti. Thanks for calling me. We're alone here, just you and me?" He had secretly hoped that Pete Webster might be part of this attempt to vindicate him.

"Yeah, we're alone, Jack. There hasn't been a police presence here for a while, so the press doesn't bother coming here anymore. Besides, they're all in town at the big press conference, waiting to hear that you're going to be arrested."

Jack wasn't sure whether her delivery indicated pleasure or sarcasm, and didn't know how to react.

"Come over here, Jack, away from those windows."

As he crossed the room to within a few steps of her, Marti stepped out from the darkness, and Jack stopped moving. She had drawn her service weapon and had both hands on it, pointing the barrel at his chest.

"Face the wall, Jack, and don't do anything stupid."

He searched for some explanation in her glowering features, but saw only determination.

"What is this, Marti? You're arresting me? Why here?"

She responded by kicking his feet apart and pushing him against the wall.

"Hands behind your back. Now!"

Marti slipped a plastic band over his hands, pulling hard on the loose end, and Jack heard the zipping sound of the ratchet teeth as his wrists were bound tightly together.

"Turn around."

She now had the gun pointed menacingly at his head, and for the first time he noticed that her eyes welled with tears.

"You owe me an apology, Jack. You ruined my life, do you know that?"

"Marti, what the hell are you talking about?"

She pulled a piece of paper from her pocket and unfolded it, dangling it in front of his face.

"Remember this, Jack?"

He looked at the paper, a blank estimate form with his business letterhead. He saw the words "I'm sorry" scrawled with a Sharpie in his handwriting, and recognized the significance of it.

"Remember that night? We agreed to meet at the Lion for a drink, and see how things went from there. I went, even though I didn't really trust you. It was like you were taking me for a test drive, deciding whether I was worthy of your attention."

"No, Marti, it wasn't like that at all! I wanted to get to know you better, and Pete said you were interested."

"Pete! Don't blame Pete, you asshole! You never even told him you were meeting me! As soon as those friends of yours stopped in, I could tell you were embarrassed to be seen with me. What, did you think they would tease you in school the next day?"

"Marti, I'm sorry, I know I should have handled it better."

She laughed at his understatement. "Really, you think so? You think that running out and leaving a frigging note on my windshield was too juvenile? Well, I agree."

CHAPTER 80

"I'M SORRY ABOUT this, Sal, but something's going on with Jack. I have to get back to the station and help out, before they over-react."

Sally kept both eyes on the narrow two-laned road in front of them and gripped the armrest tightly, as if preparing herself for a sudden stop.

"It's fine, Pete, but please slow down. These roads are so narrow, and I'm always afraid that a deer is going to jump out in front of the car. The tree-line is so close to the road here."

Pete lightened the pressure on the accelerator pedal by an almost imperceptible amount.

"What's 'going on' with Jack?"

"I don't know yet, but Rocky says they've lost track of him."

"You mean he took off, like Wainwright did?"

Pete glared at the road ahead, shaking his head as he all but dismissed the idea.

"I can't believe Jack's gone on the run, the guy is innocent. Besides, he's smarter than that, he wouldn't just freak and leave town."

Sally put a hand on his arm in reassurance, and finished the thought for him. "You mean he wouldn't do that without calling you first, for advice."

"Something like that, but I'm not so sure he would at this point."

Pete was trying to remain matter-of-fact, but Sally could see the pain of a lost friendship in his face.

"Just go straight in to headquarters, Pete, I'll take a cab from there."

Pete's phone rang before he could reply. He set it to speaker as he answered, laying it on the console between them.

"Webster."

"Detective Webster, this is Donna Mackey, sorry to bother you outside of duty hours."

"Supervisor Mackey, it's always a pleasure to hear from you." Pete had expected to hear Rocky Showle's voice, and his answer felt as insincere as it must have sounded.

"What can I do for you?"

"Webster, we've discovered something on the MP3 player, and I thought my first call should be to you."

Pete stopped the car at a flashing red light, checking the rear-view to make sure he wasn't holding anyone up. He kept his foot on the brake as he concentrated on the phone call.

"You found something that she recorded?"

"Yes, our tech found a .wav file, just what you reminded us to look for. I thought it would have been covered, but our guys missed it. They must have — "

"It doesn't matter, Mackey, what did you find?"

Pete's tone was sharper than he had intended, and his lips tightened as Sally looked on in wide-eyed excitement.

"It's incredible, she must have been able to start the memo recorder just before she was killed. It's mostly unintelligible, at least until we clean it up, but she's definitely pleading with her attacker. She says the name 'Marty' over and over."

Pete stared at the dashboard as he turned the name over in his mind. "Marty?"

"Yes. I hope that means something to you."

Pete thought for a few moments more, than looked to Sally.

"You said you saw a red Jeep in Jack's driveway. Did you mean maroon? Roof rack, big Bills decal on the back?"

"No, it was red. Fire engine red, but not real shiny. The boxy-looking kind of Jeep."

Pete squinted to read the faded green street sign across the intersection and punched the gas pedal, steering into a screeching right turn.

"Thanks Mackey, call this in to the task force, will you?"

"Got it."

Sally's exhilaration at having played a part in the discovery of important new evidence was tempered only by the frightening rate of speed at which they were traveling.

"I was right!" she cried, bracing one herself with one hand on the dash as she turned towards Pete. "She must have used that memo feature a lot, it's a pain to figure out. You have to slide the case open, and the buttons aren't really marked clearly." She realized that her babbling might distract Pete from his driving, and stopped herself.

"Sally, I'm just playing a hunch, it may turn out to be nothing. Jack's house is only a few minutes from here, and I want to check it out. There's no time to drop you in town."

She gave him her best look of utter disbelief.

"You'd better not drop me off! I want to see how this turns out!" Pete held the wheel in both hands as he negotiated the twists of Emery Road, wondering what might be taking place at the home of Jack Ferris.

CHAPTER 81

"MARTI, I'M SORRY I hurt you, I really am, but is that a reason to shoot me? That's crazy!"

His words brought her demeanor to a heightened level of contempt, bordering on rage.

"I'm not crazy, I'm pissed off! You weren't satisfied with humiliating me, were you Jack? You took Nicki away from me, too! *That's* why I'm pointing this gun at you."

"Marti, I swear I did not kill Nicki. I loved her, why would I do that?"

"Oh, shut up! I know you didn't kill her. I want to hear an apology, Jack, and it better be a good one. You think you can do that?"

"Yes, yes I can. I do apologize, Marti, for whatever it is you think I've done."

"Not good enough." She grabbed his arm and spun him around again, letting him feel the barrel against his spine. As Jack's mind raced to find the words that might allow him to reason with her, Marti slipped a GPPD knit cap over his head, pulling it down over his eyes. She pushed him forward, and Jack shuffled his feet and turned his face to the side, blinded to any obstacle she might push him into.

"The first stair is just a couple of steps in front of you. We're going up. Just so you know, the safety is off and this thing has a very light trigger, so don't make any dumb moves."

They slowly ascended eight steps to the landing, where the staircase turned ninety degrees to the right before continuing an equal distance up to the loft. As Jack turned, feeling around with his foot to locate the second set of steps, Marti stopped him. With a hand firmly grasping the collar of his jacket, she pulled him backwards a step, still on the landing, and turned him face the stairs they had just climbed.

"Take a small step forward." Jack did as he was told, and was now positioned at the edge of the stairs. He could picture where he was in a general way, but lack of sight had him disoriented and confused. He couldn't see the cable that had had been looped over one of the exposed rustic beams above him, and secured to the railing to his left. Marti quickly slipped the other end over his head, pulling the cable tight around his neck.

"Don't struggle, Jack. Those stairs are right in front of you, and you don't want to step off, do you?"

The cable was small in diameter but very strong, woven stainless steel with an eyelet crimped onto one end, the other end looped through to form a noose. Marti took up the slack by wrapping it around the newel post, pleased that the tension had forced Jack up onto his toes. She snatched the hat from his head and tossed it aside so he could see his predicament.

"How's that, Jack? Oh, forget the apology, I don't really need to hear it. I'll just leave this note on the table for everyone to see. By the way, thanks for leaving this cable lying around in your garage, it's perfect! Was it for Willy? Was that story even true, or did you just tell it to sound like a hero?"

Willy was a stray dog Jack had once taken in, an endearing story he had been recounting for her that night at the Crouching Lion, before his abrupt departure.

Jack's airway was nearly closed and he was struggling to remain upright, fighting against the blackness that encroached upon his vision. He made a few gurgling sounds, hanging on to consciousness by a thread.

"What's that, Jack? I couldn't quite make out the words. Was it 'I'm sorry?' Those are your last words?"

CHAPTER 82

"THERE IT IS, Pete! That's the red Jeep I saw here this afternoon. Do you know who it belongs to?"

They had pulled into the driveway just far enough to see the two vehicles that were parked near the house. One was an older Dodge Neon, a car that Pete had never seen before, pewter gray except for a black replacement door on the passenger side.

Parked alongside the beater was a red 2013 Jeep Patriot, one that Pete had seen many times.

"It belongs to Marti Lucas. She's a Grove Park cop. I don't recognize the Neon."

"So 'Marty' is a woman?"

"This one is."

Pete was leaning forward, peering through the windshield towards the house. He was unwilling to drive any closer, and the surrounding trees partially obscured the windows from his line of sight. It seemed odd that there didn't appear to be any light coming from inside, even in the gathering darkness.

"Are we going in?"

He pointed a finger at Sally, backing it up with a no-nonsense look.

"I'm going in, you're staying right here."

"Pete, what do you think is happening in there?"

"I don't know, but it's time to find out." He grabbed a flashlight from the glove box and unlatched his door.

"Shouldn't you call for backup?"

Pete considered the idea, and then shook his head. It was possible that Marti had been sent to retrieve something from the house, or assigned to accompany one of Mackey's techs on a follow-up search. It was strange that Marti would use her personal transportation, but not unheard of. If that was the case, calling for backup could prove to be pretty embarrassing later on.

"No, it's probably nothing. I'll leave my phone, if it makes you feel safer. I should be back in a few minutes, sit tight."

Pete left the truck without waiting for a reply, closing the door softly to avoid any noise that might resonate to the house. As he crept to a position between the two parked vehicles, Sally saw him unholster his weapon.

"That does it" she muttered, alarmed at the implication that some grave danger might be at hand. She picked up his phone to summon help. Pete might be upset with her later, but Sally was learning to err on the side of caution.

The metallic pings of a cooling engine emanated from the Neon, and Pete placed a hand on the hood to verify that it was still warm. He tested the Jeep in the same manner, finding it cold to the touch. Obviously, Marti had arrived somewhat earlier than the second party. What were they doing in there?

He approached the house carefully, feeling totally exposed to anyone watching from within, and stepped up onto the porch that surrounded the perimeter. Standing with his back against the exterior wall of stacked logs, Pete craned his neck to get a look through the expansive windows, searching for any discernible movement. Without the benefit of lights from inside he could see only the reflection of the trees behind him, swaying in the stiff breeze. Branches snapped together as the wind whipped through them, covering any sound that may have come from inside the house.

Pete had the option of continuing along the porch to the rear of the house, but increasing doubts about the basis for his concern were making him impatient. He decided to try the front entrance.

Easing the ornate brass lever down, he felt the latch retract and pushed the door inward, allowing it to pivot silently on ball-bearing hinges. Moving aside as he closed it behind him, Pete studied the room as his eyes adjusted to the decreased ambient light.

Voices from somewhere to his left, near the stairs, sent Pete into a squat position. Pointing his gun and unlit flashlight in that direction, he took another moment to evaluate before announcing his presence in a booming voice.

"Police officer, who's there?"

As Pete clicked the powerful flashlight to life, two figures were illuminated in the circle of yellowish light, posed in a shocking tableau.

Jack Ferris appeared to be bound and somehow suspended by a thin rope, struggling to maintain his perch at the edge of the stairway. Behind him stood Marti Lucas, squinting into the brightness as she pointed her handgun in Pete's direction.

Webster's initial thought was that she was trying to prevent Jack from committing suicide, but the hands tied behind his back were contradictory. Marti's stern warning confirmed the second possibility.

"Stay out of this Pete, it doesn't concern you! Just back out of here!"

Pete extended his arms to the side in a conciliatory gesture and straightened up to take a step forward, convinced that he could reason with his fellow officer.

"Take it easy, Marti. Tell me what's going on here."

The barrel of her handgun blazed as she fired a shot into the floor, inches from Pete's left foot. Shocked by the realization that a warning shot would have been aimed much further away, Pete hit the deck and rolled hard to his right, taking cover behind an overstuffed leather recliner.

The flashlight had fallen out of his hand, and as Pete reached for it he heard Marti's voice again.

"Goodbye, Jack." She pressed a hand against the small of his back and gave Jack a vicious shove, sending him out into the open space above the stairway. As he swung back toward the landing his wildly thrashing feet searched for support that was out of reach, and his legs quickly ran out of energy.

The sight of his longtime friend in the throes of death spurred Pete into action. Without regard to his own safety, he broke from cover and rushed to Jack's aid. Leaping onto the stairs, he wrapped both arms around Jack's thighs, lifting to relieve the stress of his full weight on the noose, but without help it was a wasted effort.

Looking upward, Pete saw that he was dealing with a woven steel cable rather than a rope, and his eyes followed it to its origin. It was wrapped tightly around the top of a newel post at the landing, just to the left of where Marti stood. Jack's body had gone limp.

"Marti, for God's sake, untie this thing!"

She was still pointing her gun at him, but Marti's face was a blank stare as she pondered her next move. With the post out of his reach, Pete had only one choice. He let Jack's weight down as gently as possible and dashed up to the cable's anchor point. As he did, Marti took the opportunity to run past him unchallenged and flee the house.

As Pete's frenzied fingers pried at the coils of cable the startling report of a gunshot echoed from outside the house. His immediate instinct was to rush out and intervene, but a glance at Jack's motionless silhouette made it clear that any chance to save him was slipping away.

Pete could see that a decoratively carved finial topped the post, and the cable was wrapped into a narrow groove just below it. Putting both arms out for balance, Pete aimed a mighty kick at the finial. The hardwood hardly budged, and a wave of pain shot up to his knee.

He stepped back in frustration and aimed his 9mm at the cable, firing three shots before he succeeded in severing it and shattering the wood into splinters.

Jack's limp body impacted the stairs with a sickening thud and rolled clumsily to the bottom, coming to rest on his back with one leg twisted unnaturally beneath him. By the time Pete reached him and managed to remove the garrote from his friend's neck, it looked as if Jack Ferris was already beyond help. His face was a deep shade of purple, and the unforgiving wire had left a deep impression that encircled his throat.

Pete rolled Jack's body so he could use his pocket knife to cut the tie from Jack's wrists. Pushing him onto his back once again, he aggressively launched into a CPR technique for only the third time in his career. Pete was frantically anxious to pursue Marti and investigate the meaning of the gunshot he had heard. Bringing Sally on the call, and following that by ignoring her advice to call for backup, had been a grievous error in judgment.

As he struggled to massage Jack's heart into a voluntary rhythm, Pete heard footsteps. Two county patrolmen were entering the room, weapons drawn.

"Over here, I need someone to keep the CPR going!" One of the uniforms came over and knelt at Jack's opposite side while his partner hung back, still in the ready position. He kept his eyes on the staircase as he addressed Pete.

"Is the rest of the house clear?"

"I think so. Turn a light on, will you?"

The first officer placed the heels of his palms on Jack's sternum and began a series of sharply delivered chest compressions, freeing Pete to continue his pursuit of Marti. He got to his feet, ignoring the searing pain in his right knee, and questioned the second officer as he headed for the door.

"What did you see outside?"

At that moment Rocky Showles rushed through the door, followed by a gray-haired man wearing, of all things, a blue velour sweat suit. His i.d. and badge hung from a neck lanyard, and he held a Glock 9mm to complete the outfit.

Pete grabbed Rocky's arm as he passed by.

"Did you see Marti Lucas out there?"

As he asked the question one of the sheriffs could be heard advising his partner. "This guy's gone, Davey."

Pete turned and screamed at them. "You just keep working on him until the paramedics get here!"

Rocky glanced down at the hand still clamped onto his arm, remaining totally calm in the face of his colleague's intensity.

"Lucas just had a total meltdown out there. She just keeps saying 'I'm sorry' over and over, can't stop crying. We took her weapon and put her in the back of a patrol car." He looked toward Jack. "She did this, too?"

"Yeah, when I got here she had him — what do you mean, this too?"

Showles rocked his head in the direction of the door.

"There's a woman outside, mid-thirties, dark hair, well dressed. She's been shot, told the medics Lucas did it. Do you know her?"

His question was lost on Webster, who was already running out the door.

CHAPTER 83

HANK ROWAN LOOKED up to see Pete Webster enter the squad room, looking drained and broken. Rowan broke off his conversation with David Greco and walked over to lend support. He stood silently as Pete tossed his keys on his desk and let out a long sigh, collapsing into his swivel chair for a much-needed rest. Fearing the worst, Hank posed the question that was on the mind of everyone in the suddenly quiet room.

"How is she, Pete?"

Pete started to speak, but his quivering lips forced him to stop and compose himself. He took a moment to reset and tried again. "Sally's going to be alright, she's out of danger. The bullet tore up her shoulder pretty good, but the surgeon said she could eventually regain full motion with it."

He had obviously been through a gut-wrenching experience as he waited for the woman he loved to be declared out of danger.

"It was scary, Hank. She lost so much blood, they had to keep halting the surgery until her vitals stabilized. They found that some major blood vessel had been nicked, and once that was repaired they were able to finish. Thank god, she's going to be okay."

Pete was about to recount the events leading up to the shooting, including his own poor judgment regarding Sally's safety, when he was interrupted. Hank was genuinely concerned for Sally, but his intention was to move on to enlist Pete's help with another pressing matter.

"Pete, I know you're whipped, and you've been through hell tonight. I know that you haven't even had a chance to write your report on what happened out there, but we need you to get a statement from Marti Lucas."

Pete's face reflected the revulsion he felt at the mere mention of her name.

"What? You just said I haven't even laid out my own statement yet. Why isn't someone in there already, pushing for a goddamn confession?"

The reaction was expected, and Hank's voice remained calm.

"We tried that, Pete. She says she absolutely refuses to talk to anyone but you, and no one has been able to change her mind. She hasn't even lawyered up, she's been waiting to speak to you. She's been Mirandized."

Pete shook his head in disbelief, then wearily pushed himself out of his chair as Hank pointed to the interview room.

"She's in there waiting, and the camera's rolling."

*

Pete entered the stuffy, barren room to find Marti slumped over the table, resting her head on crossed arms. He thought that she must have fallen asleep, but Marti surprised him by abruptly straightening up. She ran her fingers through her recently shaved faux hawk and contorted her face into a stretch that forced her swollen eyes to open wide.

In spite of her efforts to shake the cobwebs, Marti appeared to be completely exhausted. She looked at him with dull eyes, as if the last of her energy had been spent on the tears and hysteria that had now receded into numbness. She looked away as she acknowledged his presence in a low rasp.

"Pete."

He seated himself without offering a reply.

"They brought me some clothes from my locker, I guess they couldn't stand to see me in a uniform any longer. They look at me like they're all just disgusted." She finally made eye contact with him. "The same way you're looking at me."

"Marti, Hank said you wanted to talk to me. Do you want an attorney present?" He wanted badly to remain neutral, but it was going to be a struggle.

"No. I want to tell you everything first. I feel like I owe you that. He was your friend."

Pete had always held a high opinion of Marti Lucas, as a person and as a colleague. He had considered her a friend. Now he sat across the table from her and struggled to remember that hatred was not an emotion he could allow himself. He pulled a digital recorder from his pocket so he would have a copy of his own for later review, starting it and setting it on the pale green tabletop.

"Let's start with that, Marti. Why did you kill Jack Ferris?"

She looked away again, unable to say the words directly to him.

"I hated Jack. He humiliated me, and then he took Nicki away from me. I wanted him to feel suffering, and take the blame for Nicki's death."

Questions began leaping into Pete's mind. "Explain that to me, Marti. How did he humiliate you?"

She gave him a defiant look. "I said I wanted to tell you, try to let me tell it without interrupting! It's complicated."

Pete sat back in his chair waited for the fire in her eyes to fade away. "Go ahead."

"I met Nicki at the gym almost two years ago. We struck up a conversation one day, and we just seemed to click, to open up to each other. She was having a rough time then, she used to say she felt kind of lost. We started going out for coffee after our workouts and we'd talk for hours. She did most of the talking, really."

Pete resisted the urge to speak as Marti became lost in the memory she was recounting.

"I know people have always had questions about me, but I swear that was the first time I'd been attracted to another woman that way. Nicki said it was a first for her, too. We became lovers. It was the best two months of my life."

The next pause was longer, and Pete felt he had to keep Marti on track. "It ended after two months."

"Yeah. Nicki told me she couldn't see me anymore. She wasn't a bitch about it though, she seemed really torn. I actually told her I understood, I thought she wanted to make things right in her marriage.

"I was still in love with Nicki, and as much as I tried I couldn't stop myself from thinking about her. I wanted to talk to her at the gym, to see if there was any chance of us being together again, but that damned Jill Sherman was always there."

Pete could picture the small group huddled around the video monitor in a nearby room, reacting to the mention of yet another local woman who had died tragically.

"I followed her sometimes, so I guess they can add stalking to the charges. Eventually it became obvious to me that Nicki wasn't trying to save her marriage at all, she was replacing me with Jill Sherman. That devastated me, and I think that was when I really started to lose it.

"Not too long after that, Jack asked me out."

She looked at Pete and saw that he was, as she expected, surprised by her remark.

"I think he must have done it as a favor to you, but Jack never mentioned it, did he?"

"No, he never did."

"Didn't think so. We agreed to meet for a drink, and before we even finished it he abandoned me. He was ashamed to be seen with me, Pete."

He felt that Marti was rescinding the no-interruption rule, and might be more open to his need for a detailed explanation. "But you've continued to ask me about him, why were you still interested after that?"

"I started to see him with Nicki." She laughed derisively. "Deja vu. I had suspected it for a while, that's why I asked you about his situation. I thought maybe you knew, maybe Jack confided in you. Guys like to brag about that stuff, right?"

Pete had no comment. "I suspected it, too, but Jack never did the sort of bragging you're talking about. He only admitted it to me after her death. That's one of the reasons he was under suspicion."

Marti formed a one-sided frown and shook her head. "Even after Jill was out of the picture, Nicki didn't want me. She preferred Jack."

Pete felt sure that Marti had more to say about the accident on Powers Road. "What do you mean, about Jill being out of the picture?"

Marti sighed deeply, as if she was relieved to be able to unburden her conscience.

"Time went by, and then one night I was on patrol and on a swing through the village I thought I saw that white Jaguar pass by, headed out of town on 19. I decided to follow, to see if it was Jill, but the snow was falling so thick you could hardly see the tail lights. I started following closer and closer, until I could see that she was alone in the car. The driving conditions were horrible that night, that Jag was fishtailing all over the road. I was so angry at her, and at Nicki, I started to really enjoy it, knowing how scared she must have been. I remembered a time at the gym when she was with Nicki, and I knew she was making fun of me, and it made me so mad.

"She turned onto Powers for some reason, and I followed. Things got away from me, and I bumped her from behind a couple of times, then I pulled alongside to scream at her. That's when her car went off the road. It just disappeared into a cloud of white."

"You forced Jill Sherman off the road, to her death?"

Marti looked at him as if she had been startled out of a dream.

"I told you it was complicated." She let her words settle in and returned her gaze to the floor, as if reading the memory in the faded beige tile. "I was lucky there, I mean lucky that I got away with it."

Pete was all ears. "How so?"

She was still looking at the floor. "Ed Flanders, the old guy who spotted the wreck — I know his daughter, we're in the same spinning class at Strong's. She approached me one day and said her dad had remembered something from the night before the accident and wanted to report it. He was out late walking his dog, and the storm was getting started, visibility was poor, so he turned back for home. He remembered seeing a car like Sherman's, looked like it was being followed by a black and white. Definitely something with a light bar. That made me nervous.

"So, the next day I called him, and as soon as my shift started I stopped in and listened like I was taking a statement, told him I'd report it. Never heard any more about it, and I guess he didn't push it any further. Like I said, lucky."

Pete was silent, flashing back to that night at Woody's when a drunken Ed Flanders had gotten in Hank's face but hadn't been able to make himself understood, or hadn't been given the opportunity because of his condition. He let Marti continue without comment.

"Once that quieted down I swore that I was finished with my stupid obsession."

"But you weren't finished, right? You wanted to get back at Jack Ferris, for being so involved with Nicki Wainwright." Pete interjected only when he felt it was necessary to clarify the chain of events.

"I took advantage of that. He had set himself up so well, all I had to do was make it look like the suicide of a guilty man. I was going to cut the tie off of his wrists before I left. I even had a note to leave behind that was written by him, saying he was sorry."

She shrugged as if the story was complete, shaking her head.

"but, then you showed up."

CHAPTER 84

WEBSTER WAS ASTONISHED. Marti had confessed to two murders, and they hadn't even discussed the death of Nicki Wainwright yet.

"Tell me about Nicki. What happened that day?"

Her eyes flooded, tears fell, and she looked at the ceiling as if she dreaded the thought of verbalizing the events.

"I kept seeing her with Jack, and I couldn't stand it another day, I had to talk to Nicki one last time, just to understand what I had done wrong. She wouldn't return my calls, and she'd gotten really good at avoiding me. I didn't sleep all night thinking about what I'd want to say to her if I had the chance. I knew Nicki's running routine, and I spotted her as she turned on to Robinson. I let her run about a half-mile further and then pulled over in front of her. She came to the passenger side of the truck, but I didn't roll the window down. I wanted her to open the door to speak to me, and she did."

Pete remained silent, studying Marti as she relived the moment.

"I asked her to please get in so we could talk, just for a few minutes. Nicki looked kind of pissed, and said she didn't think that was a good idea. When I pointed the gun at her, she changed her attitude in a hurry. I was afraid she might take off running, but she didn't, she got in and closed the door, sort of cringing up against it.

"I drove for a while and then we got out and walked to the spot where you found her. We had met near there a few times, I used to call it our special place. Of course, that changed when I found out she went there with Jack, too. I followed them there once, spying on them like some lunatic, but a couple of backpackers showed up and I had to leave."

"The geocachers." Pete muttered the words to himself.

"What?"

"Nothing. Go on."

"We were out of the car, and I was trying to get Nicki to talk to me. She wouldn't though. Not about Jack, not about us, not anything. She wasn't scared anymore, she was really upset with me for bothering her.

"I asked her how she could throw away what we had, and Nicki said she liked me but it wasn't love, at least not for her. She had never been with a woman, and she had been curious."

Marti focused on Pete's face, but she seemed to be addressing Nicole Wainwright all over again.

"Curious? That's what I am to you, a freaking CURIOSITY?"

She stood up and began to relive the moment in vivid detail as she leaned against the wall.

"I snapped when she said that, and I don't know if either of us said anything more. The next thing I remember is the feeling of her throat in my hands, gripping it tight and pressing my thumbs down, choking the life out of her. She struggled and clawed at my arms and I backed her against a tree, and I kept shaking her.

"I didn't even realize that I'd been hitting her head on the tree until I saw all the blood on my hands. I let go, and she went limp."

Pete was amazed that Marti was capable of such a crime, but her telling was totally convincing. "You got away with it so cleanly. You never came up on our radar, we never connected you with Nicki. Why didn't you leave it at that?"

"Yeah, I got away with it. Nicki scratched my arm pretty badly, but I covered it with a bandage and a sling until it healed. I told the doctor that I'd pulled my shoulder out while on duty, struggling with a kid. He never looked at the other arm. He gave me a sling and ordered light duty, and I just switched the sling to the other arm. Nobody ever knew about the scratches, and I got to work inside and keep track of what was going on in the investigation."

She showed a self-satisfied grin for a moment, then her mood darkened once again.

"I could have let things play out, it looked like Ferris and Wainwright were having a competition trying to see who could look more guilty. I called Jack a few times, acting like a friend who was concerned about him. I couldn't believe he actually bought that.

"Like I said, I hated him for being with Nicki, I knew they probably talked about me and had a good laugh. I wanted to have the last one. After that, I don't know. I don't think I'd have been able to live with myself very long."

The implication of possible suicide reminded Pete of Marti's fragile state of mind, and he thought they should give her a rest.

"Marti, we've covered a lot of ground here, and we'll have a lot of questions. You'll need to fill in all of the details. Are you sure you don't want legal representation?

"I guess it's time for that, huh? One more thing though, before you go."

"What's that?" Pete wondered if there could be a fourth victim in Marti's chain of violence.

"Tell them to lighten up on Bronski, he wasn't the leak. I was the one who gathered information and fed it to Banks."

Pete could only stare at her as Marti proudly recalled her manipulations. Was she some sort of evil genius, or were they truly a bunch of fools?

"People at the station love to tell what they know, it doesn't matter how long they've been on the force. I always knew as much about that investigation as anyone, and I kept feeding it to Banks. It became fun, sort of a game to see the media reaction, the uproar. That girl is a star now!

"Bronski saw me talking to Jennifer a few times, but he didn't have a clue what was going on. He just wanted to know if she had asked about him. Bronski's a pig, but I agreed to introduce them. They dated a couple of times, and I made sure it got around the station. Voila, another egotistical male sets himself up for me.

"He never revealed anything to her, Bronski was just being a hound. Everything she reported came from me."

CHAPTER 85

"SAL, ARE YOU doing okay over there? I'm trying to avoid the bumps, but this road isn't the best. Maybe I should have taken — "

"Petey, stop, please! I'm fine, they have this arm wrapped so tight to my body I couldn't move it even if I wanted to. Besides, they gave me pills for the pain, I probably wouldn't feel it if you shot me again right now."

They laughed, and once again Pete was aware of how thankful he was to have her, and how close he had come to losing her.

"I can't wait to get home and to see Jon. I could tell how uncomfortable it made him to visit me in the hospital, he wasn't himself at all. Oh, and I promised him I'd quit smoking. I'm done with that."

Pete nodded his agreement. "That's great, hon. It was hard for him, seeing his mom like that, knowing that someone had actually tried to kill her. We had a long talk about it, I think it brought us a little closer. Don't get any ideas though, Sally, there are easier ways to find common ground between the generations."

She chuckled again, relaxing into the headrest and closing her eyes as if the medication was making her sleepy. "I keep telling you, she wasn't trying to kill me. I heard shots and ran up to see what was going on, and she bumped into me on her way out. The gun went off, I felt the burning in my shoulder, and the next thing I knew they were loading me onto the gurney. It felt so wonderfully soft, like a waterbed or a cushion of air. Jeez, I never got to thank those guys."

"You're starting to ramble, honey. Maybe you should just rest, we'll be there soon."

Sally kept her eyes closed, but her thoughts continued to spill out. "I can't believe Marti did all those horrible things, Pete. She must have had so much pain in her life, in the end she just snapped. Do you think she could be bipolar?"

Pete checked to see if her eyes were still closed as he frowned his disapproval of her theory.

"That's not something for me to decide. Some people would say she's an unfeeling sociopath. You had to hear her tell it, so matter of fact, so detached from it all. I hope she gets what she deserves, that's all."

Now Sally looked directly at him.

"I'm sorry, I don't mean to make excuses for her after she killed your best friend, and two other innocent people. I'm just having a hard time understanding how a seemingly normal person becomes a murderer."

Pete shook his head, having wondered the same thing for so many days.

"I guess we'll never know the answer to that."

CHAPTER 86

"ROSIE, BACK ME up with a shot of CC, and pour one for my buddies over there." The beefy, red-faced man, a complete stranger to the two oil field hands seated at the far end of the bar, grinned as they nodded their appreciation. Rosie deftly poured three shots of Canadian Club and slid one in front of each patron. They raised their glasses as one in a silent toast and quickly drained them, enjoying the taste of a top-shelf whiskey. Wainwright would have preferred Jack Daniels, but, when in Rome —.

"Ernie, you want another one before I step away? I got dinner orders to take." Rosie stood with the bottle in hand as she gestured towards two men seated at a corner table. She knew that Ernie had had one too many, but as long as he said he wasn't driving she was willing to keep pouring.

"Absolutely, and get one for those guys, too." He jerked a thumb toward the dining area behind him, without turning to address the recipients of his drunken generosity.

"Sure thing." She poured him another and ducked out from behind the bar, carrying the bottle and two clean shot glasses.

She crossed the room, feeling her customers' eyes checking her out from head to toe and lingering at points in between as she approached. Rosie hadn't seen these men before, and immediately noticed that the clothing they wore to fend off the brutal cold of western Canada was top quality. Their flannel shirts, down vests, and Patagonia parkas looked so new that she half-expected to spot a sales tag on one of the sleeves. Rosie's father was a native Shuswap Indian who made his living as a hunting and fishing guide, and she had spent several summers cooking for his parties. She could spot a newbie a mile away, as could most of the residents of Yellow Creek.

"What can I get you boys?" she asked, offering the smile that was reserved for potentially large tippers.

The younger one, a thirtyish blonde bodybuilder type, tore his eyes away from the strip of bare midriff above her low rider jeans and returned the smile.

"Well, the chili sounds good."

"Bison chili with black beans. Comes with a bowl of fries." She turned to his friend, a large, dark man whose salt and pepper hair put him around fifty. "And you, sir?"

He didn't answer, seemingly distracted by something at the bar. Finally, his buddy broke the spell.

"Norm, are you gonna try the chili?"

"Oh, yeah, right, I'll have the same."

Rosie showed them the label of the bottle she was holding.

"Gentleman at the bar offered to buy you guys a shot."

They both waved her off.

"No, tell him thanks anyway, the coffee's fine."

"M'kay. I'll be back to warm it up." Rosie gathered up the menus and was about to turn away when Norm tapped her on the arm.

"Listen, can I ask you something, just between us?"

The way he lowered his voice made Rosie apprehensive, but she waited to hear the question.

"That guy at the bar, the one who sent the drinks over, do you know his name?"

"Sure, that's Ernie. I think his last name is Whitman, or Riteman, something like that."

"Have you known him very long?"

Rosie pursed her lips and wrinkled her nose a bit as she came up with her estimate.

"He's been coming in for a week, maybe a little longer — he stays at a bed and breakfast down the street. I think he told me he writes magazine articles, so maybe he's going to do one about Yellow Creek. I don't know what he'd find to write about though, not much happens here."

Norm seemed satisfied with the answers, but his partner needed one more.

"Did he ever mention where he's from?"

Rosie took a quick glance towards the bar and lowered her voice.

"He says he's from Kamloops, but I think that's bullshit. His accent changes after he's had a few, I'm pretty sure he's from the States."

The two men looked at each other as if her opinion had provided some sort of confirmation.

"Thanks, honey. This is just between you and me, alright?" The blonde guy leaned towards her and stuffed a bill into one of the glasses she was holding.

Rosie instantly regretted having told them so much about Ernie, and so easily. She had been about to ask the pair why they were so interested in him, but now she decided not to get involved any further. "I'll be right back with that chili, guys. You're gonna love it."

She went the kitchen to place the food order and returned to her place behind the bar, stopping at the beer taps that were located in front of Wainwright.

"Have a beer on me, Ernie" she said, and as she poured her voice dropped to a level that only Wainwright could hear.

"Don't turn around, just listen. Those two guys at the table were asking me about you. Now, I don't know you very well but here's some advice – the door across from the men's room leads to the kitchen, and there's an exit door to the back lot. You might want to use it."

She set the beer in front of him and walked away to serve the oil workers. Wainwright slid from his bar stool and started toward the hallway to the right of the bar, turning his head to address Rosie as he left.

"Honey, pour us another shot, will ya? Gotta visit the boys' room, I'll be right back." The request was delivered somewhat louder than necessary, with a noticeable slur, for the benefit of the two strangers. He hiked up his pants and walked rather unsteadily towards the men's room. Once he was out of sight he turned and pushed through the kitchen door to make his escape.

The encounter with two men who were interested in his identity had shaken Wainwright almost into sobriety. Before they showed up he had already been questioning his plan, wondering how to proceed. Early on he had managed to trade his car for an old Durango, plates and all, which he could only hope was not a stolen vehicle. He had cash, but no safe place to keep it. Life on the run was already wearing on him, and starting over at his age was no longer a pleasant thought.

After grabbing most of his belongings from the rooming house, he took the highway south, driving long into the night until he felt safe enough to stop at a motel. By that time, he had talked himself into the belief that returning to the States might actually be an option, and he was ready to contact Al to put the wheels into motion.

CHAPTER 87

AL KAPLAN ARRIVED at One FBI Plaza, the Buffalo region field office, earlier than the scheduled appointment time of 11 a.m. Forty minutes later he was still seated in the waiting area, facing a large oak door with a nameplate that read "Special Agent in Charge Brendan Boldt". During that time two other men, presumably FBI agents, had been allowed in and now, as they opened the door to leave, Kaplan was summoned.

"Mr. Kaplan, please have a seat. What brings you here today?" Boldt's confident smile conveyed the impression that he was, as his nameplate promised, "in charge" of the situation, as if he knew something that Kaplan did not.

"Well, as you may have guessed, Agent Boldt, I'm here on behalf of my client, James Wainwright–"

Boldt interrupted before Kaplan could finish his opening declaration. "Are you ready to tell us where he is?"

Kaplan was not one to be bullied in any conversation, and continued with his original statement. "Mr. Wainwright has contacted me without divulging his present location, and asked me to reach out to you. He wishes to return home to properly grieve his late wife, and visit her grave without interference, and is willing to cooperate with your investigation of the New Century corporation. Under certain conditions, of course".

Boldt raised his brow and the corners of his mouth turned downwards as if he were impressed with the offer, but the sarcasm was obvious. "Well, that is a generous offer. Assuming he has information that we value, what are his conditions?"

"He would require the assurance of immunity from prosecution in any case involving the Cedar Ridge project."

Boldt remained aloof. " You mean things like accepting a bribe, for instance?"

"If that were part of any indictment being considered, yes."

Boldt was preoccupied with something on his computer screen, and paused to type for a few seconds. Kaplan wondered if he was searching for something on a website, or possibly communicating with a colleague in real time.

"So, Mr. Kaplan, was your client concerned at all with the homicide investigation?"

"Why would he be concerned? He's aware that Officer Lucas has been arrested and reportedly confessed to his wife's murder. He should never have been a suspect."

"Oh, I'm sorry, I should have been more specific. I meant the investigation into the murder of Paul Gotts. Any mention of that?"

Kaplan was thrown by the change of direction but maintained his composure. "Mr. Wainwright stated to me that he had absolutely nothing to do with that, and there couldn't possibly be any evidence linking him to that incident. I'm sure you realize that the local police have called it a robbery, plain and simple."

Kaplan's indignance seemed genuine, convincing Boldt that Wainwright was never forthcoming, even with his trusted friend and attorney.

"Is that what he said, there couldn't possibly be? Did he have an alibi for the time of that attack?" He referred to a notepad on his desk. "Friday, February 17th, between 7 pm and midnight?"

Kaplan was unconcerned and wished to return to the original topic.

"We didn't get into that. He wasn't there. I'm sure a man like Gotts made a lot of enemies in his lifetime, I suggest you check into that. Now let's get back on point here."

Boldt wasn't easily angered, but Kaplan was pushing him closer. He held his tongue to hear what came next, gesturing to Kaplan to continue.

"If you are open to my client's offer he wants to speak to you himself. He would call you tomorrow, at 1 p.m."

"Where is your client? You should be advising him to come in and appear for questioning, or we'll be happy to provide transportation."

Kaplan felt that the FBI agent was toying with him, and decided to knock him down a peg. "As I said, I don't know where he called from, but he did mention the two men who have been tracking him, so you undoubtedly have a better idea than I do."

Boldt showed no outward reaction to Kaplan's counterpunch, wondering if he had underestimated his adversary. He took a long pause to weigh his response, prompting Kaplan to play his trump card too soon.

"One more thing that my client wanted me to pass on to you, and I don't know the implied details. He said that in return for full immunity, he would tell where the bodies were buried."

Boldt sat back in his chair, cocking his head slightly to the side. "Bodies? What bodies? What does that even pertain to?"

An exasperated Kaplan rose from his chair, unwilling to engage any further. "As I said, I have no idea what he meant, I only agreed to relay the offer. He'll call your direct number tomorrow, you can accept the call or not. It's up to you. Let me know in advance, I'd like to listen in if that's allowed."

Boldt was intrigued by Wainwright's offer, and although he hadn't yet worked out the details he was sure that a traceable phone call would lead to Wainwright's apprehension. Surely this killer was too smart for that, he must be feeling more desperate with each passing day.

"Of course. See you tomorrow, Mr. Kaplan."

CHAPTER 88

AL KAPLAN WAS momentarily stunned by the sight. When one of Boldt's assistants finally showed up to escort him to the meeting, after another prolonged wait, Wainwright's legal representative had expected a three-party conference call. Now he felt somewhat ambushed and unprepared. The call hadn't been Kaplan's idea, in fact Wainwright had insisted that he arrange it, but now he wondered if he was adequately protecting his client's best interests.

He was led into a large conference room where no less than ten people were already seated. There were multiple conversations in progress until Kaplan entered, at which time the room went silent. A table at the far end was laden with breakfast items and beverages. Judging by the half-empty platters, this meeting had been in progress for quite some time.

Some of those present were members of the task force that had been formed to investigate Nicole Wainwright's disappearance. Kaplan recognized detectives Rowan and Webster from the Grove Park P.D. as well as detectives from the county sheriff and state police agencies. There were new faces, including an assistant to the district U.S. Attorney who introduced himself as Carter Lang. He was seated in a corner chair, giving Kaplan the impression that he would be an observer rather than an active participant.

Special Agent Boldt stood and introduced Kaplan to two of his assistant SA's and an officer of the Royal Canadian Mounted Police, then resumed his position at the center of the table directly in front of a triangular phone terminal. To his left sat two young assistants, a male and a female, staring intently at their laptop screens as they worked. They appeared to be technicians who were there to support whatever computer activity was required.

Kaplan was directed to the open chair directly across from Boldt, and after the obligatory offer of coffee the agent addressed him in a voice that was plainly intended for everyone to hear.

"Al, we're about ten minutes from the appointed time. I've already briefed the team on the situation, specifically our previous conversation and your client's demands – "

Kaplan interrupted. "Not demands, really. He is reaching out to explore the possibility of an arrangement that would benefit both sides."

Boldt continued "Right. To explore the possibility of an exchange of certain information for immunity from prosecution."

Kaplan was about to respond when the conference phone rang, startling the room into silence. A small red light on the terminal flashed on and off, somehow adding a sense of urgency as it signaled the incoming call. Boldt raised both hands dramatically as he glanced around the table.

"Remember, I do the talking, no one else speaks except Mr. Kaplan." He nodded to the techs and reached out to tap the hands-free button.

"Special Agent Boldt speaking." A few seconds of silence followed, in which Boldt began to doubt the connection. He glanced at the techs and repeated his terse greeting. A few more seconds passed before a response was heard.

"Agent Boldt, James Wainwright here."

The female tech scribbled something onto a notepad and held it up for Boldt to see, accompanying the message with a thumbs-up. "LAND-LINE". The trace was off to a good start.

"Mr. Wainwright, I'm here with Mr. Kaplan, we have you on speaker." He had no intention of announcing the presence of anyone else. That would fall to Kaplan, if he chose to do so.

"Hello Jim" was all the attorney could manage for the moment. He was distracted by the activity of the technicians, wondering if their efforts may actually lead to his client's capture before the call could be completed. It was all he could do to keep from blurting out a warning. In contrast, Wainwright's tone was admirably self-assured.

"So, I take it Al filled you in on my offer."

"He did, but just to be sure we're clear, why don't you re-state your position?" Boldt knew that the clarification of Wainwright's proposal would add more time to the conversation, a win-win.

"Well, it isn't that complicated. I want immunity from any charges relating to Cochran, Harmon, Gotts, that whole New Century mess. I'll tell you what I know, under oath."

Boldt lifted a hand to his head, adjusting a small earpiece that Kaplan hadn't noticed until now, as though he was receiving updates from a source outside the room. "Before I can agree to anything I need specifics from you. What kind of information are we talking about?"

Wainwright sounded like a man who didn't have time to waste. "Look, they use money and influence, threats and even violence to get their way. I have first-hand knowledge of that. If you can get Al something in writing today, something official signed by the D.A. or a judge or whatever, I'll tell you what I know in return for immunity and protection."

"Frankly I'm not sure that the information you're describing would rise to the level needed to justify witness protection, you have to understand that." Carter Lang was writing something onto a legal pad and nodding his head, but didn't look up. Boldt looked to the techs and turned up both palms in a silent query, hoping they would indicate that they were close to a specific location, but they both shook their head.

"Al, are you there? Did you mention the other thing?"

Kaplan was unnerved, and eager to contribute in some way. "Yes Jim, I passed on exactly what you said."

Boldt welcomed the new topic. "You say you know 'where the bodies are buried.' What bodies?"

Everyone at the table seemed to lean in closer, even though the volume was more than adequate for all to hear.

"Just that, literally. You're now familiar with Mitch Goren, right? Well, years ago he killed some girls back in Iowa and bragged to me about it. He told me where he dumped the bodies. Even showed me his little collection of trophies, little trinkets he took from the victims."

Boldt saw the chance to further expand an investigation that was already promising to advance his career to the next level.

"That may be something we can work with, if it's true."

There was an alarmingly loud crash from Wainwright's end, the sound of furniture toppling or a door being broken down.

"What the —" was all they could make out as he dropped the phone. The call was still connected and the sound remained audible, although distant. They could hear new voices indicating that at least two men had entered the room, ordering Wainwright to show his hands.

In the tension of the moment Pete ignored Boldt's ground rules and stood up, pointing to the speaker as he looked at the agent. "Are those our guys?"

In unison Boldt, the technicians, and the Canadian constable exchanged blank looks and emphatically shook their heads in a negative response.

A furious Kaplan remained silent and stared at the speaker, open-mouthed, convinced that he had been set up by the FBI.

Speaking in a hoarse whisper, Boldt stated "They're not there yet!" and angrily put his hands out, raising a forefinger on each to signal that he wanted silence in the room. Now everyone was staring at the speaker-phone, straining to hear what was being said.

"Turn around and get on your knees, Wainwright – or should we call you Ernie?"

Kaplan was horrified, whispering "Boldt, what the f – " until the Special Agent's glare stopped him short.

Wainwright could be heard pleading, and then shouting "I was just on the phone with your boss!"

Voice one could be heard asking "You mean Victor?" and then the other voice cut him off.

"Shut up, you idiot!"

Voice one issued another command; "Kneel down, I said!", followed by a cry of pain from Wainwright.

There was silence for a few beats. Boldt's hand went to his forehead as he realized he was helpless, unable to intervene.

Then voice one growled a final statement, clearly heard above Wainwright's whimpering. "This is for Paulie!"

There was a distinct sound, twice in quick succession, that the experienced law officers immediately recognized as a that of a suppressed handgun. It was followed by a thud, consistent with a body falling to the floor. A few more seconds of commotion, and then the line went dead.

A panicked Kaplan wondered aloud, "what was that?", unwilling to acknowledge what they had indirectly witnessed.

Hank Rowan voiced what all the shocked attendees now suspected.

"Double tap. Classic mob hit."

CHAPTER 89

"THE LAST FEW months have been so crazy, I still have trouble coming to terms with everything. So many people related to this case have died, including my best friend and your ex-husband, Jonathan's dad. Our peaceful little town thrust into the national spotlight, for the worst reasons you could imagine — jealousy, revenge, money – our dark side on full display. An American horror story." Pete Webster shook his head in disbelief, saddened by a chain of events that he had been unable to anticipate or fully comprehend.

Seated next to him at the kitchen table, Sally covered his hand with hers. "I can think of one good thing that came out of all this."

She leaned over and kissed him to complete her thought, then sat back to enjoy the smile she'd brought to his face. "That phone call had to be so shocking, Pete. No one could have seen that coming."

His reply was preceded by a shrug of disbelief. "The way I understand it, the FBI never had anyone near that motel room. They knew Wainwright had made calls to Kaplan the previous week from Ontario, then from Windsor. They thought he was still near the border, so that's where they stationed a couple of agents. When the call was traced, they were supposed to join with the RCMP and move in.

"Once the call came and the techs began to zero in on a location, it turned out to be in western Canada, nowhere near the U.S. border. The local guys weren't able to get there until it was all over. Boldt thinks Wainwright may have called Harmon at some point early on to feel him out, and was outsmarted. Obviously they found him long before we did, they just didn't know it was being broadcast live to a studio audience."

"So Gotts' buddies are convinced that Wainwright killed him, was the FBI going to charge him with that?" She had so many questions, that was simply the first one that came to mind.

"The FBI was convinced that Wainwright killed Gotts, but they didn't have any proof. No eyewitness to the act, no murder weapon. I'm not sure what the plan was, there'll be a lot of debriefing to try and figure out what happened and who's left to be charged with any of it.

"Wainwright and his friend Mitch were killers, we're pretty sure of that. Still, Marti is the one I can't get over. Never would have guessed it."

Sally stood behind him and began to massage his shoulders. "What you need is a vacation, a chance to process all this and find a way to move past it."

He put his hands on hers. "Exactly what I was thinking, hon. You and Jonathan and me, some fun in the sun."

EPILOGUE

ARLEN RAINES WAS standing at the end of what he hoped would become his hayfield, within a stone's throw of Route 19. Even at age seventy-four, Arlen still found excitement in the new planting season, and spring was drawing near. He'd been itching to spend some time outdoors, and today a deeply personal tradition gave him a purpose. He planned to start the 1951 Farmall Cub tractor that had belonged to his father, and take it for a nostalgic drive through the overgrown field. As he piloted the old tractor he would be rewarded with the recollection of those ever more distant memories, flashes of his boyhood, perched on his dad's lap as they bounced along, squinting into the bright sunshine at his bronzed face.

This year it was taking longer than usual to get her started. Arlen adjusted the carburetor as he had been doing for years, and the engine showed a willingness to fire. He was sure that the next turn of the key would bring a brief sputter of combustion that would quickly become the steady purr he was accustomed to. He turned the key, only to find that the battery was too weak to provide anything more than the dull click of a solenoid.

With the undaunted determination of one who had spent his life on a farm, Arlen grabbed the hand crank from its holding clamp and set it into the socket at the front of the tractor, cranking it to give the engine a boost the old-fashioned way. To his surprise, she started on the first turn.

He took a drive to the far side of the field, smiling as he enjoyed the experience yet again, and as he started into a turn the engine stalled. Arlen took the tractor out of gear and climbed down to grab the hand crank, but the clip that normally held it in place was empty, and he realized it must have dropped off along the way.

Looking back at the field he had just driven through, Arlen realized that the cast iron handle would be difficult to find in the tangles of long grass, even for a younger pair of eyes. Still, he thought he had the right tool for the job, and walked to the barn to fetch it.

When his sons had given him a metal detector as a birthday present Arlen had pretended to be pleased and even somewhat fascinated by it, but a few unrewarding excursions had tempered any enthusiasm he had been able to manufacture. Now it could serve a truly useful purpose.

Unlike the tractor, the detector's battery was fully charged, and Arlen moved it slowly back and forth as he walked the path he had driven on the FarmAll. He was more than halfway back to the Cub when he heard the shrill beeping that indicated a hit. Bending down to fish through the tangled grass, he made an unexpected find — it was a golf club.

"How the heck did this get here? It couldn't have been here last time we mowed."

Arlen had played the game only once in his life, but he knew something about it. His boys traded golf stories endlessly at every family function, and Arlen had bought their first sets of clubs. He knew that the Medalist 9-iron he held in his hands was an older style. The business end showed the scars of battle with the occasional rock or tree root, and the steel shaft had begun to corrode. If nothing else, it would be worth keeping in the barn. Maybe his grandson could hit practice balls with it, he wasn't sure if Jonathan was into golf yet. He turned it in his hands, still wondering how the club had gotten into his field.

"Bet this old thing has some stories to tell."

Holding it against the handle of the metal detector, he resumed his search. The sky had become overcast, and he heard the distant rumble of thunder, reminding him to get busy and find that crank handle.

The local TV meteorologists hadn't forecast rain, but it wasn't uncommon for a storm to quickly form over the lake and move down. Arlen was well aware that no one could truly predict what might happen south of the city.

THE END

QUESTIONS FOR DISCUSSION:

1. Before the identity of Nicole Wainwright's killer was revealed, who did you think it was and why?

2. Which, if any, characters did you identify with, have empathy for, like or dislike?

3. As an editor, what would you change about this novel, if anything?

4. After reading the first hundred pages, how compelled were you to continue reading this novel to its end, in comparison to other books? Why?

5. Was there a passage that you found memorable... something funny, poignant, insightful or profound?

6. Do you think the story was plot-based or character-driven?

Made in the USA
Lexington, KY
09 January 2018